This one's for my 20 something self;

For the girl who spent way too much time trying to be what everyone else wanted from her;

For the girl who was told how to act, how to dress and what volume her voice should be to make it in the business world;

For the girl men claimed was too much, too difficult, too emotional, too sexy, too boring, too wild, too smart (I shit you not) to be the right one;

For the girl who grew up enough to figure it out for herself

And for Erik, for building something with me

NOT
SAFE
FOR
WORK

LINDSEY LANZA

Not Safe For Work Soundtrack

The Man - Taylor Swift
Touchy Feely Fool - AJR
Tableau - Kaky
Would've, Could've, Should've - Taylor Swift
Different Kind of Beautiful - Alec Benjamin
Bejeweled - Taylor Swift
Kiss Me - Ed Sheeran
if you think i'm pretty - Artemas
"Slut!" - Taylor Swift
High - Stephen Sanchez
Dangerous Woman- Ariana Grande
Make You Mine - Madison Beer
Puzzle - Kaky
imperfect for you - Ariana Grande
golden hour - JVKE
Circles - Wyn Starks

Full List on Spotify:
https://open.spotify.com/playlist/7ocuP8zA1ruSy
QKVWeUkfW?si=bc5012c0a30743e5

"It is literally impossible to be a woman."

Barbie

AUTHORS NOTE

While this story is a work of fiction, every anecdote has been taken from my experience working in the world of tech and start-ups. All names have been changed.

DIAMOND SKY VINEYARD

BAR BOCCE

THE NSFW LOCATIONS

GOLDEN GATE BRIDGE

LOVER'S LANE

FISHERMAN'S WHARF

FOG & FOAM

GHIRADELLI SQUARE

OLIVIA'S APARTMENT

THE FERRY BUILDING

THE TONGA ROOM

SIZZL HQ

GAVIN'S APARTMENT

AERO MEXICO

N
W   E
S

PROLOGUE
OLIVIA

It has been brought to my attention that I lack enthusiasm.

Enthusiasm? Seriously?

Under normal circumstances, this would be a mediocre insult, but taking into account my current position, consider me offended.

"What did you say?" The words spill out of my mouth along with my boyfriend's dick.

"No, you can keep going. It'd just be better if you acted like you liked it more." Liked it more? How much I am supposed to enjoy giving head? It's not that I hate it, but what's to like? My knees hurt from the tile beneath me. The relative silence has me focusing on nothing but the small sounds of me gagging and the constant internal thoughts about what I'm doing wrong.

Sure, I'm loving every second of it.

"Do you want me to do something differently?" I ask.

"It's fine, just finish, okay?" He grabs the back of my head and not so gently guides himself back in my mouth. I try to force out some pleasurable sounding moans, but since he's silent—as always—I'm not sure if I succeed.

After a few more minutes of trying my best to enjoy this, I hear the telltale grunt of my job being done.

I swallow my boyfriend's *enthusiasm* and rise from the kitchen floor as he buttons his pants. And just when I lean in for a kiss, he pulls away and pecks my forehead instead.

"Sweetie," he says in the most patronizing voice I've ever heard. "We should talk."

I, OLIVIA DIAMOND, PERFECT GIRLFRIEND, HAVE BEEN dumped.

I look at my phone again because I'm dumbstruck that the conversation only lasted ten minutes. Surely, something is off. But no, the clock isn't wrong. My brain just doesn't want to admit defeat.

Ian spent a total of *ten* minutes telling me why I'm not good enough. He even listed the reasons off on his fingers. My long-term relationship has been whittled down to a thumb pointing to "bad sex", a ring finger for "too young and immature" and a *fucking pinky* to clarify that I'm "just not marriage material." And the one that hurt the most, when he quipped about me not having a real career. He said the promotion I've been working toward for months is nothing but a pipedream.

For a moment, after I grab my bag and head toward the door to leave his apartment, I think he might change his mind. That maybe I'll feel his hand on my shoulder, that he'll spin me around and apologize. That he'll ask me to stay. Instead, I hear him flop down on the couch and turn on the TV. *Unbelievable.*

My first—no, my *only* real adult relationship is over.

The guy I spent two years trying so hard to be perfect for has had enough of me. *Two years* of doing everything I could to be the girlfriend he wanted me to be. The fashion choices I made to appease him, the music I only listened to in secret, the delicious sugary drinks I gave up for "more mature" beverages. Or worst of all, wearing a tight headache-inducing bun for months at a time because my long, fiery red hair is "too wild." All of it was for absolutely nothing.

I close the door behind me and slump against the wall, willing myself not to shed a single tear. Ian isn't worth my tears, and I think I've known that for a while now. Because underneath the pain in my chest, I can feel a weight being lifted as well. It's almost as if I'm a balloon and Ian was the rock I was tied to. I only wish I would have been strong enough to cut the string myself.

Because Ian doesn't know what he's talking about. Ian doesn't know *me*. I *am* mature. I *do* live in the real world. I *will* make someone happy one day.

And I'm getting that damn promotion if it kills me.

CHAPTER ONE

OLIVIA

Two months later

"THE NEW USUAL?" KARLA ASKS AS I ENTER FOG & FOAM, my daily caffeine supplier.

"Yes, please," I reply, though she's already started making my sugar cookie latte with an extra shot and an obscene amount of whipped cream. Ian would say my drink order is ridiculous, but he's not here to judge me anymore. Somehow it makes the drink taste even sweeter.

I'm earlier than usual so I grab a seat to enjoy a few sips before heading into the office. I could save a dollar a day by going to any of the three Starbucks across the street, but I love this place. It's full of mismatched furniture and chairs that are actually comfortable. And just north of the San Francisco Ferry building, it's right on the water. The name isn't a coincidence; for most of the morning, the entire shop is surrounded by fog.

When I was young, I hated the fog. It made my hair frizzy,

my skin damp and my parents wouldn't let me ride my bike when the ground got too wet—I had a tendency for tracking mud through the estate. But then I learned that fog was the lifeblood of California wine country, the place I grew up in. All that extra warmth from the Pacific is what made my family's business a success. And it creates a damn good pinot noir.

Opening my email, I scroll through to delete the numerous automated messages I don't need and I spot a LinkedIn notification. As a sales rep pushing marketing software in San Francisco, I basically live on LinkedIn. I send tons of messages to prospective clients every single day, but for some reason I have a good feeling about this one. And when I open it up, I'm *right*.

Tristan Cross (*He/Him*) – 2nd
Chief Marketing Officer at Surf and Stream

Olivia,
I appreciate your persistence in reaching out to me. As you mentioned, I was recently appointed this position and my schedule has been full. I'm very interested in hearing more about what you do at Sizzl and how it could benefit our marketing program.

You're also correct that our offices are nearby. If you'd still like to meet for coffee, I could carve out 30 minutes tomorrow at 10:00. Fog & Foam is my favorite as well.

You can email me directly at tristan.cross@surfandstream.com for a faster reply. Please CC my EA Chelsea: chelsea.mcdonald@surfandstream.com.

Tristan Cross
CMO

surfandstream.com

I can't help it. I *squeal.*

"Hey, you okay?" Karla shouts from behind the counter.

I look back apologetically. "I'm fine, sorry. Great, actually." I grin at Karla. "Better than great." This is exactly what I've been waiting for, a chance to prove myself with a huge prospect. For the first time in weeks, I'm excited to go into the office.

I grab my coffee and practically skip down the Embarcadero to our building, sneaking a few glances at the water and the Bay Bridge—one of my favorite views. I anxiously ride the elevator up to the twenty-second floor, letting my nails tap on the wall to the beat of Aretha Franklin demanding respect. And then I burst through the doors to Sizzl HQ like I own the place.

"Morning, Sparkles."

I grimace at the typical greeting from Gavin Scott. When I first started at Sizzl, I learned quickly how nickname-forward the culture was here. Our CEO, Daanesh Khan, is mostly referred to as "DK". Most of the guys on my team get called by their last name or some version of their initials. I prayed during orientation that they didn't start calling me "OD" and that Diamond would suffice.

But then, a few months in, Gavin Scott decided to start calling me Sparkles. It only took a second to realize it was some sort of insult, the mocking tone a sure giveaway. And sadly, the best retort I could come up with was to call him Scottie. Two years later, both names have stuck.

Gavin's not my enemy, but he's definitely not my friend. He's just the extremely attractive top-performing salesman

I'm forced to stare at all day from the desk directly across from me.

I don't have anything against him, but it's tough working with people when I know they don't like me. And Gavin Scott has made it very clear that he wants nothing to do with me. Sure, he's always professional. He answers questions when I ask and he's perfectly polite to me in meetings. But when it's not required for work, he puts the rude in broody.

Last Friday, I tried being extra friendly and asked him about his plans after work. He responded with a brusque, "happy hour with the team," before promptly grabbing his stuff and walking out. *Our* team, he was referring to, the one I'm also a part of. Somehow, I don't think my invite went to spam.

I wish I didn't care so much about being his least favorite Sizzlr, but I'd be lying if I didn't admit to having a little crush when we first met. How could I not? He has these piercing aqua-adjacent eyes and a megawatt smile that's impossible not to feel in your chest. He also has this way about him. Maybe it's charisma or just the perfection of his face, but whenever he is forced to interact with me, it's impossible not to like the guy. It's irritating as hell.

"Hey, Scottie," I respond. "Here early again?"

"Early bird catches the...what's the saying again? Oh yeah, the biggest commission checks." He winks, and just like every other day, I wonder how he can get away with saying things like *that* when I get judged for so much less. *Ugh.*

I'm about to respond with a snippy comment about wondering what it's like to get those kinds of commissions, when I remember that I need him today. Surf and Stream is *his* account after all. My job is to source leads for him, set up initial meetings and then bring in the closer. I'm just a glorified tele-marketer, sending hundreds of emails a day so that when someone finally bites, I can introduce them to a *man* who'll actually do the selling.

Not just Gavin, but all four men on my team. Yes, I'm the only woman and yes, I'm the only one who hasn't been promoted to sales executive within their first year. It's *supposed* to be a one-year cycle. One year to learn from our sales counterparts along with leadership before we get promoted to run deals ourselves. I joined the team two and a half years ago, but Mitch, our vice president, still doesn't think I'm ready.

But I *am* ready. I know I am, no matter what Mitch thinks or what Ian used to say. I might hate this job most days, but I know once I get the promotion everything will change.

Gavin, along with the other guys on the team, have offered to let me work some of their territory. They each gave me a list of accounts that could be mine if I'm able to set up a meeting. My excitement about these opportunities died almost immediately when I realized they were all accounts that had basically been impossible to break into.

But then, a few months ago, I saw Surf and Stream appointed a new chief marketing officer. Every article I've read about Tristan Cross says he's young and ambitious and wants to make waves. Choosing a new marketing platform like Sizzl to expand their program sounded like a no-brainer for him, so I've been relentless in my outreach. And it paid off.

Now, I just have to confirm with Gavin that he'll still let me run with it. I want to believe he wouldn't betray me. We may not be friends, but he's always professional. The thing is, Surf and Stream is one of the fastest growing streaming platforms in the world right now. The deal size could be massive, upwards of a million dollars a year. I'm not sure if I could really blame him for not giving up that kind of money just to be a trustworthy colleague.

Shit. I should have brought him a muffin or something.

"Sparkles? You okay over there? I see your lips moving but no sound is coming out, just in case you didn't know." He smirks and I practically flinch at how sexy he looks doing it. *He is making fun of you, Olivia.*

I really hate this habit of mine. I'm horrible at concealing my emotions, and even worse, I tend to mouth the thoughts in my head way too often. Just a lovely symptom of my anxiety.

"Hey." I look up and flash him a dazzling smile. He mirrors my expression and I think once again about how much easier it would be to hate him if he didn't look like *that*. "So, I got a message back from the CMO at Surf and Stream. He wants a meeting."

Gavin's eyes flash and his mouth goes slack. I start to nibble the inside of my cheek. *Please, please, please don't say you're taking it back.*

To my shock, his smile turns genuine, but he hides it quickly with his usual look of indifference. "Cool. You still good to run the deal?"

I eye him with a bit too much skepticism. He's really letting me keep it?

"It's yours," he clarifies. "But since you haven't run a meeting before you might want to have someone sit in, or just help you prep." I would kill for someone as good as Gavin to help me prepare, but I can't tell if he's offering.

"Do you mean you would—?"

"I'm way too busy," he scoffs. "Just get Ian to make someone help you."

Yeah, right. Even if we hadn't broken up a couple months ago, he'd never offer to help me with work. I feel a little awkward not correcting Gavin, but I've yet to tell 99 percent of my co-workers that Ian and I broke up. I'm still not ready for the aftermath.

I was never prepared for the rumors when I *started* dating

Sizzl's biggest investor. I have no idea what to expect once I go public with our breakup.

"Sorry for bothering—" I start to respond, but he's already put his headphones on. I guess I shouldn't have expected one moment of kindness to turn into an actual conversation.

I respond to a few more emails and LinkedIn messages as the rest of the team starts to filter in. It's still early for other departments, but the sales team is always in first.

Except for the surprisingly empty desk to my left. Curious.

"Hey, Scottie?" I bravely ask a few minutes later.

He hears me but just points to his headphones, like he can't be bothered. Not sure why I expected any differently.

I turn to Eduardo this time, who sits diagonal to me. "Hey. Do you know what's going on here?" I gesture to the desk next to mine where Paul sits. His normally cluttered desk full of papers and fidget toys is completely empty other than an unplugged monitor and a few pens.

"Oh, umm." He leans over his desk to whisper, "Fired. On Friday." Eduardo's eyebrows shoot up, letting me know there's more to the story. I don't bother asking him for more information since I doubt he'd tell me. He's definitely not an office gossip.

Luckily for me, my best friend, Andie very much *is*.

SLACK DIRECT MESSAGE
Olivia Diamond:
Hey! I just heard about Paul. Do you know what happened?
Andie Oh:
Morning! Yes, but NSFW – I'll text you!

ANDIE OH:

OK! I can't believe I forgot to tell you this weekend! He was fired on Friday at the end of the day for "lewd behavior"

ME:

Didn't he get caught having sex in the stairwell last month? That wasn't lewd enough for HR?

ANDIE OH:

Right!? Honestly, I thought the same thing. But IT saw the sex tape and kept it somewhat under wraps. This time, he had no such luck. He was caught doing coke in the bathroom

ME:

No way

ANDIE OH:

YES WAY. The guy is so dumb, he didn't even go into a stall. He was doing lines at the sink FFS

ME:

So, who caught him? Do you know?

ANDIE OH:

That's the best part. HR did…

ME:

How? There are zero men in HR…right?

ANDIE OH:

Like I said, the best part. He must of still been drunk from the night before or something, because he was in the women's bathroom

I gasp, audibly, and when I look up, I notice Gavin's been watching me. "The Andie Express?"

I nod with a quick laugh at the team's name for Sizzl's rumor mill.

If Andie were anyone else, people would probably hate her for knowing all the company gossip, but in reality, she's more like the darling of Sizzl. She's run our marketing team since she started here, plucked from a Google internship and tasked with planning huge events and doing all our social media when the company was a little baby start-up. Now she reports directly to the CMO and has a team of three.

She also has a part-time intern who happens to be Gavin's little sister, Gabby.

ANDIE OH:

I'm heading into the office now – wanna grab coffee?

ME:

Can't. Have my 1:1 with Mitch in 10. Lunch? Noon? Sushirrito?

ANDIE OH:

See ya then buttercup!

Like most other tech companies in the Bay, we have an open office floor plan. Our co-founders both sit at a pod of desks with the other engineers. But our vice president of sales, along with a couple others on the leadership team, demanded his own office.

I lightly knock on the just-barely-open door. "Hey, Mitch. You ready for me?"

"Sure, sure. Come in," he says, without looking up from his phone.

After a few minutes of sitting in silence, he finishes up the texting and looks at me. He's probably confused as to why I'm smiling.

"You look chipper. Finally over Ian?" I hate that Mitch knows about my break-up when I've barely told anyone other than Andie. So much for HR confidentiality. I knew I shouldn't have bothered disclosing the break-up, definitely learned my lesson there. In my defense, I could never find the rulebook for dating your company's investor.

"Ian's old news. Really, no need to talk about him ever again. I have a new sales prospect."

"Okay...?"

"Surf and Stream. Their new CMO wants a meeting. Tomorrow." The words fly from my mouth. But Mitch doesn't come close to matching my excitement.

"Great. Did you tell Gavin?"

"I did, but this is one of the accounts he said I could work on my own. Remember? You said it was fine as long as he was okay with it."

"I remember. But I meant smaller deals. This is too significant to take a chance with, Livy." Ugh, I hate when he calls me that. It always sounds like he's talking down to me, like I'm a child or a pet. I actually think I prefer Sparkles.

"But—"

"What else are you working on?" he asks, skipping over this like there's absolutely nothing left to say on the topic. But I'm definitely not finished.

"Mitch." I pause to take a breath. *Don't be argumentative, but don't be a push-over. Be strong, but not so strong that he'll think you're "bitchy." Be direct. Not emotional.* I dig deep for the "big tit energy" Andie is always telling me I have hidden inside. "You said I can't get promoted until you see I can work deals on my own. Gavin's on board and the meeting is already set. I need this opportunity to show you what I can do. Please?"

My soul is crushed a tiny bit that I couldn't stop myself

from adding "please." I make a mental note to practice this conversation later and lose the p-word. *How un-manly of me.*

Mitch looks back at me like I'm the human equivalent of a dental appointment, nothing more than an annoyance but one he can't avoid forever.

"Fine. When's the meeting? I'll be joining you."

CHAPTER TWO

GAVIN

"Finally!" Gabby yells, as I walk through the door to our apartment. I haven't even finished setting down my backpack when she continues, "Why were you at the office so late?"

I ignore her for a minute and sit down at the kitchen table, rolling out my neck from the eleven-hour workday.

"Hey, Kadesha," I say to Gabby's girlfriend when she joins me. "Sorry for holding up dinner." We share a grin, both of us accustomed to my sister's extreme expectations for punctuality. Expectations that neither of us can seem to meet. "I like the hair. Pink suits you."

"Oh, I know." She flips a few braids behind her ear.

I laugh as Gabby joins us at the table, setting down a platter of lasagna. My sister is an amazing cook and I dread the day she moves out and I'm stuck with frozen dinners every night.

Once we've all had a few bites—delicious bites—Gabby starts in again. "So, why were you working so late?"

"Come on, you know I work late all the time. Just trying to make as much money as I can. How else am I supposed to pay for that fancy school of yours?" I flash a smile. "I was working on a few contract proposals."

Gabby leans so far forward on the table that Kadesha has to pull her hair back before it takes a swim in the lasagna. "Mentiroso! You, big brother, are a big fat *liar*." I shoot her a look trying to figure out what's going on, but I get nothing. A silent stand-off forms and Kadesha's gaze flies back and forth between us like she's watching a ping pong match.

"What?" I finally say back.

"Be honest. Tell us why you were really there until seven o'clock." It's a full stare down between us and I'm starting to guess she already knows exactly what I was doing.

"Who told you?"

"You know Olivia and Andie are like best friends, right?"

Yeah, I did know that. And I really shouldn't be surprised that Gabby's boss, Andie, felt the need to tell anyone—especially my sister—that I stayed late to help out Liv.

"Fine. Liv was stressing out about a meeting tomorrow and everyone else was in meetings so I offered to help her prep. Why is that such a big deal?"

Gabby levels me with a weighted look, willing me to read her mind. I just shrug. She's making a huge fuss over nothing.

She knows I wouldn't usually spend time with Liv unless it's obligatory, but she was a mess this afternoon. I'm not sure what went down with her one on one with Mitch, but ever since that meeting, she was extra fidgety and frantic.

"The holiday party was over two years ago. It's time to move on," Gabby continues. She's not wrong but her words still feel like daggers. "She has a *serious* boyfriend." And the kill shot.

"I know, okay. *I've moved on*." I exaggerate each word to help convince her. "That doesn't mean I can't be a decent human and help one of my colleagues. The more deals she can close, the better for our company, right?"

"Oh, come *on*," Gabby huffs. "I don't buy any of that. It's time to forget about her and find someone else to fall madly in love with. How will you ever meet your soulmate if you're staying late at work every night to help the girl who's unavailable?"

I sigh. Sometimes Gabby acts like finding a girlfriend is the only thing that matters in the world. Of course I love how much she cares about me, but I'm just not interested in anyone.

"This has nothing to do with my dating life—" She huffs. "Gabs, please relax. Olivia and I work together, and part of my job is coaching the rest of the team. Today it was her, tomorrow it could be Eddie needing a hand. I can't refuse to work with her just because she..." I don't finish the sentence because we all know how it ends.

"Maybe you don't remember how messed up you were over her, but I do. You're my family and I just—" Her voice breaks. "I never want to see you like that again."

I roll my eyes, just as Kadesha says, "Dark times," under her breath. Guilt swells through me, remembering how I ruined their first Christmas as a couple. Gabby and I were so excited to bring Kadesha into the mix, to show her our favorite traditions of days full of baking food from our childhood and watching cheesy holiday movies. But that Christmas, the only thing I wanted to ingest was alcohol, and the only movies I would watch ended in murder.

"It's not like that, I swear."

My sister sighs in resignation. *"Es que no confío que no te haga daño."*

"Hey," Kadesha interrupts. "No Spanish at the dinner table. You know I can't understand you."

Gabby cringes. It's not unusual for her to slip into another language. She speaks five. When it's just the two of us, it's common to switch to Spanish since it's what we both grew up speaking. Even if it has been almost twenty years since we left Argentina.

"Sorry," she apologizes. "I just said I'm worried she'll hurt him. And you know I can go a little 'mama bear' when it comes to my big brother."

"Gabby," I sigh.

"What? You need someone looking out for you. Who else is gonna do it if I don't?"

"Babe, they work together." Kadesha comes to my rescue, and I'm thankful because I'm more than tired of talking about this with my sister. She's been pushing me to keep my distance from Liv for what feels like forever. "If he's fine with it then maybe you should let it go."

My sister plops back in her chair with a pout, her arms crossed over her chest like a petulant child. I can't help but grin.

"How about a subject change?" Kadesha offers. "Any new goss at Sizzl?"

Gabby eyes me again.

"*What?*" This dinner is starting to feel like an interrogation.

"I heard a rumor about Davide..." she teases, drawing out all three syllables of his name like a song.

I let out a long exhale. How the hell did she hear about this? It's supposed to be confidential for fuck's sake.

"What'd you hear? Seriously, tell me."

"Just because you're friends doesn't mean he gets a free pass for being a douche."

Friends? I am not *friends* with Davide. And he is a douche. But he's also one of the original eight. Those of us who basically started this company.

When Daanesh and Vaughn—our co-founders—got a huge

round of funding by participating in Y Combinator, they hired eight people to build out departments and grow the company. Daanesh was a few years ahead of me at UC-Davis, but we met playing intramural rugby together. We stayed in touch after he graduated and started coding an entire marketing platform. When he reached out about a sales job, I thought he was joking, but he said that he and Vaughn both hated all the salespeople they'd interviewed and offered to give me a shot.

So there I was, fresh out of college, almost no experience, the only one out of the original eight that wasn't already a Silicon Valley success. I was nowhere near ready, nor did I have any desire to lead a sales team, so once we locked down a few early clients, they brought in Mitch to head up the department.

Daanesh and I are still close friends, but I can't stand Vaughn. He's the one who has hired all my least favorite people and is on his way to tanking the company if he keeps letting the culture take a nose-dive.

Davide, our Head of Product, is his right-hand man, and it's worth stating again, a huge douche.

"Please don't say Davide and I are friends. You know I can't stand the guy."

"But you obviously know about the affair," Gabby snaps back.

"An affair?" Kadesha asks, her big doe eyes lit up. "Like with someone from work?"

"Yeah," Gabby continues. "He cheated on his wife with Megan in recruiting and, *oh yeah,* Megan was mysteriously let go for 'performance issues.' You know she might sue."

"There is no proof that there *weren't* performance issues." I hate myself as I repeat the company line. I know it's bullshit, but there's nothing I can do about it. Gabby scoffs at me and I run a hand through my hair in annoyance. This dinner is the worst. "Look, I know Davide is horrible—"

"Horrible? He took advantage of a girl half his age and got her fired when he was done with her. How can you defend him?"

"I'm not defending him. If it was up to me, he'd be gone immediately, but that's not going to happen, and Sizzl cannot handle bad press right now. So please, for the love of god, just let it go."

"What do you mean, we can't handle bad press? Is something happening?"

Yes, something's happening. And while I love my sister and want to tell her everything, I've been keeping this one to myself. It's not that I don't trust her, but this is not a secret I can risk getting out. And Gabby talks to Andie way too much.

Daanesh confided in me a few weeks ago that the board is considering an acquisition offer, a *massive* offer. If it all goes through, I'll make so much money from my stock options that I'll never have to worry about me and Gabby again.

The last twelve years, ever since I became my sister's legal guardian, haven't exactly been easy. Between putting myself through college while working two jobs, paying off our student loans in what feels like a never-ending cycle, and now working my ass off to get us out of debt...it's fucking exhausting.

It's even harder dealing with it all alone. I should have let her take out loans when she offered, but I hated the idea of her being in debt too. And since I've also fibbed a tiny bit on my salary, and our rent, she thinks I'm covering everything without issue.

Which is why I am *desperate* for this deal to go through, even if I have to keep my mouth shut for a few more months to protect assholes like Davide. Because once it does, I'll never have to keep anything from Gabby again. I'll be able to take care of her like I promised I would the day I signed those papers declaring her my responsibility.

"Can we talk about something else, please? We can even go back to Liv if you really want to," I plead.

"I made Churro a new sweater," Kadesha offers. "I'm working on sunglasses too, but they're trickier than I thought."

"Nice. I haven't even had a chance to say hi considering Gabby's been *berating* me since I got home." I flash them both a grin to show I'm (mostly) joking, and head to the living room where we keep Churro's cage. Cage is probably not the right word. It's more like a tiny Pottery Barn styled habitat. We have a very spoiled hedgehog.

I drape the sling Kadesha made for us over my shoulder and gently grab Churro to place him inside. The sweater she knitted is red and only covers his top half. He looks like a tiny, prickly Winnie the Pooh.

"Hey pal." He makes a little chirping sound in response, letting me know he's happy to be in his sling.

"He really loves it in there." Kadesha smiles at him. "I'll have to make another, just in case."

Kadesha is some sort of crafting wizard. Her Etsy shop is killing it, selling mainly pet accessories with a few items for humans every now and then. She pulled in over twenty grand during Halloween last fall and has won numerous awards for being a top BIPOC owned small business.

"That would be great," I say, right before my phone buzzes in my pocket. I pull it out to check the message.

OLIVIA DIAMOND:

I'm SO sorry to bother you, but could you remind me about the pricing tiers for our creation team? I've been searching google docs for an hour and can't find anything. SOS!

I MUST BE GRINNING BECAUSE GABBY ACTUALLY CROONS when she says, "Who's texting you, Gav? Could it possibly be a gorgeous redhead with a loving boyfriend? Hmm?"

"Shut up, Gabby." I grab a second helping of lasagna and take it into my bedroom so I can cut up a few little pieces of meat for Churro.

And then I call Liv.

"Scottie?" she answers. "I'm so sorry I texted but Eduardo wasn't responding and you always know everyth—"

"Hey, Sparkles." That always seems to shut her up. I can't tell if she likes or despises the nickname, but I can't seem to stop either way. "First of all, take a breath." I wait a second, letting her know I want to hear it. After a few beats of silence, it comes. "Why are you even looking up pricing? You never go through pricing on a first meeting, especially customizations and add-ons."

"I know, I know. But I just keep thinking, what if they ask? And then I won't know the answer and then Mitch will say I wasn't prepared, and I don't know what I'm doing and I'm not ready to run my own deals and—"

"Jesus, Liv. *Breathe.* Seriously."

She obeys again and during this moment of silence I get a quick hit of gratification that she came to me in a time of crisis. Normally I'd blow her off, say I'm too busy to talk, but something about being alone in my room with Churro has me wanting to let my guard down for once.

"Liv," I start, but she cuts me off.

"I'm sorry," she says, her breathing even again. "I'm so sorry for texting you. I shouldn't have bothered you with this."

I can tell she's ready to hang up and I should let her. But this is the first time I've ever talked to her on the phone. It's the first time I can let myself grin at the sound of her voice without fear of her noticing. I probably shouldn't find her nervous energy as adorable as I do. But I've never been very good at pretending, which is why I usually stay away.

"It's fine. Just tell me what you need to feel prepared. I'll help you."

"Really? You want to help me?"

"Want? Definitely not. But I've got thirty minutes to kill." I look down at Churro as I say this, realizing my Monday-night plans consist of Netflix and cuddling this guy. But she doesn't need to know that.

"You're sure you don't mind? I already took up half your night." She sounds so apologetic I want to reach through the phone and hug her.

Instead, I grab the tweezers, break up a few small pieces of meat and inspect for cheese before feeding them to Churro. He's still curled up in the sling as I sink down in my bed and flip the phone to speaker. I can't show Liv the smile I get from helping her, so I show him instead.

"Tell me what you need, Sparkles."

CHAPTER THREE

OLIVIA

"What's this?" I ask to the deserted space around my desk.

I arrive to an almost-empty office right at seven-thirty in the morning, giving me two more hours to prep for my meeting. I shouldn't need to do anything else. I'm pretty sure I've memorized all my notes, but I still want to show Mitch how much effort I'm putting into this, for him to see how ready I am for this promotion.

But when I get to my desk there's a coffee sporting the Fog & Foam logo. I take a sip, surprised to discover it's my typical sugar cookie latte, extra everything. How?

"Oh, hey, Sparkles." Gavin approaches from the kitchen and runs a hand through his hair. It still looks wet from a shower.

"Did you..." I raise the cup between us. "Did you get me coffee?" I feel like an idiot even asking because of course he didn't get me coffee. It's much more likely that it came from Andie, or a stalker I don't yet know about, or maybe the tooth fairy trying to up my sugar intake to get more loot.

"Yeah, I umm...had a feeling you might be too rushed this morning. Didn't want you to screw up the meeting just because you didn't have a buzz." He sits down at his desk and throws on his headphones, completely ignoring the shock on my face.

Yesterday was the most Gavin and I had talked in months, maybe ever. I know he only helped me out for the good of the team, but I can't say I didn't enjoy it. Gavin's brilliant. The way he speaks about our product, all the analogies he uses to help marketers understand the why, how, what—"always in that order, Liv!"—of what we do, the sheer confidence in everything he says, I was captivated by it.

Working in Silicon Valley, I'm surrounded by intelligent people. But there are different types. Most common are the ones who want you to know how smart they are, who drop hints at their Stanford degree every chance they get and love to humble brag about their money, their stock options, whatever else they can think of, really.

Unfortunately, my ex is the leader of this group. The brilliance and the status sucked me in. And then it became an actual chore to stroke his ego.

Gavin definitely has a chip on his shoulder, or at least I thought he did until last night. He's great at his job and clearly smart, but he falls into a group of his own, one without arrogance and elitism. And I'm still in shock that he got me coffee.

I wave a hand to get his attention and he drags the headphones down around his neck. I don't know why exactly but the move is so sexy I can't stop my mouth from parting. Since when am I a neck person?

"Yeah?" he asks.

"Why did you...how did you...umm...how'd you know my order?"

He raises a brow. "I've got my ways." And his headphones go right back on.

"Thank you so much for meeting today," I say, shaking Tristan's hand. I grab the tray of coffees I pre-ordered from Karla and set them on the table. "This is Mitch Stevenson, our VP of Sales."

Photos of Tristan were commonplace when I was compiling my research on him and Surf and Stream. But I wasn't prepared for how intimidating he'd be in person. He's wearing all black and looks like he stepped out of a Tom Ford ad. He has one of those perfectly square jaws I thought only existed in romance novels and photoshop.

We go through a quick round of introductions as Tristan has brought two team members with him to the meeting. Priya runs their social media department while Darnell is their creative director.

The meeting goes well. I take Gavin's advice and encourage the team from Surf and Stream to do all the talking. This whole meeting is about information gathering so when I do schedule them for a platform demo, I can personalize it as much as possible.

Darnell is the most engaged. He is in charge of their current marketing platform and gives me a lot of info on what he likes and dislikes about it. It's already easy for me to see where we can fill in their gaps and provide services they're missing out on.

We agree to schedule the demo for next week in our office, but before we conclude the meeting, Tristan speaks. "I'm looking forward to seeing more, but I have to say, I heard Sizzl was the most expensive platform on the market." He leans in and his cologne hits me like a drug. I could swear it's intentional, meant to knock me off my game. It smells like money and power and hands tied to a headboard. "I know you said you'd be putting together pricing options once we decide on which features we're interested in, but can you give me a range to consider before we move further?"

My brain circles back to my conversation with Gavin last night as I try to rid the aroma from my senses. We went over so much pricing info that it's all jumbled. And then there were the talking points about why we cost more, or how to customize the package to make it more cost-effective. Fuck, I can't remember the details of anything.

Pressure starts to build in my chest, the tell-tale sign of my anxiety taking over. I take a deep breath, thinking of Gavin's words on the phone last night and will myself to get through this.

Mitch is eyeing me like he just can't wait to see me mess this up, so I blurt out the first thing that comes to mind.

"Tristan, do you mind if I ask what car you drive?"

A smirk starts to form on his face, but he hides it. He tries his best at least. The subtle grin is charming, especially on his chiseled features. I've been doing my best to ignore his face this whole meeting because Tristan is—objectively—hot as hell. He's wearing an expensive three-piece suit, and his hair is gelled to perfection. He's the epitome of tall, dark and hand-some with jet black hair, olive skin and amber eyes framed by the kind of thick lashes women are always envious of. And between the Rolex on his wrist and the Gucci sunglasses he set down on the table, I'm betting he has a designer car to match.

"A Maserati." He finally answers my question and I try to stop ogling him.

Okay, that was exactly the answer I was hoping for. Now I'll just have to see if it pays off.

"Why?" I ask. "A Prius would be cheaper. Hell, a Tesla would. Less gas, less maintenance. If you live in the city, you probably don't drive much anyway. Seems like a waste if you ask me." Now he really grins at me. "But you seem like a substance over savings guy, someone who values performance more than a good deal." I can't help but pointedly look at all his accoutrements, finally landing on the Burberry tie.

"Touché." Our eyes meet and I smile back, but something about the way his gaze locks on me feels much too intimate. I quickly divert my eyes. "I'll see you next week, Olivia," he says, standing up and extending his hand. "This has been interesting. Definitely interesting."

Mitch is mostly silent on the way back to the office, responding to a million emails on his phone. Once we reach the twenty-second floor he quickly says, "keep me posted with any updates," before going back into his office.

I thought the meeting was a success. As much as a first meeting can be, but maybe I'm missing something?

"How'd it go, Sparkles?" Gavin asks as soon as I get to my desk.

"Good? I think? I don't know. Mitch hasn't said a word." I can't stop chewing the inside of my cheek as I run through the meeting over and over in my head. They agreed to a product demo. A second meeting. Isn't that the whole point?

"I'm sure it was fine," Gavin says, not looking up from his screen. He's typing away on his laptop, reminding me I'm not too important for multi-tasking. "Mitch isn't one for praise. If he didn't tear you to pieces after, he's happy with how it went."

Okay, tucking that piece of knowledge away for next time.

The rest of the day flies. I spend way too much time drafting a follow-up email to Tristan and his team and eat lunch at my desk so I can keep working. Prepping for the second meeting is going to be even more grueling. I'm no product expert but I plan to be one by next week.

Then, at three o'clock, I receive an email no amount of planning could prepare me for.

From: Tristan Cross < tristan.cross@surfandstream.com >
To: Olivia Diamond < olivia@sizzl.com >
Subject: RE: Nice Meeting You

Olivia,

It was a pleasure meeting you today as well. We were all impressed with what you had to share. I won't be able to meet for the demo next week, but Darnell is anxious to see more. He'll be your point-person moving forward.

I would, however, like to see you again. Are you free for dinner this weekend?

-Tristan

It's now just after five-thirty and I have probably read this short message over a thousand times.

As soon as I finished the first read-through I put on my headphones and blasted my favorite playlist so that nothing could distract me. I'm sure people have tried to get my attention, or at least attempted to say "bye" as they left for the day, but I can't seem to stop re-reading this damn email.

What the hell am I supposed to do with this?

I'm supposed to be landing a deal, not landing a date.

"Olivia!" It's barely audible through the music, but I can

faintly hear my name being yelled while a finger pokes into my shoulder.

Quickly removing my headphones, I find Mitch hovering above me. "Yeah?"

"Walk with me."

He turns toward the exit, his messenger bag already strapped across his broad shoulders. I grab my keycard and chase after him.

"Sorry I didn't have time to meet this afternoon. Prepping to present at the board meeting on Friday, you know how it goes," he says, briskly walking toward the ferry building to catch his ride across the bay.

"Oh, that's okay." Even though it's not okay, because a board meeting means I'll finally have to see my least favorite human: Ian. Not only will he be spending the whole morning in our office, he'll also be joining us at our off-site in Sausalito. I used to love our quarterly board meetings. All of the leadership team is busy in the morning, creating a super lax environment, and then a fun event in the afternoon to socialize outside the office. This will be my first one sans Ian at my side. I guess that's a problem for Friday-Olivia to solve.

"What's the next step with Tristan?" Mitch asks.

Shit. I need more time to prepare for this conversation. How do I explain that Tristan won't be coming to the next meeting but asked me on a date instead? Mitch can never know about that email. I want the chance to do this job, to be brilliant like Gavin. I'm sick of people thinking the only way for me to get ahead is by seducing powerful men.

"Product team is looped in and we're syncing tomorrow to start prepping the software demo for the next meeting. And yes, Darnell confirmed the time next week still works." It feels like I'm about to break an ankle walking this fast in my pumps.

I'm trying to make some eye-contact but if I step on any uneven ground, I'm a goner.

Mitch stops suddenly and I almost slam into his side. He looks at me pointedly. "Great. Fine. I'm asking about Tristan."

"Well, Tristan said he's going to have Darnell run point moving forward. Gavin said that's normal, for executives to take a step back during the process, let their team handle things." Gavin said no such thing, but I hope it's true.

"I saw his email, Livy. I'm asking what your plan is."

Mitch glances at his watch and over at the ferry line, as if this conversation is nothing but a notch to check off on his list before heading home. He saw the email? I reach for my phone but realize I left it on my desk.

"You saw it?"

"I assume he didn't mean to reply all. I hope you don't keep him waiting too long for a response."

Tristan seriously replied all with that email? He is a successful *executive*. He shouldn't be making mistakes like that. That's something I would do, have done. *Ugh.*

Okay, try to relax. Don't let the panic take over. This is an easy fix. Just be professional. Act like it's just something silly. Big tit energy. A man would never get worked up about this.

"I'll respond before I leave tonight. Let him know I'm only interested in a professional relationship. It's no big deal." *Suck it, Ian. Look how mature I am now.*

"Livy," Mitch sighs. "You can't say no to him. You wanted to work the deal. Work it."

I *can't* say no? "Mitch, you can't be serious. He's a prospect. Not to mention that he's like fifteen years older than me and—"

"Come on Livy, we both know that's your type." He winks at me, and it feels like a worm slithering down my spine.

"You think I'm going to sleep with someone to close a sale?"

I met Ian two months *after* starting the job at Sizzl, yet

somehow people still treat me like I'm there because of him. If I really used sex to get ahead, I would hope I'd be promoted by now. Well, maybe not considering Ian's opinion on my skills in the bedroom.

"Hey." Mitch holds up his hands like he's being interrogated by a cop. "I never said you had to sleep with him. But do you really think he'll want to work with us after you turn him down?" He scoffs and starts walking again. "Look, I'm taking a big chance letting you work this. It's my ass on the line if we lose the deal because you flirted with the client and couldn't follow through. I gotta run." He looks up at the crosswalk sign changing. "You wanted this to prove you have what it takes to be in sales, right? So prove it to me."

He jogs across the street while I'm left slack-jawed and shaking.

CHAPTER FOUR

GAVIN

"Hey, what are you still doing here?" Gabby asks on her way out of the office.

I should probably lie, but I just don't have it in me.

"Please don't read into it, but I'm waiting for Liv to get back. She looked kind of upset this afternoon and it's after six, but all her stuff is still here. I just want to make sure she's okay."

"Oh, brother. You are never getting over this girl." I roll my eyes but don't respond because it's not worth another argument. I've tried staying away from Liv ever since I found out Ian was in the picture, but it's getting harder to push her away. Even if all I get to do is help her earn the promotion she's fighting for, being the one to make her smile is worth it.

"I'll see you at home, okay? I'm sure she'll be back soon."

"I'm staying at Kadesha's tonight," she replies, heading to the door. Then she turns around and yells, "Have fun pining!"

A half hour goes by and I'm really starting to worry about Liv. The entire office is empty, and I've checked every single conference room for her. Who leaves work without their phone?

I finally decide I'm being an idiot, and maybe a creep, and pack up my stuff. Ian probably surprised her and took her out for a date or something.

It's too late to go to the gym now, so I decide to take the stairs. But when I open the door to the stairwell, I find Liv. She's crouched down on the floor curled into herself the same way Churro does when he's scared. I can't tell if she's crying but she's definitely shaking.

"Liv? What's wrong?" She's breathing erratically like she can't get any air. "Can you breathe? Do you need me to call an ambulance?"

She subtly shakes her head and lifts her face to meet my gaze. Her tear-free eyes shine back at me, but I can't understand the expression. All I see is fear.

"Please, talk to me. What happened?" I beg, dropping to my knees in front of her. My voice is desperate but I need to know what's going on because I have no idea how to help her. All I can do is watch as her chest heaves up and down, the movement completely unnatural.

I reach out a hand to cup her shoulder, wanting to comfort her in any way I can. Her wide eyes track the movement. Suddenly her hand finds mine, tugging and pressing it right over her sternum. She pushes against me, adding more force to the compression until I can feel the shift in her breathing pattern.

Eventually, her head tips back and she blows out a very long and shaky breath. The hand that isn't covering mine is wrapped in a tight fist. I grab onto it and urge her to relax her grip before she digs her nails in any further.

"Liv?" I ask, because I don't know what else to say. It's clear she can breathe now, but I also know she's not fine. And I really can't ignore the fact that both of our hands are still touching. I release the one on the floor between us, but she keeps my other firmly pressed between hers and her chest.

"Just a panic attack. I'm okay. Sorry."

She finally lets go and I slump down next to her, releasing a big breath of my own. Not that a panic attack isn't serious, but I'm just relieved she finally spoke. I wrap an arm around her almost subconsciously, but she doesn't move away. Comfort is clearly what she needs.

"Want me to call Ian for you?" I spit the words out as quickly as I can because Ian is the last person I want to see today.

"What?" She turns toward me. "No, definitely, definitely not." Not sure what's going on there but I'm *definitely* not going to ask.

"Okay, what do you need? How can I help?"

"I think—" She braces her hands on the ground to move to standing but her whole body is still shaking. I bracket my hands on either side of her and help her up, letting her lean on me for support. "Thanks." She flashes a shy smile. "I just want to go home."

"Okay, I'll walk you. Let's go grab your stuff."

She clings to me as we walk back into the office, and I hate myself for how much I enjoy it. This girl is clearly going through something and I'm busy inhaling the scent of her shampoo like some sort of addict.

"You really don't need to walk me. I'm all the way over Russian Hill, by Ghirardelli. Isn't your bike here anyway?"

"And it'll be fine if it stays here. Are you hungry? Thirsty? You look a little pale."

She looks down at her stomach like she's checking to see if it's empty. "Yeah, a little."

"Okay, last question. How do you feel about ridiculously cute, tiny animals?"

She looks at me this time. At first all I see is confusion, like she's trying to figure out what I'm hiding behind my eyes. But then she smiles, really smiles. She has the prettiest smile I've ever seen. "I think I feel pretty good about them..."

"Alright, Sparkles. Come with me."

I DECIDE TO TAKE LIV BACK TO MY PLACE SINCE GABBY'S staying at her girlfriend's. It's only a few blocks from the office and one of her favorite take-out restaurants is across the street. I've seen her get their ramen for lunch about a hundred times, and a big bowl of noodles sounds like just what she needs right now. And personally, I believe Churro can cure any ailment.

She doesn't fight me on the plan, even though we've never socialized outside of the office before, minus a few company events. She also perks up quite a bit when I mention ramen for dinner.

Liv is definitely still shaken up and I can see she's having some internal conversation with herself. It's always easy to tell when she's thinking hard about something because she mouths the words in her head. I'm also tracking the finger tap thing she tends to do when her anxiety comes out, poking the pad of her thumb with each nail over and over.

I shouldn't know these things because I shouldn't pay this much attention to her. She's not mine. She never has been.

But as well as I've hidden it from her, I've never been able to stop myself from noticing.

I take her inside my apartment before I order the food so she can relax while I pick it up. And then I introduce her to Churro.

"A hedgehog? The way you talk about him I was sure he was a dog." Yeah, she's not the first person to say that.

"Gabby begged me to get us a dog when we moved here,

but with my hours it was impossible. We considered a cat but then we found out she's allergic, so after lots of consideration, we landed on...Churro."

"He really is adorable," she coos while I pick him up. "How'd you come up with his name?"

"Well, I have a weakness for desserts and my mom made churros a lot when we were little. They were always Gabby's favorite. And I have to practice rolling my r's every day or quickly lose the ability. It was a win-win," I answer.

"Oh yeah. You're both always speaking Spanish together at the office. I assumed you were just being secretive, but is there another reason?"

"Secretive? No, we're just used to speaking both languages. We were born in Argentina, and our mom always spoke to us in Spanish when we were little."

I'm really not trying to air my family history, so before she can respond, I walk her through a basic tutorial of how to handle a hedgehog. She seems eager to cuddle with him, which isn't always the case. Most people assume he can't be held without hurting them. Gabby always tells me that my love language is physical touch, and now I'm wondering if it's possible that Liv's is the same.

I grab the sling Kadesha made and let Liv use it. Once she's settled with Churro in her lap and smiling again, I run out to grab the food.

Dinner goes by easily with a bit of small talk, but as we finish and I sense her getting ready to jet, I can't stop myself from asking, "Will you tell me what happened?"

She looks back at me like I'm holding a loaded gun, like if she stares into my eyes long enough, she'll be able to know if she can trust me not to shoot.

"You can trust me," I say.

Her gaze turns thoughtful. Then she hands me her phone. "Read it."

I quickly parse through the email to see it's from the CMO at Surf and Stream. And then I— "He asked you out? What a creep."

Her arms fly up over her head. "Thank you! That's what *I* thought."

"I don't get it. Did he do something to you? Why are you so upset over this?" I don't mean to diminish her feelings, and if this guy fucking touched her, I'll kill him. I just don't think Liv is the kind of girl to freak out over a request for a date. A polite request at that.

"Mitch doesn't want me to say no. In fact, he sort of insinuated that if I reject him, and we lose this deal, I'll never get promoted."

"Are you fucking with me?" That is complete bullshit. And also... "Wait. Are you sure he wasn't joking? Ian would flip if he found out. There's no way he'd go along with you dating someone else just to help our bottom line."

Liv's gaze drops down to the sofa and she starts to chew on the inside of her cheek. She still has Churro in her lap but he's fast asleep. "Ian wouldn't care. We're not together anymore. He...he dumped me."

I clench every muscle I have trying to school my features. *He* dumped *her*?

"I haven't really told anyone," she continues. "Only Andie knows. Well, and HR. So Mitch found out right away."

"How long?" I ask, trying and failing to keep any emotion out of my voice.

"Huh?"

"How long have you been broken up for?"

"Oh. A few months now."

What the hell? Mitch knew about this for *months* and

didn't tell me? He's the only one besides Gabby who knows how I felt about Liv. So much for thinking we were friends.

"I'm really sorry," I say, only because I'm sure she's expecting me to say *something* and not jump up and down on the couch screaming "*fuck yes!*"

"I'm not. I can't believe I was with him for so long. He wasn't—sorry, never mind."

I would kill to know what she was about to say, but before I can find my words her phone chimes. She flinches when she reads the text.

"What's wrong?" I ask.

"Nothing. Just Mitch again."

I check my watch and see it's almost nine o'clock. "Does he normally text you at night?"

"All the time. It's so annoying," she whines.

"Really? Like about work or..."

"Rarely. He usually just wants to know if I'm caught up on the latest episode of *Dragon Wars* or he'll ask for advice on what to do with his ex-wife. I really, *really* wish I didn't know so much about his love life." She makes a "blech" noise.

"That's inappropriate. He shouldn't be texting you after hours like this. You should tell him to stop."

She looks up at me and starts to chuckle. At first I smile back but then her laugh turns maniacal and I realize I've chosen my words poorly. "Oh, I should? Does he text you after hours?"

"Well, yeah, but—"

"But you're a guy?"

"I mean...I didn't mean it like..." Shit. I have no idea what to say.

"Scottie, it's okay. I know you mean well. But if I tell Mitch it's inappropriate, I'll be drawing a line in the sand. I'm already on the outside of your little club. I don't get invited to golf on the weekends, or the strip club team lunches. Or the *happy hours*." She gives me a pointed look at this, and I feel like such a piece of shit. "So yeah, I put up with a few inappropriate texts and let him bitch to me about how it wasn't *his* fault he cheated. If it helps me finally get the promotion, then it's worth it."

"I'm sorry. I never really thought about all that." And this time I really *am* sorry, because I never thought about any of it. She's right. Mitch takes our team golfing all the time. I guess it never occurred to me whether she was even invited or didn't want to come. Does she play?

And I've unknowingly contributed to this too. Does she think I don't invite her because she's a woman? I want, no I *need*, to explain myself. I just don't know how to without giving myself away.

"*Ugh.*" My thoughts are interrupted as she grunts at another incoming text.

"Can I see?" I ask. She hands me the phone and I'm more than disgusted by what's on the screen.

> MITCH:
>
> Did you respond to Tristan yet?
>
> I need to know the plan Livy
>
> If you really want to be in sales you're gonna have to learn to use the assets you've got. Let's stop pretending the hair and the heels wasn't part of your strategy today
>
> Don't be such a tease

When I look up at Liv, tears swell in her eyes and her fists are wrapped around her long red hair, tucking it into a bun. She's muttering to herself, but I can't make out the words.

"What'd you say?" I ask.

She scoffs. "Just that Ian was right." Jesus. I don't even want to know.

"Is there anything in the middle?" she asks suddenly. I'm not sure what she's referring to, so I give her a questioning look. "Like, is there anything in between a slut and a tease? Because I'd really like to know. It seems like no matter what I do, I'm one of the two, so I'm just asking, is there another option?"

My lips part to respond, but nothing comes out. I have no idea what to say to her. She shouldn't have to deal with this shit, especially not from her manager.

With all of my frustration directed at Mitch, I don't think for a second before tapping on his name and hitting the call button. Liv is staring at me horrified when he answers the phone.

"Hey Livy."

"It's Gavin, actually."

"Oh, umm, hey? This is Olivia's phone, right?" I love how flustered he sounds. I want him to be nervous about this call. Even if I have no idea what I'm going to say.

"Yeah, she's at my place." Liv is watching me with wide eyes and an open mouth. She looks terrified and I hate that I'm contributing to that. But I also can't get the image of her out of my head, the one from two hours ago when she was on the floor struggling to breathe. "Stop asking her to date a prospect. You're not her fucking pimp. She isn't okay with it, and she shouldn't have to tell you twice."

"Christ, Scottie, can you just let us handle this? You're really making a big deal out of nothing."

"Are you not telling her to date this guy to close a deal?"

"What I'm doing is none of your damn business. Put Olivia on the phone."

I'm fuming. The texts he sent her, the way he's dismissing

her feelings now; she had a *panic attack* worrying about her job over this and he doesn't seem to give a shit.

It's like Davide all over again. I shouldn't even be talking to Mitch. The CEO is my closest friend. And I'm sure Daanesh would want Mitch gone if he knew this was happening. But can we really afford to lose our VP of sales with this acquisition on the line? Would the board even allow it, or just blame Liv like they did with Megan in recruiting? Mitch isn't the kind of guy that would go quietly.

I look back at Liv, trying to convey an apology with my eyes. Because I wish I could do the right thing here. I wish I could tell Mitch to go fuck himself and have his desk cleaned out tomorrow. I wish I could make our office a safer place for people like Liv. I wish I wasn't a selfish bastard who chose paying off his loans over keeping our company douche-bag free.

So I'll have to do the next best thing. I can't stop myself from what I'm about to say. It's the only option I can think of.

"Actually, it is my business. Liv and I are together."

CHAPTER FIVE

OLIVIA

What is happening right now?

Staring daggers at Gavin wasn't enough to get his attention so now I'm kicking his feet, trying to force him to look at me, all without waking Churro who's still cozied up in my lap. This hedgehog might be the only thing keeping me from a full-on anxiety spiral right now. I may need to kidnap him. Hedge-nap?

Finally, Gavin turns to me and mouths "I'm sorry" with a shrug. That's it? He just poured fuel all over the fire of my shit day and all I get is a shrug?

"We haven't told anyone yet since it's new and we didn't know how people at work would react. Yes, it's serious," he continues on the phone. There's a long pause and I am desperate to know what Mitch is saying on the other end. "Well, I'd say the second I found out she was single, actually." Another long pause. "Look Mitch, the point is that I'm not okay with you asking her to do something she's uncomfortable with, and it should have been enough when she told you herself. Now we're gonna go to HR tomorrow and disclose our relationship. Is there anything else I should be talking to them about?"

Did Gavin just threaten Mitch? Gavin Scott is morphing into an entirely new person tonight. He went from the hot colleague who hates me to my panic attack savior and now he's some sort of vigilante superhero. The longer he talks to Mitch the darker his eyes get, the more strain I can see in the set of his jaw. It's hot, so hot I'm afraid I might start fanning myself if this goes on much longer.

If I didn't want to throttle him right now I might be seriously turned on. Rage and lust aren't a great combo. I feel like I'm about to combust.

We're together. Why the hell would he say that?

"Yeah, screw you too. See you tomorrow, *pal.*" He hangs up.

"Oh my god, did you really just talk to him like that?" I guess when you're best friends with the CEO you can do whatever you want, but still.

The anger on Gavin's face starts to dissipate and he finally makes eye contact with me. "Shit. I'm so sorry, Liv. I was just really pissed and that was the first thing I could think of to get him to stop hassling you." He really does look sorry. Not that his sorrow does me any good in this situation.

The fact that Gavin tried to stand up for me says a lot. It's telling me he's not at all who I thought he was. But as good as his intentions are, he hasn't exactly helped to solve my problem. In fact, I'm positive he's made it worse.

Would it have killed him to ask me before he called Mitch and went on that tirade? But he's a man. Why would he ever need to worry about the consequences of his actions?

"It's okay," I lie. Because what's done is done. "It'll be pretty awkward when you tell him the truth though," I say through gritted teeth. Mitch will probably think we slept together or something, but it fizzled out, or he got bored with me. It took months for people to believe I was actually dating Ian, that I wasn't just some plaything.

I know what I look like. It's the big hair and the big boobs and apparently my *smile*. Men have always found it appropriate to comment on my looks as though I'm hanging on a wall instead of an actual person.

And women...well, I've been called a gold digger and a slut around the office more times than I can count, hence why I've been so quiet about the break-up. At twenty-six I'm still the youngest person at our company, minus Gabby. Starting a romantic relationship two years ago with one of our board members who's over a decade older than me created a lot of eye rolls, especially when I was so new. I try not to care about my reputation, but it still hurts when I hear what people say about me.

"We don't have to," Gavin offers, tilting his head to the side. "Tell him the truth I mean, if it'll help him leave you alone for a bit, we could just..." He shrugs.

"We could just pretend to be a couple? Are you serious?" Pretending to be his girlfriend is ridiculous. We're not even friends. I was pretty sure he hated me until this morning—when I determined the coffee wasn't poisoned.

Though it doesn't sound as horrible as I'm making it out to be, dating Gavin. I mean, he's really nice to look at. It might even soften the blow as people start to find out about Ian...oh my god, *Ian*. I almost forgot about having to see him on Friday when he comes in for the board meeting. And then after the board meeting when we all—

"Sorry, never mind. It was a stupid idea," Gavin mutters. "Please don't get upset. I'll figure something out to tell Mitch."

"Actually," I start, but he cuts me off.

"It's okay, Liv. I can see the horrified look on your face. I know what it looks like when you're anxious." He does?

"You've been through enough today. I'm not trying to make you feel worse. You can relax." He brushes a hand through his hair and falls back against the sofa. "I should never have told him that in the first place. I'll take care of it."

"*Actually*," I continue. "I was thinking maybe...maybe you could wait to come clean until next week?"

"What?" He swiftly straightens his spine, eyeing me like he's trying to find the puzzle piece he's missing.

"I was just thinking, since you already offered, it might help me out on Friday at our off-site, so I can avoid—"

"Ian?"

"Mmhmm." I squint at him, worried about how childish it might look that I'm desperate to avoid my ex. But I'm not too embarrassed to ask for Gavin's help. I have no idea what people will say when they see I'm not with Ian anymore. I'll gladly suck up my pride for a shield. "It's just, I don't know what to expect—"

"Say no more, Sparkles. I'm in." He grins back at me, and it's so genuine I want to cry. I still don't know what changed in the last twenty-four hours, but whatever made him go from hating me to becoming this fierce protector, I'm grateful for it. I'm so tired of feeling sorry for myself in the aftermath of this break-up.

Maybe Gavin's exactly the kind of distraction I need.

From: Olivia Diamond < olivia@sizzl.com >
To: Tristan Cross < tristan.cross@surfandstream.com >
Subject: RE: RE: Nice Meeting You

Hi Tristan,

Thanks for the kind reply. I hope you'll be able to join more meetings in the future and see all the capabilities Sizzl can offer you. I think you'll be especially impressed with Davide, our Head of Product.

As for this weekend, I'm very flattered. Since I'm currently seeing someone, I'll have to decline but very much appreciate the offer.

Please don't hesitate to reach out for any other questions regarding Sizzl. I'm excited to work with your team and help you reach all your marketing goals.

Cheers,

Olivia Diamond
Sales Development @ Sizzl

I SPENT HALF THE NIGHT CRAFTING THIS EMAIL AND AFTER hitting send I want to rewrite it again. Unfortunately, I could not find a template for a message that conveyed utmost professionalism, while being friendly and positive and also turning a guy down. And I searched for one *thoroughly*. Even AI couldn't help me this time around.

With the dreaded email finally sent, I walk out of Fog & Foam with my half-drunk coffee in hand and bump into my new boyfriend.

"Hey, Sparkles. Had a feeling I'd catch you here." Gavin's in his usual hoodie and jeans, white sneakers and his hair still wet from the shower. While I try to look polished and professional each day, he's my complete opposite. And yet, he pulls it off every time.

"You were...looking for me?" I realize now I did leave his

apartment a little abruptly last night. I'm beyond grateful that he's willing to fake-love me to alleviate some of the stress in my life, but once he started talking logistics, my anxiety got the best of me and I fake-yawned until he ordered me to go home and get some sleep.

"Thought it might be good to walk in together, show a united front." He winks before threading his fingers through mine and *holding* them there. Yep, we are officially holding hands.

"This okay?" he asks in a quick murmur. And I'm *frozen*. When we talked about this last night, I never really thought about the actual pretending we'd be doing. It's one thing to tell people we're together, even my company, but *showing* people, how did I not consider what that meant?

My mind flashes back to him on the floor with me last night, when he pressed his palm to my chest, when he squeezed my fingers and gently unwrapped them from my fist. For someone who's never liked me, he sure is making it a habit of touching me. I only wish I didn't enjoy it so much.

Suddenly all I can think about is Gavin's hands. His hands on mine. His hands in my hair. His hands all over—

"Sparkles?"

"Sorry. Yeah. All good." How the hell am I going to pull this off if I get this worked up over some simple hand holding? Maybe I'm not mature enough for this.

"Good. And I want Mitch to see us go to HR together, so he knows I was serious. As long as that's still okay with you."

"Yeah, it's..." I'm actually dreading going to HR. I've already had to disclose and then *un*-disclose one relationship to the team. This is getting embarrassing. But on Friday everyone at the company is going to find out Ian left me. Having Gavin around will make things easier. I think. "Let's do it."

SLACK DIRECT MESSAGE

Andie Oh:

Were you and Gavin holding hands this morning?

HOLDING HANDS

?!?!?!?!?!?!?!??!?!?!?

Olivia Diamond:

No need to panic. I'll tell you everything at lunch

Andie Oh:

Stalking your calendar now

OK 12:45 at Yank Sing – we need dumplings! Accept my invite
so no one can book over it

I click over to my calendar and find an invite for *Strategy
Session – DO NOT BOOK* with a winking emoji in the
description.

The one thing Gavin and I did discuss last night was who
we would and wouldn't be lying to. At first, he said I shouldn't
tell Andie the truth because of her penchant for gossip, but
then I reminded him that she was the only person besides
Mitch and HR who I'd confided in about my break-up and he
came around. She's also his sister's boss, and there's no way we
could lie to Gabby. She's his family.

Andie's sort of mine too. She's been my work-wife, as she
likes to say, for more than a year now. She closed the deal the
first time she invited me over for a homemade Korean dinner.
Her sugary-sweet personality also hooked me hard, but I'd be
lying if I said I didn't go to her place once a week for the tteok-
bokki alone. That, and the fact that she is one of the least judg-
mental people I've ever met in my life. She was never anything
but supportive of my relationship with Ian, at least in the beginning, before pleasing him became so tedious.

She was even more supportive about the breakup.

"How many orders of har gow do we need? Or should we just get extra soup dumplings? It's sort of chilly today," Andie says, rubbing her arms over her cream sweater. She's right. It's a very brisk fifty-four-degree day. Basically freezing for February in San Francisco.

"Let's do both. And get egg tarts. Before they sell out."

I've barely torn into the pork bun when Andie starts. "Okay, it's time to talk about the *hand holding*." She emphasizes the last two words like they're explicit. What is this, Regency England?

There's no great way to ease into this conversation so I just go for it. "It was just for show. We're fake-dating."

She squints back in response, her mouth full of shrimp. And then barely audible, says, "Like in a romcom? You know that's not a thing people do in real life, right?"

"It's kind of a long story, but Mitch was being an ass, and before I could stop him, Gavin told him we're dating." My words tumble out at lightning speed. "So now we have to keep up the ruse for a little while."

She eyes me suspiciously while demolishing a few more dumplings. The restaurant is completely full and listening to the sounds of everyone around us has me momentarily distracted while I wait for her opinion on all this. "You sure this has nothing to do with seeing Ian on Friday? Are you trying to make him jealous?"

I almost spit out my green tea. If there is one singular thing I'm sure of, it's that I don't want Ian back. If a genie miraculously came out of this teapot, I'd use all three wishes on erasing him from my life completely.

"No. *Definitely* not. I mean, yeah, it'll make avoiding Ian a lot easier, but I couldn't care less about making him jealous. You know that."

"You're right. I do," she says after studying me for a

moment. "This has been one of the healthiest breakups I've ever witnessed. You've never even mentioned texting him or trying to bump into him somewhere randomly. Hell, you've even avoided the gym and I guarantee if that man saw you in spandex he'd be begging for another chance."

I roll my eyes at her comment, but I'm also flattered. Not about the spandex but that I've handled it well. After two years with a boyfriend constantly reminding me how immature I am, it's nice to hear the opposite from someone I admire as much as Andie.

I used to think love was like a ladder. It was aspirational, something to achieve when you reached the precipice. From a birds-eye view, I always thought Ian was better than me, so being with him meant I was better too. Like if someone like him loved me, I'd go up another rung.

Now I think it's more like a house, or at least that's what I'd like it to be if I ever fall in love. Something we can build together over time.

The thing I've been working on with my therapist is pursuing what makes me happy. This might sound intuitive, but I've realized that I tend to focus on what others want from me instead of what I want for myself. That I give way too much power to those around me, to their opinions of me.

Now that I've put in the work, it's so clear that Ian never made me happy. I don't think I ever even loved him. I was just so thrilled when he said it, that I immediately reciprocated. I never actually asked myself what I felt for him.

From the very beginning, he made me feel less than, and instead of building a relationship together, I spent two years constantly trying to mold myself to fit his expectations.

"This really isn't about Ian, I swear. Just an added bonus."

"So what did the mighty Mitch do now?" she asks.

"Well, I told you about that prospect, Tristan. How he

asked me out?" She nods in response. "Mitch saw the email. I guess Tristan had replied all and I didn't notice. And Mitch told me to go out with him."

"Told you? Like ordered you?"

"Pretty much. And when I said that wasn't going to happen, he got really worked up about it and made it clear my promotion was on the line with this deal. It just sort of spiraled."

I show Andie the texts from Mitch and give her the bullet points from last night at Gavin's apartment. She whisper-yells several expletives and I see her cheeks burn pink.

She tosses my phone back to me like a hot potato and takes a deep, centering breath. "We should discuss how to murder Mitch later, but I still don't understand how Gavin's involved. Why didn't you go to HR? Or Daanesh even? Why resort to a fake boyfriend?"

"It's just for a few days. It got Mitch to stop harassing me and it'll be nice to have a buffer on Friday when the whole office finds out Ian and I are over." I don't mention how good it felt to have Gavin stand up for me, or the butterflies I felt this morning as we walked into the office together.

"Still. I just hate letting Mitch get away with treating you like that. Isn't there something we can do?"

"You know exactly what happens to women who complain about these things. I mean, what would I even say?"

"You wouldn't have to say anything. The texts speak for themselves. You know this is sexual harassment, right?" Andie argues. "Just because he's not the one hitting on you doesn't mean he's innocent."

"Sure, I know that. But I also know I'll end up being the one who gets blamed. You saw what happened to Megan after everything with Davide blew up. I can handle Mitch being Mitch if it means I get to keep my job. I've worked too hard for this promotion to just throw all that work away and start over."

Andie sighs. I can tell she's frustrated with me, but I also know she gets it. Even as a team lead, she knows what it's like being a woman in tech. Companies in the Bay Area love to tout how forward thinking and feminist they are, but it's always still men who are running the show. Women are celebrated, just as long as we play by their rules.

She pulls up the texts on my phone and reads through them again. "So, Gavin saw these and just suddenly agreed to pretend you're a couple?"

"He didn't agree to anything. I never asked. He just did it." I shrug, not really knowing how else to explain why he jumped in like that. I still don't understand it myself.

"Good for him. You need a man like that. Someone as right-eous as you are."

I do need someone like that, and for a split second I forget that this is all a façade. That no man who was actually mine has ever defended me so gallantly.

"We're not really dating, you know. He's not *my man*."

Andie twists her lips, giving me a thoughtful once over. "He got you *ramen*, Liv." She says the word like it's the equivalent of organ donation. "I'd give it a real shot." She pops another soup dumpling in her mouth and grins at me.

SLACK DIRECT MESSAGE
Gavin Scott:
How'd it go with Andie?
Olivia Diamond:
Fine. I'm glad I had a chance to explain things before the rumors started.
Did you get a chance to tell Gabby?
Gavin Scott:

Yep. All good

Gavin has been checking in on me all day. Not in an annoying way, but how an actual boyfriend might act. And not just about our arrangement. After our chat with HR he told me to come to him if Mitch ever made me feel uncomfortable again. He promised he wouldn't insert himself into the situation like last night unless I asked him, but that he wanted to make sure I had someone to talk to. If I didn't know better, I'd say Gavin Scott might care about me.

Which is the thought I'm trying to erase from my head when Mitch heads to our desk pod and asks, "How are the love birds?"

Mitch and I haven't actually spoken yet today. Just minimal eye-contact across the office. He has a good excuse, prepping for his board meeting in two days, but it's still weird.

"Mitch, should we chat for a sec?" I know it's the end of the day, and I can see he's about to head out, but I don't want this awkwardness to linger any further.

"It's fine, Livy," he says, ruffling my hair. Seriously? "So, are you gonna take the ferry with us on Friday or will you be going with your *boyfriend*?" He nudges his head at Gavin when he says the b-word. And I'm...lost.

I look to Gavin, wondering what Mitch is talking about but he just scowls. "Scottie?" I ask.

"You know I don't do boats." I try to school my features when he says it because apparently, I'm supposed to know this. Mitch laughs, loving our first Newlywed Game fail.

Trying for a save, I respond, "Oh, I thought it was just smaller boats. No ferries? Really?" Why would he not be okay with ferries?

"Goodnight, guys. Have fun getting to know each other." Mitch winks back before he walks out. *Shit.*

"Sorry, Liv. That's my bad. I should have told you considering the event on Friday."

I can't exactly fault him for this, but I am curious. "You really don't do ferries? Ever?"

"No boats." I raise my brows, urging him to explain and he sighs, resignation coating his features. "You hungry?" He swiftly changes the subject.

"A little. You wanna tell me about the boats?"

"Let's grab dinner," he says, standing and packing up his laptop. "I'll tell you all my deepest, darkest secrets."

CHAPTER SIX

GAVIN

Olivia says she doesn't feel like going out, but to my surprise, she invites me over to her place for dinner.

"I mean, we should both have some basic knowledge of our fake-partner's apartment, right?" I couldn't agree more.

Our walk there goes straight through North Beach—San Francisco's Little Italy—so we stop by a market to grab everything needed for a lazy meat and cheese board. Neither of us know how to cook.

"What kind of wine do you prefer?" she asks, perusing the rows. The way she examines each label makes it seem like she knows what she's doing, whereas my wine knowledge starts and stops with red versus white.

"You look like a pro. Just grab whatever you like," I offer.

"It's all Italian. I'm mostly familiar with French or Californian varietals." Varietals? She grabs a bottle and inspects it thoroughly. "Hmmm, I think I like Sangiovese. It's single origin, usually has nice tannins. Does that work?"

"I only know about half the words you just said, Sparkles." I grab the bottle from her hand and feel a buzz just from the briefest brush of our fingers. I squeeze my hands into fists to stop myself from seeking more contact. "My fake girlfriend is so sophisticated."

We argue over who's paying for a few minutes before she reluctantly concedes, and we head to her apartment. It's kind of surreal to think I'll finally see where she lives after two years of wondering. Wondering what she does outside of work, what she looks like when she isn't wearing her typical blazer, pointy shoes, and hair pulled tight in a bun. I've thought about it all. What music she listens to; what she watches on tv; if she's a morning person or a night owl.

"Well, this is me. Sorry it's a little cluttered," she announces when we walk inside. Cluttered isn't exactly the word I'd use. It's not messy at all. Just a small studio with a lot of décor. To my delight, she immediately kicks off her shoes and lets her hair down, before swapping the blazer for a hoodie that almost matches mine.

Her walls are covered in photography, hundreds of framed photos lining each corner of the apartment. It looks to be mainly shots of the Bay Area; bridges, the Painted ladies, Land's End. One wall is just vineyards.

"I like all the photos," I say as I walk through the space, eyeing them in more detail.

She's grabbing glasses and plates from the kitchen when she responds, "Oh, yeah. Just a hobby I can't seem to kick."

"A hobby? Wait." I squeeze around the love seat to help her in the kitchen. "You took all these?" I gesture to the walls around us.

"Yeah. I know the place looks like a mess, but I really can't choose which ones to get rid of. I love them all." She pouts and shrugs her shoulders until they go all the way up to her ears. I wonder if she knows how beautiful she looks right now.

"Why do you have to get rid of any?" I ask.

"I don't *have* to. But anyone who's ever set foot in my apartment tells me it's too much. Kind of like my brain." She mumbles the last part, but I don't miss it.

"It's not too much." I make sure to look at her when I speak, because I can tell there was hurt in her words. I've learned a lot about Liv in the last forty-eight hours and I'm realizing that kindness is something she deserves quite a bit more of. I don't really know how to convey that with my eyes but I'm trying, and the way her mouth softens makes me feel victorious.

"Well, that means you are welcome here anytime." She grins and hands me one of the glasses she just poured. "Cheers to my very supportive fake boyfriend."

"Cheers to my very beautiful fake girlfriend." She blushes as we clink the glasses together and her eyes flutter closed when she tips the glass toward her mouth. To my surprise, she doesn't take a sip. Especially not a big gulp like I just did. Instead, she tilts the glass to her nose and breathes in deeply. I continue to watch as she swirls the glass, tilts it from one side to the other and then finally brings it to her lips.

They're painted scarlet today—just a few shades lighter than the wine—and leave a perfect imprint on the glass.

"What was that?" I ask, after she finally swallows a small sip.

"What? Oh, sorry. Habit." She shrugs again. "The wine's pretty good. Do you like it?"

"Are you some sort of wine expert? What do you mean, habit?" I'm thoroughly confused.

"My family owns a winery up in Sonoma. Diamond Sky?" I shake my head, not entirely sure which words go together. "I assumed you knew. People in the office are always asking me for free wine."

"I've never been much of a wine drinker," I respond, which

is true, but then she looks at the glass and back at me with an apology in her eyes. "I like this though. You picked a good one."

"You should've told me." She nudges my shoulder and I grab onto her hand before she can pull it back.

"I like it. I swear. You'll have to recommend some others for me to try. Maybe I can be as fancy as you."

I help her plate up all the food and move it over to the coffee table. Her apartment's too small for a dining set, but I'm glad for the tight space. It feels more comfortable, sitting on the couch, snacking together. It's nice seeing Liv in her comfort zone, her body relaxed as she tucks her feet under her legs and falls into the couch.

"I always bring a ton of wine back when I visit. I'll make sure to put a bottle on your desk so everyone knows how special you are."

I watch her tear off a chunk of bread and try to remind myself she's only pretending that I'm special, that this whole arrangement is going to end in a few days. When I came up with the idea last night, I don't think I considered what I'd have to give up once it ended.

I like hanging out with Liv. I've always had a thing for her but now that I get to see this side of her, in her own environment, I like her even more.

Part of me wants to run before I become even more pathetically gone for her, but a stronger part of me wants to enjoy this while I can.

"So, I think we need to go over some ground rules," she says, interrupting my thoughts.

"Rules?" I grab a few almonds from the platter while she nods her head several times, mouthing a few words I can't make out. "Go ahead. Tell me."

"Touching." The word flies through her lips and her eyes bulge. "Sorry, I meant, umm…"

"You've got to stop apologizing, Liv. You say sorry more than anyone I've ever met."

"Sor—" She just barely stops herself and we both grin. "I can't help it."

"Just tell me what's on your mind," I urge her to continue, because my thoughts are still snagging on the word *touching*.

"When you held my hand today," she begins. "It sort of caught me off guard. I guess I just wanted to know what to expect on Friday."

"You want to know how much I plan on touching you?" Each of her features scrunch together as she nods, her hands in tight fists by her sides on the couch. She looks nervous as hell. About me touching her? Shit.

"I mean, I'm good with it, if you are." Okay, I can breathe again. "And it's a work-sponsored event so I don't think anyone is expecting us to be going at it, but I just need a heads up if you want to start making out or something."

I really wish I hadn't just taken a sip of wine because it bursts through my mouth as I choke on her words. *Or something?*

"Oh no. I'm so sorry!" I glare at her. "Not sorry, just...apologetic. Let me get you a towel." Luckily, I saved her from the spray by blocking it with my arm. My arm that's now covered in wine. I really should take smaller sips.

"Just to be clear, you'd like a heads up before I stick my tongue in your mouth? Or...more?" I ask, trying and failing to clean my stained sleeve with the paper towel she hands me. I give up and reach for the hem of my hoodie, taking the whole thing off.

"Preferably, yes. Umm, why are you taking off your clothes? I feel like a heads up there would be nice too."

Now that I know she's not nearly as timid as I thought, I feel like messing with her a bit. I stand up and pull her with me, wrapping an arm around her waist and lifting her up until her feet dangle against me. She makes a little shriek.

"What are you doing?"

"Ravaging you, of course. Is this enough of a *heads up*?"

She punches at my shoulder. "Oh my god. Put me down, Scottie!" I love it when she calls me that. I love that she has a comeback for everything, even the first time I gave her a nickname.

I set her down, both of us laughing, and take my sweatshirt over to the sink. I never knew how much I'd enjoy making her flustered. It's not exactly a great recipe for fooling people we're dating, but I'll have to enjoy it behind the scenes.

"As for your rules," I yell over my shoulder, loud enough for her to hear with the running water. "If there's anything you don't want me to do, anything you're uncomfortable with, just tell me. But no, I don't think anyone expects us to be making out at the off-site." I leave the wet sweatshirt hanging off the counter to dry and sit back down on the couch. "Unless you want to, of course." I can't help it. I wiggle my brows a bit to see if I can make her blush again. And she does. Hell, maybe she does want to kiss me.

"I think I'll pass," she says, scooting away from me an inch or two. "At least until I know why you're so scared of the *big bad ferry boats*."

"I am not *scared* of ferry boats," I bark back. "I just get motion sickness, okay? Boats, buses, planes, cars. They're all my enemy."

Her face softens and I realize I just killed the mood. "That really sucks, Scottie. You can't be in a car at all? Or fly?"

"I can. But I usually take medicine that puts me to sleep. That's why I got the bike. Only thing I can ride that never messes with my head."

"That's not embarrassing, you know. You promised deep

and dark," she says, arms crossed over her chest. She's eyeing me like I just stole her favorite toy. It's cute as hell.

"Fine. I'm terrified of snakes. I will scream like a little baby if I ever see one. Gabby puts a fake one in my bed every so often just to remind me she has all the power in our relationship." Liv laughs and while I'm not thrilled to be sharing the most unattractive qualities about myself, I am enjoying letting her know me better. "I sing along to every Disney movie. They remind me of when Gabby was little, so we still watch them all the time." I shrug. She giggles. I love this. "You've already seen my pet hedgehog and the personal sling I use to carry him around."

"That's not embarrassing! It's adorable," she interjects.

"Well, you haven't seen me give him a bedtime story yet, so..."

"I would really like to see that."

Noted.

"Maybe you can give me something here? I'm feeling very vulnerable." I frown. Or try to. Vulnerability isn't really my thing. "Do you even have any embarrassing stuff?"

She scoffs. "How long have we got?" Now I scoff. "Okay, fine. I only listen to French music. Everyone I know thinks it's crazy."

"I didn't know you spoke French."

"I don't," she deadpans.

"That's not embarrassing." I'm more intrigued than anything. "Why do you listen to it?"

"It helps me relax, get out of my head. I don't know. I think I just feel the music more when I'm not focusing on the lyrics. Does that make sense?"

"I guess so. Why not classical? Or instrumental? Why French?"

"It's hard to explain, but I like to hear them sing even if I can't understand it. I think I just like the way it makes me feel. It helps me shut off my brain. Makes me less anxious."

I've seen Liv's anxiety get the best of her. It makes me glad she's found a coping mechanism.

"French music, wine, photography." I list them off on my fingers. "You're an artist."

A laugh bubbles out of her that catches me off guard. "I don't think so."

"Why is that funny? You are."

"No. Everyone else in my family is an artist. And everyone agrees that I am the black sheep. I'm basically the opposite of my parents and all three of my brothers." Three brothers? That's not intimidating or anything.

"They're all artists?"

"Yeah, pretty much. Or at least in the sense that they believe any real job is 'done with your hands.' My dad's family goes back three generations as winemakers, ever since his grandparents emigrated here from France. My mom's a painter. She designs all the bottle labels and did all the murals at the winery—people come just to see them. My brothers all work the vineyard and Deacon—the oldest—is also the head chef there."

"That's where you grew up? Surrounded by that?" It sounds like a dream compared to what Gabby and I have been through. But I'm not about to bring up any of that.

"Yeah. It was a little slow for me. Again, black sheep." She points her thumbs back at herself and makes a face.

"I remember now, your interview. You said you were desperate to live in the city and would take any job to make it happen."

"I don't think I said desperate," she argues, indignation spreading across her features. "But yeah, I was."

"Well, I'm really glad I went against all better judgment and hired you."

She punches my shoulder. "You are so lucky you hired me! How many deals did I source for you last year?"

"Most of them," I concede. "You're a rockstar. And I'm sorry Mitch hasn't realized that yet."

She doesn't respond, just offers a half-smile. I take a moment to look around the room again at all the photos she's taken. It feels like I'm reading a treasure map to all her favorite spots in the bay.

"I've got an idea. Let's blow off work Friday morning."

"I can't just blow off work, Scottie. I'm not you."

"Everyone will be busy with the board meeting, they won't even notice. I'll tell Mitch we're both working from home since we'll be riding to the off-site together."

"We will?"

"Yep. We're going on a field trip. Ever been on a motorcycle?"

CHAPTER SEVEN

OLIVIA

27 Months Ago

"Were you surprised that I asked you out?" Ian inquires from across the table.

I'm not sure how to answer the question. I was definitely surprised when one of our board members decided to speak to me at all. But once he started hitting on me, no, getting my number wasn't exactly a surprise.

"Definitely," I reply. It feels like the response he's looking for.

"Do you like wine?"

"Actually—"

"Don't worry, I'll order. I know it's confusing. They have excellent wine here. I bet I can find something you'll love."

I'm not sure why I don't speak up, but it feels like he wants to impress me. It feels kind of nice that he wants to impress me. Well, it feels nice until he orders a cab that's extremely over-priced and way too dry. But I can look past that.

"You know you're the most beautiful woman in the restaurant, right?" It doesn't feel like a question, so I don't respond, but my cheeks heat nonetheless. "Everyone here is probably wondering what you could possibly be doing with me."

"I doubt anyone would think that." And it's true. Ian's not just handsome, he has this air about him that lets you know he's won at life.

He grins. I like it when he grins at me.

When the waiter returns, Ian whispers to him, ordering both of us something that's not even on the menu. Our server actually winks before he walks away.

"What was that?" I ask, hoping he didn't order one of the many things I'm allergic to.

"A surprise." He takes my hand in his over the table. "Just humor me and pretend like it isn't painfully obvious how hard I'm trying here."

Our date continues with him showering me with compliments. I'm not sure how well we get to know each other, but I do learn a lot about his job. It's impressive that he's the youngest partner at his venture capitalist firm. He gets to work with clients all over the world.

The furthest I've traveled from home is Colorado.

When our meal arrives, Ian's excitement only grows. He explains every detail of the three raw courses we'll be sharing as if I've never eaten fish before.

"They only serve this to five tables a night. That's why it's not on the main menu. Do you know how lucky you are that you came with me?" he asks before popping another piece of flounder in his mouth. This man really loves rhetorical questions.

I've always enjoyed food. My oldest brother is an incredible chef and because of him, I've understood wine pairings since I was old enough to drink—which in my family was age nine.

Ian made it clear his special order was expensive, so I know

I shouldn't complain, but the delicate scallop crudo being washed down by the heavy tannins in this cabernet is honestly the *worst*. I didn't plan on ordering dessert, but I get a slice of flourless chocolate cake just so my taste buds don't go on strike.

And when he feeds me a bite of cake from across the table, his eyes glued to my lips the whole time, all is forgiven. I've forgotten anything that didn't contribute to this being the perfect date.

As soon as we leave the restaurant, he takes my hand and pulls my body against him.

"There's something I've been thinking about all night."

I open my mouth to respond but his lips find mine before I can ask the question. His kiss is hungry and demanding, his tongue finding mine almost instantly. His hand slides down my back until it rests on my hip and squeezes.

"Come home with me." Again, it's not a question, but my answer would be yes all the same. My first date since living in San Francisco feels like a dream. And Ian Thompson is the weaver.

ANDIE OH:

How'd it go

ME:

I just got home ;)

IT'S ELEVEN IN THE MORNING SO I THINK SHE GETS THE hint.

The truth is I never wanted to leave his apartment. It was this beautiful space with all floor-to-ceiling windows on top of

Russian Hill. The views alone were drool-worthy. It's exactly the kind of place I always imagined when I pictured living in the city.

Unfortunately, with my salary, and even quite a bit of financial help from my parents, all I can afford is a tiny studio. After talking to people at work, I just feel fortunate to not have multiple roommates.

ANDIE OH:

I need details!

I mean, not those details, well, unless you want to share ;)

But did you have fun? Will you see him again?

ME:

Lots of fun

And I'm seeing him again today

He wants to take me shopping

A few seconds later my phone starts buzzing.

"Shopping?" Andie screeches into my ear.

"Yeah, he said he knows some stores I might like that will help elevate my wardrobe." I repeat his words exactly because I'm still not sure what he meant.

My family has always made fun of my fashion choices, but that's because they all dress like they live on a farm. Dresses and heels are half the reason I wanted to move to the city.

"You have great style," Andie says, her voice defensive. And then a little softer, "But I guess I'd never turn down a shopping trip on someone else's dime."

My thoughts exactly.

"It just annoys me," she continues. "Men always feel like they should get an opinion on how women dress."

"They do?" I ask. Of course, this has happened to me, mainly at the holiday party when I wore the most sparkly dress I could find that wouldn't blind anyone permanently. But I thought it was a "me" thing.

"Ugh, yes. You know Davide, right? Head of Product? He's always telling me I shouldn't wear chunky sweaters, that they're not *flattering* on me." She huffs. "I am *always* cold, and why would I care what he thinks about me anyway? I'm not at work looking for a husband."

That's so rude. I would never have the gall to say something like that, especially to a coworker. I've only met Davide once. Hopefully it stays that way.

"Sorry, just venting," Andie continues. "I hope you have the best shopping trip ever. You better call me after and tell me all about it."

IAN PICKS ME UP AN HOUR LATER, BUT INSTEAD OF heading downtown, we drive to the airport.

He's taking me shopping in LA.

CHAPTER EIGHT

OLIVIA

When Friday morning comes, I am most definitely *not* ready. I'm not ready to see Ian and even less ready to spend the day pretending to date Gavin. I'm barely even ready to leave the house on time because I can't seem to decide how to wear my hair.

I refuse to wear it in a bun anymore. I'm done caring how anyone else wants me to look, and I hate pulling it tight anyway. But then I wonder if I keep it down how much it'll whip me in the face on the back of Gavin's bike.

A braid. Yep, I'm officially a genius. Or an idiot for taking thirty minutes to come up with that idea.

"Liv!" That would be Gavin banging on my door. I answer it even though I'm still in sweats.

"Hey, sor—hello! I'll be ready in a minute." He's been calling me out on every "sorry" I've said since the other night. I had no idea how much I said it and I'm actually thankful for his persistence in helping me stop. What the hell am I so sorry about, anyway?

"I like the braid," he comments, giving it a little tug. I've gotten slightly more used to him touching me in the last two days and I may or may not have had a very explicit dream about his hands last night.

"Well, you said the bun made me look uptight," I quip.

"Nah. All the blazers make you look uptight." He grins back and I wonder if he's right. My work uniform has always been based on the saying "dress for the job you want, not the one you have." Though considering I want Gavin's job and I've never seen him in so much as a collar, I may have been doing it wrong. Just a little more of Ian's influence I need to shake off.

"You know I'm kidding, right?" he continues. "You should wear whatever you want. You just look a lot more comfortable like this." He touches me again. A little pull on the hem of my sweatshirt.

"Well, I'm not wearing this to the off-site. This is what I sleep in, Scottie."

"You look good to me." He gives me a full once over and another smile tugs at his lips. It makes one tug at mine too.

"Just give me a minute so I can figure out what to wear, okay?"

I walk into my room where several outfits are already laid out on the bed. Only one includes a blazer. Since my apartment is basically a studio, my bedroom only has three walls and Gavin follows me in.

"I like these," he says, his hands combing through the dresses on my hanging wardrobe. My closet is tiny, so I built a rack on one side of the room for my dresses. I have *a lot* of dresses. When I was younger, one of the reasons I was so set on moving to the city was so I could dress up, be fashionable, stand out. I grew up with a mom who wore overalls seven days a week and I refused to follow in her footsteps. Fashion has always been my favorite way to express myself.

Little did I know that leggings and a vest were suitable for a night out here in San Francisco. But I still love my dresses, especially the sequined ones and anything with a bow. I may have limited occasions to wear them, but I still collect them like rare artifacts.

Gavin moves to the bed and peruses the outfits laying there like he's a judge at an art show. He picks up the black silk slip dress and runs the fabric through his hands. "I really like this. Might be a bit fancy for playing bocce ball though."

I grab the dress from him and lay it back down. "This is for tomorrow. I have to go to a charity event."

"Need a date?" he asks. He's obviously joking. The truth is I would love to have a date, but there is no reason I can come up with to make him join me. It's probably for the best, since my whole family will be attending.

"No one from work will be there. You're off the hook."

He almost looks disappointed as he grabs a pair of jeans and a sweater off the bed. "Wear these," he says. "I'll wait outside so you can have some privacy. And bring your camera."

"You scared?" Gavin asks, clipping my helmet on. He's already secured my purse and camera bag under the seat.

"No," I say, grinning ear to ear. "I'm excited." I've always been a bit of an adrenaline junkie, and I grew up riding dirt bikes and four-wheelers with my brothers. But I've never had a chance to ride on a motorcycle. Gavin's sex appeal also rises ten notches every time I see him on the bike. The man can really rock a helmet.

"Thatta girl." He gently squeezes my chin with his thumb and forefinger. "Just follow my lead and you'll be golden."

He circles my block twice at ten miles an hour so I can get used to the feel of his bike before we get on Bay Street and head toward the bridge. He still hasn't told me why we're leaving so early. It's only ten-thirty and the off-site starts at one o'clock.

"Tighter," Gavin says when he turns back to me at the first stoplight. He grabs my hand and pulls it further around his torso. "Don't be shy, Sparkles."

I squeeze my arms around him as we speed forward again. To my disappointment, we're not going very fast, and I don't anticipate we will at all. It's a beautiful Friday with clear skies all over the bay. I'm sure all the tourists will keep the roads slow the entire way to Sausalito. But even though my safety isn't a concern, I keep squeezing.

Luckily, the view outside is a good distraction from our current closeness. I keep my head swiveled to the right to stare toward the water. Marina Green is one of my favorite places to bring my camera on a nice day. It's a huge field right next to the water and there's always something *happening*. Festivals, food trucks, volleyball games, people picnicking with their dogs. It's one of the many places in this city that's always teaming with life, with energy. I can't get enough.

But just when I think that's where we're headed, he keeps going. Maybe we're stopping at the Palace of Fine Arts? It's another favorite spot, great for photos. Honestly, my favorite part is usually feeding the ducks. Andie and I walk over sometimes after brunch when we have leftovers.

And still he keeps going, following the 101 toward the bridge. Then he makes a last minute turn into the Presidio, keeping us on this side of the bay.

"Where are we going?" I yell through the loud breeze. The wind started whipping hard as we got closer to the water and I'm thankful I didn't attempt to leave my hair down. Even the tail end of my braid has smacked my chin a few times.

He doesn't respond until we come to a stop. I have no idea where we are other than in the woods. Leaves crunch beneath my feet as Gavin helps me slide off the bike. He carefully pulls off my helmet next, tucking wayward hairs behind my ear.

"You have photos of all the best spots around the city. Except this one." He lifts up the seat to hand me my camera. "Hopefully it's not too artsy for you." He winks and I shove a hand against his chest hard enough that he takes a step back.

"It smells so good over here." I take the deepest breath I can, all but inhaling the trees around me. I do a little spin to try and get my bearings and see a sign pointing to the walking path. "Lover's Lane?"

"Yeah," he replies. "It's a short loop. There's this winding tree sculpture on the way back. I always see people taking pictures."

"How often do you come here?" I ask, as we start the hike.

"Not so much anymore. Daanesh and I used to come over here all the time to smoke. His old apartment was in the Marina, like a five-minute walk."

"You two would get high and go on walks together at Lover's Lane?" He nods. "That's adorable."

"Shut up, it's just a name." The wind whistles around us as he takes in the scene. "I like nature."

He moves behind me and squeezes my shoulders just enough to steer me in a new direction. We walk over a short bridge that empties onto the main path. There's no impressive view from here, the water completely hidden. But I can see why he likes it so much. It showcases how special San Francisco is. That we're in the woods surrounded by the scent of pine and eucalyptus, yet we're minutes from the Pacific and we could get to the heart of the city on foot in under an hour.

There's nothing more exciting than discovering some new part of San Francisco. But I'm never going to be able to enjoy it with all the confusion rattling around in my head. It's one of my least favorite forms of anxiety, when something I do not want to think about refuses to leave my mind. No matter how hard I try to whisk it away, it's all I can focus on.

"Scottie?" I ask, stopping for a moment. I've had this specific question on my mind for two days and if I don't ask it now, it might actually burst out of me.

"What's up?"

"Why are you doing this? Helping me?"

"Why not?" he replies, like that's all there is to it.

"Come on, I'm serious," I continue. "First you offered to help with Mitch, and then Ian, and now you're just going out of your way to be nice to me. Why did you bring me here?"

His brow furrows. "I thought you'd like it."

"I do like it. It's beautiful," I respond, because he looks defeated. The last thing I want him to think is that I'm ungrateful. "But we're not friends. You don't even like me. And suddenly you're willing to be my pretend boyfriend?"

He looks thoughtful for a moment, and he bites his lip, but then the playful grin reappears. "Of course, I like you. And I figured if we hung out now, you wouldn't be as anxious being together at the off-site. Can't I just enjoy being helpful?"

"No," I argue. "No one's that nice. And I don't want to take advantage of you."

"You are not taking advantage of me. It was my idea, remember? Just look at it this way. I might not be the one putting you in a shit situation at work, but I'm still part of the problem. If I can't fix it, I'm going to do whatever I can to make things better for you. Really, you're doing me the favor, helping me rid my guilty conscience."

"But—"

"Don't overthink it."

His words are so soft, too soft to be mocking me. And the smile that follows warms my bones. He's right. Why am I so worried about the reasons behind everything when I could just enjoy the day instead?

I take a deep breath and look around me, willing my mind to focus on the sounds, the smells, the sight of this gorgeous man who's slowly becoming a friend.

The next hour goes by in a blink. I find beautiful light filtering through the massive trees and want to snap pictures from every angle. I'm not sure if Gavin has worked out my issues with decision paralysis just yet, but he's being really patient with me. I'm used to getting eye rolls or having people snap their fingers at me, letting me know it's time to move on. It's almost disconcerting that it isn't happening today.

"Sorry, I'll be done soon," I promise, not wanting to look a gift horse in the mouth.

"There's no rush, Sparkles. Hey, come over here, there's almost a rainbow if you squint really hard."

Gavin might not realize how difficult it is to follow his lead, to not overthink everything happening around me, but it feels a bit easier when I'm in his presence. Breathing feels easier in his presence.

When we get to the winding trees, I put the camera down and we compete to see who can balance for longer on the zig-zag walkway.

"This is so much easier sober," he says when we both make it to the end. He looks at his phone then. "Shit. I was hoping we could hike up to the Spire, but I don't think we have time anymore. It's after noon."

I've never seen the Spire he keeps mentioning, another art installation at the highest point of the Presidio. He looks disappointed, so I offer, "Another time? I'd still like to go."

"Definitely."

By the time we reach the Golden Gate Bridge I'm obsessed with the bike and want to start saving for my own. My brothers and I have an annual dirt bike race each year and I'm wondering how hard it would be to convince them to up the ante on the prize.

We still haven't gone more than forty miles an hour with the traffic, so whenever the road opens up, I squeeze Gavin a little tighter hoping he'll hit the gas. I'm tempted to ask if he'll let me drive, but considering how nice he's been today, I don't want to push my luck.

For the first time since I've known him, it feels like Gavin and I are friends. And yes, I might still fantasize about his hands every time I close my eyes, but I'm enjoying this new *friendly* side of him too.

Our company off-site is at one of my favorite spots outside the city, Bar Bocce. It's a restaurant that sits right on the beach with a huge outdoor patio and several bocce ball courts. The water in this area is exceptionally calm, so you can also take kayaks out right from the beach, which Andie and I have done on multiple occasions.

But my excitement about being here dies when Ian is the first person I see at the entrance.

"You okay?" Gavin whispers in my ear as he slides an arm around me.

"Yep," I lie, forcing my eyes up from the ground.

People always warn you not to "dip your pen in the company ink." They say how awkward it will be to see your ex everyday if things don't work out, how even a minor fight can be extremely uncomfortable when they're also your co-worker.

But no one ever warns you about dating the investors. They don't work in the office so interaction is minimal. But when they are around, everyone is expected to treat them like gods. Ian has never been my boss and we've never had to work together. No, it's just his money that furnishes my paychecks.

I didn't realize how much I was fidgeting until Gavin squeezes my hand and threads our fingers together. The gesture isn't for show. He's just trying to calm my nerves. Just like he did a few days ago in the office. His hands are turning into my own personal wonder drug. Move over Xanax, I've found something stronger.

"Olivia," Ian croons as we walk in. We have no choice but to confront him to get inside the venue.

"Hey, Ian." I tilt my chin up as high as I can. I want to keep this interaction as short as possible, but I also refuse to cower in front of him. Not after everything he said to me.

"You doing okay?" Ian asks me in a hushed tone. Is he trying to imply that I'm still not *okay* from our breakup? "You look," he continues, giving me a once over. "Winded."

"Yeah, we rode my bike here," Gavin offers, combing a few fingers through my hair and smoothing it back. "You're a little speed demon, aren't you?" I can't tell if this is for Ian to hear or just me, because his voice is lower when he says it. And then he winks again. *Hot.*

Ian clears his throat, louder than anyone actually needs to. He's never appreciated being pushed out of a conversation.

Gavin ignores him and steps toward the bar, tugging gently on my hand. "What do you want to drink, babe?"

I track Ian's eyes as they shoot down to our hands. I brace myself for him to ask what's going on, but instead he just smirks. He pats Gavin on the shoulder and says, "Nice to see that initiative, Gav." And before I can figure out what the hell that meant, he's heading toward the patio.

Gavin squeezes my hand again, seemingly ignoring Ian's remark. "You like Aperol Spritz, right?"

"I do. How'd you know that?"

"Just remember you getting it the last time we were here." Gavin must have a photographic memory or something because the last time we were here together was for another off-site at least a year and a half ago.

After we collect our drinks and head outside, I have to ask, "What was Ian talking about?"

"Oh, just Ian being an asshole as usual." He takes a long sip of his beer and looks back at me. "I can say that now, right?"

"Of course. Wait, do you guys know each other? Like outside of work?" I remember now mentioning Gavin to Ian, recounting work stories and what not. Ian didn't have the kindest things to say about most people—he clearly felt like he was above them—but he always referred to Gavin as "the kid." Maybe there was more to it than his usual elitism.

"Umm, we've bumped into each other a decent amount through work. Honestly, I never liked the guy, Liv. He just thinks he's better than everyone else. For a while, I was hoping to—you know what?" He pauses and tugs on the end of my braid again. "We're here together to avoid Ian, right? To let people know you're with *me* now. A much better option if you want my opinion."

I laugh, and silently agree, even as I remind myself this is one hundred percent *fake*.

He throws an arm around me again. "So screw Ian. Let's not waste our time on him. Wanna play a round of bocce?"

We find Gabby, who won't stop glaring at me for some reason, and then Daanesh so we have a foursome. And then we wait in line with everyone else who's looking to play.

"So, I heard Churro has a new *bestie*," Gabby says, nudging my arm. The guys went to get another round of drinks, and I'm not feeling great about being alone with Gabby. Her tone feels accusatory, like I've wronged her in some way.

"He's adorable. And I love all his little accessories. Gavin said your girlfriend made them all?"

"Yeah. She's incredible. I know." Gabby's reply is about as friendly as a wasp.

"Did I, umm, do something to offend you?" We've never interacted much at work, but I hang out by the marketing pod a lot and we've never had an issue.

"Just be nice to my brother, okay?"

"Okay...you know we're just—"

I'm cut off when the guys return, Gavin handing me another Aperol Spritz.

"Olivia, Gavin just told me the news," Daanesh says, leaning into the middle of our little foursome. "You can't tell anyone I said this, but he's a nice upgrade. I mean, we all love Ian," he clarifies, his eyes bobbing over my head searching for eavesdroppers. Then he drops his voice to a whisper. "But I wouldn't want to date him."

We all start to laugh, though I'm pretty sure Gabby's is fake —still no idea what's going on there—when we're interrupted again, by *another* founder.

"Hey, Vaughn," Gavin says.

"Just heard the news. What could this beautiful girl be doing with your sorry ass?"

Vaughn, who I've never actually had a conversation with, decides it's okay to wrap an arm around my shoulders, while simultaneously talking about me as if I'm not here. Not wanting to engage, I turn to Gabby, who actually looks sympathetic.

But Gavin takes it in stride. "I know. I'm a lucky man, what can I say?" He expertly removes me from Vaughn's arm and starts fiddling with my braid again. I wonder if all these little touches give him the same kind of comfort they do for me. I lean into him a bit, partially to play the part and partially because I just want to.

"I'm the lucky one." I don't know where the line comes from. Maybe I'm a better actress than I thought. Gavin's smile seals it. We're crushing the fake-dating trope right now.

"So, how did you get together anyway?" Vaughn asks Gavin, still not acknowledging me.

And then I panic, because of all the things we have discussed to get to know each other better, not once did we come up with a story to tell. Pros, we are not.

I try to catch Gavin's gaze and momentarily get lost in his eyes. They're the same color as the bay right now, the sun making them glow. He's still smiling, those perfect dimples making an appearance. Damn, my fake boyfriend is hot.

Gavin doesn't seem to be having the internal crises that I am though. He coolly replies, "We've been sitting across from each other for two and a half years. Have you seen her? She's like...a different kind of beautiful. The second I found out she was single I made my move."

A different kind of beautiful. What does that mean? I try to catch Gavin's eyes but he's still looking at Vaughn.

"So you've just been pining away all this time?" Vaughn mocks.

"Pretty much." This time, Gavin's eyes meet mine. I can't tell if he's trying to sell the story or just urging me to go along with it, but there's definitely some hidden meaning, some silent language he wants me to understand with this look. "I would've asked her out during her interview, but I think that's frowned upon."

CHAPTER NINE

GAVIN

32 Months ago

ANOTHER ONE? I'VE ALREADY DONE FOUR INTERVIEWS today and I'm damn near exhausted. I really do try my best to be engaged with each person, but recruiting has passed through some major duds lately.

Sure, sales development roles are entry-level, but the goal is to promote them over time. Experience isn't necessary. I just need someone who can carry on a conversation. The airport test is my rule. Could I be stuck sitting next to this person in an airport, waiting out a delayed flight? If yes, they might make it in sales. We can teach the product, but we can't teach having a personality.

Just before I get up from my desk, my cell vibrates in my pocket.

GABBY:

> I got in!!! I can't believe it but I actually got in.
> I'm GOING TO STANFORD!!!!

Holy shit. My baby sister is getting her MBA from Stanford. Her dream is finally coming true. I feel like I might cry.

ME:

> You're amazing. I never doubted you

GABBY:

> You totally doubted me

> But I love you anyway! I'm making you alfajores tonight – don't work too late!

Before I realize what I'm doing, the cell is ringing in my ear.

"Wow," Gabby's voice comes through the phone. "My brother actually has time to call me?"

"I needed you to hear how proud of you I am. You amaze me. Truly."

"Shut up! You're gonna make me cry. Are you sure about paying the tuition? I'm twenty-one now. I can take out a loan."

I squeeze my eyes shut. There's nothing I hate more than lying to my sister, but there's also nothing I won't do for her. "Don't you dare. I make more than enough to cover it. We'll be fine."

"I love you! Hey, before you go, how was the date last night?"

Ugh. Gabby and her friend Kadesha have made it their mission to find me a girlfriend. Every time we go out, they fight over who's the better wing woman.

"It was fine. Don't think I'll be seeing her again though."

"Why not?" Gabby screeches into the phone. "She was gorgeous. And she spoke Spanish!"

"And she was exactly the same as every other girl I've gone out with." I don't know if it's a San Francisco thing, but all the women I meet seem to blur together. Is there some sort of rule that requires them all to order espresso martinis and work in marketing? They all wear the same Bay Area uniform, listen to the same music, and the only weekend activities they know of are brunch and hiking. It's not that I have anything against hiking, I'm just...bored.

Mainly, I get the sense that they're all just telling me what I want to hear, like it could take years to puzzle out who they are beneath the curated version they show me.

Maybe I've been in sales too long.

Or maybe it's that I don't have space in my chest to care about anyone besides my sister. Maybe I don't want to. As long as I know Gabby is safe and happy, there's little else I need.

"I know you have these incredibly high standards, but I'm worried my brother will be alone forever."

"I'll never be alone. I have you," I quip.

"That doesn't—"

"Gotta go Gabs. Have another interview. See you tonight."

Luckily this wasn't a lie. I'm even two minutes late. I march back down to reception to grab the next candidate while I peruse over her resume. Olivia Diamond. Damn, what a name. Sounds like a popstar or something.

Business major, Sonoma State, captain of the archery club? Okay, that's pretty cool. No work experience at all. The only thing listed is her certification as a service dog trainer. Might not be relevant but that's really fucking cool.

"Olivia?" I ask, seeing a few people sitting in the waiting area. The girl who stands up is breathtaking. Red hair hangs down to her waist, layered over a black sweater and sparkling black skirt. If I didn't know better, I'd say she was applying for a job at a fashion magazine, not Sizzl. I'm tempted to peek at her resume again. Sonoma State is a mostly local college, but she's got to be from New York, maybe Boston.

"Hi, that's me." She offers a little wave. Her face is veiled in soft features, smooth skin, a smile that makes me want to say "yes" to anything she asks. And her curves. I stop myself just in time before doing a full once-over and hold out my hand instead.

"I'm Gavin Scott. I'll be interviewing you today."

"Great. Nice to meet you, Gavin." Fuck, even her voice is sexy.

I lead the way up one flight of stairs to the main office. We start every interview with a quick tour.

"All our sales and customer success teams are on this side. Kitchen's in the middle. Then the rest of go-to-market here." I say it all while walking, anxious to get my last interview of the day over with.

"Go-to-market?" she asks.

Right, because she has no experience in tech. "Just means all teams that have a hand in the customer experience. So all the customer-facing teams like sales and support, plus marketing and product."

"That makes sense. Thanks for explaining it." She lowers her gaze when we stop walking and I wonder if I made her feel like she should have known the answer.

"It was a good question, Olivia. No one else ever asks it but I have a feeling most candidates don't know all the terms we throw around here."

She smiles up at me and I'm a fucking *goner*. I want to offer her a job on the spot just to see her face light up again.

"Cute skirt!" Our tour is interrupted when Andie, our solo marketing team, pops into the kitchen. "Are you interviewing here?"

"Yeah, for sales," Olivia clarifies.

I let them chat for a minute while I check my email on my phone. I've been waiting for two days to get this latest contract signed and the quarter ends tomorrow.

Andie grabs a pack of carrots from the fridge before leaving. "I like this one," she says on the way back to her desk. "You could use some feminine influence on your team."

Shit. Most of the female candidates become wary once they hear we're still trying to hire the first. It's not that I don't want to. There are just a lot less women who want to sell software, less who have experience, and unsurprisingly not many who want to be the first one. They must think we have one big circle jerk at lunch every day.

Honestly, I'm kind of desperate to hire a woman. It doesn't look good that we don't have any and it comes up every quarter when HR releases our latest diversity report. But I also refuse to hire someone just because they're a woman. Isn't that just as bad?

I do my best to ignore Andie's comment and show Olivia the rest of the office.

"Do you really train service dogs?" I start once we're seated in the conference room. I'm too curious not to ask.

"Yeah. My whole family does. As part of a charity organization they run."

"That's so cool. I love dogs." I was hoping we could move up to Marin at some point, get a place with some land, maybe a dog or two. Now that Gabby will be commuting down to Stanford three days a week and I'll be paying off loans for eternity, that seems unlikely. At least I have the world's greatest hedgehog for now.

"Me too. I grew up with golden retrievers. They're the best."

It's difficult to stop myself from asking about them, because I find myself wanting to know more about Olivia, but none of the questions on my mind are related to the job.

"So, tell me why you're interested in sales," I pivot, quickly.

"It's a grind."

"I think it sounds exciting."

"It can be, but it's a lot of rejection. It gets draining, trust me. Are you sure you're up for that?"

"Are you trying to sell me *against* the job?" she asks, with a healthy dose of incredulity.

"Not at all. But you haven't worked in sales before. I feel like it's my duty to warn you of the pitfalls. Closing deals, even just securing a meeting can make you feel like you're on top of the world. But as soon as the celebration's over, you're back to an eighty percent rejection rate."

She purses her lips and when she looks back at me, I can see a hundred thoughts floating through her eyes.

Finally, she says, "Do you have an eighty percent rejection rate?" I force myself not to grin. That was unexpected.

"Mine's closer to fifty, but I'm the best."

She straightens in her seat, placing her hands on the table between us. Her nails are dark blue and as glittery as her skirt. "Then I'll be the best too."

I laugh. "Love the confidence, but even fifty percent is a lot of rejection. It's grueling."

"Why do you do it then?" she asks. I'm starting to feel like I'm the one being interviewed. Maybe that's a good sign. The best salespeople get their prospect to do all the talking.

"Money," I say plainly. And it's true because there are a million jobs I'd rather do if I wasn't so focused on getting paid. Sales equals survival for me and Gabby right now. "Are you motivated by money?"

"I guess so. Well, not really." Wrong answer. She just dug her own grave because that's the dealbreaker in any sales interview.

"But I'm motivated by power," she continues.

That's one I haven't heard before and I've been doing ten plus interviews a week for months. Power? I'm definitely intrigued.

"This is an entry-level job, remember?"

"Yeah, but, doesn't sales give you a sense of power?" She crosses her legs and pins her eyes on me. They're this bluish gray color that I swear didn't exist until today. "You're the face of the company. You represent every department when you're the one selling. You're influencing how much money comes in, what everyone's paycheck looks like, even how good the benefits are. There's power in that. I mean, at least I think there is."

"Yeah, I never thought of it that way, but it's nice calling the shots sometimes." There are a million questions I want to ask this girl but none of them are appropriate, so I go with an old standard. "Do you see yourself as a leader?"

"Umm...I was captain of the archery club in college?" Her gusto is fading. As much as I want to believe she has what it takes for this job, confidence is the most important asset. Well, that and wanting to make money. "And I like to boss around my brothers."

I can't help but laugh at that one.

"Where are you from?"

She lets out a long sigh. "So that's it? You've already decided I'm a no and now I get the fluff questions?"

She's not entirely wrong, even if I was asking more out of curiosity than killing time.

"Olivia—"

"This is my tenth interview, okay? I'm desperate. And I know I shouldn't say that, but it's true, and it doesn't make me any less qualified for this job. I already got an apartment and if I don't get a job soon my parents will make me move back home. I refuse to give up. I need to live in the city and work in the city and just be a *part of this city.*

"I know I don't have any experience, but I work hard. Harder than anyone. I want to learn and grow and be the best salesperson here, even better than you. I just need someone to believe in me. I need someone to give me a chance. You want to give me a chance, don't you Gavin?"

As far as a hard close, it's not bad. I'm not sure if Mitch would be impressed, but he handed off hiring responsibilities to me when he decided hiring sales development reps wasn't worth his time.

I'm trying my best to imagine Olivia saying all of this, without her being the first woman I've been attracted to in months. I'm even trying to imagine her with a beard and a combover in my attempt to be objective.

But the truth is that the world isn't objective. Especially in sales. People buy from people they like, and if there is one thing I'm sure of today, it's that I *like* this girl.

In fact, I can't seem to find anything I don't like. Nothing at all.

CHAPTER TEN

OLIVIA

After Gavin fooled everyone around us with his romantic declaration, one of the bocce courts opened up. We played three rounds while I learned all the perks of being his fake girlfriend.

People can think what they want, but dating Ian never got me closer to socializing with our CEO. The only exec I ever saw outside of work was Davide. He and Ian are decent friends and liked to double date. I really hated all the nights we spent with him and his wife considering how much Davide flaunts his infidelity.

Daanesh on the other hand is a joy to be around. I had no idea he was so funny. It's a quiet, kind of dry sense of humor, but my cheeks hurt from the little time we've spent together. He even offered to be my bocce partner because Gavin and Gabby are too competitive to be on opposing teams.

I know playing bocce with Daanesh has no effect on my job, but that was never the point. I'm not fake-dating Gavin to get chummy with the CEO, just like I was never using Ian, but it felt nice to be part of this inner circle for a little while.

Now, Andie and I are sitting by the fire pit having another round of pretty orange cocktails while Gavin stays back to play with another group.

"I just have to say it. You and Gavin are hella cute together." I bite my lip in an attempt not to smile. "I mean, the matching motorcycle helmets? You look like you both just came from some edgy photoshoot."

"He does look good on the bike," I admit, nibbling my cheek.

She eyes me. "So do you." She takes a long sip of her cocktail, looking around the patio. "Well, how's it been seeing Ian?" she asks.

"Weird, but not that bad. He's kept his mouth shut, so that's a plus."

Andie bites her lip, making a face that tells me I'm so very wrong.

"Shit. What's he been saying?"

"Nothing too bad. Just, you know, the usual stuff."

I pin her with a stare. "Andie."

"There you are," Mitch's voice sounds from above. "I need to borrow Livy for a minute," he says to Andie before turning around. What's it like to have that kind of power? To not even have to wait and see if people will do what you ask.

I look at her half apologetically and half scared as I stand up. She mouths *big tit energy* before I jog after Mitch.

I follow him to the other side of the patio where there's more privacy. The further we get away from the group, the brighter my anxiety burns. Why do I have a feeling he's about to fire me?

We sit down at a small table and Mitch takes a long pull of his drink.

"Just wanted to let you know I'm gonna be out next week. Ellen wants me up in Portland." Oh god. He wants to talk about his ex-wife? This is getting so annoying. Mitch never treats me like his friend, not like he does with the rest of our team. The only exception is when he wants to vent or needs advice about his ex. Like because I'm the only one with ovaries that I'm more qualified for the topic. I'm not a fucking couple's therapist.

"Okay, well, I'm glad she's talking to you again," I reply, trying to nip this conversation in the bud. Half the time he's upset she won't talk to him or see him. Then he complains because she wants him to come back to Portland—where they have a home and a *child*—instead of her coming down here.

"Yeah, we'll see. Anyway, I won't be able to oversee your product demo, so you'll need someone else to join."

Oh.

"I'm sure Gavin will sit in if he's free, but I'm prepared to run the demo myself," I offer.

"I'm sure he will." His words have an edge that I don't quite understand. "You can cut the shit with Gavin, by the way. Ian might have offered some protection, but if you were hoping to keep that job insurance, you should've aimed a little higher."

From the way he's raising his brows and tilting his head I'm wondering if he's actually referring to himself. *Gross.*

I picture Andie's face as best I can. *Big tit energy.*

"I like Gavin. He's kind and thoughtful, and I'm not using him for job insurance." Well, the first two were true. But I'm not *using* him, am I? I don't want to be. He's just helping me out with a tough situation. And now I realize the whole ordeal is going to be even worse than I thought when we come clean. Will Mitch think I ended it because he called me out?

"Look, you wanna throw Gavin a bone so he'll be your little helper? Be my guest. All I give a shit about are results. *You* chose to alienate the CMO at the company you're selling to. So show me some progress with the deal, and soon, or it'll be clear this job isn't for you."

"Mitch—"

He stands up and throws back the rest of his beer. "Gotta get to the airport, Livy. Text me any updates with Surf and Stream."

And apparently, another lovely conversation with Mitch is over.

I slump down on the bench, not wanting anyone to see me. I've mastered the art of holding in tears, but my anxiety always makes me fidgety.

Have I somehow made this situation worse? Mitch wanted me to use a man's attraction to me to close a deal. Now he's threatening me because he thinks I'm using a man to keep my job? How does he not see the hypocrisy here? I'm so sick of all these double standards. It feels like any decision I make is wrong, like just being a woman is wrong.

All I want is to be taken seriously, to prove myself in the business world. I want to play by the same rules as the men.

I never asked Gavin for an assist and now I'm wondering if I should be pissed at him for playing white knight. But I know he was only trying to help. And without him stepping in, my promotion was already on the line. I was never going to go to HR to complain about Mitch. I don't want to be another Silicon Valley story that people use as anecdotes at happy hour. I don't want my career to become the memoir I'm forced to write to stay relevant.

How did everything get so twisted?

Looking down at my hands, I realize I've dug my nails into my palm so hard that little crescent moons mar my skin.

I dig through my bag to find my AirPods, grateful I made the last-minute decision to bring them. As soon as I turn on my "chill out" playlist, I can feel my heartbeat slow down. I will not have a panic attack out here.

Closing my eyes, I let the French lyrics and slow beat drown out the thoughts in my head, and do a few breathing exercises my therapist taught me.

And then I feel a hand on my shoulder.

"Sparkles? You okay?" I crack open my lids to find a very concerned Gavin peering down at me. Before I can respond he points to my ear. "Can I?"

I nod and he pulls the tiny headphone out of my ear. I thought he just wanted to talk, but instead he sits down on the bench next to me—so close our arms and thighs are touching—and pops the bud in.

The song I'm listening to is my favorite. I have no idea what it's about, but the melody feels like that first sip of rosé, like walking barefoot in soft grass or sliding into bed under freshly laundered crisp sheets. It's not sensual exactly but it's the kind of song I'd want to cuddle to. It's one that immediately relaxes me, which is why it's the first on the playlist.

Gavin presses a little harder against my side and I realize he's swaying to the beat.

I relax my shoulders and let him guide me side to side until a smile breaks free from my lips.

"Better?" he asks, turning to face me.

"Yeah. Thanks." A new song starts, and I turn it off, placing my AirPods back in their case after Gavin hands me his.

"I liked the song."

"It's one of my favorites," I admit.

"What's it called?"

"Tableau. I think it might mean desk, but I try to pretend it's something more romantic."

"You've never looked up the translation? Not even for a favorite song?" He looks incredulous. I wonder if the patience and the curiosity has worn off, if he just thinks it's weird now. He pulls out his phone and starts typing vigorously. "Yeah, that's what I thought. It means *painting*."

The emphasis he places on the word makes it seem like I should understand. Is there a joke I'm not getting?

"Okay?"

"Liv. You say you're not an artist, yet your favorite *French* song means *painting*. You've got to see the irony here."

He laughs a bit, and the sound rings through me. I've always loved his laugh. It's never mocking, never at anyone else's expense. He rarely cracks a smile most days at work, but when it does happen, he laughs for joy and joy alone.

"Maybe you're right. I tried the sales thing, but I can always fall back on painting murals with Mom."

"Nope. I'd miss you too much." His words feel genuine, no matter how well I know he's joking. "I saw you talking to Mitch over here. What happened?"

"Oh, just my career imploding. He thinks I'm using you as leverage so he can't fire me."

"What? Since when is your job at risk?"

"No idea," I respond. Because I can't even keep track of the mess I'm in. "I don't think he actually wants to fire me, but he likes to screw with my head. Let's just come clean soon, because as soon as we do it's gonna be such a shit storm for me." I huff out a long breath and try my best not to imagine what those rumors will look like.

"So let's not."

A breeze rolls by and a loose lock of hair escapes my braid, brushing against my lips. Gavin is right there, ready to tuck it behind my ear. He's so tactile with me and I find myself enjoying it more each day.

But it's messing with my head. Is he like this with everyone?

"Why?" I ask. "Why would you want to keep this up indefinitely?"

"Why not?"

"Gavin," I say with a bit more force than intended. I can't handle his laissez faire attitude about this anymore.

"Olivia," he mocks. I give him a pleading look. "Just tell me what you want to do, and I'll back you up one hundred percent."

"But I'm in over my head here. I have no idea what I should do." I stop to take a breath because I can feel the spiral coming. "If we come clean, Mitch will think he was right. And if I can't close Surf and Stream, and at record speed apparently, I'll never get promoted and I'll have to find a new job and start all over."

"That's not going to ha—"

"Gavin."

"Olivia."

"Oh my god, stop. You know I'm right. You know how Mitch treats me, how he sees me. I don't get to play by the same rules as you do."

"Fine," he concedes, his jaw clenched. "Then I repeat, let's not come clean."

"Gavin—" I start.

"I really prefer Scottie. Every time you say Gavin, I feel like you're about to scold me."

"Fine, *Scottie*. We can't just pretend to be dating forever."

I stare down at my empty drink, wishing we weren't having this conversation, wishing I had a simple way out of this whole situation, wishing I could enjoy my first company off-site without Ian by my side critiquing every interaction with my colleagues.

"Not forever," he muses. "How about for a few months? Or

how about just until you close this deal, and he can finally see how amazing you are."

Fake, fake, fake. How many times is he going to do something or say something like that to me? Something that makes this relationship feel way too real.

"Seriously, Scottie. Why would you do that for me? You're getting nothing out of this."

He turns to me and flexes his jaw.

"I'm starting to realize that me trying to help the other night only made things worse for you. I got you into this mess." He wraps an arm around me, pulling me in close. "Let me get you out."

DAD:

Thanks for filling in tonight. You know Deacon hates public speaking

ME:

Of course. I'm happy to help

Happy? Definitely not. I had one day to come up with a welcome speech for tonight's gala. It's true that I'm the only one of my siblings who doesn't get total stage fright, but I'd still like to be prepared.

The plus side? I've been too busy prepping for the charity event that I haven't had a moment to think about Gavin. Well except for the moments I *did* think about him. Is it cute or creepy to dream about your co-worker slash fake boyfriend braiding your hair? Asking for a friend.

After he drove me home from Sausalito he asked if I wanted to hang out, which of course I'm still reading into, but then I saw the family group text asking me to take over the welcome speech at tonight's event and told him I had to work on something.

So that's what I've been doing for the last twenty-four hours. Writing the speech, practicing the speech, recording myself practicing the speech, scrutinizing the recording of myself practicing the speech. It's been a fun day.

At least I'm finally at the good part, where I get to play with makeup and put together my outfit. Deacon—the oldest of the Diamond siblings—called a few days ago to ask me not to wear anything "too girly." He specifically requested no glitter or bows. My family has never appreciated my style, but I'm following orders and wearing the black silk dress Gavin had his hands all over yesterday morning. And I'm *definitely* not going to read into that.

Deacon never mentioned gemstones, so to go with the simple black slip, I'm wearing my favorite bejeweled pumps. They're completely encrusted with gems of every color, and while difficult to walk in, they aren't impossible.

I finish the look with loose waves and a nude lip before I take a selfie to send to Andie. I would normally ask her to come over and help me decide on my look, but she's in Santa Barbara with the mystery man she's been keeping hidden for months. I'm positive he's a celebrity who made her sign an NDA, but I can't for the life of me come up with a guess as to who.

ANDIE OH:

HOT HOT HOT

Is Gavin going with you?

ME:

Of course not. This isn't a work event so it's not like we need to be fooling anyone

ANDIE OH:

> Well I imagine looking like that you'll have a
> date by the end of the night anyway ;)

> I'm heading back tonight so let me know if
> you get bored and wanna bail

Tonight's event is at the Fairmont Hotel, one of my favorite venues. I have to Uber there since it's at the top of Nob Hill. Also, these heels could take me about two blocks max.

As soon as I enter the main ballroom I find Deacon, who looks calm as a cucumber as he bosses around multiple event coordinators. For some reason I'm the only one in my family who isn't perfectly comfortable in their own skin.

"Hey, Deac. Where can I help?"

"Ollie!" He wraps me in a bear hug before squeezing my shoulders and inspecting my outfit. "Good to see you, Sis. You look great."

"Thanks."

"No idea where Mom and Dad are. Owen and Phil are still unloading the truck, but they'll be dealing with the auction all night. Guests are starting to arrive so why don't you hang by the entrance and help greet, show people how to find their tables. You know the drill."

My family, along with Sonoma County Animal Rescue started Pawsability when I was in elementary school. And this will be our fifth wine auction gala in support of the cause. I definitely "know the drill." But it'll also be the first time I give the welcome speech.

I perform my duty as greeter while I run through the order of events tonight in my head. We start with a cocktail reception, though I'm not sure why we insist on calling it that when we're serving 90 percent wine. Then I'll give my welcome speech as dinner starts, followed by a video that will be sure to leave zero dry eyes in the audience. The band will start playing during dessert and the silent auction—after my announcement—will end promptly at ten.

"What are we serving tonight?" I ask the bartender, anxious to sip my liquid courage.

"We have a few options," he replies, presenting a laminated drink list. My parents really pulled out all the stops for this one.

We specialize in pinot noir and have around seven different wines from the grape each harvest. Though I do see we're not serving my favorite. The Vega isn't our bestseller, but that would be impossible considering its price tag and batch size. It comes from the smallest block in our vineyard and produces the richest pinot I've ever tasted.

But tonight, the selections are three of our more moderately priced pinots—Orion, Polaris and Rigel—along with our rosé and the Capella chardonnay that isn't nearly buttery enough for my liking. I always wonder if people find the names of our wines to be strange. My family really leaned into the Diamond Sky name.

"I'll do the Lyra, please," I say excitedly. I take a healthy sip of my favorite rosé and scan the room for Deacon again. I figure if I stay by his side there's no way I'll miss my cue to start the speech.

"There you are," Deacon says, finding me first. "There's someone I want you to meet. One of our newest donors."

He guides me through the maze of the crowd as my senses are attacked by heavy-handed perfume and cologne. And finally we reach a table filled with a group of extremely attractive people and one of the cutest dogs I've ever seen.

That's my favorite part of these galas. There are always at least a few dogs in attendance.

"Hello, my fluffy boy," I say, kneeling as low as I can in this dress. "Is it okay if I pet him?" I ask the blonde holding his leash.

"Of course." She smiles back at me, and I wonder if I've met her before. She looks familiar but in that super distant way that makes it impossible to know why.

"Aren't you just the sweetest?" I continue with the dog as he gives my fingers a lick. He's gray and white with the softest fluff that makes him look like a toy I had as a kid. "What's your name, pal?"

"This is Rowan," the woman continues.

"Ollie, stand up," Deacon orders, using his infamous brotherly whisper-yell. "Remember I wanted to introduce you to the new donors?" I grab his hand for balance since my shoes aren't really intended for deep squats. Once I'm standing, he turns back to the guests. "This is my sister, Olivia. Olivia, I'd like you to meet Lucy and Henry Turner."

"It's Gold, actually, "Lucy says with a shy smile. "I kept my last name." She does a little shrug and shoots a conspiratorial grin to the man next to her. Henry, I presume.

I shake both of their hands, but Henry never says a word, and then I realize where I know her.

"You're Lucy Gold? Like, *Beautiful Beasts*, Lucy Gold?" My voice pitches a little higher than intended, but I can't help myself.

"Ollie!" Deacon scolds at my less than gala-level behavior.

"Guilty," Lucy chirps.

Ignoring Deacon, I refuse not to enjoy my fan-girl moment. "I stayed up until like, four in the morning reading that. It was amazing. I've read all your books, actually."

Deacon is shaking his head, horrified that I've embarrassed him, so I try to salvage what I can.

"Lucy," I say. "On behalf of my family, we're so grateful for your donation, and personally I'm just really excited to have my favorite author here."

"I love this organization. When I read about what your family has done to help people match with service dogs....well, having Rowan changed my life. Anything we can do to help more people get that kind of support."

"Sorry to interrupt," Deacon mumbles, "But, it's time for you to get up there."

"It was so nice meeting you," I say to Lucy and Henry. "Let's have a drink together after dinner."

Deacon rushes me to the stage area. I'm happy to see that it's not actually elevated, just a mic set up on the dance floor.

"Break a leg, Ollie," Deacon whispers with a quick pat to my back. He rushes to the side of the ballroom and suddenly I realize that all eyes are on me.

My anxiety can get the best of me sometimes. There may not seem like a good reason for it, like the most random thing can set it off. But one thing that's never been an issue is this. It's like I feed off of it, being the person commanding the room. I love stealing everyone's attention, knowing they're all about to listen to what I have to say.

"Hello, everyone," I begin. "I'm Olivia Diamond, and I'm thrilled to welcome you to our fifth annual Sips for Service gala." I pause for a few moments of applause.

"My family founded Pawsability almost seventeen years ago. Our mission was simple: make it easier to train and place service animals. My parents, brothers and I have personally trained over fifty animals that have gone on to help people live a more fulfilling life. And our goal is that anyone who could benefit from a service dog, or other animal, will have the ability to be matched with one.

"Since we started this organization, with the help of the Sonoma County Animal Rescue,"—I pause again for a quick applause—"we have facilitated the training and placement of over nine hundred animals. These furry superheroes support numerous disabilities and come in all shapes and sizes. If you're lucky, you can even spot a few tonight.

"If you've been blessed to experience the love of an animal, you'll know that it's priceless. But tonight, we ask that you do put a price on it, and that you be as generous as you can. Remember, not only are you changing someone's life for the better, you are giving these animals an extremely fulfilling life as well.

"Plus, I have it on good authority that the wine we're auctioning is pretty tasty." This elicits a few laughs. So far so good. Just need a strong finish.

"I'd like to thank all the incredible wineries and vineyards who are here and donated tonight. Your contribution to this event means the world to me and my family. And with that, let's start the auction."

I ring the little cowbell that my mom insists we use, then I exit the stage and find my table. My parents are usually so busy at these events I barely see them, so I'm surprised to find them at the table when I sit down for dinner.

"You were amazing, sweetie," Dad says, giving me a quick hug.

"Thanks. I hope it was the right length. I couldn't really remember what Deacon did last year."

"It was perfect. Wasn't it, Sandra?" Dad poses the question to my mom on his other side.

"Oh, yes, lovely. Olivia, those shoes are ridiculous," she says, right before she stands up to go greet another guest. Dad follows almost immediately. Par for the course.

My parents are great people. They have always felt fortunate to achieve such success in winemaking and make a huge effort to give back when they can. Sometimes I think this charity is more important to them than their own business.

But for some reason, we've just never really connected. My brothers have always been close with them, and I've always been...somewhere else.

The only family member that's ever seemed to get me is my brother, Owen. We were really close throughout childhood and even college, but he's become more and more distant the longer I've lived in the city.

I enjoy my dinner in solitude while my family schmoozes and gives their little wine tasting lessons table to table.

And after my third glass of rosé, I make an announcement to get in final bids as the auction ends abruptly at ten o'clock.

Alone again at the table, I'm thoroughly enjoying my white chocolate raspberry mousse when I sense someone come up behind my chair. The scent hits me first, that heady cologne that must cost a fortune. And then I hear his voice.

"Olivia Diamond. It appears you're free after all."

CHAPTER ELEVEN

OLIVIA

"Tristan."

I turn just as Tristan Cross takes the seat next to me. His expression screams smug as he looks back into my eyes.

His whole vibe is the same from our meeting, perfectly polished from head to toe, all black everything. We almost match.

"I'm obviously not 'free.' My family is running this event."

"I gathered as much from your speech. You look stunning by the way, in case no one else has said it yet."

My cheeks burn at the compliment. He has such an easy confidence about him, the kind of confidence I would kill for.

"Thank you," I reply.

"Nothing you don't already know," he muses. "I couldn't help but notice you ate dinner alone. Mind if I join you for dessert?"

Before I can find a polite excuse to leave, my mother is back.

"Olivia, who's your friend?"

"This is—"

"Tristan Cross." He cuts me off, standing to offer Mom his hand.

"Oh!" she exclaims. Then drops to a whisper. "I believe you're about to win the 2007 Vega. Excellent taste."

Eww. Is she flirting with him? My mom has always been a free spirit, completely uninhibited. I'm used to it, but the way she's batting her eyelashes at my current prospect is giving me the ick.

The band has started playing and I think that maybe the noise will help me escape. I take one final bite of the raspberry mousse and stand.

"I actually need to—"

"Dance with me." Tristan cuts me off again. I can't decide if it's attractive or annoying when he attempts to finish my sentences.

"I don't think that's a good idea."

"Oh, don't be silly," Mom butts in. "I'm sure Olivia would love to dance with you." Then she physically pushes me toward him like I'm a child who needs encouragement to play.

"Wonderful," Tristan says, holding an arm out for me. Unfortunately, I latch on to him tighter than I mean to, but after Mom's little shove, I'm having trouble balancing on these heels.

I love to dance. At home, in the kitchen, to the music everyone else finds so strange. Well, everyone except Gavin. The jazz band playing tonight isn't really my jam. Tristan, on the other hand, seems completely in his element.

"Have I already mentioned how beautiful you look tonight?" he whispers, his mouth dangerously close to my ear. He's placed one of my hands on his shoulder and seems to be holding it there for good measure. Until he lets it drop down to my waist.

"Yes, thank you," I reply, my cheeks heating again. How the

hell am I supposed to exude professionalism right now? "You'll love the Vega," I offer, wanting to talk about anything other than myself. "It's always been my favorite of our collection."

"I'm quite familiar with your wine. If I'd have known who your family was last week, I'm sure I would have been talking your ear off about the vineyard the entire meeting. I'm a bit of a collector."

He takes hold of my free hand and spins me. The move is flawless with little effort, and I can't help but grin as we come back together. He flashes his perfect white teeth, pleased with my response.

Maybe I shouldn't be fighting so hard against this. I'm not sure if going out with Tristan would actually promise a closed deal, but it would make Mitch happy with me. And how bad could it be dating this man?

Tristan's handsome, confident, he smells really nice. A date with anyone who enjoys good wine would be easy to endure. I meet his eyes as he grips my waist, trying to decipher if there's something here worth exploring.

"You're really good at this," I admit, thankful for such a competent dance partner. He smirks and twirls me again.

Allowing myself to lean in a little closer, I imagine what a night with him would be like. Fancy dinner, fast car, delicious wine, definitely sex. By the way he's looking at me I could probably convince him to find a coat closet right now.

Would he be like Ian? I can already see myself wearing a mask for him, not wanting any of my "quirks" to come out. Wanting to be as perfect as he seems.

It feels easy, slipping back into old habits. To wonder about where Tristan might take me, what kind of interesting people I'd meet in his circle. But would he make me laugh? Would he make me *feel* beautiful, or just let me hear it all the time?

I could justify a million reasons for testing the waters, for seeing where this could go, but that's not who I am anymore. My choices are for me, not to please everyone else. And this isn't who I want.

I avert my gaze over his shoulder and vow to keep this professional for the rest of the night.

"Well, if you have questions about the wine or the terroir, I'm more than happy to answer them for you," I continue, hoping it sends the right message. This is good, this is professional. We may not be talking about my work at Sizzl, but educating about wine has been my job since I was nine. It's the most natural thing in the world for me.

"I do have a question, actually," Tristan continues. The music has slowed down again, and he tugs me a little closer, letting his hands slip over the silky material of my dress. "Why are you here alone tonight?"

So, not exactly a professional conversation then. "Oh, Gavin doesn't really care for these events. He hates wearing a suit." I don't know where that comes from, but now I can't help picturing Gavin in a suit. I wonder what he's doing tonight, if he has his hands on another girl, just like Tristan's are on me.

Tristan somehow leans in even closer, so much that I have to tip my head back to avoid us touching. "Gavin, huh?" He says the name like it's a bad taste in his mouth. It's oddly offensive.

"Yes, Gavin." It may just be a fake relationship for Mitch's sake, but each day I'm finding myself happier for the shield he creates. His friendship means something to me.

Tristan must not hear the conviction in my voice, or maybe he just doesn't care. He strikes me as a man who's used to getting anything he wants. Just like the 2007 Vega he bid on that rarely goes for anything under five grand.

"Now, why would you be with a man who wants to be anywhere else but with you?"

I can feel his breath on the shell of my ear. It makes me shiver in a way that I can't decide is good or bad. His brazen flirting might be hot if it wasn't for my job, but I've never felt more uncomfortable in my life.

"Excuse me. I just need to run to the restroom."

I move as quickly as these beautiful shoes will allow and grab my purse from the table. Finding a dark corner to hide in is all I want right now.

Once I'm settled in the women's sitting room, I pull out my phone, looking for a distraction. My heart skips a beat when I see a new text from Gavin.

Shit. Do I have a crush on my fake boyfriend?

GAVIN SCOTT:

Everything quill be all right

Beneath the words is a photo of Churro. It looks like Gavin is holding him in the palm of his hand. I know from my experience with dogs that it's not real, but I could swear Churro has a huge smile plastered on his face.

Something compels me to hit call before I have the chance to talk myself out of it.

"Hey, Sparkles."

Shit. I have absolutely no reason to be calling this man. I don't have anything to say. My palms are getting sweaty with each second the silence continues. *Jesus, Liv. Say something!*

"Did you get the pic?" Gavin asks, saving me from further embarrassment. "Sorry about the cheesy line, I just know it's been a tough week for you."

Damn, that's sweet. It's Saturday night and I'm sure he has plans, but just knowing he took a moment to think about me makes me feel all gooey inside. I really do have a crush.

"Liv? Hello?"

"Sorry, I'm here."

"Thought you pocket-dialed me for a sec." He sounds relieved and it makes me happier than it should.

"Nope, no pockets tonight."

"Oh yeah? What are you wearing?" Flirting with Tristan made me nervous, but this feels fun. Gavin's voice is so playful that it makes me want to play back.

"Why don't you come find out?" As soon as the words leave my lips I'm mortified. *Who am I right now?* "I'm just k—"

"Yeah? You at home?"

"No. Sorry. I umm...I don't know why I said that. I don't even know why I called you. I'm at a charity event, my family's event, actually." Great, and now I'm rambling.

"Not having a good time, then?" he asks. I can't decide if I should tell him about running into Tristan here.

"I guess."

"So why did you call me?"

"I'm not sure. I saw the text and..." I trail off, still not really knowing why I called.

"And you thought your night would be better with me in it?"

"Exactly." Maybe he's on to something.

"Where's the event?" he asks.

"Nob Hill. The Fairmont."

"Really?" His voice sounds overly eager. "Can you get away?"

"Yeah, all the important parts are over." I could just go home now, which is probably what I should do.

"Meet me in the lobby in twenty minutes." And he hangs up.

CHAPTER TWELVE

GAVIN

"You're leaving in the middle of game night?" Gabby pouts at me from across the table. Then she throws her cards up in the air. As dramatic as ever.

"Sorry Gabs. If it's between Uno and a Mai Tai, I'm going Mai Tai every time."

I head to my room to change. The Fairmont is one of the nicer hotels in San Francisco, so I assume Liv is dressed up. Probably can't show up in my usual uniform. Locating a clean and wrinkle-free pair of pants takes a few minutes. Luckily a shirt's easier.

I call an Uber so I don't show up sweating buckets from climbing Nob Hill, but it's still five minutes away. More than enough time for Gabby to scold me some more.

"You're completely falling for her again, aren't you?"

"Kadesha, can you please be more attentive to my sister? She is spending way too much time worrying about me."

Kadesha pulls Gabby into a hug. "She is very well attended to, I promise. We just care about you. Neither of us want you to get hurt again."

Oh god, now it's both of them. "No one is hurting me. Liv and I are friends now. And she sounded like she needed one."

My phone buzzes, alerting me that Dale in a silver Jetta is now two minutes away. "Gotta go. Have fun girls."

I took some adorable pictures of Churro tonight, so I fire another one off to Liv, along with the message "Quill be there soon." She might think my puns are stupid, but I'm pretty sure the last one got me a phone call. Now I just need to work on some better lines.

Entering the Fairmont is a little trippy. It's like decoration overload. But it only takes me a second to spot Liv and her diamond-covered shoes.

"Hi," I say, tapping her on the shoulder. She turns to face me, and her wide smile is absolutely everything.

"Scottie!" She hugs me. Well, she sort of falls onto me with open arms. "I wasn't sure if you were actually coming."

"Didn't you get my text?"

"Phone died." She shrugs. "You're here."

"I'm here."

"And you're all...fancy." Her gaze follows the length of my body. I have to remind myself a few times that she's admiring the outfit and not me. "I'm not sure you want to go to the event though. It's sort of stuffy and it's all jazz music and—"

I place my hands on her shoulders. "It's all good, Sparkles. I have another plan anyway." She takes a quick breath and relaxes a bit. "Ever been to the Tonga Room?"

"No, what's that?"

"It's in the hotel. My second favorite tiki bar in the city." I let go of her shoulders but offer an arm for her to hold on to. She's looking a little wobbly on her feet, though I can't tell if it's the shoes or if she's been drinking.

"What's your first favorite?" she asks when we start walking through the hotel.

"Let's see how you handle this one first."

We head downstairs and follow a long corridor to get to the restaurant. Liv never lets go of my arm. Based on the hiccups that started in the elevator, I'm positive she's been drinking, but she doesn't seem too drunk. Either way, she can use me for balance any time she wants.

The Tonga Room is one of my favorite places in the city. I'm definitely biased, because I love a good tiki bar, but there's something about it, being in the basement of the fancy Fairmont hotel, that makes it extra special.

I had a feeling Liv would love it, but when we walk in and she sees the boat floating in the middle of the restaurant, her shriek still catches me off guard. The restaurant itself is one big square-shaped bridge, so every table has a clear view of the water in the middle, where a small boat houses a band playing reggae. As soon as you walk in, you're immediately on a tropical vacation. Even the air is sticky with humidity and rum. The scents of coconut and pineapple swirling all around us.

Unfortunately, I forgot how busy this place gets on the weekends. There's an hour and a half wait for a table.

"That's okay," Liv says when she sees my disappointment. "Let's just grab a spot at the bar."

The bar is slammed too. We walk the full length of the restaurant, but every seat is taken.

"Olivia!" I turn toward the voice and find a pretty blonde sitting at one of the tables closest to the water. She's flanked by two men in expensive suits.

"Oh my god, she remembers me," Liv squeals. She takes a few sharp breaths like she's hyperventilating. "That's Lucy Gold, my favorite author. Can we go say hi?"

"Of course."

"Hey, Lucy," Liv says, her nerves on display. I run my hand

down her spine to help settle them. "Did you have a good time at the gala?"

"It was an amazing event. Henry's getting over some jet lag, so he took Rowan upstairs a while ago, but these are my friends, Jayce and Graham."

The men stand and we all greet each other. They seem nice enough, even if I'm a little jealous they're stealing some of Liv's attention.

"Why don't you join us?" Graham offers, his Australian accent throwing me for a sec. "I'm sure the wait for a table is ages."

She looks at me, her eyes pleading a bit. No idea who Lucy Gold is, but if it makes Liv happy, I'll talk about books for the rest of the night.

"Thanks, that'd be great actually." I pull out a chair for Liv and once we're seated, I throw an arm around her back. Maybe I feel a little possessive because of the guys sitting across from us, but she's my pretend girlfriend, not theirs.

"I just have to say," Liv starts, leaning toward Lucy. "I have read *Beautiful Beasts* at least three times. I actually just finished my last read about a month ago. After my break-up, it really spoke to me. Like, I wanna be the villain of my own story, you know?"

What the hell? There are a million questions I want to ask her about this. I decide that I'll try to remember them later, because there's no way I'm cutting into Liv having her moment right now.

Lucy laughs a little. "I love that. I don't think I've ever heard someone phrase it that way before, but I was actually going through a tough break-up when I wrote it. I was tired of focusing on the happy ending, and I wanted my lead to have her moment without a man to make it happen."

"Ugh, *yes*," Liv replies, completely lit up. She licks her lips a few times and I turn around to try and flag down a server. "I know you don't know me and I'm sure I sound ridiculous, but I think I could feel that through the book. It's just so empowering and it really made me want to find a better story for myself too. Not killing people, obviously. But just taking control of my narrative. You're such an incredible writer."

Lucy looks down at her drink before taking a long pull from the pink straw. "The best feeling is just knowing my words resonated with you. But no more talking about me or I'll get very weird, very fast."

"That's just because she'll drink until she's comfortable getting compliments," Jayce says, smoothly sliding Lucy's coconut drink toward himself.

A waitress pops by to take our order and Liv looks to me. "What should I get?"

"Oh, get this!" Lucy offers, stealing her drink back. "It's called the *Divine Dragon*." She says the last two words with a flair, and I can immediately see that she's a storyteller.

"You're a divine dragon, Luce," Graham says, ruffling her hair. No one has made it clear if either of these guys is "with" Lucy, but I'm getting major brother and sister vibes.

"Ooh, that sounds good," Liv replies, reading the menu. "But I can't decide between that and a Mai Tai."

"I'll get the Mai Tai," I tell her. "We can share."

She must be tipsier than I thought because she looks up at me with glistening eyes. "That's so nice of you."

"I'm a nice guy," I say back.

"Yeah, you are," she murmurs, still gazing at me. "It's very unsettling." She narrows her eyes and purses her lips before her face transforms into a grin.

I give her shoulder a squeeze, tucking her a bit closer. "Brat."

I never let myself flirt with Liv before this week. At first, I didn't want her to be uncomfortable starting a new job, and then, once our working relationship felt more settled, she got herself a boyfriend. I've waited over two years to be able to do this and it feels amazing.

"So, Olivia," Jayce muses, pulling me out of my daze. "Do you work at the winery?"

"No, I'm in sales with this one." She tilts her head toward me almost close enough for us to touch. "What about you guys? Are you all writers?"

"*Song* writers." Jayce raises an eyebrow and a muscle in my jaw starts to tick, because with two words I can already tell he's about to hit on her. Does he not fucking see me here?

"Graham and I work with Lucy's husband. We mostly score movies or high production TV series." He bites his lip this time. "Do you like music?"

What kind of question is that? Who doesn't like music?

"Of course. That's such a cool job. What instruments do you play?" she asks them, somehow unaware of Jayce's intentions.

"I do strings," Graham says just as Jayce replies, "A little bit of everything." He licks his lips and I feel like smashing his head in. Thankfully our drinks just came so I can chug some rum and ignore this guy.

I take a long pull of the Mai Tai and offer it to Liv. Her eyes flare up at me when she takes a sip and I grin.

"Delicious, right?" I ask, our eyes still connected.

"I pegged you more for a 'whiskey, neat' kind of guy to be honest." I nudge her shoulder. "You're really full of surprises, Scottie."

I keep smiling at her. My face feels stuck this way.

"Olivia," Jayce continues, ignoring the fucking *moment* we're having. And this time he reaches out to grab her hand on the table. "If you could be any instrument, what would you be, and how would I—"

He's cut off when Lucy and Graham both yell "stop it!" and Graham smacks Jayce over his head. I like the Australian one.

Liv turns to me with wide eyes and we both laugh.

"So, Olivia," Lucy says, ignoring Jayce's pleas for her to "play nice." "It looks like you landed a new boyfriend, huh?" She tilts her head and eyes me.

"Oh, no, we're just friends," Liv offers. It only hurts for a moment because a week ago, I'm not sure she'd even call me a friend.

Graham chuckles, also ignoring Jayce when he shouts "see!"

But then he eyes Liv, then me, and Liv again. "Have you told him that?" And I take it back. I do not like the Australian one.

"I CANNOT BELIEVE I JUST SPENT THE NIGHT DRINKING with Lucy Gold. She gave me her number. Her *number*."

Liv has been gushing non-stop since we left the musicians. After the second round of drinks, I could tell it was time to go. Though I'm still feeling grateful she was tipsy enough to not bat an eye at Graham's comment.

"Should I call an Uber?" I ask, tugging gently on her hand. She's been holding on to me since we left the restaurant.

She looks up at me, a perfect angel, twisting her lips in indecision.

"What is it?"

"Are you hungry at all?" she asks.

"Always. Wanna get some pizza? Golden Boy isn't too far from here."

She grins back, nodding her head vigorously.

I offer to get a car, but she says she can walk it. Halfway down the hill she stumbles, and I just barely catch her before she rolls all the way to Chinatown.

"Want a piggyback ride?" I offer. "We've only got a few blocks left."

"Yeah, but I'm afraid my dress will rip. I'll just take these off." She bends down to slip off her shoes.

"All right, princess." She gives a little shriek when I pick her up, but there's no way in hell I'm letting her walk outside barefoot.

We walk like that the rest of the way, her body pressed against my chest, until we reach the long line of every other drunk person in the city wanting pizza.

"Maybe this was a bad idea. It could take forever with this line."

"Nope," the guy in front of us says, turning around. "Some douchebag just bought three pies for the whole line. As long as you like pepperoni we're all about to get slices."

"That's...generous," I reply. But the guy just laughs.

"Yeah, right. He said he doesn't wait in lines. Offered to buy for everyone so he could cut."

"Huh. Do you like pepperoni, Sparkles?"

She wraps her arms a little tighter around my neck. I can tell she's minutes away from sleep. "Mhmm."

As promised, employees start handing out slices to everyone in line. I let Liv feed me while I use one hand to hold her and the other to call an Uber. I definitely don't want to wait and compete for a car with this group.

When I get to the end of my slice, I bite down gently on her fingers. She squeals but it morphs into a laugh and our eyes lock. I'll do anything to keep recreating these little moments, like the one Jayce stole from me earlier.

Max in a black Tesla arrives a few minutes later and I carry her into the car. She sort of falls into my lap. I guess it wasn't the smoothest move, but I was only worried about keeping her feet off the ground.

To my surprise, she doesn't try to move, just settles in, wrapping her arms around me and burrowing into my chest.

"This was the best night. Thank you for coming out," she says against the collar of my shirt.

"Thanks for tempting me with your choice of clothing."

"You never told me. Did you like the dress?"

"Of course. You look stunning." She just responds with an "mmm" sound, and I wonder if she's disappointed in my answer, so I might as well be honest with her. "It's so plain though, compared to everything else I saw in your closet. Where's the sparkle?"

She laughs, or exhales, or does something that vibrates against my chest. I swear she nuzzles in a little closer.

"You get me." It's the last thing she says before promptly falling asleep.

CHAPTER THIRTEEN

OLIVIA

THE SEAGULLS OUTSIDE MY WINDOW SOUND LIKE pterodactyls this morning. I wake up and immediately cover my ears with the pillow. The screeching feels like it's burrowing into my skull.

It only takes a second to remember why my head is pounding. Mixing wine and rum was not the best idea.

A quick check to my phone confirms that it is thankfully Sunday, and I can stay in bed as long as I wish. It's only nine-thirty. But seeing I have several unread text messages has me upright and alert.

I decide to click on Gavin's first. It's from an hour ago and I might as well rip off the Band-Aid to see if I did something embarrassing last night.

GAVIN SCOTT:

Hope your hangover isn't too prickly

Of course, it's followed by another adorable picture of Churro, and then another text.

GAVIN SCOTT:

> Left your keys on the kitchen counter

My brain is trying to quickly figure out what this text means. Gavin was in my apartment? This is when I realize I'm still wearing my dress from last night. He must have brought me back here after I passed out or something.

I guess it could be worse but I'm still a bit rattled by it. I rarely drink that much. But I also rarely have that much fun. And then I remember Lucy. *Oh no...*

(232) 018-9779:

> THIS IS LUCY GOLDS PHONE. YOUR
> PHONE DIED BUT SHE WANTS YOU TO
> HAVE HER NUMBER. YOURE BASICALLY
> BEST FRIENDS NOW OMG OMG OMG

Oh my god. Do I message her back to apologize? Or never use the number in hopes that she doesn't actually see this message? I decide to let that simmer, but I save her name in my phone, just in case. And then, to my absolute shock, a new message comes in.

LUCY GOLD:

> Hi Olivia! It was great meeting you last night.
> We're in town until tomorrow and decided it
> would be fun to visit wine country. Could you
> recommend some places that are dog
> friendly? And if you're free, I'd love for you to
> join us. Let me know!

I chug a glass of water to clear away the tiny daggers in my throat and pull up her contact. I may feel like I spent the night being pummeled by a stampede, but I will not turn down another chance to hang out with Lucy Gold.

ME:

Mind if I call you?

A few moments later my phone rings.

"Hey, Lucy."

"Liv! I'm so glad you're not one of those 'I only text' people. It's so much easier having an actual conversation sometimes."

"I couldn't agree more." I know we aren't hosting any events today so I tell Lucy that I can give them a special tour of Diamond Sky, and that there are several other wineries close to my family's that we can check out. And while Napa can get a little snooty, most places in Sonoma are dog friendly.

"Amazing!" She squeals over the phone. "Henry's finding us a limo now, so no one has to drive. I'll text you when we have an ETA."

I jump in the shower even as my body is screaming at me to go back to bed. Adrenaline is my best friend right now.

Trying to decide what to wear, I can't help thinking of Gavin and his comment about my dress last night. I should text him back.

ME:

I'm so sorry if I fell asleep on you. Thanks for getting me home safe!

He immediately responds.

GAVIN SCOTT:

Isn't that what fake boyfriends are for?

I'm sure he's sick of me by now, but I feel compelled to invite him. We were all together last night, so I doubt Lucy would mind.

ME:

Going to stop by the winery today with Lucy
and her friends. Do you wanna come?

Promise I won't be drinking too much – no
fake boyfriend duties

The typing bubble appears but minutes pass before I get an answer.

GAVIN SCOTT:

Can't. Rugby

I wait again, assuming more is coming. His other texts always feel so warm and friendly. But I get nothing.

He's busy, I tell myself, and also, *not* my boyfriend. Sure, we had fun last night, but that doesn't make this relationship suddenly real.

I check the weather app to find it's the perfect day for a sundress in Sonoma. I grab one from my closet that my mother hates. It's bright yellow and the entire hem is lined in frothy pink bows. I add a denim jacket on top that's studded with pearls and tiny crystals, mimicking a clear night sky, and some simple white sneakers because my feet are still throbbing from last night.

I have five minutes before Lucy's group arrives, based on her last text, so I do a quick once-over in the big mirror to make sure I look okay.

I love this outfit. My hair is still wet from the shower but I leave it down to dry in natural curls, even if it'll be a little wild. The jacket sparkles every time I turn, and another crystal catches the light.

Feeling the best I have in a long time, I take a quick video to send Gavin, popping my shoulder back and forth to show off how it glimmers.

ME:

Sparkly enough for ya?

Excitement rolls through me as I see a limo pull up outside my window. I toss my phone in the crossbody bag I'm wearing, and I head out the door.

EXHAUSTION HITS ME HARD WHEN I GET HOME AND FLOP down on my bed. But I have zero regrets. Running around Sonoma with Lucy was almost as fun as last night. At one point, after she was pretty sloshed, she opened up to me about her ex, and how she fell in love with Henry. Her story was so hopeful it made me believe in real life fairy tales.

Then she went on and on about the way Gavin looked at me last night. She said that if she had to describe it in a book, she would write that his eyes were full of more pine than a Christmas tree farm.

I did my best to pretend like her words didn't matter, but I spent the whole ride home forcing myself not to check my phone and see if he'd responded. Graham and Jayce were also great distractions. They went crazy for the archery practice field on our property. They loved it so much we never actually made it to another winery. We only left to have a picnic in Sonoma Square.

Now that I'm alone and free to process my emotions without any judgment, I open up my messaging app with the same fervor of opening a birthday present.

Nothing. Well, nothing from Gavin.

I do have a couple messages from an unknown number though.

(473) 860-5515:

I have thought of nothing all day but you in that black dress

Put me out of my misery and call me back?

I check my call log and see two missed calls from the same number. One is from last night around ten-thirty, right before my phone died, and another from this afternoon.

It must be a wrong number, except the comment about the black dress has me curious. I'm sure lots of women wore a black dress this weekend. It just seems a little too convenient. I think, deep down, I know it's Tristan. But I find myself searching for any other scenario that doesn't further complicate this entire situation.

Maybe I should just delete the messages. Or maybe I should get it over with.

ME:

Who is this?

My phone starts ringing a few seconds later, making me jump off the bed. It's the same number as the texts.

"Hello?"

"Olivia," Tristan says, stretching my name into something overtly sensual. "She lives."

I want to ask how he got my number, but I'm also still worried about coming off rude. Mitch might think I pissed him off with the initial rejection, but that doesn't seem to be the case. Now I'm just trying to salvage whatever weird working relationship we still have.

"I was worried about you," he continues. "When you ran off last night, I asked the group at your table if anyone had your number."

"Sounds like I need to give my family members a lesson on

privacy." I immediately regret my words because they're sure to offend him, but he just starts laughing.

"I guess I lucked out, then. Have dinner with me." It's not a question. The confidence he showed last night is still there, like the multiple times I've turned him down don't exist. It's not *not* attractive.

"Tonight? It's a little late." My clock just turned nine.

"Any night you want, Olivia." The way he says my name makes me sound like a rich chocolate dessert, or maybe a fine wine, something to be savored.

"Sorry, I think I have plans," I reply, grinning into my phone.

"Sounds like I'll just have to wait until those other plans get boring. I'll see you soon, Olivia." He hangs up before I can say another word.

CHAPTER FOURTEEN

GAVIN

Liv is going to kill me.

I get up extra early Monday morning so I can wait for her at Fog & Foam. I know she doesn't go every day, but Monday's a sure thing. And I really need to chat with her away from our co-workers.

I probably should have just responded to her texts or called her last night, but after having such a good time together on Saturday, I wasn't ready for her to hate me yet.

Now I'm out of time. I have to tell her what I did.

It's 9:00 a.m. and I'm waiting for Daanesh at Marina Green. Our pickup rugby game starts in an hour. This is why my Saturday plans were game night with Gabby and Kadesha, staying in and going to bed early. Playing hungover is not going to be pretty.

"Hey Daan. Thanks man," I say as he walks up and hands me a cup of coffee.

"Morning." His tone is much too cheery. He definitely

wasn't out drinking all night. "Sorry I missed game night. You look like shit."

I grimace and hold my coffee up toward him. "To Mai Tai's."

"Mai Tai's, huh? That's different."

"Actually, I went out with Liv. Tonga Room."

"With Liv?" he asks, looking back at me with confusion. For a second, I have to remind myself that I did in fact tell him we were dating just two days ago. Not sure why he sounds so surprised I'd be out with her.

"Yeah. She had some charity event at the Fairmont. I met up with her after."

"With people from work?"

"No? Just us, and some random guys from LA I guess."

"Actually," he says, his brows pulled together. I'm honestly struggling to decipher what kind of look he's giving me. "Stacey emailed me the final list for Mexico yesterday. Olivia's not on it. Did you forget to book her flights?"

Shit. Century Club is next week, the annual trip where our exec team and board take the top performers from each department on a tropical getaway. And we all get plus ones. No one turns down that trip willingly. It's not only a free vacation, but a chance to party with the leadership.

How the fuck do I tell Daanesh she's not coming? If people at work are supposed to believe we're dating, why wouldn't she come with me? Would she come with me? The thought of spending a weekend with Olivia in Mexico...

"Shit, look at your face. You forgot, didn't you?" Daanesh shoves me against the chest. "You finally get a girlfriend, and you forget all about her? Is there something I'm missing here?" His tone is playful. He thinks I'm an idiot. In reality, I just don't know what the hell to say. The line, "oh, she's allergic to Mexico," hovers on my lips. "Hey, you okay?"

"Yep. You're right, I'm an idiot," is all I can say.

"It's cool, I got you. If you book something now and expense it, I'll make sure it gets approved."

"Right now? Like you want me to book her flights on my phone right now?"

I must sound like the idiot he thinks I am, because he's looking at me like I belong in a straitjacket.

"Is that a problem? Do you not want to bring her?" I pin him with a look. "Shit, you do know her birthday, don't you? Do you need me to look it up in the company directory so you can book it without calling her?"

I pull out my phone and navigate to the travel app. Sadly, that is not the problem. I've known her birthday ever since Gabby and Kadesha decided to do a star chart for me during the "dark days." Apparently, Liv being a Libra was all they needed to know to explain why we'd never work.

"You good?" Daanesh asks just as I show him the booking confirmation. "Why do you look so nervous? This team sucks."

"You try playing hungover." I shove him and start jogging toward the field.

"Hey, Scottie," Liv greets me. The words are drawn out and I can tell she's confused to see me.

"Morning," I say, handing her the coffee I just bought. I track her eyes going to the barista who actually winks back at us. Interesting. "Sorry I didn't get back to you—"

"It's okay. It's my fault," she says, sitting down on the chair next to me. Her fault? "I made it weird, right? You've been so nice and helpful, and I swear I know that this is all pretend. I promise I wasn't trying to make something more of it."

She starts chugging her coffee, pointing her eyes anywhere but me.

"Liv, I don't know what you're talking about. I was trying to apologize. I did something stupid yesterday and I was afraid to tell you about it."

"So, you're not annoyed about taking care of me on Saturday?"

"Annoyed? I thought we had fun."

"I might have had a little too much fun," she murmurs. "I swear I never drink that much."

"If carrying you down a hill is the worst thing I have to deal with, I'll be happy to go out with you every Saturday night."

She stops grinning and our eyes meet. I need to stop being so honest with her. Sometimes I forget I'm the only one with real feelings here.

"So what was the stupid thing you did? It can't be worse than passing out in an Uber."

She really has way too much faith in me.

"You had fun on Saturday, right?" I ask.

"Right." She stretches the word like taffy. And now she looks suspicious, like I'm trying to get her to admit some hidden secret.

"Well, what do you think about hanging out like that again, but for three days in Mexico next week?"

"Scottie."

"Sparkles."

"Ugh, don't do that! What are you talking about?"

"Next week is Century Club. You know, the top performers' trip? I'm going to Punta Mita and, well, Daanesh thought I fucked up and forgot to book you as my plus one. He did me a favor by letting me get your flights after the deadline. I'm sorry, Liv. I didn't know what to say."

She looks pensive, her brows scrunched together while she works all this out in her head.

"You're telling me you just booked a flight for me to go to

Mexico next week? Our pretend relationship that was supposed to be over by now is going *international?*"

"Maybe?" I cringe, waiting for her to scream at me.

But she doesn't scream or yell or look angry at all. She actually looks sad.

"I've always wanted to go on that trip," she says, barely audible.

And then I think, "Why haven't you come before? Ian could've brought you."

"He said it wouldn't be right to bring me as his date when I didn't earn the trip."

Liv looks down at her coffee again and starts to fidget, while I think back to Ian's behavior on those trips. He might have gotten away with feeding her a bullshit line, but I know what he and Vaughn get up to. He probably just wanted an excuse to play single in Mexico.

"What a dipshit," I reply. "You can't even qualify to go until you're a sales executive. It's not like anyone else in your position would be there." I knew Ian was a dick, but what kind of asshole does that to his own girlfriend? "You deserve to go just as much as anyone, probably more so."

"Still, I shouldn't go. Just say I got sick or something." Her voice, her entire demeanor is deflated. It's the opposite of how she was Saturday night. "I don't want to piss anyone off by being there when I didn't qualify. That's how the rules work."

"Fuck the rules, Liv." She bites her cheek, trying to hide the grin. I think she likes the idea of being a little reckless. "Screw anyone who thinks you shouldn't be there. Come to Mexico with me."

CHAPTER FIFTEEN

OLIVIA

23 months ago

"You better get in the shower if you want time to do all your primping. Town car picks us up in an hour." Ian rolls back on top of me in his bed, laying kisses across my neck.

"How am I supposed to get up when you're doing that?"

"Fine. I release you." He kneels on the bed and I roll off before things get heated again.

"Are you gonna tell me where we're going yet?" I ask, before I slip into the bathroom.

"Not a chance. You know how I love to surprise my girl."

My girl. He's been calling me that for weeks now. We haven't had any real talk about defining our relationship, but Ian made it clear that I'm his girlfriend after only a few dates. He's been bringing me to client dinners and work events ever since our first, and he always introduces me as "his." *My lovely girlfriend, my Olivia, my beauty queen.* I could really do without the last one, but I still feel giddy every time he claims me as *his.*

I've never felt like I belonged to someone before.

After I shower, I ask Ian how I should wear my hair. He usually tells me to wear it back in a bun so it's not so wild, but sometimes on the weekends he likes it down.

"Down is fine, just not too big," he replies. "And I laid out an outfit for you on the bed."

He's pulled a crisp white sundress with a sweetheart neckline and a black stripe around the waist. After our first shopping trip, he started buying me clothes on his own. I have an entire wardrobe in his closet now, with new surprises every week. I haven't been to my own apartment in days.

The dress fits perfectly, even if it's kind of boring. I pull half my hair back in a clip to tame it a bit, and swipe on some simple makeup.

"Car's here," Ian calls out. I grab a pair of sandals and we speed out the door.

WE'RE IN THE CAR FOR OVER AN HOUR AND THE RIDE IS almost silent. Ian spends half the time talking to some client in Dubai and the other half firing off a million emails.

I don't say anything because I know how important his job is, I just get so frustrated when this happens on our dates. It happens all the time.

Instead of being bored, I figure I should check my email too. No responses from prospects today, but I do have an email from Gavin Scott. He's been especially cold lately, ever since the holidays. I'm almost nervous to read it.

To: Olivia Diamond < olivia@sizzl.com >
From: Gavin Scott < gavin@sizzl.com >
Subject: Nice Work

Olivia,

The first call with FoodRush went well. Thanks for setting up the meeting. Since they're local, they want to come into our office for the demo next week, Wednesday at 10. You can join if you want to see how a demo meeting goes.

-G

I try to school my features as I respond.

To: Gavin Scott < gavin@sizzl.com >
From: Olivia Diamond < olivia@sizzl.com >
Subject: RE: Nice Work

YES! Thank you so much for thinking of me. If there's any prep work I can do to help, let me know. Here for whatever you need. How long do these meetings usually last? If they're with us for lunchtime I thought it could be a nice touch to order in using their delivery app? Or if lunch is too late I could just do an order of coffees or snacks?

Let me know what you think.

Thanks again!

-Liv

His reply comes almost immediately.

To: Olivia Diamond < olivia@sizzl.com >
From: Gavin Scott < gavin@sizzl.com >
Subject: RE: RE: Nice Work

Not a bad idea. Submit a ticket with marketing to get budget approved. If you don't know how to do it, I'm sure Andie can help you. Coffees and snacks would be great.

-G

To: Gavin Scott < gavin@sizzl.com >
From: Olivia Diamond < olivia@sizzl.com >
Subject: RE: RE: RE: Nice Work

I'll take care of it first thing Monday morning. I'm thinking Blue Bottle for coffee and small bites from Onigilly. Their marketing director is from Japan and his brother owns a sushi restaurant in Marin.

Let me know if you want to make any changes!

-Liv

> A few moments after I hit send, another notification pops up.

SLACK DIRECT MESSAGE
Gavin Scott:
Do you always work on Saturdays?
Olivia Diamond:
Do you?
Gavin Scott:
Yes
Olivia Diamond:
Well, I'm on a long car ride and figured I'd check email to pass the time

Thank you again for letting me join the meeting

Gavin Scott:

Mitch told me to. Part of my job is getting you ready for sales

Can't he just pretend to be nice?

Olivia Diamond:

I'll be sure to thank him then

Gavin Scott:

How do you know all that about their marketing director?

Olivia Diamond:

I do my research

Have to go above and beyond to be the best right?

Gavin Scott:

You're killing it

So where's the long drive to?

Olivia Diamond:

I'm not sure actually. It's a surprise

Gavin Scott:

Oh

I wait for another response from Gavin, but it never comes. So now I'm back to looking out the window.

I realized we were heading toward wine country a while ago. If Ian hadn't been so preoccupied, we could have stopped by my parents' place a few miles back, but by the time he puts down his phone we've already entered Napa and turned onto the Silverado Trail.

The worst part is that it looks like we're pulling into La Fantasia, one of my least favorite wineries in Napa. I must be mumbling to myself without realizing it, because Ian gives me a funny look.

"Have you ever been here?" he asks when we get out of the car.

Unfortunately, yes. "Not in a *very* long time," I reply. He looks at me quizzically, like he thinks I'm lying. Maybe because I've only been twenty-one for two years.

Shoot. Was I supposed to pretend I've never been to wine country?

I've learned that Ian loves to teach me things, to help me experience something for the first time. And I love that he loves it, so every so often, I fib a little. Nothing major, just saying it's the first time I've eaten some type of food or visited a landmark in The Bay. The only one I really feel bad about is pretending I've never shot an arrow before. But in my defense, archery shooting for a date *really* caught me off guard.

It might be time to come clean on a few of these.

"Ian, I've been to a lot of wineries. I grew up in Sonoma, actually." It's a little wild this hasn't come up, but Ian never asks about my family. I like it that way, I think. It makes me feel more like an adult, like I'm my own person and not just a daughter or a sister. But Sonoma and winemaking are also part of my blood. It's not something I would ever choose to hide.

"Oh," he replies, stretching the word out for a few beats. "Well, you've never experienced wine country with me."

When we get to the entrance, we're greeted by the owner, a man named Dave that I've known since birth and seen annually at different competitions and events. He's probably perfectly fine, but he and my dad have never gotten along. My dad's family emigrated here from France and pride themselves on old world style wines using the best terroir in California. We don't mass-produce or outsource anything.

Our prices reflect that.

La Fantasia has had a habit of calling us overpriced, not that theirs are much cheaper. And their name is a façade.

Nothing about the winery, the family, or the wines themselves are Italian. They make overpriced red blends and use names like "Climax" and "The Villain" for shock value. I admit, their labels are eye-catching, but their wine is the beverage equivalent of a butter face.

"Olivia Diamond!" Dave croons, holding his arms out like I'm expected to run into them for a hug.

"Hi, Dave," I reply, not moving an inch. Out of the corner of my eye, I can see Ian's mouth hanging ajar. "Good to see you."

"It's been a few years. You're all grown up now. And coming to taste my wines. Do your parents know?" He smirks, like there is any chance in hell I came here by choice.

"Actually, this is my boyfriend, Ian. He brought me here as a surprise." I let the men shake hands. And then, because I can't help myself, "If I'd have known we were coming up here I'd have brought him to Diamond Sky, for some really special wine."

Dave grimaces but Ian's eyes flash. "You've been there? I tried to book a tour, but they didn't have anything available for months."

A huge, genuine smile tugs at my lips when I see Dave's displeasure. I can't wait to tell Dad about this whole encounter. Each of my muscles is strained as I try not to laugh.

"Ian, that's my family's winery."

DAVE FOUND A POLITE EXIT WHEN ANOTHER CUSTOMER walked in and now Ian is pulling me outside.

"Why didn't you tell me who your family was?" he asks, though it feels more like an accusation than a question.

"I don't know. It didn't really come up. If you asked me about my family I would never lie."

He huffs out a breath of exasperation. "But you're Olivia fucking Diamond, *heiress* to Diamond Sky Vineyards. You should have told me."

"I'm really sorry. I wasn't trying to hide anything from you. But I'm definitely no heiress. I have three older brothers, Ian. I don't even work there with them."

He's still shaking his head at me in disbelief. But then a smile forms.

"Can we go?"

"I thought you'd never ask."

CHAPTER SIXTEEN

OLIVIA

For the second day in a row, my favorite barista has denied me my morning caffeine fix. She didn't even say a word today, just shook her head when I walked in the door. Though she was grinning ear to ear.

SLACK DIRECT MESSAGE

Olivia Diamond:
You know you really don't have to get me coffee every day

Gavin Scott:
But that's what a good boyfriend would do

Olivia Diamond:
You're not actually my boyfriend, remember? You don't have to do stuff like that

Gavin Scott:
Just because it's pretend doesn't mean I shouldn't treat you the way you deserve

My little Gavin crush is turning into a full-blown

avalanche. But I don't feel like it's entirely one-sided. This whole week he has been the perfect boyfriend, and while he says it's just for show, I'm starting to question that.

On Tuesday, when I came into work, there was a sticker on my monitor that said "property of my Scottie"—with the "my" crossed out. He must have found it at a pet store because there was a picture of a Scottish terrier in the background.

Wednesday, it was a mug with the same design, except it read "I love my Scottie." Again, with the "my" crossed out.

He brought me lunch when I was too busy prepping for my demo, coffee multiple days in a row, and every morning when I wake up, there's a new picture of Churro waiting for me on my phone.

The texts are probably my favorite, especially the "hedge-hugs," but maybe it's just their juxtaposition to the other texts I keep getting. The ones from Tristan that are far from innocent.

They are the reason I begged Andie to get happy hour today. She and I have both been so busy this week, we've barely had time to catch up, and I desperately need her advice.

My Sunday night chat with Tristan hasn't deterred him at all. In fact, it's only seemed to fuel the fire. The texts he sends me have gotten more explicit each day this week.

"I don't understand. How did Tristan get your number?" Andie asks. We just sat down on the patio at B Bar and imme-diately ordered two dozen oysters and a bottle of rosé.

I cringe, thinking about what Tristan told me. "I think it was my mom. She was under the impression that we're friends."

"Creepy," Andie says, cringing right along with me. "All right, let me see them." She reaches for my phone.

"Okay, but just a disclaimer. I've been trying to respond as neutrally as I can, just so I don't offend him, you know?"

"Okaaaay." She drags out the word and snatches the phone from my hands. And then, as expected, her eyes bulge.

"Olivia!" She whisper-yells. "You sound like a freaking Teletubby. What the hell is this?"

I shrug, while simultaneously chewing my cheek so hard that it bleeds. Our waitress comes by with the wine and I thank her with full sincerity.

"I just didn't know what to say."

She slides the phone closer to me. "The angel face emoji? Really?"

I take a huge glug of wine and slump down in my chair. Then I look through the messages again.

TRISTAN CROSS:

When can I see you in that black dress again?

And when can I see you out of it?

ME:

Wow

blushing face emoji

I still have a boyfriend

TRISTAN CROSS:

Have those plans started to bore you yet?
Because I promise I can keep you up all night
screaming my name

ME:

Oh my

TRISTAN CROSS:

I'm a generous man, Olivia. Especially in the
bedroom. Let me find out how many times I
can make you come

ME:

> Umm no thank you *angel face emoji*

I push the phone back to her, not wanting to read the rest.

She's right. I could have handled that better. Why isn't there a guru for situations like this? Maybe I need a life coach.

"How does he think it's okay to send you those texts?" Andie asks, quiet rage seeping through her lips.

"Because he's a man?" And a rich and powerful one at that. She "tsks" in silent agreement.

"I know you're worried about closing this deal," she continues. "But this is getting creepy. You should tell Mitch."

"No way. He'll take it away from me for sure."

Our oysters come and we both demolish a few in silence. There is truly nothing better on a Friday afternoon than sitting on the rooftop patio at B Bar, slurping oysters and rosè. Even if we are dissecting the mess of my life.

"There will always be other deals, Liv."

"Not for me. Not like this. I really don't think there will be. If I lose it, that proves to Mitch that I'm not ready, and if I start somewhere new, it'll be at least another year in the trenches before I'm given a shot like this."

She looks like she's about to say something else when my phone chimes with another text. It's a picture from Gavin and Andie opens it immediately. I don't know why I hold my breath. Of course, it's just a photo of Churro. Well, technically it's Churro balancing on top of Gavin's head. Its fucking adorable and makes me want to kiss the smirk right off his perfect face.

GAVIN SCOTT:

> We needle you to join us for game night.
> Hedge over whenever you're free

I can't stop from grinning. He's so wholesome. Why is he the one I'm always fantasizing about at night when Tristan is practically sexting me?

"Oh my god!" Andie squeals. "You love him. I knew it!"

"You knew nothing," I argue, taking my phone back. "We're just friends."

"Since when?"

"Since now."

I quickly fill her in on Saturday since in her mind, Gavin and I haven't actually hung out before, minus the off-site.

"You met Lucy Gold? We've been talking about these stupid men for an hour and *now* you tell me the most important thing I missed last weekend?"

"I'm sorry, truly. I shouldn't gate-keep. She was exactly what you'd imagine, maybe cooler. She even invited me to come visit her in LA."

I almost forgot that Andie was the one who introduced me to Lucy's books. Andie isn't a fan of open-door romance like I am, but she is a YA Romantasy fiend; I think Lucy's title *Sleeping Darlings* is her favorite book ever. Her copy has about a thousand tabs in it.

"I'm never going out of town again." She sighs, her lips forming a dramatic pout. "I missed so much."

Shit. I haven't even told her the biggest piece of news.

"Well, before we head out, there's one more thing," I say.

"Really?"

"Yep. I'm coming with you to Mexico."

CHAPTER SEVENTEEN

GAVIN

"Gav!" Gabby yells from the kitchen. "Your phone's ringing."

"Can you answer it for me?" I yell back. "I just got out of the shower."

"Nope! It's your fake girlfriend who you wish was your real girlfriend who I still think will definitely break your heart again if you—"

"I got it," I say, grabbing the phone off the island. I glare at Gabby and shake my wet hair at her.

"Hello?"

"Hi." I must be smiling already because Gabby pokes me in the chest with a wooden spoon. I back away and head toward my room to get dressed. I can't help it. I like Liv's voice. "You really want me to come over?"

"Of course. Churro asked for you specifically, and I hate disappointing him."

Her laugh rings through the phone and I swear I can feel the sound in my entire body.

"Well, I wouldn't want to let down my favorite hedgehog. What can I bring?"

"Just you. And maybe some luck because Gabby and I are both masters at Sushi Go."

"Sushi Go?" Liv asks through the phone.

"Yeah, it's a card game. Don't worry, it's really easy, definitely meant for children. But we love it."

"Can't wait."

I hang up the phone and throw on some sweatpants and a T-shirt. I'm freshly showered but somehow also sweating. Liv and I have hung out together several times now, but something about having her here with Gabby and Kadesha changes things. There's no pretending to be cool when I'm playing a children's card game with my sister.

The funny thing is, I invited her over thinking it would be helpful to *her*. That if we're going to be sharing a hotel room together in a week, we should get to know each other as much as we can. I hate the idea of contributing to Liv's anxiety and I want her to feel as comfortable around me as possible. Luckily I was able to call the hotel and secure a room with two beds.

But now I'm the one who's anxious and jittery. Liv and I are friends now. We flirt. Am I going to ruin that tonight when she sees how Gabby and I fight over cards covered in smiling tempura shrimp?

My thought spiral must be worse than I thought, because what feels like thirty seconds later, someone's knocking on our door.

"What's with the watermelon?"

Liv arrives just after seven. She's still in the same clothes from work and has her laptop bag slung over her shoulder. But she's also carrying a whole watermelon, something my sister points out oh so graciously.

"It's for Churro. I read they're a healthy treat for hedgies," she answers, her voice small and unsure. I flash a quick glare at Gabby.

"I'm sure he'll love it. Come on in." I grab the watermelon from Liv and offer it to Gabby but she swiftly turns away.

"I'll cut some up for him," Kadesha offers. She takes the melon and places it on the counter, and extends a hand to Liv. "I'm Kadesha, Gabby's girlfriend. We're so excited you're here."

Liv looks skeptical, and I don't blame her after the greeting from my sister, but she offers a smile and lets me take her bag to set down by the door.

"Do you want to change?" I ask. We're all in sweats and pajamas but Liv's got on the typical blazer and pointy heels. There's no way she's going to be comfortable in that.

"Umm, I'm okay. I didn't want to go all the way home. I was down in SOMA after work so..." She trails off. I look at Gabby, hoping she'll get the hint and offer something to Liv. They're about the same size. She either doesn't understand, or she's still very much anti-Olivia.

"Come on, you can borrow something of mine. I want you to be comfortable."

"Okay," she says with a hefty amount of hesitation, following me into my room.

I grab a few options. Sweatpants, sweatshirts, shorts, T-shirts, throw them all on the bed. "Wear whatever you want," I say before closing the door so she can have some privacy.

Gabby rolls her eyes at me when I come back to the living room. They go so high I'm worried they'll get stuck that way.

"Shut up."

"I didn't say anything."

"Your face says it all."

"Can you two behave for one night?" Kadesha scolds.

"Sorry," we both mutter back.

Olivia comes out a second later. She is drowning in my clothes. Sweatpants that are clearly rolled a few times at her hips and a hoodie that reaches her knees hang loosely off her body. She looks ridiculous, but also happy. She's grinning from ear to ear.

"Thanks, Scottie," she says, taking a seat next to me on the floor. "I feel like I'm living in a cloud right now." She crosses her legs—well, I think she does; it's honestly hard to tell—and wraps her arms around herself. "Can I wear your clothes every day?"

"Yes." Gabby and Kadesha both stare daggers at me and I realize that was not just an internal thought. Shit. "I mean, keep 'em, if you want."

She beams and...shit. I shouldn't have offered the Messi hoodie. It might be my favorite but I already know I'll never be asking for it back.

Gabby pulls out Sushi Go and expertly explains the rules to Liv. What she doesn't say is that game nights are sacred to us. When we were young, we didn't have a lot of luxuries, but I taught Gabby every card game I could. She probably would have preferred playing with dolls or stuffed animals, but we couldn't afford anything like that. So we played card games, even made up our own games to keep ourselves entertained.

Things are different now, but we're all about traditions. We've branched out on different games, and for some reason, Sushi Go has been our favorite for a while. I'm pretty sure Gabby just likes how it allows for sabotage.

"The cards are so cute." Liv "ooh's" and "ahh's" when we run her through the deck. "Oh!" She suddenly jumps up and we all stare. "Sorry. I just, umm, forgot about the watermelon. Sorry."

"Stop apologizing," I say, standing up too. "Let's go get it for him."

Gabby grabs all the snacks she made while we make up a tiny plate for Churro. Liv goes crazy for the actual tiny plates Kadesha got us. She asks if she can hold on to Churro so I give her the sling and we all settle back in the living room.

"Hey Chunk," Liv coos, holding Churro up in his sling. "How would you like a tasty treat?" She offers him the plate and we all watch as he nibbles it up.

"I guess he likes it," I say. "Thanks for bringing it over."

"I will never get over how cute he is. And I still want to hear the bedtime story."

I gulp, notice Gabby and Kadesha snickering, and grab the plate to put in the sink.

We're on our fifth round of the game when Gabby starts screaming at me in Spanish. I'm actually impressed she waited this long. Apparently, she thinks Liv and I have been sneaking each other sashimi cards when she's not looking.

We have been.

"Los dos son unos tramposos! Lo sabía! Gavin, nunca has ganado tres veces seguido."

We all laugh, tossing the remaining cards into the pile. *"Cálmate,"* I whisper to Gabby. "We're just having a little fun."

Of course, Liv is apologizing profusely, saying I made her do it, but Gabby just keeps muttering under her breath. She switched to Italian for a moment but now the hard vowels are making me wonder if she's practicing her Danish.

"Damn, how many languages do you speak?" Liv asks a moment later.

"Five. Six...ish." Gabby shrugs. She's never understood how

impressive it is. Learning new languages is Gabby's favorite pastime.

"That's incredible. How'd you get into that? I mean, where did you even start?" Liv's eyes are full of wonder, but Gabby's cloud over.

I decide to answer for her. "We were both bilingual as kids. Our dad mainly spoke English so our mom only spoke to us in Spanish. When we moved to the States it was a tough transition, especially for Gabby since she was so young."

"Tough?" Gabby looks at me, daring me to be more honest. "I was in first grade and couldn't really differentiate one language from the other. Kids were mean." She looks at me again and her face softens this time. "But lucky for me, I have the best big brother in the world. He spent every afternoon and weekend helping me adjust. And the more time we spent in the library reading about languages, I guess I developed a knack for them. We taught ourselves French, but of course Gavin lost it immediately. I practiced a lot more. Then Italian and Portuguese were pretty easy to pick up with a couple online classes. I'm working on a few more. Hoping it helps me get better job offers."

My heart warms with Gabby's admission. "Without my brilliant sister, I probably would have lost my Spanish by now. I'm glad I get to keep that part of our family though."

"That's amazing," Liv replies. "I wish my family held on to more of their culture. I think my grandparents spoke a little French but it sort of died with them. At least my brother cooks authentic French food sometimes."

"Did you try the Alfajores yet?" Gabby extends the plate of cookies to Liv and I don't miss the change in her tone. Maybe she's warming up to her. "They're our mom's recipe."

Liv takes a small bite, then a larger one. "Wow. These are insane."

Gabby looks at me again, with a softness that makes my chest ache. "Did I mention I have the best brother? He made sure to save her recipe book for me."

I sniff, cover it up by taking a long pull of my beer.

Liv turns to me and smiles softly. "He is the best, huh? I wish I could have dated him instead of my shitty ex."

And for the second time this month, I spit out my drink at Liv's words. The plus side, I think the sound of it covered up the gasps from Gabby and Kadesha.

Liv turns crimson. "I meant, like, hypothetically. Like I wish I had dated someone as nice as you. Oh my god, I'm so sorry." She pops up to follow Gabby who's already grabbing paper towels. My arm saved most of the cards, but there's still beer everywhere.

"It's fine, Liv," I say when she comes back, wiping down my sleeve. "Just went down the wrong pipe."

She scrunches her whole face at me, another silent apology.

Kadesha hands me a new beer and motions to clink our bottles together. She shoots me a mischievous grin. "Best game night ever!"

CHAPTER EIGHTEEN

OLIVIA

ANOTHER WEEK FLIES BY WITH WORK CONSUMING MY life. Work and texts actually. Every time I hear that little chime I salivate like Pavlov's dog. The problem is I never know what I'm going to get. It's fifty-fifty odds between an adorable hedgehog pun or a very direct promise of an orgasm.

My physiological receptors are a mess.

But tonight, as soon as I get home, I silence my phone and blast my favorite playlist. My flight to Mexico leaves in the morning and I haven't started packing yet. The chances of sleep tonight are slim.

All morning, I tried googling what to wear to a work event that's also a tropical vacation where you're bound to see your ex multiple times a day. The results were less than helpful.

So here I am, digging through my tiny closet for the perfect pair of shoes I definitely don't own, when I hear someone banging on my door.

I'm only wearing a sports bra and joggers, so I grab a shirt and run to the door, trying to untangle it as I yank it over my head.

My hair is an actual rats' nest by the time I get the shirt on and open the door.

"Scottie?"

"I've been calling you. I was worried."

"Oh, umm, come in?" Not sure why I posed it as a question. "Sorry. I mean, hi. I had my notifications off. Didn't want to be distracted."

"Are you working on something?" He looks around my apartment, totally confused. He's probably wondering why I need to be focused. But he's a man. And he's not about to be in Mexico with thirty-five co-workers who know he didn't earn the trip. He'll probably wait to pack in the morning since it'll only take him five minutes.

"Just need to pack."

"That's what I figured. I came over to help."

"To help me pack?" I ask.

"Yeah. I know you have trouble making decisions sometimes, and...look, I did call first."

He drops his gaze and my heart tumbles after it. Gavin is an actual sweetheart. I never knew offering to help pack was my kink, but here we are.

So much for a crush. I am very into Gavin Scott.

"You okay?" he continues. "You look a little hot?" He reaches out to feel my cheek.

"I'm fine. That was really nice of you. To come over."

His hand is still on my face, but his fingers move down to my mouth. I didn't realize I was biting my lower lip until he releases it from my teeth. Just a little tug with the pad of his thumb. His eyes lock on my lips, and I forget how to breathe for a moment. Heat creeps up my spine until I feel like my entire body has been turned up several degrees.

"I should go turn down the music," I say, a little breathier than I'd like. But as soon as I break away to turn it off, I'm reminded of the sounds it was drowning out.

"What the hell is that?" Gavin asks, spinning in a circle to try and place the noise. I laugh, knowing how jarring it is for people who don't live this close to the wharf.

"Sea lions."

"No way. You can hear them from here?"

"Yep. Every night. I'm pretty used to it, but they're also why I always have music playing."

"I like your music. Keep it on." He turns toward my bedroom—if you can call it that—and throws me an optimistic smile. "So? Where should we start?"

Hesitantly, I show him the current packing situation. All I've got so far is a couple pairs of sandals and thirteen different swimsuits on the bed.

"The Sonoma Seals?" Gavin holds up my speedo I still have from middle school swim team. I'm not sure it even fits, but it's the most conservative suit I own. Not that my others are particularly scandalous, but when you have double d's, everything looks overly revealing.

"It's a work trip. I don't want to wear anything inappropriate," I argue.

"*This* is inappropriate." He throws the suit back on the bed. "Which one of these is your favorite?"

"Well, it depends on where I'm going and who I'm with and what I'm—"

"You're going to the beach, alone, with your favorite book. Which one would you bring?"

I look through the selection, nibbling my cheek. There's one that's hot barbie pink. The top is a triangle style that ties in the middle instead of the back, with thick strings that create a large bow. It's totally impractical and would give me horrible tan lines, which is why I've never worn it. But I'm also obsessed with the look.

"That one," I say, pointing to it.

"Great." He grabs the suit and tosses it into the open suitcase next to my bed. "And if you found out your parents were about to show up, which one would you want then?"

I laugh. His method is silly but extremely helpful. "The blue one."

He tosses the blue suit into my bag, and I grab the rest to put back in my closet.

He follows the same instructions for a few more outfits, specifically asking for my most comfortable clothes for the travel days, and shoes that don't hurt to walk in. Whenever I struggle between options, he's cutthroat. The whole process of packing for a trip is something I dread, but it's like he turned it into a game. The kind of game I can't lose.

"The first night is dressy-casual," he says looking at his phone. He pulled up the itinerary for me, so I don't miss anything. "And the second night says cocktail attire. That's the awards dinner."

"That's easy. I just need two dresses." I step toward my dress rack and slide all the casual sundresses to one side so I can see the fancier ones.

"You really like fashion, huh?" Gavin is sliding his hands through each hanger to inspect all my garments. He's currently in my favorite section with all the sparkly and colorful dresses.

"Yeah, don't worry. I won't bring those. I have some simpler ones." I grab the black silk dress from the other night, but then I put it back. It will feel too weird wearing it after all of Tristan's comments. I reach for another plain one instead. It's navy blue, nothing special, but shouldn't offend anyone either.

"Why? I like these," he says, taking the navy dress out of my hand and hanging it back up. "What about this one? He grabs a pink strappy slip that's covered in sequins and little feathers. It has this modern-day flapper appeal that initially caught my eye. It's gorgeous.

But way too much.

"I don't think I want to draw that much attention to myself."

"Come on, Sparkles." He does a little shimmy, shaking the dress so it glitters even more. "A diamond's gotta shine."

My suitcase is packed in record time and my anxiety seems to be packed away in it too. We don't have work tomorrow and I have nothing to do except make it to the airport, so I ask Gavin if he wants to have a glass of wine.

"I actually have a couple bottles I picked up last weekend, if you want to try something from our vineyard."

"That sounds great."

"What jersey is that?" I ask, sort of abruptly while I grab the wine. I've been eyeing his baby blue and white striped tee since he got here, the color matching his hoodie I stole almost exactly.

"It's a Messi jersey," he says, turning around to show me the name on the back. I shrug, clueless to what he means. "Football. Soccer, I guess. He plays for Argentina."

"Oh," I say, realizing quickly it's a shit response. "*Oh*, right. That's where you're from. Are you a big fan? I've never really followed soccer."

"Yeah, I guess. Can I try the wine now?"

I'm starting to realize he quickly changes the subject anytime our conversation shifts to his background. Not wanting to push, I pour two glasses of the Vega and slice up my last chunk of Midnight Moon, my very favorite California cheese.

I can't help it, but I watch closely when he takes his first sip. This wine has always been special to me, ever since I was a little girl and my brothers showed me how to find Vega in the night sky.

"Sirius is bigger," Owen would say.

"But if you find Vega, you can see the whole Lyra constellation. It looks like a harp," Deacon always countered.

"What do you think?" I ask Gavin.

"That's really good. It tastes like...umm...sorry, I can't describe it. It reminds me of Christmas though."

"Yes!" I practically jump off the couch. "You tasted baking spices. Cinnamon, nutmeg, that's what makes it so complex."

"What's my prize?" he asks.

Before I even realize what I'm doing, I grab a square of cheese and feed it to him.

His eyes flash as his lips part and my finger brushes against them. As soon as I realize what I'm doing I pull my arm back. *Jesus, Olivia.* But Gavin doesn't let me. He grabs onto my wrist, holding it in place and takes the cheese out of my hand with his teeth.

My entire body freezes. Even my eyes refuse to look anywhere but straight into Gavin's. He holds my gaze along with my wrist until he finishes chewing. I watch his Adam's apple bob when he finally swallows and I reluctantly pull away.

"Sorry," I murmur.

"Liv."

"Sor—how do you like the cheese?"

"It's as delicious as the wine. Thank you."

I smile, grateful for how he just played that off. That's twice tonight he's turned me on more than I ever have been before. And he's barely even touched me. I take a deep breath and try to slow my pounding heart.

"I'm glad you like it. This is my favorite combo, even if they don't technically pair well together."

He takes another sip, and I can tell he really enjoys it by the way his eyes squeeze shut, just for a moment. And then he takes another bite of cheese and chews thoughtfully.

"I guess sometimes opposites attract."

CHAPTER NINETEEN

GAVIN

"I don't need both of these," I say to Gabby when she hands me two massive breakfast sandwiches wrapped in foil.

"One's for Olivia, you doof."

"Wow. You're finally coming around to her?" I ask. I know they bonded a little during game night, but Gabby has been so against this fake relationship that it's made me worry she'd be just as against a real one. Not that I'm delusional enough to think Liv wants to be my girlfriend. But I'd be lying if I said there haven't been moments.

Liv is always a bit frazzled. Ever since the first interview with her I've been aware of the energy she gives off. I find it endearing, but I also love how relaxed she is when we're together. That has to mean something.

"I'll admit, she was a very helpful addition to game night," Gabby replies. "Now that Daanesh is always too busy for us, having a fourth really opens up the game options." I give her a look. She's really going to act like she's coming around just because Liv is another warm body? "And she's fun, okay? And like, stupid hot. I get why you like her. Just please don't let her break your heart. I'd really prefer not to commit a felony before I'm twenty-five."

"Thanks for looking out, Gabs. But I'm the one who takes care of you, remember?"

I grab my bags and head to the door when I notice the Uber's waiting.

"It doesn't always have to be a one-way street, you know," Gabby yells as I leave.

Liv is just as surprised about Gabby's breakfast sandwich as I was.

"Thank god your sister doesn't hate me anymore. I was starving. And this is delicious."

"Yeah, she's a really good cook. I don't know what I would eat if we didn't live together," I reply.

"You'd live off wine and cheese like I do," Liv offers, a wide smile stretching from her lips. Last night was the third time we've shared wine and cheese together. She calls it "girl dinner," whatever that means.

"That doesn't sound so bad." And it doesn't, if it always includes her.

"So tell me what I need to know about flying with you," she says, turning to me in the back of the car. "You take medicine, right?"

This catches me off guard, but I guess I did tell her about my motion sickness a couple weeks ago. The truth is that I get migraines. I can't tell if they make the motion sickness worse or if it's the motion sickness that sets off the migraines. Either way, it isn't pretty.

I don't love the idea of Liv seeing me in my weakest state, but with a four-hour flight ahead of us, I don't have much choice.

"It's no big deal," I lie, wanting to downplay it as much as I can. "I have some pills I'll take before we leave that help a lot. But they make me pretty sleepy so don't be surprised if I zonk out right away."

"I can handle that," she says with a cheery expression. I definitely appreciate the optimism.

MAYBE LIV HAS SOME MAGICAL POWERS BECAUSE THE flight does go well. I sleep the whole time and only wake up once to find myself leaning on her shoulder. This medicine knocks me out hard. I really hope I didn't drool.

I'm still drowsy as hell when we get off the plane in Puerto Vallarta, and we still have another hour ride to the resort in Punta Mita. I'm not looking forward to more moving vehicles, but at least the medicine is still doing its thing.

My van nap is woken up by my favorite voice and a squeeze to my bicep. "We're here."

Liv helps drag me out of the van and we enter the nicest resort I've ever seen. It looks like our budget went up from last year. The St. Regis lobby mimics a tropical castle more than a hotel, and we're all handed freshly made margaritas while we wait to check in.

After a few sips, she nudges me. "Do you mind if I go find a bathroom while you check in?" She starts bouncing with her legs squeezed together. "I really gotta go."

I laugh and let her know it's no problem. And moments after she escapes, I'm called to the front desk.

"Good afternoon, Mr. Scott," the receptionist says, eyeing my passport. "I see you've requested a room with two queens."

I hear someone snicker behind me and turn to find Ian and Vaughn. "Guess someone's not getting laid," Vaughn mumbles to Ian, but it's more than loud enough for everyone around us to hear.

Turning back to the front desk, I loudly say, "There must be some confusion. I called to confirm that we had a king bed."

"No, Mr. Scott. I have the notes right here and it says—"

"Your notes must be wrong." I feel like an asshole right now, but Ian and Vaughn are still giggling behind me like a couple of high school mean girls. I think about switching to Spanish, trying to explain the situation, but with all of Ian's fancy degrees I wouldn't be surprised if he could understand me.

"I'm sorry sir. I'm sure we can accommodate the change. Just let me get a manager."

By the time Liv gets back I've secured a room with one bed, as well as a free upgrade to their beachfront villa with a private pool—for the trouble they caused.

I really am an asshole.

"What's wrong?" she asks, as we leave the main building. There's no tower at this hotel, just tons of winding paths to take you to your villa. Since ours is right on the beach it's the furthest away. "Wow, this place is beautiful," she adds, distracted by the views.

"Well, I'm glad you think so. I got us an upgrade, one of their nicest suites."

"Really? You're awesome." She nudges my shoulder. "But how?"

"Don't thank me yet."

We find our villa and it *is* awesome. The entire thing is an indoor-outdoor space with a full living room and separate bedroom. The bathroom is massive with a deep soaking tub and oversized shower and looks fancy as hell with marble tile everywhere.

The living space opens straight into the private pool which faces the ocean, and there's an enclosed outdoor shower as well.

The bedroom is probably bigger than Liv's whole apartment and—

"There's only one bed," she says, looking around like there might be another one hiding in the closet.

"Like I said…"

"But you called and asked for two, right?" I quickly explain the fiasco at the front desk and how we were able to upgrade. "Oh. Well, that's okay. I can sleep on the couch."

"I will sleep on the couch, Sparkles."

"But it's your trip."

"That I forced you to go on."

"Gavin."

"Olivia."

"Ugh, fine!" She dramatically flops down on the king-size bed and huffs. "I guess if you insist, I will have to endure the most luxurious sleep of my life."

LIV MEETS ANDIE FOR A DRINK BY THE POOL WHILE I TAKE a nap in the luxurious bed. The drugs usually wear off after five or six hours so I should be fine for dinner tonight.

I'm just about dressed and ready to go when Liv bursts into the villa in a state of distress. I think I can see a vein popping on her forehead.

"What's wrong?" I ask, finishing the last button on my shirt.

"Do I have to go tonight? Everyone's talking about me."

"Everyone? What do you mean?"

"Andie and I were sitting by the pool, and you know how water carries sound? Well, some idiots don't seem to know that. Like everyone who's here from the HR team."

"What were they saying?" My voice comes out raspy,

deeper than usual. There's a part of me that feels fiercely protective over Liv. I can't let anyone hurt her, not after I was the one that got her in this situation.

I motion for her to sit on the couch with me and she sniffles a few times but doesn't let any tears slip. I hold on to her hands in between us and she stares down at the connection. After a few moments she finally looks up at me and lets our eyes meet.

"They said I *finally* got a man to bring me here. And they called me a slut, which I'm used to by now but still."

Yeah, that's rough. Especially because I know how wrong they are.

"That's really shitty, Liv. I'm sorry they said that. But you know they're all just jealous of you, right?"

"What? They're not jealous. They think I'm a joke. It's not like this is the first time people at work have said that about me."

"Was Stacey one of them?" I ask.

"Yeah, why?"

"She's asked me out like ten times. Last year on this same trip, she showed up to my room in the middle of the night with a bottle of tequila. She's jealous."

"Really? You're not just making this up so I feel better?"

"I swear. I can show you some of her Slack messages. For someone in HR, they are very inappropriate."

Olivia starts to laugh. At first, it's just a light chuckle but then it grows until her whole body is shaking with it.

"Thank you," she says. "For telling me that. Even if it isn't true—"

"It's true. Don't you trust me?"

"Yeah, I do, actually. I know you wouldn't lie to me."

"Just remember, when people talk shit, it's always more about them than it is about you."

"That is incredibly wise, Scottie."

"I have my moments. Now go put on one of those gorgeous

dresses I picked out." I wiggle my brows. "If they're gonna be talking about you, they might as well be looking at you too."

I stay on the couch to give her some privacy, but when she comes out to show me her outfit she might as well be naked. I can't imagine her looking better than she does right now. It feels like the wind was knocked out of me.

"You don't like it?" she asks, nibbling her cheek. I remember helping her pick this one last night, but I had no idea what it would look like on her. The top is a sheer black mesh, highlighting her curves, and the bottom is a metallic green skirt that hugs her hips and thighs. I simultaneously want to rip it off and glue it on her so she can never wear anything else.

"There is absolutely nothing I don't like about that," I reply, a little breathless.

She likes my response. I can tell by the way her face changes, adding a little more pink to her cheeks. She's trying to hide her smile but it's plain to see. She's still fidgeting though, doing the nail tap thing I know so well.

"Are you still feeling anxious about seeing everyone tonight?"

"Yeah, a little."

I'm pretty sure it's more than a little.

"I brought some edibles. Do you want one?" I ask. I hope she doesn't judge me for bringing them. I always need a little help getting through these events. But I never want my co-workers to see me shit-faced, so I usually limit myself to a few drinks. Weed tends to keep my migraines at bay too.

Her reaction has me worried because for a second, she looks a little stunned. It's not like it's illegal. It's barely even frowned upon in San Francisco. But then she runs toward me and throws her arms around my neck.

"Thank you, Scottie. I can't think of anything that sounds better right now."

Once she's finished getting ready, I hand her one of the gummies I brought. "We can share—" I freeze when she pops the whole thing in her mouth. "Umm, I usually just take half."

"Oh, I'll be fine. I take them all the time."

I guess we'll see about that.

"I know you're nervous, but don't let those girls ruin your trip." She twists her lips and I can tell she's deciding how difficult it will be not to think about it. It's hard for me to understand what she's going through, and for the umpteenth time I think about how much worse I've made things for her by trying to help. So I just keep trying to make up for it. "We're gonna have fun, right?"

"Right," she says, slipping on her sandals. "Let's do this."

"See," Liv whispers in my ear. "Everyone is looking at me."

"That's because you look gorgeous." She scoffs. "Sparkles, you literally took my breath away earlier. You just have to give everyone else a chance to catch theirs."

She loops her arm through mine and clings to me a little more. We've never really discussed how to do this fake relationship thing, how often we should be holding hands or showing affection. Not since the night she asked about us making out. *Or more.*

But it never feels forced with Liv. I don't think she does anything for show. Maybe we're just friends, or maybe there's something more here. Either way, we feel good together.

"Want a drink?" I ask.

"Yes, please. These edibles are taking forever." Weed might help her anxiety but mine's on alert waiting for the edibles to kick in. I'm not really sure what to expect. After she popped a whole one, I took a quarter. I figure one of us needs to keep their wits tonight.

We make our way over to the bar area. Tonight's event is the welcome reception, so it's basically a cocktail party. They have people passing around appetizers and a bar is set up next to the beach. Instead of dining tables there are lots of smaller high-tops to use while standing. In the past, we've all gone out for dinner in large groups once this winds down, but I'm not sure what Liv will want to do so I haven't agreed to anything yet.

Unfortunately, Stacey and her HR trio had the same idea about ordering drinks right now. We bump into them as soon as we order.

"Wow, Olivia," Stacey croons. "That dress is amazing. You really went for it, huh."

Then Marissa has to add her two cents. "I could never wear something so showy. Good for you."

"Thanks," Liv replies curtly. I don't blame her for being short with those kinds of backhanded compliments.

I wrap an arm around her tightly, so snug that she has to bend a little at the hip. "Thanks ladies. I picked it out. Liv's way too modest, but I love seeing her shine." Without thinking, I kiss the tip of her nose. I'm elated when she doesn't flinch, just drops her eyes while a small grin forms.

Stacey clears her throat, but I don't give a fuck if our little display of affection bothers her. I just squeeze tighter.

"Olivia, we heard you got a meeting with Surf and Stream. How'd you get so lucky?" Stacey asks.

I really need to get away from these women, but before I can find a polite way to exit, Liv straightens and looks directly at them.

"You think I got lucky?"

Stacey and Marissa both laugh uncomfortably, just a little chuckle that shows they have no idea what to say.

I don't know where this newfound confidence comes from, but Liv continues, "Would you tell Gavin he got lucky? Or Eduardo? Or any of the men on my team?"

"She didn't mean anything—" Marissa says, before getting cut off.

"She meant exactly what she said. And my answer is no, I didn't get fucking *lucky*. I put in hours of work to research that company, to find the right contact and to message him again and again and *again* until he agreed to take a meeting. Luck had nothing to do with it. It was hard work, and perseverance, and plain old grit that got me that meeting. So next time you're chatting about me, those are some words you can use." Olivia looks down at her margarita for a moment and then she chugs the whole thing. "You know, besides just calling me a slut."

Stacey and Marissa both go bug-eyed, but Liv is already dragging me away. She pulls me all the way onto the beach where a fire pit is roaring to life. And then she not-so-elegantly plops down directly in the sand.

"Sparkles?" I sit down next to her.

"I am so high right now."

Oh. Well, that was bound to happen. "So when you're stoned, the filter turns off? Because that shit was awesome. I wish I had it on tape."

"Scottie!"

"What do you need?" I ask.

"Just five minutes to get my limbs working again. Then, maybe a quesadilla. I've gone too long without cheese."

I lean into her and laugh. She'll be fine.

"I bet they have some pretty good wine at this hotel. We could skip this thing and order room service if you want," I offer.

She squints at me, but I can tell she's mulling it over. "You'd really want to leave the party?"

"I don't give a shit about anyone here but you." Fuck. I hope she's buzzed enough to let that one fly. Though if I'm honest, I'm starting to care less and less about hiding my feelings from her. She's single. We have fun together. How long am I supposed to pretend I don't think about kissing her every damn day?

"We do have our own pool," she muses.

"We do. And if I'm correct, you have two swimsuits to choose from."

"I'm not positive I can walk," she says, completely serious. She pushes out her lips, trying to solve the dilemma.

"Let's start with standing." I haul her up and try to brush as much sand as I can off her dress. She leans on me but it's definitely not all her weight. "Can you take a few steps? You can hold on to me."

It feels like I'm teaching a toddler. Liv gives me a skeptical eye roll but hesitantly takes a step. Then another, and another, letting go of me entirely.

"Yep. I'm perfect," she says, right before falling back into the sand.

We wait about ten minutes before trying again. Luckily no one has noticed us over here, everyone consumed with the bar for now.

This time, when I get her up, her balance is back to normal. She also doesn't let go of my arm as we walk toward the other side of the beach.

On the way to our villa, Liv quizzes me over and over on our new agenda.

"Quesadillas, then swimming? Or swimming first? Or *wine* first!"

Once we get inside, I get her settled on the couch and hand

her the room service menu. "How about you look at the menu and the wine list and tell me what to order. Then we can swim while we wait for them to bring it."

"Scottie?"

"Sparkles?"

"You're a genius."

I can't stop laughing at her serious tone, even when I've left the room to change into trunks.

Then I hear Liv start huffing.

"What's wrong?" I ask when I get back, trying not to laugh. She's frustrated about something but the faces she keeps making are so overly animated it's making me chuckle.

"Well, they have one of my favorite wines, the Goldeneye Pinot. But I'm pretty sure the price is marked up by a thousand percent."

I take the menu from her. "I'm sure it's fine. What do you want to eat?"

She grunts again and covers her face in her hands. "They have seven different quesadillas. I can't decide."

I eye the menu to check because seven seems excessive. But she's right.

"I'll decide for you, okay? Go get your swimsuit on."

She hops up and throws me a grin full of gratitude. Once she's in the other room I call for room service. And I order all seven quesadillas.

The wine arrives almost immediately via butler and the quesadillas soon after, so we hold off on getting in the pool. It's a blessing and a curse because instead of swimming, Liv is sitting cross legged on the bed in her bikini.

I asked If she wanted to sit on the couch. The coffee table seemed like a better place to put the food. But she insisted.

"Scottie, it's not room service if you don't eat it in bed."

I open up each container until she realizes what I ordered.

"You got every kind?" I nod. "I swear I could kiss you right now." I honest to god seal my lips shut so I don't say "please."

We polish off about a third of the quesadillas, which is pretty impressive, and half the wine while we watch some Disney movie in Spanish. Liv can't understand it, but she says she likes it anyway, and apparently enjoys having me translate.

Before we both pass out from a food coma, I ask if she still wants to go swimming.

"Definitely." She immediately pops off the bed and runs outside like she just heard the ice cream truck was here. I quickly clean up the food and pour some more wine into each of our glasses before I go out and join her.

The night rolled in, murky and silent, while we were laughing over quesadillas. Liv is floating on her back under a star-filled sky. I'm tempted to take a picture because it fits perfectly with the labels on her family's wine bottles. Each one I've seen has a different starry-night styled image. She said all the bottles are named after different stars or constellations. But from where I'm standing, they need one called The Olivia.

"Hey, beautiful," I announce when I hop in and hand her the glass of wine.

"Thanks." She takes a few small sips and places it on the ledge.

"I'm sorry if I've made things worse for you, Liv. The way those girls talked to you. It's fucked up."

"It's not your fault."

"But—is that always what it's like? Being a woman? I mean, Marissa is always talking at our company meetings about the women's group she started. I swear she uses the word *empowerment* so much I could make a drinking game from it. But then she talks to you like that? What the fuck?"

"Yeah," she sighs. "Misogyny isn't always from men. It's so internalized at this point, it's like all the shitty men from yesteryear found a way to outsource it. They can just sit back and watch us tear each other apart now." She grabs the glass and takes another long sip of wine. "I'm just glad I have Andie. No one else at Sizzl likes me."

"That's not true."

I lean against the edge of the pool, half-hoping she didn't hear the conviction in my voice. She sets down her glass and swims closer to me, stopping just short of my personal space.

"You know you're the nicest guy I've ever dated." Her voice is sad when she says it, each word coated thick with shame. "I mean, we're not even actually dating. And you're still the best boyfriend I've ever had."

I'm not sure how to respond so I don't. It feels like she's trying to work something out, and I want to let her.

"Are you always this nice?" She places a hand on my shoulder, and I feel the contact roll through every inch of my body. I could swear each hair on my legs stands at attention. "Are you like this with everyone?"

"No," I state simply. Because it's true. Because I've barely dated since we moved to the city, haven't made friends outside of the office. All I've cared about for most of my life is making sure my sister has everything she needs. Making sure she's happy and healthy and has a roof over her head.

My crush on Olivia awakened something in me when we first met, but it was snuffed out as quickly as it began. Now, all these feelings she's stirring up in me, they make me feel like anything is possible.

She puts her free hand on my other shoulder, boxing me in just enough to make me sweat.

"Then why are you so nice to me?" she asks.

"I think you know why."

And I hope that's true, because I really don't feel like

spelling it out right now. I don't feel like talking at all with how close she is.

She slides forward until it's her forearms that are resting on my shoulders, our lips only a few breaths apart. The water in this pool is chilly, the perfect contrast to the balmy air, but my body feels like it's on fire.

"I think I might kiss you," she whispers. The words land on my lips and I push forward, barely an inch. But she doesn't make a move.

"I think I might let you," I admit.

"Really?"

"Really."

"But do you think it'd be bad? You and me kissing?"

"No, Sparkles. I don't think it'd be bad at all."

I'm tired of this waiting game. I reach for her waist and pull her toward me. Her lips quickly find mine in a tentative press. It's soft, teasing and makes my pulse beat like a drum.

Our heads tilt at opposite angles and her mouth softens a little more against mine.

It's killing me a little to go at her pace, but I'm still not sure what this is, so I let her move as slowly as she wants. She leans in again and this time I can feel her insecurities melt away. Her arms press against my shoulders and she wraps her legs around my hips, her lips parting just enough to let me know she wants more.

So I give it to her.

Our tongues meet and it feels like my entire body sighs in relief. She tastes like lazy mornings and daydreams, like I could stay here forever and be the happiest man alive.

My hands trail down her back and under the water until I can fiddle with her bikini bottoms. She gives a little gasp when I squeeze her ass, but I can tell it's the good kind.

"You were right," she whispers into my mouth.

"About what?"

"This isn't bad." She grins against my mouth, so wide I can feel it. I let my hands wander while I kiss a path down her throat, eliciting more gasps and sighs.

"I love how responsive you are," I say on a breath, letting my tongue glide along her collarbone. I stop to suck on every new spot I find, creeping down to the hollow of her breasts. I'm tempted to go lower. This hot pink bikini has been torturing me all night, her half-naked body wrapped in a bow. I want nothing more than to destroy it, ripping it apart piece by tiny piece. "Nothing about this will be bad."

She swallows thickly against my mouth before she pulls herself back. I take in the sight of her: swollen lips, heaving chest, hair a wet and tangled mess that's entirely my doing. Pride swells through me.

"Fuck, you're sexy."

"We should stop," she says, still panting each breath. "That was..." she trails off. Amazing? Incredible? Something we should actually *never* stop doing? "A lot."

Shit.

"I'm sorry," I say, immediately taking my hands off of her. "Did I misread something?"

"No! Not at all. It was just going a little fast." She bites her lip and yeah, she's right. I was ready to spend all night between her legs. I still am.

"You're right. We should probably...umm, call it a night."

She climbs out of the pool, but I stay behind and try to catch my breath. What the hell just happened? For a second it felt like every dream I've had for the last two years was coming true, and then I woke up with a splash of cold water.

I finish off the rest of my wine and grab a towel.

I change into sweats while Liv is in the bathroom, most likely doing the same. Part of me wonders if I should leave, give her some space. A bigger part of me wants to stay, talk out whatever's going through her head.

"Hey," she says, coming out of the bathroom. "Just wanted to rinse off real quick." Her hair is still wet, but it's brushed out, perfectly smooth. And she's swapped my nemesis bikini for shorts and a T-shirt. "Are you tired?"

"A little," I reply. It's after midnight, but with everything that just happened I'm not sure sleep will be so easy. I also napped for half the day. I grab a pillow from the bed anyway. "I'll go in the other room. See you in the morn—"

"Will you stay in here?" she asks.

"You want me to sleep in the bed with you?"

She nods, repeatedly. "If that's okay with you."

My lips tug into a grin.

"Sure, Sparkles. Whatever you want."

CHAPTER TWENTY

OLIVIA

GAVIN SCOTT LIKES TO CUDDLE.

Or maybe he just likes me. Ian always said no men actually like to cuddle. But I'm starting to think Ian was mostly full of shit.

When we slid into bed last night, all I could think about was kissing Gavin again. I wanted his mouth all over me like it was in the pool. His kisses tasted like belonging. Every stroke of his tongue made my heart shimmer.

I hate that I let my insecurities take over. I was just hellbent on not ruining the most perfect kiss of my life.

But Gavin didn't seem fazed by any of it, like hitting pause wasn't nearly impossible like it was for me. I started to worry the kiss meant nothing to him, that it was just a way to pass time with the woman he shared a room with. Then he pulled me toward him and wrapped an arm around me. And as far as I can tell that hasn't changed all night.

He's holding me like a promise he intends to keep. Which is probably why I wake up with aching cheeks. I cannot stop smiling.

"Morning, Sparkles," Gavin mumbles, his words muffled by the skin of my shoulder. He lightly kisses the spot and pulls me in a little closer. I love the way this feels. The way *he* feels. Every time he holds me, I swear it's like bright morning light seeping into my skin. His touch feels like the safest place in the world.

"Is this okay?" he asks on a whisper, his lips pressing lightly against my shoulder.

"Yeah," I respond, but it's so breathless I'm not sure if he hears me. I press my body back into him to make sure he knows I'm in agreement.

His hands start to roam over my hip, his thumb finding the waistband of my shorts. "When do you have to leave?"

"Huh? Oh shit." I grab my phone off the nightstand to see it's nine forty-three. That gives me seventeen minutes to get ready for my boating excursion.

I jump out of bed, grab the more conservative swimsuit, and flee into the bathroom. Signing up for a yacht tour seemed like a great idea when Gavin sent me the itinerary options. I knew he wouldn't be doing it, but Andie begged me to join her. And how could I pass up a free ride on a yacht with my best friend?

But now, I'd give anything for five more minutes curled up with Gavin in that bed.

I throw on the suit and a cover up, and the plain sandals Gavin picked out because they're easy to walk in. My hair is still a tangled mess, but I really don't have time to fix it.

"Do you remember if I packed a hat?" I ask, rummaging through everything still in my bag.

He climbs out of bed and grabs the Warriors hat he wore yesterday on the plane. "Here, use mine," he murmurs, placing it on my head. He pulls down the brim since it's a little big on me before flipping it around to wear backwards. His eyes roam over my face and I think he might kiss me. Instead, he just pinches my chin between his thumb and forefinger. "You look great, Sparkles. Have fun."

I MAY BE THE LAST PERSON TO MAKE IT TO THE BOAT, BUT everyone else looks tired and hungover. I can smell the alcohol wafting off of them.

Not me. I had the best sleep of my life.

"Why are you so cheery? It's ten in the morning," Andie whines, laying her head on my shoulder.

"I don't think I drank nearly as much as you did. What'd you get into last night?"

"I'm not sure," she mumbles. "I think we went downtown? I do remember a lot of tequila shots though."

Our group is run through a safety training before we board the boat and within a few minutes we're moving. I wish I could have convinced Gavin to come, but after seeing two guys throw up over the side of the boat, I know he made the right call.

Andie tugs me all the way to the bow because she wants to have a private conversation, and because it looks like the best place to sunbathe. Unsurprisingly, everyone else is hanging out by the bar, starting their day with mimosas and bloody marys.

"Okay, so I heard some stuff last night," Andie whispers.

Shit. "About me?"

"Did you really make Stacey cry?"

"What? No, of course not. I mean, I don't think I did?"

"Well, she's not calling you a slut anymore, so that's a plus. But she did throw around the words 'stuck up bitch,' just FYI."

"Honestly, I'll take it. She was being rude and I...I stood up for myself. After we heard them talking about me yesterday, I was sick of being a doormat. I'll be more than happy to be a bitch instead."

Andie's eyes widen. "I like this take-no-shit Olivia. If you do it again though, can I be there to see? She's the worst."

I think back to Gavin saying Stacy is into him. It's not like I'm jealous, but I am curious why Andie doesn't like her. We've never really talked about her before.

"Has she done anything to you?"

"Not me, but I think she's kind of homophobic, or just an asshole. She complained to me a few months ago that Gabby was hitting on her in the bathroom and said it made her uncomfortable, that I needed to talk to her about it. She made a formal complaint."

"What?" This time I shout because I am outraged.

"Yeah, Gabby said she had offered her a piece of gum because her breath was rank, and that was all that happened. I completely believed her."

"You should. Gabby loves her girlfriend. She wouldn't do that." I pause, letting my anger simmer. "But also, that's such a double standard. Like, Stacey thinks it's okay for her to hit on Gavin, but Gabby can't do the same thing because she's gay? How is she our people manager?"

"So true. Also, since when is she hitting on Gavin?" Andie asks with a bit too much enthusiasm.

"Oh, I don't know. He just said she has a few times."

Andie sits up and squints at me, her eyes roaming my face for a clue. "I knew it. You do like him."

"Andie," I argue, but I know it's pointless, because I still cannot stop smiling. There has been a constant loop in my head this morning of Gavin kissing my neck, of his hands slowly sliding down my bare back. I start to shiver at the thought. "Okay, fine. I might like him. A little."

She squeals. "I love this for you, for us really. Think about all the double dates!" I eye her with a confused look. I have never even met her mystery boyfriend.

"You know what I mean. Like maybe one day," she says flipping her hand around like it's all a hypothetical. "So...did something happen?"

I'm dying to tell her—anyone, really—about the kiss. In a moment of insanity, I almost texted Lucy Gold on the way to the marina. If anyone could understand the magic I felt last night, it'd be her.

But before I can get a word out, Stacey and Marissa join us on the bunny pad.

Once I see them, I shake my head. "I'll tell you later."

It's then I notice that Andie's been vigorously texting on her phone. The name Kenneth Dane pops up, the one I know to be an alias for her secret man. "Boyfriend drama?"

"No drama," she replies.

"This resort is so private. Why didn't you invite him here?" I ask.

"Come on, Liv. You know I can't tell anyone we're dating."

"Who are you dating?" Stacey asks, and Andie gives me a major eye roll.

"I have a boyfriend that's sort of in the public eye. So we're keeping things private for now."

Stacey and Marissa share a look that reminds me of my dogs salivating over family dinner. I mouth an apology to Andie.

"There you are!" Daanesh yells, stepping on to the bow. "I had no idea what you meant by bunny pad."

Andie looks at me and mumbles, "He should really watch more reality TV."

"Can I borrow you? Just to go over some of the logistics for tonight?" he asks Andie.

She looks back at me, then him, then me again, then grabs my hand and pulls me off the mat.

"Fine, but Liv's coming." She turns to me and whispers, "I will not leave you alone with those vultures."

I follow Andie and Daanesh to a deck area on the other side of the boat. Most of our co-workers are enjoying drinks out here, but it's a large enough space to give us some privacy still.

I'm especially glad for this when I see Ian and Vaughn in a fit of laughter, both with a cigar hanging out of their mouths.

My face must give me away, because Daanesh says, "Do you want to go somewhere else? I didn't realize Ian was over here."

It's nice of him to be concerned about me, but I'm done hiding from Ian.

"It's fine. I couldn't care less if he's here." And it's the truth.

"It's easy to get over someone when you're under someone new," Andie trills, smirking at me.

"Andie!" I shove her lightly. Not the kind of conversation I want to have in front of our CEO, *and* one of Gavin's best friends.

"I'm glad I reminded him to book your flight in time to join us," Daanesh says to me, eyeing me a little more intensely than usual. "He must have felt pretty bad about it, got obliterated at our game."

"Your game?"

"We play rugby together in a local club."

It had crossed my mind a few times what Gavin meant by his "rugby" text. It felt like he was blowing me off to watch TV, but now it makes more sense why he went dark on me that day.

"That's really cool," I reply. "I thought all you did together was take romantic walks down Lover's Lane."

Daanesh's jaw flies open and his nostrils flair. "I can't believe he told you about our spot. That's sacred."

Andie and I share a laugh at his incredulity.

"Boys and their bromance," she muses.

"He didn't just tell me, Daan," I continue. Because it's fun chatting with him like this. It's fun being his friend. "He took me there on the way to Sausalito."

"Really?" he asks, and this time he sounds incredulous, like he thinks I might be lying. I nod, and then I catch Andie eyeing me with more suspicion. Her tongue slides along the inside of her teeth.

"Well," she says. "He really must be in love with you then."

I END UP SPENDING THE REST OF THE DAY WITH ANDIE and Daanesh. I enjoy a mimosa while they talk work stuff, and we stay in our trio when we start the snorkeling part of the tour.

It's nice getting to spend time with one of Gavin's closest friends. Deep down, I know last night doesn't mean we're together. This is all still pretend.

But I can't deny this sparkling effervescence I've been feeling every time I'm in Gavin's orbit. It makes me hope that something real could be on the horizon.

Without giving away the whole story, I let Andie and Daanesh know about our surprise upgrade to a beach villa, so once the boat docks, Andie insists she come back with me to check it out.

Gavin opted for the surfing lesson this afternoon in lieu of the boat, so I knew he'd still be gone when we showed up. And I was grateful for it, because once we were alone, I finally got to tell her about the kiss.

She reacted about as calmly as I expected, so not at all. And soon we were jumping up and down on the couch together having a full-on dance party.

I'm not sure when Gavin walks in but it's to both of us belting out a song I barely remember from high school.

"I thought you only listened to French music," he says, announcing himself. I hope he's not mad I brought Andie here. It is technically his room.

"Hey," I reply with a smile. It's hard not to grin when I look at him. Especially now, when he's wearing nothing but swim trunks and flip flops. For all the time I've spent today thinking about our night together, this is the first time I really get to look at him.

The man has abs. How the hell didn't I notice that before? His skin is perfectly tanned, not pasty like mine. Just one day he's spent in the sun and every bit of him shines like a golden god. His hair looks lighter, like he's been freshly balayaged. And those eyes. Kill me now. They're glowing like two pale blue beacons, beckoning me to get naked and climb him.

I swallow and tell myself this is not the time to be having these thoughts. I'm about to apologize about Andie being here but she cuts me off.

"Not with me," she says, hopping off the couch. "I make her listen to stuff we can actually dance to. Sorry for crashing your suite."

"Oh, it's no problem."

"When Liv told me about the upgrade you got, I had to see it for myself.

That private pool is amazing."

"It was," I murmur, not loud enough for anyone to hear.

Or maybe it was louder than I thought. Because Gavin *winks* at me. "I'm gonna jump in the shower," he says. "Don't hurt yourselves."

It doesn't feel like he's avoiding me, but Gavin and I are like ships in the night as we get ready. Andie left when he was showering, and then as soon as he was done it was my turn. I cracked the door to the bathroom once I was decent so that he could move about while I did my hair and makeup. But he hasn't come in here once.

After everything that conspired last night, I feel like I have a little spring in my step, my confidence blooming like an eager peony in March.

I decide to celebrate the feeling by curling my hair into voluminous Hollywood waves and staining my lips a bold shade of red called *dangerous woman.*

I like what I see when I look in the mirror.

Gavin's on the couch watching TV when I grab my dress. I should be happy he's given me so much privacy, but I'm still wondering how things are going to be between us now that we've made out. *Don't overthink it.*

I slide on the sequin dress he encouraged me to bring and grab my heels that he begged me not to. They're incredibly uncomfortable, but they have huge bows on the back of the ankles, and I freaking adore them.

I carry the shoes over to the living room, anxious to finally share some space with Gavin again.

"Hey," I announce, walking into his line of sight.

His jaw works but he doesn't say anything. And I quickly realize that I'd be fine if it stayed like that. This dress makes me happy. I don't need his approval.

For so long, I've been concerned with what my outfit said about me, with what Ian or anyone else who shared an opinion on my wardrobe thought. I would stress over if it made me look like I was trying too hard or if it wasn't perfectly appropriate for the occasion.

But as I wait for Gavin's response, sliding on my ridiculous six-inch heels and seeing my bright copper hair shine back at me in the window's reflection, I feel like a siren. And if I do lure anyone to their death tonight, it's their fault for staring, not mine.

"Jesus, Sparkles. Are you trying to kill me?"

I bite my lip, trying and failing to suppress a massive grin.

He really does get me.

CHAPTER TWENTY-ONE

GAVIN

I have never been so tempted to blow off a work event in my life. I'm kicking myself for being good at my job, because if I wasn't going to be accepting an award, I could stay in this room with Liv for the rest of the night and no one would care about my absence.

"You like it?" she asks, like there is some alternate reality where I don't think she looks incredible.

I nod my head dumbly, like a cartoon character who just got shot with cupid's arrow. "People might stare. You okay with that?"

"Will you be one of the people staring?"

"You could try and stop me."

She beams. Part of me wants to talk before we leave for dinner, to figure out what's happening with us, because this relationship is feeling more real by the minute, and I need to know if it's the same for her.

But she starts shimmying her shoulders and her hips, showing off the feathers of her dress. I've never seen her giddy like this and the feeling is contagious. She's never looked better.

"You ready to go?" I ask.

"Yep. Just—" She reaches for my hand. "Please don't let me fall."

"I wouldn't dream of it." As if I have the self-control to keep my hands to myself right now.

"Four years in a row, this guy has held the title. Sure, he had a little bit of a scare when the New York office brought on the NFL last year, but Gavin Scott wasn't about to let someone else claim the top spot on the sales team.

"It's no surprise why he's won this award four times. Gavin is first in the office every morning and usually the last one to leave. When a deal falls through, he never makes excuses, just moves on to the next opportunity and tries to learn from his mistakes.

"I'll keep this short since it is the fourth time I've done it. Gavin, get up here." Vaughn ends the announcement just as we're finishing dinner.

I jog up to the head of the three long tables we're sitting at so I can collect my check. People seem to think I just enjoy being the best. Which I do, but not enough to work as hard as I have been. What really drives me is the extra ten grand I get each year when I win this. Another chunk of Gabby's tuition will be paid off with this money, and it couldn't come at a better time. Our rent just went up. Again.

"Thanks, Vaughn," I say, knowing they'll want me to speak to everyone. "It's a team effort. I wouldn't be able to sell anything without the hard work of everyone here." I glance around the room and find Ian laughing. He's not talking to anyone either, just trying to show me what he thinks of my award, what he thinks of *me*.

I really hate that guy.

"Especially Liv," I continue and clear my throat. "Olivia sourced seventeen deals for me last year that closed within nine months or less. And I'll admit, I probably wouldn't be in so early every day if it wasn't to spend more time with her." That elicits a few laughs, but Ian is just glaring at me now. Awesome. "Cheers, everyone."

"You didn't have to say that," Liv says when I get back to my seat.

I throw an arm around her chair, squeeze her shoulder a bit because I just feel better when we're connected. "It's true."

ONCE THE DINNER ENDS, OUR WHOLE GROUP MIGRATES across the beach to the resort next door, where a nightclub is blasting a mix of rap and electronic music.

I'm honestly not sure if this is the kind of thing Liv likes or not. I'm about to ask what she wants to do, but Andie grabs her hand and drags her onto the dance floor.

She turns back to look at me, and I take a mental snapshot. The way she flips her head has her wavy hair catching the air around her just as her dress swishes with the movement. She's a fucking goddess.

But the best part is the way she looks at me. Her gaze is filled with promise. It's telling me, "I'll be yours again soon."

I suck my bottom lip into my mouth and nod. *Mine.* After all this time. What a fucking feeling.

Daanesh finds me a minute later and we grab drinks by the bar. It's so loud in here, we can barely talk to each other, so we end up doing a few shots.

Then Liv appears at my side, grabbing my hand and tugging. "Come dance with me."

It's impossible not to indulge her so I abandon Daanesh immediately. Her skin is flushed but she can't stop smiling. She throws her arms over her head and circles her hips against me. I spent half the day wondering how things would change between us after last night, if she'd write it off as a mistake, but this doesn't feel like it.

Especially when she lays her arms over my shoulders, pulling me against her.

I think Liv asks me a question, but I can't make out the words with the volume in here.

"What?"

This time she slides closer until our bodies are flush, and she whispers in my ear.

"Thanks for bringing me to Mexico." She brushes her nose against my cheek, and I get a satisfying hit of déjà vu from last night.

She pivots until our bodies do a one-eighty and I find Ian staring from the bar. Did she see him? Is that why she's doing this?

"Ian's watching us," I murmur, curious to see her reaction. She doesn't move an inch.

"I don't care." She's practically nuzzling me, her hips still swishing enough to give me a semi. My mind and body are at war right now with how to react to her.

"Are you trying to make him jealous?" I hate that I ask, but I have to. Ian's dumb little smirk won't get out of my head. I dare to look up and find him still staring, still seething. If he wants to throw down, I'm more than ready. Just have to make sure he gets in the first hit.

Liv pulls back from me, but I keep my arms around her

waist, not letting her go anywhere. I might even let my hands drop a bit. This dress, that ass. I can't help it.

"It's okay. You can tell me," I continue. Because I'm not sure I would stop either way.

"I don't miss him," she says, those gray-blue eyes making solid contact. "I don't care what he thinks about me, not anymore." I'm afraid to break this little spell we're under, so I don't ask what I'm really thinking, but she seems to figure it out anyway. "I like the way you make me feel, Scottie."

She presses her face against my cheek, and I squeeze my arms around her, pulling her close again. I kiss her nose and she leans into me a little more. I'm aware there are people all around us and I'm sure Ian is still watching, but in this moment no one else exists.

"How do I make you feel?"

She pulls back an inch or two, just enough for our eyes to meet. I drag my fingers through her hair, pulling it behind her shoulder, greedy for more bare skin.

"Beautiful." She swallows. "Capable. Powerful." I can't tell if she's finished. Maybe I don't want her to be. There are a million things I could add to that list. A million ways I want to make her feel. My knuckles graze her bare shoulder and I can just barely hear her breath catch. "Sexy," she whispers against me.

"You are all those things, Sparkles. With or without me." We both lean into each other, our lips close enough to share breath.

"I lied last night," she continues. I feel the words brush against my jaw.

"What did you lie about?"

"I didn't want to stop."

I swallow thickly. "Then why did you?"

"I was scared of ruining it." I wait for her to explain but she doesn't speak, just blinks a few times, tickling me with her eyelashes. "I might kiss you again."

"I dare you."

"Not now," she whispers. "I want you to know it's not for anyone but us."

"Then why are we still here?"

WE SPRINT ALONG THE BEACH AS A SHORTCUT BACK TO our villa.

"You're sure about this?" I ask as soon as we're inside.

"Very." We're both a little winded from our jog but the way she pants just reminds me of her breathing last night. Her cheeks are flushed to the perfect shade of pink. Against her creamy skin and fiery hair, she looks like a goddamn sunset.

"Kiss me, Scottie."

I obey and press her against the door for leverage. As soon as our lips meet, I know last night wasn't a fluke. There's something otherworldly between us, something that feels like fate.

She isn't hesitant tonight. As soon as our lips collide, she throws her hands over my shoulders and digs her nails into my back. It's just short of painful but so fucking hot.

"Sparkles." I actually groan into her mouth. I kiss my way across her jaw until I can gently bite down on her ear. "I love the dress. Can I please take it off?"

She nods and makes some cute little sounds in agreement. My mouth moves down to her collarbones as I slide each strap off her shoulders, one side at a time. I lay kisses down each arm following the path of her straps as I go lower. Then I reach behind her and pull down the zipper.

She shivers when my fingers graze the dip in her lower back, and she gasps when I yank the dress down all the way.

I get to my knees and help her step out of it. To my delight, she wasn't wearing a bra. All that's between us now is a lacy black thong and her heels.

She bends down and reaches for one of the buckles. "Here, let me help."

"Can you leave them on?" I ask, kissing her ankle. I drag my lips up her calf, then her thigh, and do it again on the other side.

"I can barely stand up, Scottie," she pants.

"Not a problem." I pick her up at the waist, urging her legs to wrap around me until I hear her heels click when they knock together.

"How's this?" I ask. I press her harder against the door and grip her thighs. She digs her nails into my back again and then moves her hands up until they're scraping through my hair.

"Better." She grins right before she bites my bottom lip. Her legs tighten around me until we're pressed together as much as this position will allow. It might be time to leave the doorway.

"Don't let go of me," I whisper in her ear and start walking us into the other room.

I lay her down on the bed, kick off my own shoes and yank off the shirt she's already started to unbutton. But when I lay down and reach for her, she's shaking. "Are you cold? What's wrong?"

"I just need to warn you, I'm bad at this." Her words come out so fast, it takes me a second to put them together.

"Bad at...?"

"Sex."

I almost laugh. "I don't think that's possible."

"It is," she argues. "It's kind of why Ian...you know. So, I just want to umm...temper your expectations. I guess."

She throws an arm over her eyes. She might be embarrassed but all I feel is rage.

"He said that to you? That you were bad in bed?"

"Basically. He said it was boring, that I...lacked enthusiasm." She cringes.

"Sounds like he didn't give you much to be enthusiastic about." I pin her arms above her head so she's forced to look at me. Kiss the tip of her nose because I can. "And Sparkles?" She blinks, her teeth digging into her lower lip. "That's the last time I want to hear that asshole's name tonight."

I refuse to let Ian kill the mood, so I go right back to kissing her neck. I say a silent *thank you* to the dress that didn't require a bra and move lower. And lower. Until I can circle her nipple with my tongue.

"Oh," she whimpers, her hand reaching for my shoulder. I circle again and drag my teeth against her pebbled skin.

I draw a hand up her thigh until I feel the lace of her thong and pull on it, letting it snap. Based on the sounds she's making, I think she likes being teased. I dip a finger under the lace, dragging it up slowly until she throws her head back and gasps. She's soaked.

"I really don't think enthusiasm's going to be a problem here."

She laughs and I hope I've gotten her out of her head a little.

"God, that feels good," she moans, her hips starting to writhe.

"Yeah? I only want to make you feel good, Liv," I say, touching her again the same way. "Just tell me what you like." Because it sounds like she hasn't been taken care of in the past. And there is nothing more I want to do right now.

"I like you," she replies, still breathless.

I rip off the thong.

CHAPTER TWENTY-TWO

OLIVIA

I can't keep up. Can't catch my breath. So much is happening at once. His hands, his lips, his words.

"You taste so fucking good, Olivia," he says, sucking on the skin along my hip. "Can I?"

He looks up at me before his eyes shoot down to where my thong used to be. And for a second, I hold my breath. He wants to go down on me? This isn't something Ian and I really did together, another thing he said guys don't actually like.

I can feel my body shaking again, not in the good way. "You don't have to—"

"Olivia, *quiero probar cada centímetro de tu cuerpo.*" He lifts his head and crawls further up the bed, just until he can rest his cheek against my chest. He never stops kissing me. "*No tienes idea de cuanto tiempo he estado esperando este momento.*"

"Is that...Spanish?" At first, when he spoke, I thought my brain was just foggy from this lust-filled room, but those definitely weren't words I know.

He reaches up to claim my mouth in another tender kiss. "I

thought it might help you relax. I could try French, but it's pretty rusty."

For a moment I'm frozen in disbelief. Gavin really does get me. In a way that maybe no one else ever has.

I throw my arms around him and pull him in closer. He's so sweet I feel like I might cry. Instead, I pour every emotion I'm feeling into the press of my lips, the drift of my tongue, the way my nails scrape through his hair.

"*Eres hermosa, tan perfecta.*"

I don't know what he's saying but he's right, it does relax me. It's easy to follow the emotion of his words without knowing their translation. How does Gavin Scott know what I like, what I need, even more than I know myself?

His kisses turn molten as he smoothly slips back down my body, each one hotter than the last. "*Te sientes como el Cielo, Olivia.*"

I get turned on a little more each time he says my name. Nothing has ever felt like this before. Everything he does makes me feel like I'm going to explode.

By the time his mouth is between my legs, I've lost all control of my head. Every thought is consumed by where he's touching me or licking me or biting me. The way he keeps dragging his teeth against my skin is making me wild.

He makes slow circles with his tongue exactly where I need it, his hands massaging my thighs. I close my eyes, giving in to every sensation, my usual worries a million miles away. Tension rises through all my muscles, and I can sense my body twist and writhe, chasing some sort of release.

"I feel like—" My words get stuck in a breathy moan. Like I might combust at any second.

When I start to squirm, he grabs my hips, holding me in place, and sucks my delicate skin into his mouth. One of his hands coasts around my thigh and he slides a finger inside me.

"Oh, god. Gavin," I pant his name, along with a few more expletives that are barely audible.

He lifts his head. "No. Say Scottie when you come."

And I do.

The orgasm rips through me until every one of my senses are shot. For a moment, it feels like time stands still, like hot is cold and up is down and gravity is just a myth. My lungs forget how to breathe. My heart forgets how to beat. The only thing I can feel are tiny fireworks igniting beneath every inch of my skin.

Little stars are still clouding my vision when Gavin climbs back up the bed.

"Good?" he asks.

"Good?" I laugh. "That was...wow."

He doesn't respond, just starts kissing me again. I'm starting to realize I'm obsessed with Gavin's mouth. He kisses me like he never wants to stop.

"Scottie," I say, pausing the brush of our lips. "I've never felt anything like that before. Can we?" I finish the thought by reaching for his zipper. I can't believe his pants are still on.

He bites his lip, like he's hesitant to go further. But I'm not. I've never wanted sex more than I do at this very moment.

"I umm...I don't have a condom. I really didn't think this was going to happen." He grins, a shy little quirk of his mouth.

"Didn't you see the intimacy kit in the bathroom?" I ask.

"No...they have condoms?"

"Yep!" I jump out of bed and realize my heels are still on. I either look ridiculous or like a porn star, but my post-orgasm glow has me feeling way too good to care. I even swish my hips a little as I walk away from the bed and I hear him grunt out a few curses, making me grin.

I find the kit in the bathroom, full of condoms and small

tubes of lube and I grab a foil packet before running back to the bed.

Overly confident, and way too eager, I pull Gavin's pants off before climbing on top of him and straddling his hips. And maybe it's the heels, or just how he affects me, but I'm feeling so hot that I rip open the condom with my teeth.

He's staring up at me with an open mouth like I'm his favorite dessert just out of reach. It's the sexiest I've ever felt in my life, until I realize, "I have no idea what I'm doing."

"You've never put one on before?" he asks.

I shake my head but keep it held high, still feeling too good to be ashamed by my lack of experience.

He bites his lip and reaches up to kiss me gently. "I'll show you."

And I like this even better. The way he is so patient with me is one of my favorite things about him. Gavin Scott, sex teacher, is almost too much. He doesn't just guide me to put it on; he shows me exactly how he likes to be touched.

"Do you see how hard you make me?" He grips my hand and glides it along his shaft. "Only you, Olivia."

He reaches up for my shoulders like he's ready to flip us, but I ask if I can be on top.

"I want to try it with you." I've never enjoyed it before, but something tells me it could be different with him. Everything feels different with Gavin.

"You want to ride me, Sparkles?"

I bite my lip and grin at him. I really, really do.

In lightning speed, he repositions us and enters me slowly. I sink down, taking him deeper and deeper until I'm fully seated. I exhale, letting myself adjust to the feel of him inside me. Once I start to roll my hips, he groans and grabs my ass, helping me find the right rhythm.

His breathing quickens and his cheeks flush. I love being

the one affecting him like this, but the position still isn't working for me.

"Lean back," he orders, stilling my hips.

"What?"

"I know what it looks like when you're enjoying yourself. Let me make it good for you." He pushes up to balance on his forearms. "Lean back. Hold on to my legs."

I follow his instructions and tilt at the waist until I feel an entirely new sensation in my core. This angle feels incredible, and I start to rock my hips again out of sheer need.

"Just like that, Sparkles. Don't stop until you come."

One of his hands still rests on my hip, guiding each movement and thrust, but the other floats between us and finds my center.

He circles and circles my sensitive skin, before adding even more pressure with his thumb. And then he pinches me.

I whimper and throw my head back, feeling that perfect pressure start to build in me again. Every muscle in my core tightens. Even my legs are begging me to let them squeeze shut. I flex anything I can, searching for some kind of relief.

"Fuck, Olivia. Do that again." Gavin's eyes are locked on me, more piercing than usual. I clench my muscles and watch his head roll back.

The hand on my hip slides to my back and he runs his nails down my spine. The touch is so featherlight, almost ticklish, but it makes my back bow and hips push forward even more.

He pinches me again, sending every one of my nerves into overdrive.

I ride each wave higher and higher until I shatter completely.

Some people see stars when they have a mind-bending orgasm. All I see is Gavin Scott. And he looks good.

He watches me ride it out like I'm performing a magic trick.

And once my body stops shaking with pleasure, he flips us in one swift movement. His mouth comes down, kissing me hard. And he doesn't stop when he thrusts inside me, again and again until he falls apart.

Gavin groans through his orgasm, but never takes his lips off mine. He doesn't even move them when he starts talking.

"Olivia Diamond," he breathes. Our noses brush against each other. "You are *exceptionally* good at that. Five stars. Eleven out of ten." He pants hard on the last few words. "Let's never leave this bed."

I laugh as he rolls off of me and throws an arm across my chest.

We lay together, completely boneless for a long moment, listening to nothing but our racing hearts and the ocean breeze. I finally get up to slip off my heels, glad they've officially been put to good use, and get right back into bed.

"I really need a shower," he says softly against my side. "But I don't like the idea of not being able to kiss you."

I laugh and turn to face him. "Sounds like a real prisoner's dilemma."

"Join me?" he asks.

I try and decide how much it would kill the mood to say I don't want to wash my hair again. It really takes forever to dry.

"How about a bath?" I offer. "I've been eyeing that tub since we got here yesterday."

He slowly starts to nod, and then he's kissing me again, and suddenly he hops out of bed and glides into the bathroom. I hear the water running a second later.

CHAPTER TWENTY-THREE

GAVIN

Saturday night turns into Sunday and we both blow off our planned activities. I feel a little guilty remembering how excited Liv was for a spa day, but I figure I'm helping her release tension too.

It's a weird feeling, to finally get what you've wanted for so long. You worry that your expectations are too high, or you've built something up in your head that doesn't fit the reality. Being with Liv feels like the opposite, like I never had a fucking clue how amazing this girl is.

We almost miss the shuttle back to Puerto Vallarta, but luckily Daanesh has them hold it for us. And when we get on, we're met with a bunch of hushed whispers.

Liv gives me a questioning look when we sit, but I don't have a clue what to say. Then Andie is there shoving Liv onto my lap so she can sit with us.

"What's going on?" Liv asks her friend.

Andie looks sheepish, like she's not sure she wants to answer the question, even though she came over here on her own.

"I heard a few of the guys talking."

"And?" I ask.

"So, I don't know if he was drunk or just being petty but Ian was talking about you a lot last night. After you two left the club. Which, by the way...not a very subtle exit."

I grin, remembering how badly I wanted to get Liv alone that we actually started running.

"What was he saying?" Liv asks.

"Just the usual bullshit. How you're pretending to be into Gavin to try and make Ian jealous. That he's above the childish gimmicks, blah blah."

What a dick. He just doesn't want to admit he wants her back.

"Sounds like Ian," Liv replies coolly. "But why all the whispers?"

"I wasn't around for this part," Andie continues. "But I guess a bunch of people were partying on the beach doing acid,"—no surprise there—"and someone pointed out your villa. I think they were just mentioning the upgrade, but Ian like ran over and tried to get in."

"What the hell?" Liv whisper-yells.

"He didn't. Get in, I mean. Obviously, you know that. I heard Vaughn caught up with him in time to stop him kicking the door, but..."

"Andie. What are they telling people?"

He went to *spy* on us? What the fuck was he hoping to see? I have a lot of thoughts about this but let the girls talk it out.

"Honestly, it's not that bad. I mean, everyone knows you two are together so why wouldn't you be *together*, right?"

"Andie," Liv seethes.

"Okay, okay. This morning, they were telling a few people about it and how they *heard* you and Ian said something like,

"All he did was bring her to Mexico. You should hear what she did for a trip to Singapore."

"I'm gonna fucking kill him." I mean to say it in my head but when both girls turn to me, I realize I let the words slip. I guess I can't kill him. But the second I'm done with this job I'll be clocking him in the face so hard he can never smirk at anyone again.

The shuttle hits a long series of potholes and Andie goes back to her original seat so Liv can get off my lap.

"You okay?" I ask. It's a stupid question because of course she's not okay. I run my hands through her hair to try and help her relax.

"I'm fine. He may have everyone else fooled, but I know the truth. That trip to Singapore sucked." She chuckles to herself. "I didn't even want to go. It was summer and like a million degrees with a thousand percent humidity. But he begged me to go because the clients were big wine collectors. It was basically a work trip that I had to take PTO for." She scoffs, and I'm surprised she's not more anxious over the rumors.

"He took me all over the world," she muses, and then she turns to me until her face is tucked into the crook of my neck, her nose brushing against my skin. "But this was the best trip I've ever been on, Scottie."

I grin against her. And then I lean down to whisper, "Do you think he just got pissed because he heard how enthusiastic you were?"

She giggles and smacks me lightly against the chest. I can feel my eyes get heavy as the medicine starts to kick in and I wrap my arm around her. She stays tucked into my side for the whole ride.

I MIGHT HAVE BEEN PASSED OUT THE ENTIRE FLIGHT home, but I know I enjoyed it. Because when I wake up, Liv's hand is still in mine.

I try to brush off the drowsiness when we land and start by turning on my phone. I have three new messages from Gabby.

> **GABBY:**
>
> What the hell is this?
>
> WTF Gav
>
> How long have you been lying to me?

They're punctuated by a photo she took of my mail. Apparently, I was denied for that new line of credit I applied for last month. *Fuck.*

Gabby was never supposed to know about this.

"What's wrong?" Liv asks.

"Nothing, just trying to wake up."

We're both standing in that awkward scrunched position waiting to deplane. She grabs on to my shoulders and tries to shake me, shimmying her hips at the same time.

"Damn, you're stiff as a board."

"Yeah." What's that saying? Dead as a doornail, stiff as a board? Doesn't sound right but that's how I feel right now.

When we got denied any form of financial aid for Stanford, I decided not to tell Gabby. I knew she wouldn't want to put more pressure on me, and she'd already offered to take out a loan or just go somewhere cheaper, but that's not what I wanted for *her.* I was happy to bear the financial burden so she could enjoy school without worrying about money every day.

Gabby's had a tough life, and she deserves everything. I'm the only parent she's had since she was ten years old. There was no way in hell I would take Stanford away from her, not after all the work she put in to get there.

But without any aid, and with almost half my salary still going toward undergrad student loans, my debt started to spiral. I thought I had it under control and then our rent went up, and then it went up again.

I feel like I'm going to be sick.

"Come on sleepyhead," Liv chirps, taking my hand as we walk off the plane.

I pull my hand away when I feel my phone vibrate with another message.

GABBY:

When will you be home? We need to talk about this

ME:

Just landed. I'll see you soon

"Are you sure you're okay?" Liv asks once we get in the Uber. I know I'm being a dick and have barely said a word since we landed, but all I can think about is how this conversation is going to go with Gabby.

I can't let her give up school.

"Yeah, I'm sorry. I'm just really tired still." I rest my head against the backseat window and close my eyes. It's not a lie. I am tired. Exhausted, really. Just not the way she's thinking.

She lays her hand over mine and for a split second I forget about my sister and debt and everything in the world that sucks right now. All I see behind my eyelids is the amazing weekend I spent with the girl of my dreams.

I should be happy right now, but I can't enjoy this feeling anymore until I talk to Gabby. Until I'm sure she's not going to do something drastic to her future.

The car pulls to a stop, and I open my eyes.

"Do you wanna stay here? I have a very comfy bed you

could be laying on in less than ninety seconds." She taps her fingers across the back of my hand.

"I can't. I gotta get home. I'll see you tomorrow." I lean forward and ask the driver if we can make another stop.

"How could you?" Gabby greets me at the door.

I take a deep breath to steady myself and march past her so I can put my stuff down. "I want to talk about this. I really do. Can you let me shower off the drugs first?" I can barely keep my eyes open.

She huffs, which doesn't surprise me, but I need a few minutes of solitude to figure this out. I shower quickly, and when I step out of the bathroom, Gabby has a suitcase by the front door.

"What's going on?"

"I'm staying at Kadesha's. She's coming to get me in a few."

"Okay, but what's with the jumbo-size suitcase? Don't you have stuff there already?" I ask.

"I'm not just staying tonight, Gav. I don't want to be anywhere near you. Casi que ni te puedo ver la cara."

"I thought you wanted to talk," I argue. Because that's what her last text said. "Can we please discuss this? Just let me explain what's going on."

She walks over to the couch and sits. "We can talk, but I know what's going on. After I saw the mail, I decided to do a little digging. How are you paying for my school, Gav?"

From the tone of her voice, it's obvious she knows the answer.

"Gabby," I start, sitting down next to her. "I have the

payments under control. There's nothing you need to worry about."

"You think this is about the money?" she bellows. "We've had nothing, and we survived. Hell, we *thrived*," she laughs. "You and I can get through anything together. But not if I can't trust you."

Her voice breaks on the last word and tears start to pool in her eyes. It breaks my fucking heart.

"Gav, you never lie to me. We never lie to *each other*. Never about the big stuff. Never about the stuff that matters. I could have taken out a loan myself. I could have chosen a different school. I could have done a million things if you'd just talked to me instead of coddling me like you always have."

We both turn at the sound of someone knocking on the door, Kadesha I assume.

"Gabby, please don't leave like this."

"I know you're worried I'm suddenly going to drop out of school, and I'm not. So you can relax. I'll figure out something else. I just need some space right now."

When she opens the door, Kadesha offers a sad smile my way. I think she mouths something like "it'll be okay," just before they both leave and the door closes again.

I'm putting Churro in his sling when my phone buzzes. I say a quick prayer it's Gabby wanting to talk now that she's cooled down.

OLIVIA DIAMOND:

> I swear my bed feels less comfortable now. I miss Mexico *crying face emoji*

> Sure you don't wanna hang out?

No, I'm not sure at all. I would love nothing more than to share a bed with Liv again tonight. But the only thing that matters right now is Gabby, and I don't think I'm ready to dump all my family drama on Liv just yet.

It's tempting.

Part of me wants to share my predicament. Maybe she could help me figure out how to talk to Gabby, how to apologize, how to make things right. But I also like the fact that Liv doesn't know anything about my sad story yet. I doubt she'd think of me the same way after hearing about the year Gabby and I were almost homeless.

ME:

Sorry I can't. See you at work, beautiful

The truth is that as much as I want Liv, Gabby is the most important person in my life. I have to fix this with her before I can even try being with Olivia.

I GET INTO THE OFFICE AT SEVEN ON MONDAY MORNING. Gabby has class Mondays until noon and only works at Sizzl Tuesdays and Thursdays, so my plan is to get all my work done by lunchtime and head over to Kadesha's place.

This is already the longest Gabby and I have ever fought for, and I refuse to let it go on any further.

With my bike, I barely hit any traffic on the Bay Bridge and make it to her place outside Berkeley in record time.

"Had a feeling you'd show up today," Kadesha says when she opens the door. She's smiling so I take it as a good sign.

"Is she back from class yet?" I ask.

"Says she's staying late tonight. A study group or something." I appreciate that she actually looks disappointed for me. "Come on in. Let's chat."

Kadesha's apartment is full of color, just like her. It's always been easy to see why Gabby loves her so much. She has this vibrant, yet somehow calming energy.

"I fucked up," I admit, falling onto the sofa.

"Oh, I know."

"Wanna take pity on your future brother-in-law and help me?" Her eyes flash. "Come on, there's no way you two don't end up together. Plus, I already consider you a sister. You're stuck with me now."

She sits down next to me and lays her head on my shoulder. "You're stuck with me too. I'd miss Churro too much."

We both laugh, because we know it's true.

"Gabby loves you. She's hurt *because* she loves you. Just give her some time, she'll come around."

"I just don't want her to do anything drastic."

"She won't," Kadesha says. "She's not a kid anymore."

"I know that."

"Do you?" She looks at me pointedly. "Have you thought about the fact that she's almost twenty-five years old and might not need you to take care of her anymore? Have you considered that she's upset because she doesn't think *you* trusted *her*?"

"What? Of course I trust her. That's ridiculous."

"Then why wouldn't you tell her about paying for school? Why keep it all a secret?"

"Because I didn't want to give her a reason to not take this opportunity. I didn't want her to feel like a burden."

"And by not telling her, that's exactly how she feels, Gav."

"Shit." There's nothing else for me to say because Kadesha's right. I let my head fall back against the couch. "I really am an asshole."

"You're not an asshole."

I scoff.

"Can I ask you something?" she says.

"Of course."

"Do you think of Gabby as your sister or your kid?"

"What? What kind of question is that? Of course she's my sister."

"I know. But you've also been like a dad to her for a long time. When we first met, she told me you raised her."

"Well, someone had to. Gabby was only four when mom died. Our dad was pretty useless after that, but he left for good when she was ten. Was I not supposed to take care of us?"

"Please don't get defensive." Kadesha reaches for my hands between us. "I'm not sure if I've ever actually told you how amazing of a brother you are. You're a superhero." My throat feels tight, like there's something lodged in there. Maybe it's guilt, or just exhaustion. "Gabby loves you for stepping into that role when she needed you, but I think she was hoping that you'd see her as more of an equal now."

That guts me. Because we are equals. Gabby's smarter than I'll ever be. Which is why I've been so adamant about her following her dreams. I hate that there's any scenario where she doesn't see that.

"I have to run," Kadesha interrupts my thoughts. "I'll talk to her, okay? Just don't stop reaching out. She's upset right now, but she would never want you out of her life. I think it would kill her if she actually thought you wouldn't be there for her."

"Okay. I will."

I send the first message as soon as I get home.

ME:

Let me know when you're free to talk. I'll meet you wherever you want

Another day passes with no response. How long is Gabby planning to freeze me out? I work from home on Tuesday just hoping Gabby might show up to the apartment.

OLIVIA DIAMOND:

Where have you been? My desk feels lonely

ME:

Sorry, beautiful. It's a crazy week

Do you mind asking Eddie to join your meeting tomorrow? I'm not sure I'll be able to make it

OLIVIA DIAMOND:

Oh sure. Is everything ok?

Fuck. I know I need to talk to Liv, explain what's going on. I'm just not ready. I reply with a thumbs up and click over to my thread with Gabby to try again. I refuse to let her ignore me for another twenty-four hours.

ME:

I need you to know how bad I feel about this. I was an idiot, and I should have been honest with you from the start. I just wanted to take care of you Gabs

Please call me back

Can we meet tomorrow? Your Wednesday class ends at 1:30 right? I'll take the afternoon off and meet you at that coffee place you love

Please say yes

I'm lying in bed on Tuesday night when my phone rings, making me jolt.

"Hello?"

"Hey, brother."

CHAPTER TWENTY-FOUR

OLIVIA

"You did great, Olivia. They're definitely gonna buy," Eduardo says as we leave the meeting.

When I'd asked Gavin to join another demo with Darnell from Surf and Stream on Wednesday, he said he was too busy.

Just like he was too busy to hang out when we got home from Mexico, and yesterday at work when he was never at his desk, *and* the day before. He's been avoiding me so well, it's like he hasn't even been working this week.

Gavin is either playing the most extreme version of hard-to-get, or he's already lost interest and is too much of a dick to tell me.

"Thanks for stepping in at the last minute. I really appreciate it," I reply to Eduardo.

"No problem at all."

The meeting ran forty minutes longer than expected, which I assume is a good sign, but by the time we make it back to our desks, half the office has already gone home.

Of course, Gavin is here, finally showing up once I've admitted defeat. It feels like he's taunting me, sitting so close. I don't think I have unrealistic expectations but my experience with dating is limited to Ian.

I just don't get it. What happened in Mexico didn't feel like a random hook-up. He said things to me, things that felt...

Well, it doesn't matter. Limited experience or not, when you sleep with a guy and get the cold shoulder a day later, his intentions are very clear. The worst part is that people at work still think we're a couple. If our relationship suddenly ends after the trip to Mexico, won't all the rumors about me using him seem true?

"Hey, Sparkles."

My internal thoughts must have been spiraling for longer than I realized because Gavin is standing right next to me, stealing my attention.

"Hey," I reply coolly, keeping my eyes on my computer. Because he's blown me off for three days and I don't really feel like being flirty anymore.

"Wanna get dinner?" he asks.

What?

"Sorry. I have plans." With a bottle of wine and an entire wheel of cheese.

"Liv—"

"I gotta run." Feeling way too confused for this interaction, I grab my stuff and jet.

I SPEND HALF THE NIGHT WONDERING WHAT GAVIN WAS going to say.

And the other half berating myself for not waiting to hear it.

It scares me—how much I like him.

I didn't realize how bad I wanted him until I had him, but now have I lost him entirely? Was I too clingy? Were my expectations too high? Was Ian right, and I'm too immature for anyone to take me seriously? Am I not even *girlfriend* material?

Fuck, my brain hurts. I just want to flip it off.

My phone keeps buzzing, but every time I look, hoping it's Gavin with a detailed explanation for his behavior, it's just Tristan, hot in his pursuit to get me to dinner.

I silence my phone and turn on my music as loud as it will go without the neighbors complaining. After a long shower to wash away my feelings, I dive into the bed that never feels warm enough anymore.

When I close my eyes, I don't even try to push out the thought of being wrapped in Gavin's arms.

SLACK DIRECT MESSAGE

Gavin Scott:

Why are you avoiding me?

Olivia Diamond:

I'm not avoiding you

Gavin Scott:

You literally ran out of Fog & Foam this morning when you saw me

Olivia Diamond:

I didn't see you. I was just running late

Gavin Scott:

We made eye contact

And now you won't even look at me

I STRAIGHTEN MY SPINE AND LOOK UP FROM MY LAPTOP. I'm not afraid of him, and definitely not avoiding him. Just giving him the same treatment he's given me all week. Last night, I decided that I don't want to completely give up on this thing between us, that I can't pretend I don't have feelings for him. If I have to fake a little aloofness to keep him interested, so be it.

Maybe it's petty that I had my headphones on all morning, or that I texted Andie multiple times so Gavin could see me giggling at my phone. But maybe it was the right move, because I've definitely gotten his attention.

Gavin stares back at me with a smirk. Then he tilts his head down toward the computer.

Gavin Scott:
You ran away from me last night and you've barely spoken to me all day. Why won't you talk to me?
Olivia Diamond:
It's been a busy week for both of us. I'm not gonna be all clingy just because we...you know
Gavin Scott:
Because we had amazing sex?
Thrice ;)
Olivia Diamond:
NSFW!!!
Gavin Scott:
You're avoiding me because of the sex?
Olivia Diamond:
Not avoiding you. I'm just not going to make a big deal out of it. I know it was casual and just a one-time vacation thing and I didn't want to give you the impression otherwise

I'm pretty sure I hear him grunt under his breath.
He stands up but doesn't say anything, just marches toward

the exit. I chase after him until we're both standing in the elevator bank.

"Where are you going?" I ask.

"Taking a walk." His jaw works, anger coating his features.

"Scottie, I—"

"You didn't need to follow me. I'm just going to get some air."

"But we were talking," I say. "We were kind of in the middle of a conversation?"

His eyes narrow on me and he folds his arms over his chest. He shakes his head a few times like he's battling his own thoughts. I know the feeling all too well. But I'd give anything for a peek inside his head right now.

"It wasn't casual for me. And it definitely wasn't a one-time thing." His words come out raspy, like they had a treacherous journey up his throat. "Is that what it was to you?"

"No," I murmur. It's so quiet I'm not sure if he hears me.

When the doors open, he breezes into the elevator. I run in right before it closes.

"No," I say louder this time.

"Then, what was it?" he asks through a deep whisper. He stalks toward me, inching closer and closer until I'm backed up against the wall, until his lips are so close to mine, I can almost taste him.

"It was..." I take a deep breath because I don't know what to say. I'm still confused about his demeanor since we got home, but I can't keep up with my cool girl façade when he looks at me this way. "It was...it didn't feel casual to me. But since we got back, I felt like it might have meant more to me than to you."

He blinks, his pupils dilating. He parts his lips and I'm desperate to know if it's for more words or to kiss me. But the doors open before I can find out.

Gavin turns to the bank, where three people on the fifth floor are waiting to join us.

"Take the next one." He presses the close door button and once we're sealed back in the metal box, he slams the emergency stop.

He is impossibly close now, his forehead pressing against my own. He tugs on a loose piece of hair and tucks it behind my ear.

"I'm sorry I've been...preoccupied this week. I shouldn't have left the way I did when we got back from Mexico." He pauses and kisses my nose. "Please don't think for a second that it means last weekend wasn't monumental for me. Okay?"

"Ok—"

The word is stolen from my lips when his mouth crashes into mine. The kiss is intense, but sweet, his lips unbearably soft against me. His hands come up to cradle my jaw, squeezing gently around my neck. He tilts my head back and sucks on my bottom lip, biting softly before releasing it.

"I've wanted to do this all day," he rasps, moving from my lips down to my throat. "And you wouldn't even talk to me."

He kisses me again, this time parting my lips with his tongue until we're completely tangled up in each other.

"Scottie," I say, swallowing hard. "We can't do this here. Someone will come."

"This building has twelve elevators. We're fine." He sucks on the spot right beneath my ear and I care a little less about getting caught. "I need you," he breathes. And I feel the same way.

His head dips to kiss my collarbone and he slides off my blazer, letting it pool on the floor. Then he starts to unbutton my shirt.

"Scottie—"

"Just two, okay? No, three. Maybe four." I assume he's

referring to the number of buttons because he stops as soon as he can spread the shirt enough to reveal my bra. My lilac bra studded with lots of tiny black bows that I wore for a self-esteem boost.

"Your tits are wrapped up like a present," he says, licking his lips. He leans down and sucks one nipple into his mouth. It's somehow even hotter when he does it over my bra. "Are they for me?"

"Property of Scottie," I breathe, my head falling back against the wall.

"Hello? Is there an emergency?" My body jolts when I hear a deep voice over the speaker in the elevator, though it sounds more bored than worried.

"Ignore it," Gavin says, his words melting on my skin. I know we shouldn't ignore it but it's impossible to think straight when Gavin's mouth is on me.

His lips find mine again and my whole body starts to heat up. I reach down between us to find his erection rock hard against his joggers.

"I'm sorry I let you down," he whispers on my neck. His hips rock forward against my hand. "I should have told you what was going on. I'm an asshole." But he sure doesn't feel like one, his mouth clinging to the lace of my bra again. He sucks on the fabric like it's his favorite flavor, like he'll never have enough. "If you're ever feeling unsure, just talk to me, Sparkles."

His hand comes down to squeeze my ass and he lifts my leg to wrap around him. We're almost lined up too perfectly. It almost feels too good. How does it feel so good when all my clothes are still on?

"Hello? Stand back, we're opening the doors," comes a voice on the other side of the elevator. It's followed by the click of a key and in seconds we are not alone anymore.

I shove Gavin away from me and grab my blazer from the floor.

"Hey, Gino," Gavin says with a smirk. How is he not mortified?

"So sorry," I say, trying to discreetly button my shirt. "I was feeling a little sick."

"Yeah," Gino drones. "Looked real under the weather on the cameras."

Oh god.

He looks at Gavin. "Need me to escort you back to twenty-two?"

"I've got it," Gavin says, chuckling. He swipes his thumb along his bottom lip. "We'll behave."

WORK IS IMPOSSIBLE THE REST OF THE DAY. GAVIN AND I can't stop smiling at each other.

If anyone didn't buy our relationship before, they will now.

And then it hits me. What *is* our relationship now? I've been so worried all week about him wanting nothing but vacation sex, but he made it clear today that's not the case. That still doesn't mean we're a real couple.

How the hell do you define a fake relationship between two people who are sleeping together and also might have feelings? I'll have to google it later when I'm not at work.

SLACK DIRECT MESSAGE:

Gavin Scott:

Finished updating your reports yet?

Olivia Diamond:

Yep

Gavin Scott:

Wanna get out of here?

Olivia Diamond:

Yes please

Gavin brought his bike to work today so the second five o'clock comes, we ride back to my place. I try my best not to grope him the whole way home. I fail. His leather jacket must be vintage because it's as soft as butter.

It also easily slides off of him as soon as we get inside.

Ever since we got caught in the elevator, I've felt feverish, my skin uber sensitive to any contact. Now that we're alone, I wrap my arms around him immediately, wanting to fuse our lips together again.

He must feel the same because his kisses are hungry and demanding. He pulls off my blazer and throws it across the couch like he has a personal vendetta against linen.

"Wait," he says, not actually pausing anything. He's already unbuttoning my shirt for the second time today. "I need to explain."

"It's okay."

He ignores me and kisses a trail across my neck. Then he unzips my skirt and drops to his knees.

"Gabby wasn't talking to me," he says, looking up into my eyes. He slowly slides off my shoes and plants a kiss on each ankle. "I'm not sure if you realize how close we are. It was killing me that we weren't speaking. It was all I could think about."

My skirt comes down next and he licks his lips when he sees the underwear that matches my bra. Apparently, Gavin is a big fan of lilac lace and tiny black bows.

"Is it okay if I don't tell you the whole story? I will, I promise, just not yet."

He stands up until his gaze meets mine and threads his fingers through my hair. His eyes hold the question in them and the sincerity I see makes me melt. Whatever this is between us is still new. I won't be burdening him with my family drama anytime soon.

"Of course. I just hope you and Gabby are okay."

"We are. We will be." He trails his hands down my back, squeezes my ass and picks me up, walking us toward my bed. "All I want to think about for the rest of the night is you."

WE SKIP DINNER.

But when my stomach starts rumbling, Gavin offers to go get snacks. He comes back with a hot fudge sundae from Ghirardelli. When you live as close as I do, it's hard not to be tempted. All the air outside my apartment smells like chocolate and whipped cream.

"Have I atoned?" he asks, feeding me another bite.

"As much as I enjoy the groveling, we're all good. I'm partially to blame as well."

He sets down the empty cup on the nightstand and spreads out on my bed, pulling me down with him.

"Please tell me how you're at fault for me keeping secrets."

"We all have secrets, Scottie. You're not required to tell me everything going on in your life." I swallow thickly, hoping he agrees. The image of all of Tristan's texts sits heavy in my chest. "And I don't...never mind."

"Tell me. What were you about to say?"

"I just—ugh. I have no experience doing this. I hate to agree with anything Ian said to me, but maybe I *am* immature. At least when it comes to...this. I never really dated in college. My brother Owen was only a year above me and he was so protective that I never had the chance. Every guy was terrified of him.

"And dating Ian was like a fucking minefield. It felt like I was always playing some game, but I was ten steps behind wherever he was. I never knew how I was supposed to act or look or what version of girlfriend he wanted."

I blow out a breath, exhausted just thinking about it. I probably shouldn't be spilling all of this to Gavin, but it feels good to do it. It feels even better that he's actually listening.

"And with you, I don't know. I've never had to be anything but myself with you. But suddenly, you're MIA for two days and I got all weird. I was so in my head about it and then I'm the one playing mind games and I hate myself for it."

"Mind games?"

"Yes! I mean, *of course* I wanted to get dinner with you last night. And instead, I sat at home, hoping you were missing me? Like what the fuck is that about? I don't want to do that. That's not who I am. I just want to be me, and if that's not good enough, then so be it."

"Just for the record," Gavin says. "I was missing you. And I don't blame you for wanting to make me sweat a little. I could have at least given you a heads up when I was barely at the office for two days. Family stuff has just always been hard for me."

"I understand," I say, even as I'm thinking that I don't. "Or —I want to, at least. If you ever feel like talking about it."

He kisses me, just a soft brush of his lips.

"You're not immature, Liv. And I'm begging you, please don't try to be anything but yourself around me, okay? *You* are my favorite thing."

"Okay," I breathe out, feeling lighter than I have all week. I yawn, suddenly, realizing how tired I am. "Do you wanna sleep here?"

"What kind of question is that, Sparkles?" He pulls me toward him until our bodies are fused together. "I want to live here."

"But your apartment's so much bigger."

He nuzzles into the spot between my neck and shoulder. "I'm not talking about your apartment."

ON FRIDAY, WE'RE BACK TO OUR USUAL WORKING environment, and keep our elevator riding to a minimum. We both care too much about our jobs to let our chemistry get in the way. But he does insist that we get lunch together. He even invites Andie to join us. Who then invites Daanesh.

SLACK GROUP MESSAGE
#SUSHI-SIZZLRS
Olivia Diamond:
Did you just create a group chat for lunch today?
Andie Oh:
I did. I want sushi. Have I incepted you all yet?
Daanesh Khan:
Works for me
Gavin Scott:
I'm in. But not that place all the way down 3rd. Liv's wearing the crazy heels

SLACK DIRECT MESSAGE
Olivia Diamond:
You asked me to wear these heels!
Gavin Scott:
And I really like the view under our desks
Can't have your feet hurting though

"You never told me how Wednesday's meeting went," Andie asks once our food comes. I was worried this lunch would be awkward, but we've all fallen into a good rhythm together. And after Mexico, it doesn't feel strange socializing with our CEO.

"Good. Darnell seems impressed with our platform. Eduardo said the technical questions he asked were all a really good sign for them wanting to buy."

"I'm sorry I missed it," Gavin says, regret etched over his face. I notice Daanesh give him a questioning look, but he doesn't say anything.

"I didn't really need help, but it was good to have someone there to confirm it went well. I'm still figuring it all out."

"I'm so proud of you," Andie says, before pausing to take a bite. "I just wish I could have snagged you for the marketing team before sales pulled you to the dark side."

Daanesh and Gavin are sitting across from us, so I turn to see Gavin's reaction, if he remembers my interview as well I do. But they're both in some deep conversation about rugby now.

I turn back to Andie. "I like sales. And I know nothing about marketing."

"It's really not that different. Oh, I've been meaning to ask. Have you still been hearing from Tri—"

I shake my head vigorously to stop her mid-sentence. She gives me a strange look and I nod at Gavin as inconspicuously as possible.

She mouths back, "Oh."

"I have to pee," I say, a bit too loudly. The guys both look at me with narrowed eyes, like I'm a child asking for assistance. "Andie?"

"Yeah, me too. Be right back, boys."

"Here," I hand her my phone with the texts pulled up as soon as we enter the bathroom. I've been chewing the inside of my cheek constantly, worried about what's on my phone. Now, I run my tongue along the tender flesh wondering if I've caused permanent damage.

I know I'm not cheating. I haven't actually done anything but respond to the texts. And our relationship title is still one hundred percent fake...I think. But I know I can't let Gavin see these messages.

TRISTAN CROSS:

Dinner? Tonight? You'll love it, I promise.

ME:

Sorry, can't. I'm in Mexico!

TRISTAN CROSS:

How about a pic of your favorite bikini then?

ME:

I only wear one-pieces. Body image issues, you know how it is

TRISTAN CROSS:

I bet I can make you feel very good about your body. If you let me, I'll make you feel incredible

ME:

It's a deep insecurity

TRISTAN CROSS:

Stop fighting me on this. You know we'll be great together

ME:

I agree. We would make excellent business partners. Will you be at the meeting on Wednesday?

TRISTAN CROSS:

I heard you were nothing short of impressive today. Let me show you my appreciation for your hard work

Can I have you for dinner, Olivia?

ME:

I'm not on the menu

TRISTAN CROSS:

Yet

Andie hands me back my phone and glares at me.

"What? No Teletubby noises. I'm maturing."

"You're flirting," she murmurs.

"I think I've made it really clear I won't go out with him," I defend, even though I know she's right. "I'm just trying to be friendly enough that I don't totally offend him."

She purses her lips.

Mitch has been on me for days about getting him to come to our client event next month. I just have to get Tristan there, and then I can cut off this weird texting thing. But until then, I can't shut him out completely.

"You like Gavin. I know you do. Why are you doing this?"

"It's just until I can make some progress with the account, then I'll block him and never speak to him again. It's not like I want to be doing this."

She hands me back my phone and grabs the door. "You're playing with fire, Liv."

I know she's right, I *know* this. But I'm not sure I have it in me to give up on this deal just yet.

We both plaster on smiles when we get back to the table and enjoy our sushi while we discuss some upcoming work events and the guys' next rugby match.

When we leave the restaurant, I push Tristan clear out of my mind. Gavin and I are hand in hand and I'm feeling giddy about wherever this is going. I don't even bat an eye when he stops on the street corner to grab my face and kiss me.

"Ollie?" *Oh no.*

I pull out of Gavin's embrace to find my brother inspecting me. "Hey, Owen."

We stare at each other for a few moments. Owen is the youngest of my older brothers, and the one who was the most hurt when I decided to move to San Francisco instead of staying at the winery to work with him.

"What are you doing in the city?" I ask.

"Dad had me fill in for some restaurant meetings. Who are your...friends?"

"Oh! Well, you remember Andie." She's come with me to the winery several times. "And Daanesh, he's actually the CEO of my company. And umm—" I track Owen's gaze and realize Gavin and I are still holding hands. "This is Gavin, my boyfriend."

I swallow hard, terrified of what Gavin might think that I used our fake relationship status on my brother. But with Daanesh right here, what was I supposed to say? Luckily, he seems unfazed. I watch as everyone shakes hands and gets introduced.

Daanesh and Andie let us know they have a meeting to get back to, but Gavin stays by my side so I can awkwardly catch up with my brother.

"Sorry, I didn't realize you broke up with the last one," Owen murmurs. I give him a look that hopefully says "let's not talk about my ex."

"Well, this is new and—"

"Are you coming to Passover, then?" he asks Gavin, cutting me off.

"Yes?" Gavin looks at me with narrowed eyes. *Why would he say yes?*

"Awesome. Our parents will be excited to meet you. We all hated the last one, so there shouldn't be too much pressure."

"Owen!"

"What? He called the wine *obtuse*, Ollie. If there's anything worse than a snobby visitor, it's one who doesn't actually know what they're talking about."

He's not wrong. We all cringed when Ian said he tasted notes of cobalt in the Vega, but I hoped he just misspoke and meant cherry or charcoal. Then, after he called the mouthfeel obtuse, my brothers said he wasn't invited back.

My family aren't snobs. They don't expect everyone to be wine experts. In fact, they have always loved when we bring friends who have no wine education because they all love to teach. But in true Ian form, how could you teach someone something who already knows everything about everything?

"Okay, I gotta get to my next meeting and it's all the way over Nob Hill," Owen says.

"Oh, where at?" I ask, intrigued.

"House of Prime Rib. The Vega's been selling well there, so we're trying to double their order."

"Nice. See if you can get me a reservation!" I yell when the light changes and we're forced to run in different directions.

"What did I just agree to?" Gavin asks as we cross the street.

"Passover. It's the only Jewish holiday my parents really celebrate. They've sort of turned it into an exclusive wine tasting slash dinner party for their closest friends and family."

"I've never celebrated Passover before."

"It's okay. I'll get you out of it. I can always say you're sick or something."

"So you're uninviting me?" he asks.

"No? Do you really want to spend next weekend at my family's vineyard? They are loud, and invasive and have absolutely no filter. They think my job is a joke. And yeah, they will definitely quiz you about the wine."

"I guess that gives you a week to teach me."

CHAPTER TWENTY-FIVE

OLIVIA

WE DON'T HAVE A WEEK TOGETHER TO PRACTICE WINE-tasting.

We don't even have a day.

I leave for Carmel after work, a girls' weekend to celebrate Andie's birthday. And before I get back on Sunday, Gavin will be catching a flight to New York, where he's meeting with clients until he returns Thursday night.

If it was anyone other than Andie I might cancel, but we've been talking about going to the Monterey Bay Aquarium and playing Spanish Bay for months. Andie and I golf together in Half Moon Bay all the time, but we never plan ahead enough to get tee times in Carmel. It's finally happening.

Maybe it's too early to be disappointed about being apart for one week, but this thing with Gavin is feeling more real by the minute.

SATURDAY

GAVIN SCOTT:

Hey

I miss you

Is it weird to say that?

ME:

I miss you too

Sharing a bed with Andie just isn't the same

GAVIN SCOTT:

It better not be

Sure you can't get home a little earlier tomorrow? I don't have to be at the airport until seven

ME:

Doubt it. Our tee time's not until one. We couldn't get anything earlier

GAVIN SCOTT:

You play golf? How the hell didn't I know this?

ME:

I'm full of surprises ;)

GAVIN SCOTT:

Send pics!

SUNDAY

GAVIN SCOTT:

You are an exceptionally cute golfer. Can you wear the visor next time we... ?

ME:

Scottie!

GAVIN SCOTT:

;)

About to take off

ME:

Call me when you land

MONDAY

ME:

How'd you sleep? Are you feeling better?

GAVIN SCOTT:

Not really. Already missed my first meeting

ME:

That sucks, I'm sorry. Anything I can do?

GAVIN SCOTT:

Yeah, actually

Stop apologizing!

ME:

I'm not at all sorry about your recent misfortune, but would like to share my deepest sympathies and offer anything I can to cheer you up

GAVIN SCOTT:

More golf pics?

TUESDAY

GAVIN SCOTT:

Closed the deal

Wish you were here to celebrate with me

ME:

Congrats!

We'll celebrate when you get back

In Sonoma! *wine emoji* *grapes emoji*

GAVIN SCOTT:

What are you doing now?

ME:

Just got out of the shower

GAVIN SCOTT:

Pics or it didn't happen

ME:

Nice try. You'll have to use your imagination

GAVIN SCOTT:

Getting pretty good at that actually

ME:

Yeah?

GAVIN SCOTT:

Of course. Don't you ever think about me
when you're alone?

ME:

Maybe

GAVIN SCOTT:

What do you think about?

ME:

You really wanna know?

GAVIN SCOTT:

Absolutely

ME:

The night before we went to Mexico

GAVIN SCOTT:

Be more specific Sparkles

ME:

When you tugged at my bottom lip with your thumb. It was the hottest thing I'd ever felt. I wanted you to kiss me so bad that I picture it in my head and pretend you did

GAVIN SCOTT:

Are you thinking about it now?

ME:

Maybe

GAVIN SCOTT:

Are you touching yourself?

ME:

Do you want me to be?

GAVIN SCOTT:

Fuck yes

ME:

Are you touching yourself?

GAVIN SCOTT:

I've never been so hard in my life

ME:

What are you picturing?

GAVIN SCOTT:

You

Those heels wrapped around my shoulders

Your hand between your legs

ME:

I could go get the heels if you want but I don't feel like moving

GAVIN SCOTT:

Don't you dare

ME:

I'm thinking about the elevator now

What would you have done if no one interrupted us?

GAVIN SCOTT:

Gotten on my knees and worshiped you

I would have made you come even with all that lace between us

ME:

I wish it was you making me come now

GAVIN SCOTT:

It will be in two days

Are you close?

ME:

Yes

GAVIN SCOTT:

Can I call? I wanna hear you

ME:

Better hurry

WEDNESDAY

GAVIN SCOTT:

Sorry if I fell asleep on the phone last night

This time change kills me

ME:

That's okay. I just figured you were bored. I don't think I've ever talked on the phone that long in my life

GAVIN SCOTT:

Nothing about you is boring

Especially last night

ME:

Not even all the random stories about my brothers?

GAVIN SCOTT:

Are you kidding?

The one about them throwing you in a wine barrel...priceless

ME:

That was very traumatic! I thought I was going to drown

My brothers can be horrible sometimes

GAVIN SCOTT:

I promise I'll keep you safe this weekend

THURSDAY

GAVIN SCOTT:

Are you still awake?

ME:

Are you back?

GAVIN SCOTT:

Just leaving the airport

ME:

Come over

GAVIN SCOTT:

It's late, are you sure?

ME:

<< selfie wearing the golf visor >>

GAVIN SCOTT:

ETA says 22 minutes

CHAPTER TWENTY-SIX

GAVIN

I'VE BARELY KNOCKED WHEN OLIVIA OPENS THE DOOR.

"Hey, beautiful," I say, setting my bags down. I quickly wrap my arms around her and let my hands get tangled in her hair. For a split second, I think about taking a step back, that I'm being too forward, too assuming. But then I remember that everything has changed in the last few weeks.

"Are you feeling okay from the flight?" She looks up at me with sincerity swimming in her eyes and I get hit with another wave of *I really fucking like this girl.*

"Yeah, slept the whole time." I kiss her nose. "Do you mind if I take a quick shower? I always feel gross after a long flight."

"Of course."

I've never been reserved so I leave the bathroom door cracked open. But I'm still shocked when Liv comes in to join me a few minutes later.

"Is it okay if I come in?" she asks with a shy smile.

"Much more than okay." I grab her hand and guide her under the water with me.

When Liv kisses me, I feel like I'm flying. Like she's imbuing some sort of magic into me with each brush of her lips.

And it's not just her lips. Her hands wander freely, hungrily around my body. She pulls me with her until her back is up against the sliding door.

"Did you miss me, Sparkles?"

"A little."

My mouth travels down the column of her throat, stopping to suck on all her favorite spots.

"Please don't be angry with me," I say, looking up at her. "I didn't bring anything."

"You really never think you're going to get lucky, do you?"

I raise my head until we're eye-level. "I never thought I'd get this lucky."

Our lips meet again, and this kiss is more heated, more urgent, more everything.

"Well, *lucky* for you, we don't need a condom."

"We don't?" I give her a questioning look, but she only responds by grabbing onto my shoulders and moving us in a half-circle. She presses me against the glass.

"There's something I've been wanting to try with you."

She turns off the shower. And then she drops to her knees.

With zero hesitation, she drags her tongue up my length. I practically slam my head against the door behind me. Jesus. This girl really is going to kill me.

"Are you okay?" she asks, looking up at me like a perfect angel.

"All good," I grunt. My mind's in a tailspin with Liv in front of me like this. I look down, memorizing every detail, and then I notice her knees wobbling. "Here." I reach over the door to grab a folded towel off the shelf and place it down at my feet. "For your knees."

She bites her lip and re-balances on top of the folded towel. "Thanks, Scottie." She grins and licks me again.

"Fuck."

She licks her lips, drops her eyes from mine and says, "You might want to hold on to the door."

I chuckle and follow her instructions, but my laughter dissipates immediately when she takes me into her mouth.

"God, Olivia," I groan, watching her. "You have the prettiest mouth I've ever seen."

I can feel her lips stretch when I say it. She likes when I talk to her.

"Could you be any more perfect?" I ask, running a hand through her wet hair. I try to massage her scalp while I use my other hand for balance, but she's making my brain too foggy to concentrate on much more than her lips.

She circles her tongue around me, and I can feel a moan vibrate from her throat.

"Does this turn you on, Sparkles?"

She releases me slowly and looks up. "Yes," she admits, a grin playing at her lips. "A lot."

Just her saying that makes me harder. I can feel myself twitch in her hand.

"Touch yourself."

"What?"

"Spread your legs, Olivia. Tell me how wet you are."

Her gaze hooks on mine as she moves each knee a little wider. I swallow, watching her hand slide dangerously slow down her body. My lips part and I lean forward, greedy for the show.

She gasps, just one quick breath, and her mouth is on me again.

I feel drunk, dazed, out of my mind. The wet heat of her

mouth, the sounds she's making. Each puff of her breath has my muscles clenching.

A low moan escapes her lips, and my eyes are drawn back to her hand. The one making slow circles between her thighs.

"Are you close?" I ask.

Her eyes find mine and she nods. God, she's making the same circles with her tongue.

"Stop." I press my hands on her shoulders.

"What's wrong?"

"Absolutely nothing. Come here." I pull her up against me. "You're really good at that too."

"Then why'd you stop me?" She pouts and it's adorable.

"I was getting jealous." I tilt my head in a nod.

"Of my hand?" She laughs, and the movement brings our bodies even closer.

"I haven't seen you in a week. If anyone's hand is getting you off, it's mine."

Liv's alarm goes off at 9:00 a.m. and we both groan.

Her cheek still rests against my chest and our legs are completely entwined. I'm not sure how we actually slept in this position, but it goes to show how tired we were.

"Are you sure we have to leave so early?" I whine, because I'd prefer to stay in bed with her all day than drive to Sonoma.

"I told you. If we're not there by noon they'll disqualify me. It's exactly what they want, and I will not give it to them."

Liv and her brothers sound more competitive than me and Gabby. When she told me the other night about their annual dirt bike race, I was sure she was joking. I should have known. This girl is always surprising me.

And as tired as I am, I'm champing at the bit to see Liv on a dirt bike. No wonder she was so calm on the motorcycle.

"All right, Sparkles." I sit up, yawn, and stretch my arms. I give my head a good shake to try and wake myself up. "I'll run home and grab the bike. Sure you can fit everything you need in a backpack?"

"Yep. I have everything I need there, just bringing a couple essentials." She kisses my cheek. "Like you."

LIV'S HOUSE IS JUST NORTH OF THE MAIN TOWN IN Sonoma, so the drive only takes about an hour. I haven't really considered what her place might look like, being a home on a vineyard, but I feel like a fool when we arrive.

"It's a castle," I say, dumbfounded. She doesn't hear me because she's already jumped off the bike and is running toward three men who I really hope are her brothers and two golden retrievers that I really hope I can spend the weekend with.

I'm quickly introduced to the brothers, the dogs, the parents and a few other people who are hanging around. Then I lay on the ground and let Carat and Cork slobber all over me. And before I even get a chance to go inside, we're all whisked off to get ready for the big race.

Liv wasn't lying when she said she loved dirt bikes. She and her brothers are all decked out in full motocross gear from the boots to the helmet, Liv in hot pink from head to toe.

Not that I ever thought she was lying. But the girl whose closet is full of silk bows and sparkly dresses doesn't scream "I like to drive fast and get muddy."

She in fact does like to drive fast and get muddy. And it's hot. My mind is spinning on where I should take her next on the motorcycle. Hell, maybe I'll let her drive.

She smokes her brothers in the race, earning herself major bragging rights and a solid chunk of my dignity. She would have smoked me too.

"Gavin, come join us, will you?" Sandra, Liv's mom, asks shortly after we get back to the estate. Then she looks to Liv. "Can we borrow him while you get cleaned up?"

Damn, I was looking forward to helping Liv get cleaned up. After last night I never want to shower alone again. Probably not appropriate at her parents' house though.

"Sure," Liv replies. And then, "Go easy on him." She runs outside leaving me with nothing but a smirk.

Sandra gives me a quick tour and then I follow her down the stairs to their cellar which seems to double as a dining room, and maybe a tasting room too? There are three long dining tables but a few other areas with couches and low tables where people are currently drinking. From what I've learned, this main building is where they give tours and tastings, but they live in the other estate next door.

"Gavin!" Liv's dad shouts. He introduced himself as Mr. Diamond, so I still don't know his first name. "Come, come. Grab a glass."

He pours me a hefty glass of red wine and introduces me to more friends, some other winemakers from the area. And then he does the one thing I've been dreading.

"Tell us what you think about the wine."

"It's good," I reply, but he just stares at me. "Great," I offer. Still not good enough apparently. "I know it's not the one that's Liv's favorite. This one's sweeter, I think?"

They all smile at me, and I feel like I just cracked the DaVinci code. I can tell they want more but all I keep thinking is *do not say obtuse*.

I take another sip and swirl the wine to mimic what I've seen Liv do a hundred times now. I stick my nose in the glass, hoping it looks sophisticated and not as ridiculous as I feel. But when I breathe it in through my nose I get hit with a memory.

"Alfajores." I don't mean to say it aloud, but I do, attracting everyone's attention even further.

"What was that?" Mr. Diamond asks.

"Something about this reminds me of the cookies my mom used to make."

His eyes gleam. Am I onto something? Does the wine taste like cookies?

"What kind of cookies?" Sandra urges.

"Alfajores. They're these crumbly sandwich cookies filled with dulce de leche. It's like a creamy caramel."

"Ollie!" Mr. Diamond yells, his gaze traveling over my head. "You found one with a palette. He's a keeper."

I turn to find Liv standing behind me, freshly showered and gorgeous. She rests a hand on one of my shoulders and grabs the wine glass with her other.

She takes a slow sip.

"Mmm, is this the new Orion?" Her dad nods. "Love the caramel notes."

The chair I'm in is oversized but not wide enough for two. Liv comes around and sits with me anyway, half her body in my lap.

No one seems to mind, especially not me.

"Why does everyone call you Ollie?" I ask. I heard Owen say it last week, but I've noticed everyone's been using the name for her today.

"My fault," Owen says, taking the chair across from us. "When we were little, I couldn't say Olivia and started calling her Ollie. It just stuck."

Liv shrugs. "And when I was a toddler, I called you 'Money' and Deacon 'Dick.' Somehow I was able to grow out of it."

"You really hate it?" I ask.

"It makes me sound like a dog."

"I love it."

"Oh no, are you gonna start calling me Ollie now, too?"

"Nah, they can have it." I lean in closer to whisper in her ear. "Sparkles is just for me."

Mr. Diamond stands up and clears his throat, grabbing everyone's attention. "Let's make our way to the table. Dinner should be ready soon."

When I stand, he comes over and pats a hand on my shoulder. "Ever been to a Passover seder, Gavin?" he asks.

"No, sir. I'm excited for my first though." First of what I hope to be many.

He tells everyone where to sit and of course I'm next to him with Olivia on my other side. I've never been grilled by a girlfriend's dad before. I've never really had a girlfriend, or anyone I'd cared about enough to try and impress their family. It's intimidating as hell.

"So, Gavin," he continues. It's clear he's been drinking for a while from his breath, but I imagine in this line of work he can really handle his booze. "Passover is all about wine."

"Dad!" Liv scolds. "It's not about wine. It's literally about the Jews escaping slavery and returning to their ancestral homeland."

"Yes, yes, that. And *wine*," he repeats, holding up his glass like he's giving a toast.

Liv rests her chin on my shoulder.

"Sorry, he's drunk."

"It's all good."

Deacon and the other brothers start bringing out the food. It looks like we're about to have a feast. I'm not sure what anything is, but I've never had an issue trying something new.

"All right, Liv, you're up," Deacon says. "You're still the youngest."

"You know there are like ten other steps before the four questions," she replies.

"But the food's ready and we're hungry so just give us a little taste of what we *should* be doing, okay?"

"I swear, it's like I'm the only person in this family who went to Sunday school," she mutters. "How about this?" She stands. "Why is this night different from all other nights? Why do we eat unleavened bread and bitter herbs and dip the herbs and lean back in our chairs?" She finishes with a curtsy and sits back down. No idea what that was.

"Amen," her brothers all chant.

"Not *Amen*, you're supposed to answer the four questions, you idiots."

"Can we eat now?" Owen asks.

Liv's dad stands up and holds out a glass. "L'chaim. Let's eat."

Liv drops her elbows to the table and covers her face in her hands. I can hear little grunts wafting off of her.

"You'll have to explain that to me some other time," I say.

She picks up her head and looks at me. "If a Jewish person ever asks what you know about Passover, do not use this night as an example."

"I'm having fun."

She beams. "You'll love the food. Deacon's an insanely good cook. Mom, can you pass the brisket?"

The whole table falls silent as everyone takes their first few bites. It really is delicious, especially these little dumplings that I've never heard of. I'm trying to pace myself with wine, but her dad keeps refilling my glass after every sip.

"So, Gavin," Sandra starts in. "Tell us about yourself. Where are you from?"

I should have been prepared for this but I'm not. Just another reason I don't get close to people. Then I never have to talk about my past. But I don't want to hide shit from Liv, not anymore.

"I was born in Argentina, actually. That's where my mom's from. We didn't move to California until I was nine."

"Oh, we love Argentina. Mendoza has some of the most wonderful vineyards in the world." Sandra goes on some tangent about her favorite South American vineyards, mainly talking to her friends. Her hand gestures grow bigger with every word, like she's sculpting an Argentine vineyard from invisible clay.

"Sorry, she's high," Olivia mutters. Sandra already offered me a joint on our tour, so this doesn't shock me.

"You don't have to apologize for your family," I whisper. "They seem great."

Sandra finishes her air-sculpture and turns back to me. "Do you still have family in Argentina?"

"No."

Liv must hear the clipped tone in my voice because she grabs my hand under the table. We haven't discussed my childhood before, but I know she can infer enough.

"Then your parents are in California too? What part?"

"No, umm, my mom died before we moved here. And my dad's gone. It's just me and my sister now."

"Oh, I'm sorry to hear that."

"Me, too," Liv whispers. I squeeze her hand in return, and luckily her parents get caught up in another conversation right away.

"You okay?" Liv asks a moment later.

"Of course. All this wine is making me a little sleepy though."

"It's not like we were well-rested when we got here either."
She leans into me, laughing a bit. "Wanna call it a night?"

"I CAN'T BELIEVE THIS IS WHERE YOU GREW UP."

We take a winding staircase to the second floor of the
private estate where all the bedrooms are. The walls here are
covered in photographs of her family. All of her childhood
memories immortalized.

My eyes snag on one with Liv inside a wine barrel. Her
face is stained pink, and her brothers are all laughing. You can
see a sliver of her dad looking like he's about to take someone's
eye out. Then I remember the story she told me. It feels like I'm
getting a behind-the-scenes tour right now.

"It's weird, huh."

"Weird is not the word I'd use. You're lucky, Liv. This
whole house feels so alive, like I can't imagine you ever had a
quiet moment here."

"You're definitely right about that. Not with my brothers."
She opens the door to her bedroom and the size of it alone has
me reeling again. Our lives could not be more different. "Can I
show you something?" she asks.

"Of course." I wrap an arm around her shoulders and kiss
her temple. It's nice finally having a moment alone together.

She walks us over to the opposite end of her room where
double doors open to a small balcony. The air outside is crisp, a
gentle breezing cascading around us. There's a large tarp that
Liv pulls down to reveal a telescope.

"Fancy," I murmur.

"When I was little, my brothers and I would camp out in
the vineyard and count the stars. It became kind of an obsession
for me, so they got me this for my thirteenth birthday. It's still
my favorite part about coming home."

I look up, realizing there are about a hundred stars visible from where we are standing. "Wow."

"You're lucky it's a clear night. When the fog rolls in, sometimes it can be impossible to see anything. But the views will be incredible now."

She starts tinkering with the telescope before looking through it and making some more adjustments. "There," she says. "Come look."

I peer through the lens and find myself utterly speechless. I've never seen anything like this. I take in as much as I can, feeling so small in the moment compared to the vastness of the universe. Finally, I pull myself away.

"It's cool, right?" she asks. "I know it's kind of silly, all the wine names and the stars and—"

"It's very cool," I say, cutting her off. "I guess we both have an affinity for sparkly things."

She smiles. "When I was younger, I said I was going to be an astronomer. I was so desperate to get away from this small town that I wanted the whole universe. But then I kept failing science, so I settled on San Francisco."

I laugh, watching as she repositions the telescope a few more times to show me different views, finally showing me the constellation Lyra, her favorite rosé's namesake.

"For someone who was desperate to get away, you seem to like it here," I offer. How could she not? It's idyllic in the most basic sense of the word.

"I appreciate it more now. Sometimes you don't know how great one thing is until you have something else to compare it to."

As soon as we get back inside, she quickly changes into a T-shirt and slides into bed. "Come lay with me?"

I follow suit and join her under the covers. I almost moan, it feels so good to lie down. After the trip to New York, our late night and early drive this morning, I'm beyond exhausted.

Liv rolls toward me and leans in for a kiss. It's just a quick brush of her lips, nothing more. "You don't like talking about your family, do you?"

My lips part, but nothing comes out because I don't know what to say.

"It's okay. I wasn't trying to pry or anything. I shouldn't—"

"No, you're right. I never talk about them. I didn't grow up like you did." I slide a few pieces of hair away from her face. "But I'd like to tell you."

"You don't have to tell me anything, Scottie."

"I want to. I've actually *been* wanting to, because I might need some advice."

She tucks her arms into her chest, those blue-gray eyes sparkling back at me. "Well, I can't say I'm great at advice considering I do not have my shit together, but I have a damn good therapist. Hopefully she's been rubbing off on me."

I smile and she kisses me again, followed by an encouraging nod.

"Okay. So—sorry, I honestly don't even know where to start because I've never told anyone this before."

"Just start talking," she urges. I guess I can do that.

"Our mom died when Gabby and I were little. I guess you already know that. It happened suddenly, something bleeding in her brain. She was just...gone. Like it all happened so fast that I'd wake up in the morning and forget she wasn't there anymore. For months."

Liv pulls one of my hands into hers but doesn't say anything.

"My dad hadn't been around much before that. I mean he was always around, but—my parents weren't married. We weren't like some big happy family is what I'm trying to say.

When I was young, I don't think I realized exactly what was going on, but he was violent. And whenever he got that way, Mom would kick him out and he'd be gone for days, weeks sometimes. But he always came back. And after she died, he was all we had left.

"He moved us to Sacramento into his parents' house. We'd never met them before, and they didn't seem very happy to take us in. Dad never had a steady job, so money was tight. All I remember from that time was screaming. My grandparents would yell at my dad, and he'd yell back. Then Gabby would get scared, and she'd be screaming too. It was just absolute shit."

I realize I've had my eyes closed this whole time and when I open them to look at Liv there are tears shining in hers.

"I'm sorry. This is not a fun thing to talk about. I don't know what I was thinking."

"No, keep going. You haven't even gotten to the advice part yet."

I sniff, try to make it sound like a laugh.

"The short of it is that he left. Honestly, I don't even know if he's alive or dead, he just disappeared on us. It's not like he was much of a father-figure before that, but he could not have abandoned us at a worse time.

"I was barely fifteen and had to beg my grandparents to let us stay with them until I could get a job and take care of Gabby myself. The second it was legal, I started working as many jobs as there are hours in the day. People joke about how early I get in or how late I stay at the office sometimes and I just laugh, because I know they've never worked a triple in their life.

"As soon as I turned eighteen I filed for guardianship of Gabby, got us a shitty apartment as close to Davis as I could afford because I got a partial scholarship there. Then Gabby, the little brainiac she is, graduated high school early and got accepted to Cal. I still don't understand why we were denied financial aid, but no way in hell was I going to make her go somewhere else. And she was barely seventeen so I took out another loan. I've been playing catch up ever since.

"So that's what I've been doing for the last decade and a half, taking care of Gabby, of us. But I think she's starting to hate me for it, for playing the role of her father or something."

"I'm sure that's not true," Liv whispers. I scoff. "Who doesn't want to be taken care of, Scottie? To feel safe and secure? How could she ever be mad at you for that?"

"I've kept things from her. A lot of the financial stuff. I thought I was protecting her, but...I don't know."

"That's what your fight was about last week?"

"Yeah. She said she forgave me, but I can still feel this rift, like I've lost a part of her."

"She'll come back." Liv brushes my hair back and it's the softest touch I've ever felt in my life. "It's easy to see how much she cares about you. I actually thought *she* was the protective one."

"I think we're both protective of each other. Sorry if she hasn't been the friendliest toward you."

Liv chuckles. "I don't know. It's kind of nice knowing I earned it with her, that she didn't just immediately warm to me because you told her to." Her gaze floats up, like she's lost in thought. "I'm really glad you two are so close. I think that happens when you lose someone. You hold on extra tight to the ones who are still around. You might just need to relax your grip sometimes."

"Now who's the wise one?" I murmur.

Liv slides closer and wraps an arm around my shoulder. She pulls me in until our foreheads are pressed together.

"Thanks for telling me all that," she says. "It means a lot

that you trust me. Well, I shouldn't make assumptions. But I think you kind of trust me."

"I kind of love you."

She sucks in a breath and I'm frozen. Why the hell did I say that? I've never told anyone I loved them before besides Gabby. Can I take it back? I look down at the sliver of space between us, praying if I just wait long enough, she'll let me pretend it never slipped out.

"Only kind of?" The corners of her mouth pull into a teasing grin.

Immediate relief hits me, and I exhale so heavily it pushes our lips together.

This time, when she kisses me, it feels different. Like there's no destination, like we're both just here to enjoy the ride. After many pointed comments from her brothers about thin walls, I know tonight will be tame, but I really don't care. I could stay like this forever.

I slide my hand up to her neck and cup her jaw, reveling in the feel of her soft skin.

"Scottie," she whispers against my lips. "I might love you a little bit too."

CHAPTER TWENTY-SEVEN

OLIVIA

GAVIN FALLS ASLEEP QUICKLY, HIS HAND STILL TUCKED against my chest, our faces so close we share each breath.

Not me. I'm wired.

It feels like I swallowed starlight. Like I reached through the telescope and stole every shimmering ball of fire from the sky. If I'm not careful I might start glowing, a neon sign wrapped around me telling the world I'm in love.

Love. Is this my first time feeling it?

When I got serious with Ian there was this constant buzzing under my skin. Every time he invited me on a new trip or to go to some special event, I'd get hit hard with it, this zing of possibilities.

But if that was a spark, this is a flood, extinguishing any last remnants of my old flame.

I'm not just falling for Gavin. I'm drowning in him. His hold on me feels like cool rain on a hot day, an icy drink after a run. It doesn't feel like something I want, but something I need. Like something I never want to go without.

I must doze off thinking about this. But my blissful dream of crisp rain pouring over me turns scalding when I wake.

Hot, hot, hot. Not the good kind. The pillow beneath me is damp and I pull back, realizing Gavin and I slept most of the night pressed up against each other.

The heat subsides when I get some space and I reach to touch his face. It's burning.

"Scottie, wake up," I say, gently pressing against him.

"Mmm?" he mumbles, his eyes still closed. He shivers and reaches a hand to pull me back into him.

Feeling a hit of satisfaction for him wanting my comfort, I let myself curl into him for a moment. The sigh he releases makes me beam. But then I realize this isn't helping the situation.

"Do you feel okay?" I ask, wiggling out of his embrace. "You're really hot."

"Thanks, Sparkles. You're not so bad yourself." His eyes are still closed but he grins. "And you love me a little bit." Now my face is the one burning.

"See. You're clearly delusional. I better take you to the hospital immediately before you lose any more brain function."

"She makes jokes," he says, pulling me in even tighter. "I know you wanted to go explore but would you be okay heading back early? I've got a headache."

"Maybe you shouldn't be driving if you feel sick, Scottie."

"You drive. I saw you yesterday. My girl's a pro with a clutch."

Something about that singular word *my* has me heating up again. Maybe whatever he has is contagious.

"If you're sure," I murmur, more excited about driving than I want to let on.

"Positive." He kisses my cheek before stretching out of bed and cracking his neck. "Yeah, let's get out of here."

GAVIN DOESN'T SAY MUCH ON THE WAY BACK TO THE CITY, just a thirty-second tutorial on the nuances of his motorcycle. He's definitely been downplaying how bad he feels. I can tell by the way he grips my middle the entire ride.

I drive us straight to his apartment. It's a nice enough day that I can walk home, and I want him to get back to bed as quickly as possible. To my surprise, he tugs my hand to pull me through the door with him.

"Stay with me for a bit?"

"Okay."

He immediately shuts off all the lights and grabs some medicine from an orange bottle in the kitchen. He must notice my eyes tracking him.

"Just a migraine. Will you lay down with me?"

I look around for Gabby since I'm wondering what the protocol is here. If he gets migraines often, maybe there's something I should be doing to help him. But the place is empty.

"Want me to grab Churro?" I ask.

"Yeah. Just put him in the sling first. He gets scared when he's out of the cage and not wrapped up."

Carefully, I pick up my favorite hedgehog and give him a little smooch. "Hey, Chunk." He titters back at me, and I hope it means he likes me. I slide him into the sling and wrap it over my shoulders. By the time I turn around, Gavin's already in bed.

"You're sure you don't wanna be alone?"

"Why would I want to be alone if I could be with you?"

Gavin has already propped up his pillows in the perfect position. I carefully fold myself into the bed, making sure Churro is protected and happy.

We lay there for a few heartbeats without saying anything, and then Gavin really surprises me.

"Can you play some of that French music you like?"

"Really?"

"Yeah, it's relaxing. Just keep it low."

I let the music play on my phone and lay it at the foot of the bed. Churro must like the music too because I can feel him start to purr. I had no idea hedgehogs did that.

"I like this one," Gavin says softly during the second song. "It's perfect for you."

"Why do you think that?" I whisper back.

"It's about a girl who doesn't realize how amazing she is."

For a second, I'm stunned. Maybe the drugs are giving him loose lips, or maybe after last night we crossed an invisible barrier where we can say whatever we're feeling. *A girl who doesn't realize how amazing she is.* Gavin makes me feel amazing, he makes me feel a lot of things. And here I thought the song was about a puzzle. That's the name anyway.

Wait a second...

"Do you speak French, Scottie?"

"I used to. A little bit. Gabby's fluent." He mumbles the words as he turns his face into the pillow, pressing in closer to me. "I've been practicing." I remember now, him and Gabby explaining her affinity for languages at game night. That Gavin did speak French at one point, that Gabby still does.

He extends an arm to rest over me but instead, lays a hand on my breast...and squeezes.

"Umm, Scottie?" I ask, stunned.

"It's my security boob. It helps my head," is all the explanation he provides.

By the third song, he's fast asleep.

I'm not tired, but I don't want to leave him when he asked me to stay. It's kind of nice watching him sleep. He looks so calm and non intimidating. Big bad Gavin Scott is curled up like a puppy in my arms. What a difference a few weeks makes.

I've just started combing my fingers through his hair when I hear someone clear their throat. I startle and turn toward the door we left open.

"Hey Gabby," I whisper.

She raises her brows at me, one hand on her cocked hip. Maybe she hasn't fully warmed to me yet.

I hold up a finger letting her know I need a second and I untangle myself from Gavin so I can get out of bed without waking him up.

Once I'm out of the room I close the door so we don't disturb him, and then I tell Gabby the events of this morning.

"He let you drive the bike?" she shrieks. "He doesn't let anyone touch that thing. And all the way from Sonoma?"

"I ride dirt bikes. He trusted me." This earns me another stern look, but it softens quickly.

"Thanks for taking care of him. When he gets migraines, they're really bad. I always feel so helpless."

I exhale. "I have felt like that all morning." We share a look. Maybe this is some good common ground for us. And maybe it'll earn me some points if I let her take over. "I'll head out. No need for me now that you're here."

"Kadesha's on her way over. Wanna hang out with us? I'm gonna make tacos for lunch."

"That's really nice of you, but—"

"Gav's drugs keep him knocked out for a few hours. But I'm sure he'd be really happy if you were here when he wakes up. Stay." I have no idea what Gavin has told his sister about us. Like he told me, they're obviously close, but as far as she knows this is still a fake relationship, or maybe just a friendship. Does this mean he's told her things between us have changed?

"Oh my god, are you blushing right now?" she interjects my thoughts. "Wow, you really do like him."

I think I've clearly admitted as much to him already. No point trying to hide it. "Yeah. I really do."

Gabby's expression is unreadable. That is until I see tears falling from her eyes. But even their presence doesn't give me much to go on. I can't tell if she's happy for us or falling into a deep pit of despair.

Before I can puzzle it out, the front door opens and Kadesha walks in.

We met when I came over for a game night a couple weeks ago. Her personality is just as bright as her pink hair.

"Babe, are you crying?" Kadesha drops the bag she was carrying and runs into the kitchen, hugging Gabby. "What's wrong?"

Yes, Gabby. What's wrong? Am I really not good enough for your brother?

"Nothing," Gabby sobs. "Nothing at all. I'm just so happy." I think that's what she says but it's hard to tell with all the crying. She's a blubbering mess.

Kadesha looks at me, a question in her eyes. I shrug. And then suddenly Gabby is hugging *me*.

"Welcome to the family," she says into my hair. I hug her back, relief settling into my bones. "If you hurt him, I'll destroy you."

Kadesha leans against the island and laughs.

WE ALL CHIP IN TO MAKE THE TACOS. WELL, SINCE I have no actual cooking skills, I make margaritas. And I offer to press the button that blends Gabby's "famous" chimichurri.

After we eat, Kadesha shows us the contents of her bag: new accessories for Churro. The guy has been chilling in his sling on me all day and he's so quiet I almost forgot.

Kadesha shows us a new sling she concocted for him that is made out of a fabric printed with tiny churros—very meta, and then she pulls out the cutest miniature sunglasses I've ever seen. The lenses are shaped like hearts.

"Ahh, we need to get pictures of this," Gabby says, grabbing her phone.

"Hold that thought," I say. I hand Churro to Gabby and tip toe back into Gavin's room to grab my camera out of his bag.

I thought I was stealth enough to not wake him up, but after our photoshoot begins, he pokes his head out.

"What's going on?" he asks groggily. I don't blame him for being confused. Kadesha has the churro-printed sling draped over her head while she uses the bottom to hold him up. It's a full backdrop. The sunglasses hang off his tiny little face and he looks exactly like the diva he is.

We all laugh at Gavin's expression, and I finally put the camera down.

"How are you feeling?" I ask, walking over to him.

"All better." He tucks some hair behind my ear and kisses my nose. "I'm gonna grab a quick shower. Don't leave, okay?"

"Wouldn't dream of it."

The photoshoot continues as we find all sorts of props for Churro to pose with. Gabby glares at me when I wrap him in a tortilla but apologizes when she sees how cute the photos are. Gavin even joins us after his shower and lets me get some incredible photos of Churro resting on his head.

As I snap each one, I think I might never be able to have Gavin over again. My wall is about to be covered in photos of his face.

We order a pizza for dinner. Every time I mention leaving, all three of them encourage me not to go. It's starting to feel like I couldn't outstay my welcome if I tried.

We finally get into bed a little after eleven, Gavin promising he'll let me go home in the morning.

"I feel like I completely wasted the last twenty-four hours I had with you. I need tonight at the very least."

"*You* had a four-hour nap," I reply. "Don't expect another all-nighter."

"That's okay." He kisses me softly and dips his head, pressing his mouth to my jaw, then my neck. "I kind of like doing all the work." It's the last thing he says before expertly sliding off all my clothes.

"Thank you," he says a few moments after we finish. I roll over to face him.

"You don't have to thank me, Scottie. That was mutually beneficial."

"Well, I'm glad to hear that, but that's not what I was thanking you for, beautiful."

"Oh."

He wraps an arm around my waist and tugs me close again. His hand wanders up my back and over my shoulder until he has my face in his palm.

"You took care of me today. No one ever takes care of me."

"I barely—"

"You know it's not easy for me to let my guard down. Just let me thank you."

"Okay," I whisper.

"And about last night..."

I wait for him to finish the thought as I listen to my heart beat like a woodpecker. *He's taking it back. He didn't mean it. I humiliated myself by responding the way I did. I love you a little? Who the hell says something like that?*

"It's okay, you don't have to explain. This is still so new and we're figuring things out. We can just forget we ever said anything at all. Really, it's no big deal."

"Sparkles?"

"Yeah?"

"You've really got to stop assuming you know what I'm about to say."

"Oh." Oh no, could it be worse than I thought?

His hand reaches out to cradle my face, his eyes roaming over each of my features.

"I wanted to say that it felt like a cop out. Like I was afraid to tell the truth. And there's not much I'm afraid of, definitely not being honest with you, not anymore. The truth is I do love you. I really, really love you. Not kind of. Not just a little bit. I love you a whole damn lot. And whether or not you feel the same way, I just wanted you to know that."

"I—"

"And one more thing, since I'm done keeping anything to myself. Because what the hell is the point of that? So I think you should know that...that this isn't new for me at all."

CHAPTER TWENTY-EIGHT

GAVIN

27 months ago

"Is that her?"

Gabby asks the question as soon as we enter The View. It's the first time we've held our holiday party here, in the lounge on the top floor of the Marriot Marquis hotel. Until now, our company wasn't big enough to rent our own space.

And while this does offer some of the most incredible views of the city, my eyes are exactly where Gabby's have landed, on Olivia Diamond.

"Yep." I gulp. I've told my sister all about Olivia. Well, everything I know, which isn't a whole hell of a lot. But everything I do know, I like. I've wanted to ask her out for weeks, but I've been too worried about making her feel uncomfortable at work. Though with Gabby's urging, and Mitch's incessant "just man-up and get it out of your system" complaints, I've decided to finally go for it.

Yes, this is a work event, and maybe not the most appropriate time to do it. But it's the closest thing I have to seeing her outside the office. And she looks fucking incredible. Her wavy hair drapes around her shoulders, shining like firelight. She's got so much of it that she's constantly tucking it behind her ears and every time she does it my fingers itch, wanting in on the action. And the dress she's wearing. She's glittering as much as the city lights outside the window.

Gabby starts tugging on my hand, but I'm too lost in thought to realize where she's dragging me until the sparkling dress is directly in my line of sight.

"Hey, Gavin," Liv greets me. "Wow, I don't think I've ever seen you in anything but a hoodie."

I chuckle, but I'm not sure how to respond.

"You have no idea how hard it was for him to agree to wear the jacket," Gabby replies. "He's all about comfort."

"I'm Liv," she says, stretching a hand to Gabby. "Are you Gavin's girlfriend?"

We both sputter.

"Absolutely not," I practically shout. Gabby glares at me.

"Siblings," Gabby clarifies. She laces an arm through mine and tugs me toward her. "He's very single." Christ. "Actually, Gav was telling me—"

"Gavin," Mitch interrupts with a hand to my shoulder. "Are you busy?" He looks toward Gabby, then Liv and seems to decide on the answer himself. "There's someone I want you to meet."

I'm nervous about leaving Gabby and Liv alone together, but luckily Andie comes over to chat right as I leave. She hired Gabby last week to be a part-time intern.

"Ask her out yet?" Mitch snickers as we walk toward the bar.

"Not yet."

"Pussy."

"Fuck off. Who do you want me to meet?"

"You should be nicer to me, you know. How many times have you told me you want to work for a Venture Capitalist firm next?"

Shit. I've told him that a hundred times. I've never been afraid to use connections and Mitch has more contacts in Silicon Valley than anyone else at Sizzl. Probably because he's one of the only people over forty, but still. He's worked at four different start-ups, two of which have hit unicorn status.

"Is someone here?" I ask

"All our investors are. Haven't you ever met them before?"

"Only Caleb from Spangled. But not since we got our big round from AngelBak in February. I missed the last off-site they came to." I was pissed about it, but I had a migraine that kept me in bed for two days. AngelBak is where I plan to be in two years. Hell, maybe less if Mitch can help me.

"Well, I guess it's your lucky night." Mitch turns to the bar and calls a server. "Three tequila sodas." Another man comes over to us from the other side of the bar and Mitch hands him one of the drinks. "Ian, I want you to meet Gavin Scott, our top seller. Gavin, this is Ian Thompson."

Ian Thompson is the youngest partner AngelBak has ever had. He's thirty-five and has already backed three start-ups through their IPO. He literally has my dream job. Possibly my dream *life*. You can just tell by the way he carries himself that he doesn't go home at night and stress about paying the rent. He probably owns. And he probably paid all cash.

"Great to meet you, Ian," I say, shaking his hand. "I'm really fascinated by what you do at AngelBak."

He responds with a raised brow and not much else, so I continue. "I sort of fell into sales after college. But talking to so many different companies each day, I'm always thinking about what makes them successful, or what might make them fail. Especially when I look at their growth trajectories and—"

"Truly. He won't shut up about it," Mitch says. "The kid's gonna be working for you one day, as much as I'd love to convince him to stay. Pulled in ten million this year."

Mitch claps me on the back and walks away, seeing someone who's apparently more interesting than me or Ian.

"So, you're looking for a job?" Ian asks, his voice tinged in mockery.

"No? Sorry if it came off that way. I really just find it interesting. I'd love to work for a VC firm one day, but I'm happy at Sizzl for now."

"Where'd you go to school?" he asks.

"UC-Davis. With Daanesh, that's how we know each other." I smile, hoping my friendship with our CEO can make this conversation a bit less awkward.

"That's how you got the job? You guys are buddies?"

"Umm, sort of. That's how I got the interview at least. I'd say it's worked out well though." Did he not hear Mitch just mention the ten million dollars I closed this year?

Ian licks his teeth, his face overtly smug. Suddenly I want nothing to do with this conversation or this guy. There are plenty of firms around the Bay Area; I'll have to pick a different one to strive for.

My eyes snag on Olivia for the zillionth time since I was dragged away. I'm going to blame her dress that keeps catching the light.

"What about grad school?" Ian says, surprising me.

"Oh, no grad school. I started working right after college."

He smirks again. I'm really starting to hate this guy.

"You might wanna stick to sales with that background."

Fuck this guy.

I hope by some miracle he plays rugby because I'd love to see him again on the field. Considering his firm is our largest investor, it might not be a good look if I punched him in the face right now.

Olivia's dress catches my eye again. At least I have that conversation to look forward to when I can get away from Ian.

"Who's the girl you keep looking at?" Ian asks, thankfully changing the subject.

"Olivia? She's the newest member of our team, started a few months ago."

"You sleeping with her?"

"What? No, why would you say that?"

"You want to sleep with her, then. I don't blame you. Nice rack." Now we're both staring at her and I'm praying she doesn't notice.

"Gav, come on. We're getting a group pic," Daanesh shouts over my shoulder. "Oh, hey Ian. Mind if I borrow this guy? Sort of a tradition for the original eight."

I raise my glass as a farewell to Ian the Asshole and follow Daanesh to the area with a photobooth set up.

It is tradition. Every year since I started here, we all take a ridiculous photo together and then do a shot of Don Julio 1942. Though I would have left that conversation for some questionable moonshine.

"Ian's great, right?" Daanesh asks after the second round of shots. "I really think he's gonna take us to the next level."

"Yeah, seems like he knows what he's doing," I murmur.

I realize it's been at least ten minutes since I've spotted Olivia. My eyes drag through the space in search of something sparkly. They finally land on her tucked into a small table in a dark corner.

With Ian the Asshole.

She's giggling.

And his hand is in her fucking hair.

Seething, I look back at Daanesh. "Any chance he plays rugby?"

CHAPTER TWENTY-NINE

OLIVIA

"You...I...but..." Words fail me as I take in everything Gavin just unveiled. "I thought you hated me."

"What? Why would you think that?"

"You were just always *so* professional. We never talked about anything but work. You weren't like that with anyone else in the office."

He drags a hand through his hair and rolls on to his back. "Yeah, I was worried about making you uncomfortable. It was your first real job." He pauses, sighs. "And then once you started dating Ian...I'm sorry. I know I was a dick sometimes. I —"

"Can we go back to the part where you love me?"

Gavin reaches a hand around my middle and tugs me until I'm on top of him.

"Are you really gonna make me say it again?" he teases.

"I like when you say it," I murmur, settling between his legs.

"Yeah? Why's that?"

Why? Because his feelings mirror my own. Because Gavin

Scott knows me, the real me. Because there's no part of myself I've hidden from him, nothing I've downplayed or exaggerated, nothing that isn't honest and bare. What could ever be better than someone loving you through all the layers, never wanting to change a single one?

"Because I can tell you mean it." I lay my hand on his chest, dragging my nails across his skin. He hums his approval, but then he starts laughing. "What?"

"It's just kind of surreal."

"What is?"

"For so long I just watched you," he says.

"Watched me? Should I be concerned?"

"Not like that, smartass," he continues. "I mean I've sat across from you for two years. I see you." He drops his voice and wraps my hand in his. "I notice you. When you tap your nails or nibble your cheek. When your lips move in silence, and I try with bated effort to puzzle out what you're saying. It still doesn't feel real that I get to be a part of it now. That your nails are tapping on me. It's like I finally get to be on the other side of the window."

His words sit heavy in my chest, but the rest of my body melts.

"You should have thrown a rock or something. I would've let you in."

He reaches over and kisses my nose, and so quietly I almost miss it says, "I love you, Sparkles."

I whisper back, "I love you too, Scottie."

I don't go home in the morning.

We spend Sunday in bed, only leaving for meals. What I worried might be a fluke was not, and Gabby, still giddy over our fake-turned-real relationship, lets me borrow clothes so I never have to leave.

A real relationship. That's what Gavin told me he wanted last night, or maybe it was this morning. He really shouldn't keep having important conversations with his hand between my legs.

"This is real now, Sparkles. There better not be any doubt when you say you have a boyfriend."

I wasn't sure if it was his words or his touch that made me breathless, unable to respond. But I'm positive he knows I'm in agreement.

We walk into work on Monday hand in hand. And even though it's not the first time, everything feels different. Even the air around us is shimmering with possibility.

SLACK DIRECT MESSAGE
Gavin Scott:
Miss you
Olivia Diamond:
I'm sitting across from you
Gavin Scott:
Miss you naked in my bed
Olivia Diamond:
NSFW!

I click out of my Slack window knowing this conversation isn't going anywhere productive and open my email. This might be the first time since starting at Sizzl that I didn't catch up on email over the weekend. I didn't open a laptop once.

It's a weird feeling. Part of me is happy for enjoying my weekend, spending quality time with Gavin, his sister, my family. And another part of me feels guilty for not being my usual workaholic-self, especially when I see what's waiting for me in my inbox.

From: Tristan Cross < tristan.cross@surfandstream.com >
To: Olivia Diamond < olivia@sizzl.com >
Subject: Re: Exclusive Invitation to the Sizzl Spring Showcase

Olivia,
I appreciate the invitation, but I'll have to decline. Unless of course you'll be attending? You know how to reach me.

-Tristan

I keep my face neutral while I silently roar. I was positive Tristan would come to this. It's an exclusive event and offers a sneak peek into our roadmap for the next year. And I *thought* I did a good job of wording my invitation with vague enough language that he might think I *would* be there. He must have read through the event's landing page. Executives only.

Mitch made it perfectly clear last week that Tristan's presence was expected, that if he didn't come it was basically him saying the deal is dead.

It might be time for a hail mary.

ME:

> Sure I can't convince you to come to the event? You'll get to see a lot of interesting tech that hasn't been released yet

I get a response almost immediately.

TRISTAN CROSS:

> The only thing I want to see is what's under your dress.

Fuck.

"What's wrong?" Gavin asks across our desks.

Shit. "Did I say that aloud?"

"No, but you mouthed it." He mimics me, mouthing an overly exaggerated *fuck.*

Guilt pours over me. Gavin is my boyfriend. Nothing fake about it. It suddenly feels dirty to keep these messages a secret from him. I need to come clean, but I have no idea how he'll react.

"I'm okay. But I have something I need to talk to you about. Maybe tonight? We could get dinner?"

"Can't, Sparkles. I have a thing with Daanesh."

"Oh. Okay."

He looks toward Mitch's office but it's still empty. None of us know if he's still in Portland or planning to come in late. He's been managing the whole team by email for the last three weeks.

"Let's go get a coffee. I can't go all day wondering why you're upset."

"Okay, just give me fifteen minutes."

I fire off another email to Darnell. I shared a pricing proposal after our last meeting, and he told me the next step would just be landing on the right start date and getting approval from leadership. Leadership equals Tristan.

This time I copy Tristan back into the thread to ask for an update and any outstanding questions or concerns. I also throw in a few of my favorite value points—*never stop selling!*

My stomach is full of butterflies, the evil kind, as I think about what I'll say to Gavin. Everything about this situation has turned to shit. I have no idea if the deal will close, if my promotion or even my job is still in danger. Gavin is my only bright light these days. What if he's pissed I've been hiding this from him?

My phone buzzes, interrupting my internal pity-party.

MITCH STEVENSON:

Did Tristan RSVP yet?

What's the latest update?

I motion to Gavin that I need another minute and take my phone into the closest conference room to call Mitch. I know this is going to suck, but I'd honestly just rather get it over with.

"Hey Livy," he answers. It sounds like he's in an arcade or something, lots of ringing bells and buzzers in the background.

"Hey. So I just heard back from Tristan and he can't make it. But I think—"

"I'm gonna email Gavin to take over on this, Livy. I can't let you fuck around anymore."

"Excuse me? I'm—"

"You gave it a shot, now—"

"No. I didn't give it a shot. I am *actively* shooting and about to score. Just give me the chance to get open. I will close this deal, Mitch."

"Appreciate the sports knowledge Livy, but—what?"

I hear a squeaky voice come through Mitch's end of the line. "I can use the company card again, right baby?"

It sounds like something is rubbing against his phone, like maybe he's trying to cover it. "Get anything you want. Just give me a minute," he says, voice slightly muffled.

"Hello?" I ask, wondering if we're still in the middle of this conversation.

"Sorry. Tif—Ellen's on my case again."

"Okay." I draw out the word, confused as hell, because that didn't sound like a couple who argues as much as Mitch does with his ex.

"Why isn't Tristan coming to the showcase?" Mitch continues.

"He's going to be out of town," I lie. "But I know how to get him to the next meeting," I lie again. It's getting easy with how fired up I am.

For some unknown reason, Mitch starts to laugh. "You're going to go out with him, aren't you?"

"What? Of course not! Do you honestly think that's the only thing I'm good for?"

"I think it's your best shot to get Tristan to sign a contract."

I can't believe this is still what he thinks of me. "That's not fair, Mitch. You wouldn't do this with the rest of the team. You would never ask Gavin or Eduardo to—"

"I wouldn't have to. If a prospect started hitting on Eddie he'd close the deal in record speed."

"How can you say that? He's married."

"Oh, don't be so fucking naïve. Look, I gotta go. I'll give you two more weeks. If I don't see something tangible happening, Gavin's taking over, end of story."

He hangs up.

Ugh. I walk back to my desk and see Eduardo smiling down at his phone. I really hope Mitch is wrong about him.

Two weeks. Is there any way I can pull this off? If not, I might as well start looking for a new job. I don't think Mitch would actually fire me. I'm still our best sales development rep. But if the promotion's off the table, what would I even be doing here? Some days, I wonder if sales is actually what I want, or if I just refuse to quit something that I've been working so hard for.

Sometimes it feels like I have so much to prove that I don't even *know* what I want anymore.

I make a mental note to reschedule my therapy session I had to cancel last week. My progress with Dr. Plath has been good, great even. She's the reason I haven't let my breakup with Ian turn my life sour. She's probably the reason I let myself fall for Gavin. She's definitely the reason I've been so open with him, even if there's still something I've been hiding.

"You ready to go?" Gavin asks. Ready? *Only if you're planning to forgive me,* I want to say.

Might as well rip off another Band-Aid. I already feel numb.

CHAPTER THIRTY

GAVIN

I want to light this phone on fire.

It's all I can see right now when I close my eyes. Because I never want to see these texts again.

First Mitch's bullshit, then this fuckface who doesn't seem to understand the word "no."

"*Why* didn't you tell me about this?" I don't ask the question, I beg.

"I'm so sorry. I just knew you'd try and take care of it. He's really harmless, just texts. I was hoping I could close this deal and then I could block him after that."

My mouth falls open and I look around the coffeeshop, trying to collect myself. She's talking about this like it's normal, like it's just another day at work. And it's not just texts. Before she showed me her phone, she filled me in on Tristan's surprise appearance at her charity event.

"Harmless? He had his hands on you, Liv. He thinks you're playing some fucking cat and mouse game with him. I think he gets off on it."

I shove the phone across the table like it might actually

burn me to touch it again. My eyes squeeze shut as I lean back in the chair. Fighting the urge to punch something, I squeeze my hands a few times before running them over the top of my head.

"Scottie?" Liv's voice, small and breaking, pulls me out of my rage. When I open my eyes, I see tears streaming out of hers. "I'm so sorry. And I know you told me to stop saying sorry, but I think you can make an exception here because all I feel is sorry." She pauses, sniffs. "I know I should have told you sooner. I know I got in over my head. Just please know that my intention has never been to do anything but my job."

The urge to punch something flies into my head again. How is this fair? Why does she have to put up with so much shit to do the same job as everyone else on our team? Just because she's a woman? Because she's hot?

"Please don't give up on me," she continues, her tears flowing freely. "I never planned on keeping anything from you. I just didn't know the right time, or the right way. And I swear if you give me the chance, I'll—"

"Do you think I'm ending things with you?" I interrupt.

"I was a little worried you might be. You seem pretty mad."

"Sparkles."

"Scottie?"

I pull her onto my lap, not giving a shit if we're in public. "I'm mad at the situation, at the fact that you had to put up with this for weeks. I'm sad that you didn't trust me enough to tell me until now. I'm mad at Mitch. But not at you. Never at you. Not sure I have it in me."

"Really?"

"Really. I love you, remember? And not just a little bit."

I kiss her nose, because I know she loves it. She lets out a deep breath, like she was truly worried and nuzzles into the crook of my neck.

She whispers, "A whole damn lot," and I smile for the first time since we walked in here.

"You've gotta tell someone what's going on though. This is getting out of hand. Mitch absolutely cannot fire you if this deal falls through when the client is harassing you. It's insane."

"I know," she replies quietly. "But I think I have an idea. I really want to try and handle this myself, my way. Can you let me do that?"

I let out a shuddering breath.

"No more secrets," she continues. "I promise I'll tell you everything. Just give me a night to work this out. Please?"

"You realize I can't say no to you, right? That I'm completely powerless here?"

She grabs my face in her hands and tugs until our eyes meet. "That's not what I want, Scottie. I've been in a relationship where one person has all the power and I'm not doing it again. You and I are a team. I'm just asking for a day, for a few more hours to make sense of an idea in my head. The rest, we'll figure out together. You and me. Okay?"

I pull her close, because I'm not sure I want her to see the emotion in my eyes. I'm not sure I'm ready to admit how much I needed to hear those words from her.

"You and me, beautiful."

"THIS FEELS WEIRD," GABBY SAYS, SITTING DOWN AT THE kitchen table. "You've never made me dinner."

True. I really do have the best sister ever, cooking for me almost every day. "I wouldn't exactly call this cooking."

I went to Liv's favorite market after work to get some cheeses and meats that blow the Safeway deli section out of the water. It's important that I do something nice for Gabby, and I wanted to start with dinner. Though actual cooking wouldn't be very nice at all. I'd most likely poison her and burn down our apartment at the same time.

I bring the charcuterie board to the table and grab a bottle of wine Liv gave me from her vineyard.

"I love you having a fancy girlfriend." *Me too*, I think. "But what's this all for? Are you about to ask me to commit a crime together? I mean I will. I just draw the line at murder, depending on the target, obviously."

"No murder this month, Gabs." She actually pouts. "I told you things would change around here, that I'd be honest with you about everything. So that's what I'm doing. There are still a few things you need to know."

I've been meaning to have this conversation with Gabby, and after Liv confided in me earlier, I decided it's time all the secrets stop. Because Liv said we're a team. And so are me and Gabby. I never meant to have a power imbalance with my sister, but I created it anyway. That stops now.

"Oh." My sister who never stops talking looks like she's been rendered speechless. "Okay." She smiles.

I unload everything.

Starting with the real reason Liv and I had a fake relationship. Initially I'd just told Gabby it was to help her with the Ian stuff, not wanting the whole story to get out. Once I explain the details, Gabby's kicking and screaming on Liv's behalf.

"Mitch. Let's murder *Mitch*. I actually think I know how we could—"

"Gabby."

"Sorry. Please continue." She swaps her vigilante smolder for an angelic grin. My baby sister can be scary as hell sometimes.

"So, like I said, I didn't want to protect Mitch, just like I didn't want to protect Davide." Her eyes narrow again. "And the only reason I did is because Daanesh and the board are working on an acquisition offer. You know Mojave? That huge company that went public last year? They're making a massive offer to buy Sizzl."

"That's great, but why all the secrecy?"

"The term sheets for these kinds of deals are insane. Our board's been back and forth negotiating the legalese for months, and I have no idea how long the whole thing will take. Nothing is a done deal yet. So while it's all in the works, it's important our company stays just as desirable as it did when they made the initial offer. Until it's signed, anyone can back out."

"How much money are we talking about, Gav?" she asks. Maybe now she'll be on board with my behavior, once she realizes what it means for us.

"A lot. Multiple seven figures a lot. We'd be set, Gabs. School, loans, all the debt wiped clean. We'd have *savings*. Can you imagine?"

"Savings. Wow." She sighs through the words like I just told her we'd be spending a year vacationing in Santorini.

And now that her feelings toward me have brightened, I share the rest. The loans and lines of credit, the increases in rent every year I kept a secret because I knew how much she loves this apartment.

By the time I'm done, I've unburdened myself with anything I've ever kept from Gabby. It feels fucking amazing.

"We can make this work," Gabby says. She stands from the table and shoves a piece of bread in her mouth as she jogs over to her room.

She returns a few moments later with a notebook and a handful of pens and highlighters.

"What are you doing?" I ask.

"Planning!" she practically screeches. "It's not like you

don't make good money. However much time stands between now and the big pay day, we can figure it out. I'm going to put together a budget and I'll do a better job of meal planning so we stop wasting groceries. No more Ubers to Kadesha's place. I'm not too good for the train."

Gabby continues to ramble on, furiously scribbling notes to her pages. But she's right. We can make this work. I never should've doubted letting her in, letting her help me.

I'm done trying to do everything alone.

Pride flares through me as I watch Gabby finalize our new budget. I'm so entranced that I jump when my phone buzzes.

DAANESH KHAN:
You still on for the U Club?

Daanesh has been a member at the University Club since he moved to SF. Whenever we get drinks together, we meet there. It's not a scene like the bars around the city, and we can shoot pool in peace. I completely forgot we had plans tonight, Gabby occupying my mind again.

ME:
Sure. I can be there in thirty

I'd normally Uber there, but after Gabby's rant, I decide to walk it.

"What's up, Daan?" I greet my friend with a hug. We haven't been spending as much time together lately and it's nice to get back into old habits. Even if everything in my world feels like it's changing.

We grab a couple drinks at the bar and head to the billiards room.

"Wanna break?" he asks.

I take the offer, and then am immediately reminded of how shitty I am at pool.

Luckily, he's not much better. Knowing we can both take a rugby hit tends to soften the blow.

"What'd you get into this weekend?" he asks, almost sinking the first cup.

"I was in Sonoma, actually. With Liv's family. Did you know they own a vineyard?"

Daanesh narrows his eyes at me. "Yeah. I've heard of Diamond Sky. What were you doing there?"

"Celebrating Passover. Kind of, I guess. I don't know. It was honestly confusing as hell." I finally make a decent shot and scratch. I grunt out my frustration with this game. Finesse, I have not. "It was fun though. Anything with Liv is. Did you know she rides dirt bikes? That girl never stops surprising me."

"Okay, enough." Daanesh murmurs. His voice is quiet but there's a sharp edge to it, hitting me square in the chest. He drops his cue on the table. "You can cut the shit with me, man."

"What are you talking about?"

"I know this thing with Olivia is all for show. I don't care what you do with everyone else, but you can stop lying to me about it."

"What?" It's all I can say because I'm completely caught off guard. How would he know it was fake? And does it even matter anymore? Because there is nothing fake about our relationship now.

"I've known for weeks. I was hoping you'd just tell me what the deal is at some point, but apparently, you're planning on keeping up the lie forever. What the fuck?"

"What do you mean you've known for weeks? Did someone say something to you?"

"I saw a text she sent Andie a while ago. Something about

not needing you at an event because no one from work would be there. So are you gonna tell me what the hell is going on?"

"What did Andie tell you?" I ask. Because Andie knows everything. Does that mean Daanesh does too? Even as I think it, I know he doesn't. He'd never stay quiet knowing what Mitch was up to.

"Nothing. She told me I misread it, but I know what I saw. Look, I know we don't really talk about relationships, but you work for me. Olivia works for me. If there's some scheme happening within my company, with one of my best friends, I'd like to know what's going on."

"It's not a scheme," I tell him. "And you know I wouldn't lie to you unless I had to, right? I was just trying to protect Liv."

He picks up the cue, but it looks like it's just for something to do with his hands. Our game is on pause until I come clean.

So I do. Every detail from the moment I found Olivia barely breathing in the stairwell. From the moment I knew I couldn't stay away from her anymore.

"Why the hell wouldn't you come to me? You should have called me that night. You really don't think I would have helped her?"

"I mean, yeah, but, it just felt kind of similar to the Davide thing, and—"

"You know where I stood there."

"I know where *you* stood. But what about Vaughn? The board? I honestly wasn't sure what would happen."

"Davide's a board member. It's different. I couldn't overrule him on my own. Mitch can be replaced like that." He snaps his fingers, his tone still full of quiet rage.

"Liv's asshole ex is on the fucking board!" I yell. "This whole thing is fucked, okay? Maybe I screwed it up even worse but there was no easy way out. And Liv didn't want to go to you, or HR, so it wasn't my decision anyway."

It looks like he's about to say something else but changes his mind, his mouth still open. Instead, he shakes his head and kicks the leg of the pool table. "Fuck."

"Hurt yourself?" I ask.

"Fuck off."

"I really am sorry about lying to you. And for what it's worth, Liv and I are together now. It's not just for show."

He looks up at me. "Yeah? Well, at least something good came out of this. Too bad I'm disgusted by my own company."

"A few bad apples don't make an entire company, Daan. It's still a great place to work."

"If a single employee doesn't feel like they can speak up against their boss, even just to go to HR, then it's all to shit. I have to fix this. Mitch is gone."

Part of me is ready to fist bump Daanesh. I'd love nothing more than to watch Mitch get the axe. But then I think about my conversation earlier today with Olivia. I promised I'd let her handle this her way.

"Is there any way I could convince you to, umm, hold off on that for a bit?" I ask.

"You've gotta be kidding me." He actually huffs this time.

"Just let me talk to Liv first. There's a reason this all started, remember? This isn't how she wants to solve this."

"That isn't her decision, Gav. I have to speak with her about it."

CHAPTER THIRTY-ONE

OLIVIA

GAVIN SCOTT:

Can you meet for coffee this morning?

ME:

Already went! I came in early today to work on something. Let's get lunch

GAVIN SCOTT:

Why aren't you answering your phone?

I really need to talk to you. You never called me back last night

ME:

I promise we'll talk later. I'm on a roll right now and I can't have any more distractions. Going to turn off my phone

I FEEL A LITTLE GUILTY BLOWING OFF GAVIN, BUT I CAN'T afford distractions right now. I spent last night formulating a plan. The best plan I could think of for getting Tristan engaged in an actual work conversation. A plan to save my job, and maybe even force Mitch into considering that promotion.

And now I need to execute that plan before something else gets in my way.

It wasn't difficult to find a new strategy. I just had to stop boxing myself into this idea of what I *should* be doing. I can't just be another Gavin or Eduardo. I've always known I don't get to play by their rules, so why was I trying to, knowing I'll always be ten steps behind?

The fact is, they have their strengths, and I have mine. And I'm finally going to use them.

I'm Olivia fucking *Diamond*, heiress to Diamond Sky Vineyards. Well, kind of. But there's one thing I am sure of. I am *brimming* with big tit energy.

SLACK DIRECT MESSAGE

Olivia Diamond:

I'm sorry again for calling so late last night. And for the texts this morning. But were you able to come up with that client list yet?

Andie Oh:

Seriously, when do you sleep? Is my best friend a vampire? And yes, I just emailed you the file. It's password protected since it has everyone's contact info, but the pw is just SIZZL

Olivia Diamond:

THANK YOU!!! I'll sleep once I get the promotion

Andie Oh:

I also secured budget for transport. You're sure you can handle everything else? It might be tight but Mario thought this was a great idea. He was impressed you came up with it

Olivia Diamond:

The CMO knows my name!?

And no budget needed, I got everything taken care of minus the shuttles. I really owe you for this!

Andie Oh:

You owe me nothing. I'm excited to spend a Friday in Sonoma

Budget's taken care of, email list ready to go, PowerPoint presentation in the works. There's just one more thing to set this plan in motion.

ME:

How would you like an exclusive tour of Diamond Sky?

TRISTAN CROSS:

What makes it exclusive?

ME:

Possible barrel tasting – you probably know we never do those

A tour of my family's private cellar

Oh, and I'll be the one leading it

TRISTAN CROSS:

When is this happening?

ME:

Next Friday. Tour starts at eleven

TRISTAN CROSS:

I'll be there

I hover over Gavin's name in my iMessage window. My phone is still off so I screenshot the conversation on my laptop and send it to him. I can explain the details later, but I don't even want to be tempted to hide it.

ME:

> I'll explain my devious plan at lunch today,
> just wanted to loop you in

A message bubble pops up on the screen immediately, but to my surprise, it's not a response from Gavin.

SLACK DIRECT MESSAGE
Daanesh Khan:
Good morning, Olivia. Do you have a minute to chat?

What the hell? Daanesh and I have definitely gotten friendlier over the last few weeks, but we've almost never interacted at work. He's the CEO, and an engineer at that. He never has a reason to talk to me. This can't be good.

Olivia Diamond:
Sure. Right now?
Daanesh Khan:
Yep. Meet me in conference room B

B? Shit. I'm pretty sure that's the soundproof one.

"Hey, Daan," I say, walking in. I was shooting for casual, but in the current setting it feels like a possible mistake. "What's up?"

I take a seat across from him and try to decipher anything I can from his expression. He looks tired, a little sad maybe?

"Is everything okay?" I ask. He still hasn't spoken, but he really does look beat up about something. I know he was with Gavin last night. Maybe a rugby match gone bad?

"Not really," he finally replies. "Do you feel safe here, Olivia?"

My eyes dart around the room like I might find some sort of weapon.

"Yes?"

"I mean at this company. At *my* company."

"Oh. Of course, I feel safe." I'm starting to wonder if this is a new style for our quarterly reviews. I've heard of other companies in the Bay Area letting employees review their leadership. Maybe I got picked by the random generator.

"Look, I promised Gavin I would wait to talk to you, but I don't want to lose any more sleep over this. I need to know exactly what happened with Mitch, and why you didn't feel comfortable coming to me or to HR."

I see red.

He promised *Gavin*? Gavin promised *me*. What the hell is this, some sort of ambush? Gavin trying to save the day *again* and failing miserably *again*?

"I'm not sure what Gavin told you, but nothing happened with Mitch. And there's nothing I need to talk to HR about. I'd really just like to get back to work." I stand.

"Liv," he says quickly and pauses. "Please."

When I sit back down, I cross my arms over my chest, hoping it sends the right message.

"Can we talk as friends for a minute?" he continues. "Just forget this is my company. Our roles don't exist."

"That's not exactly easy to do but sure."

"Did you know I have three sisters?" he asks, catching me off guard. I shake my head. There's very little I know about Daanesh outside of work. "When Gavin told me how Mitch has been treating you, all I could think about was them. Two are still in school but the oldest, Sana, she just started working as a data scientist for a company in Dallas. If I knew her job was threatened for anything other than performance, I'd be livid. And I don't want anyone working for me that feels otherwise. I just want to make it clear that I will never condone misogynistic behavior, and you should never be afraid to come to me if something like that happens."

He nods his head, announcing my turn to speak.

"I appreciate you saying all this, I do. But it doesn't change anything."

"Why not?" he asks.

"Okay, let's just play this out. *Hypothetically*. Because I have not made a complaint and I don't plan to." I let my eyes flare. "But let's say I tell you Mitch is threatening me, harassing me, being inappropriate, whatever. What do you do then? You fire him, I assume?"

"*Yes*." Daanesh thinks this is the response I want, but he still doesn't get it.

"So, then what happens to me? I get a new boss?"

He nods, shrugs, like of course I would. No big deal.

"Great. Now I have a new boss who knows I got the last one fired. That sounds like a great start to our relationship. Mitch will be gone, and sure, people might talk about him, but he'll move on to another VP role somewhere else, no problem. I'll be the one living with the rumors. The girl who got the VP of sales fired. People will love to speculate about what happened; if it was really even his fault at all. Maybe I'm just too sensitive or couldn't take a joke. If I ever do get promoted, it'll be because the company is scared of a lawsuit, or hell, maybe it's because I started sleeping with *you* to get what I want." He shudders at this. It's nice to know where he stands, but it still doesn't change anything.

"The rumors will be endless, and I'll hate it here even more than I do working for Mitch. Eventually, I'll leave, and start over at the bottom somewhere else. Tell me if any part of that scenario sounds like a win for me."

He swallows thickly. "I don't know if that's exactly how it would go, but I see your point. You're really not going to work with me on this? You don't want Mitch gone? I'll do everything in my power to not let it affect you."

I take a second to think about it. "Of course I want him gone, but not like this. Not because of me. All I want right now is to do my job and make some magic happen, all on my own."

"If this is about the promotion you've been working toward, I—"

"Nope. Don't even say it. I do not want to win that way. Can you please keep this between us?"

He nods and something about his expression makes me want to believe him.

I stand up and leave the room before he can dangle any more carrots in front of me. Because I don't want his help, or Gavin's or anyone else's.

I want *zero* doubt. I want to erase the possibility of whispers and lies that spread like wildfire. I want it to be perfectly fucking clear that I earned that position, that it wasn't because some man likes the way I look, or feels sorry for me, or wants to make up for someone else's indiscretions.

I pass the wall of fame on my way back to my desk, the wall covered in velvet portraits of every sales rep who's closed a million-dollar deal. Gavin has a whole damn row.

Seven portraits of him I have to pass on the walk, seven times to feel the betrayal, seven expletives escaping my lips.

"Liv?"

Make that eight.

"Hey, asshole."

"Can we talk? Please?" It's not even nine in the morning and he's already begging. At least I can take a little pleasure in that.

"I actually have a lot of work to do," I say, bee-lining it to my desk.

As soon as I sit down, I put on my headphones, drowning out his pleas.

SLACK DIRECT MESSAGE
Gavin Scott:
Please let me explain
Olivia Diamond:
Explain what? Your need to run to Daanesh and betray me?
Gavin Scott:
I didn't betray you! He cornered me. Demanded to know why I lied about dating you. He found out weeks ago.

This surprises me and I briefly glance up from my computer. Gavin raises his brows in an attempt to talk, but I deny him. There's no way Daanesh has known for weeks.

Olivia Diamond:
That's impossible. Nice try though
Gavin Scott:
I swear, Liv. He said he saw a text you sent Andie, totally by accident. I think it must have been when you were going to that charity event because you said something about not having to bring me since no one from work would be there

What? That's way too specific to be made up but it has to be a lie. Andie was in Santa Barbara with her boyfriend when...

I yank off my headphones and fall back into my chair. *Unbelievable.*

"What's wrong?" Gavin's staring at me. He's doing it in that sweet "I'm just here for you" way that makes me melt. But I don't want to melt for him right now.

"There's no one I can trust anymore."

"Sparkles." He gets up and comes over to sit in Paul's old chair. "You can trust me, you can. This was all just one big clusterfuck, but that doesn't mean you can't trust me. I've only ever had your best interest in mind. You know that."

I realize the office is starting to fill up and I look around, hoping this conversation isn't being overheard. Gavin notices and grabs both of my hands to pull me up. "Come here." He drags me into the closest conference room.

"How can I make this right, Liv?"

Make it right? Does he think he has the power to turn back time?

"Yesterday," I announce. "I told you I had a plan *yesterday.* You couldn't even give me a whole twenty-four hours to fix this myself?"

"Liv, I told you. I never planned to tell him anything—"

"I believe you, that you didn't go to Daanesh by choice, but you didn't have to tell him everything. You just wanted to fix it."

I pin him with a stare, daring him to lie to me.

"Of course, I did! How do you expect me to stand by and watch as these guys take advantage of you?" He throws up his arms, his voice laced with vitriol. "Do you think it's easy for me to see the texts from Mitch disrespecting you? The ones from Tristan? How could you expect me to see that and not want to do anything about it? I love you, for fuck's sake."

I've never felt so conflicted. Everything he's saying has me wanting to run to him, to let him wrap me in his arms and make everything better.

But would that mean I'm giving up on myself?

"I love you too," I whisper in reply. "But I'm done feeling like a possession. I don't want you to fix everything for me. You're not my keeper. I don't belong to you."

"You think you belong to me?" he asks incredulously. "Is that a joke? I belong to *you*. I lied to one of my best friends for weeks, for *you*. I was—I *still* am on board with you figuring this situation out on your own, and I told you I'll be there to help as much or as little as you want. I would do anything for you. Don't you get that?"

He's been inching closer to me with every word and suddenly he's right here, sharing breath. His hands reach up to cup me face as he says, "You're in charge, Sparkles. I'm just along for the ride."

"Really?" I ask, trying not to grin. It's impossible with the way he makes me feel, sunlight begging to pour out of me. "You'll let me do this my way? No fixing?"

"I only have one request," he adds.

I narrow my eyes. "What?"

"I got your text. This thing in Sonoma you have planned. Whatever it is, let me be there. I'll keep my distance, won't say a word. I just can't stand the thought of him near you. I want to be close if you need me."

"I guess chivalry isn't dead," I muse. I like the idea of him being close. There is always a solid possibility of me getting in over my head. Again. "I can work with that."

"One more request."

"Really, Scottie?"

"What if I said my life depended on it?"

I scoff, dropping my head to the side. "Fine, what is it?"

"Kiss me."

His request surprises me. But my body reacts instantly. My eyes dart behind him to the door of the conference room. Luckily, we happen to be in one of the two rooms without windows and glass doors.

"It's just us, Sparkles," he whispers against my lips. He drops one hand to my waist and lets the other thread through my hair to cup the back of my neck. "Please," he begs. "Put me out of my misery."

My lips curl into a grin. "I thought we agreed to keep *this* out of the office. Getting caught in the elevator was bad enough."

"This doesn't count," he says, pressing into me until my back's against the wall. "Didn't you hear the part about my life depending on it? Don't you care about my survival?"

I shake my head, still grinning, and pull him toward me until I'm perfectly sandwiched between Gavin and the whiteboard. "If your survival's at stake..."

I know we should stop this before it starts. I know this. I'm just too turned on to care. Gavin's hot, and he's really good with his mouth, but the lack of control he places over me is what's really doing it for me right now.

I grip the shirt at his chest, and pull him even closer, our lips finally coming together. His hands roam from the hem of my dress up, up until he's fiddling with my bra while his lips move to my neck.

I wrap an ankle around his calf and tug, positioning his leg between mine. He quickly takes the hint and presses into me, his lips forming a grin I can feel under my jaw.

"Am I still in charge?" I ask, tilting my head back to give him better access.

"As long as you want to be."

"Good." I grab his hand and pull it under my dress. "I have a ton of work to do, Scottie. Let's make this quick."

CHAPTER THIRTY-TWO

OLIVIA

"I can't believe we're doing this right now," Andie says, dipping her feet into the warm water. "Have you ever taken more than an hour for lunch?"

"Nope."

I usually have lunch at my desk, squeezing out every last minute of my time to work. And where has that gotten me? Everyone else on the team takes half days, works from home whenever they want, which, let's be honest, means they're barely working at all. Not me. I follow the rules like it's an Olympic sport.

Not anymore. Tomorrow is the day, my own personal D Day. And a fresh mani-pedi is just what I need to prepare for battle.

"Did you pick a color yet?" Andie asks. "I think I'm going with a burgundy shade so I can match the wine."

I look at the woman currently softening my cuticles. "What's the most sparkly polish you have?"

Andie helps me decide on a peachy-pink micro glitter.

"Blinding, but still professional," is what she said. And once all of our limbs are locked in place, I decide it's time to spill the beans.

"I know about Daanesh."

Andie stills at my abrupt declaration. I've been holding this in for a week, trying to decide if and how I should bring it up. But we're going to Sonoma tomorrow and I'm honestly worried if I don't say something now, it'll pop out at the worst time.

"You know? How?"

Her voice is small and shaking with nervous energy. "I'm not mad. I get why you didn't tell me."

"I wanted to. I wanted to so badly. But we swore we would never tell anyone, not unless it got serious. And then it did but there are still reasons why—"

"I get it." I really do. It's no different from Gavin keeping our arrangement from Daanesh. We're all in this huge, twisted web of secrets, and I'm glad it's being untangled. It's fucking exhausting.

"Really though, how'd you know?" she asks. Her voice is still lower than usual, like she's worried someone might be spying on us.

I match her tone. "An accident, I guess. He saw a text from me on your phone. When you asked if I was bringing Gavin to the Pawsability gala. So he told Gavin he knew our thing was fake, and when Gavin told me," I pause to take a breath. "You were in Santa Barbara that weekend with your *boyfriend*. I knew you'd never go as far to lie about where you were. So he had to be there with you."

"That's some serious detective shit," she replies. "I thought he bought it when I told him you were joking. I'm so sorry."

"I'll be honest. When I first found out, I was hurt. Because we tell each other everything. But then I remembered our chat in Mexico. You said something about double dates, and you were so excited. So I think we should just skip ahead to that part, yeah?"

"I mean, obviously. But I also need to talk to Daan. He still thinks we've been—wait. Is this how Daanesh found out about Mitch? It's *my* fault?"

"It's no one's fault but my own. But yeah, Daanesh told Gavin he knew about our arrangement and demanded to know why."

"I'm really sorry for my part in that. But now it makes sense why you forgave Gavin so quickly. He didn't really do anything wrong."

"If I've learned anything from the last few months, it's that no secret stays hidden forever. Does the secrecy with you and Daan have an expiration date?"

"I think so?" Her smile wavers. "This has to stay between us, but he and Vaughn might be selling the company. So he wants to wait to come out until that's final. Just in case."

"Oh, I guess that makes sense. Double date TBD then."

"Yeah, TBD," she says wistfully. "But when the time finally comes, it's going to be glorious."

I grin, knowing she'll plan something over the top and amazing.

"Has Daanesh said anything to you this week, about the Mitch situation?" I ask.

She sighs, tilting her head. "He's really torn up about it, Liv. He wants to fire him, but he doesn't want you to feel betrayed either."

"I might be able to help with that, actually."

"What do you mean?"

"Well, I'm not sure exactly, but I talked to Mitch on the phone last week. And I'm pretty sure he's not with his ex-wife and kid. He might not even be in Portland. I would tell Daan to look at his charges on the company card. There might be something worth investigating."

"WE SHOULD COME HERE EVERY WEEK," GAVIN SAYS, sprawling out on the picnic blanket.

We drove up to Sonoma after work so I have extra time to set everything up for tomorrow. With Gavin's help and the rest of our sales team, we have thirty current customers and prospects coming to the event I'm hosting at Diamond Sky.

I called the event Sip & Sizzl in the invitation, an opportunity to meet with like-minded senior-level marketers while getting an exclusive behind the scenes tour of Diamond Sky. Andie and her boss Mario will be joining as well, coming on the shuttles tomorrow. But this is *my* event, my chance to show Sizzl what I'm made of.

"Well," I reply. "We always have a place to stay if you can handle my family."

"I love your family. Do you think we could bring Gabby some time?"

"Of course."

He takes one of my hands and pulls it to his mouth, pressing his lips against my skin. The simple motion has tears swelling in my eyes. I brought him to The Meritage in Napa for dinner. Since our last trip to wine country was cut short, I wanted to show him one of my favorite places. There are several wineries and shops here, all surrounding a large outdoor area where you can lounge with their food and wine.

Everything about this moment is perfect, and somehow my anxiety is trying to ruin it.

"What's wrong?" he asks, swiping at a tear on my cheek. It takes me a minute to even organize my thoughts, but once I do, I'm not sure how to articulate them. I don't even know why I'm thinking about this. Because we're talking about family? Because I love him? Because I can't let things go?

"Tell me, please?" he urges.

"Okay," I start. "I'm going to ask you something. And I need you to trust me that it's not what you think."

He takes my hand again and nods for me to go on.

"Do you think I'm marriage material?" I catch a quick flare in his eyes before he hides it. "I'm not asking about you specifically. Just, do you think I'm the kind of person *someone* would want to marry?" I blow out a breath. I know I sound ridiculous right now, but I can't push away this feeling in my head. I can't push away Ian's voice.

His features turn thoughtful, and I'm reminded again why I love this man. He's considering my question. He's coming up with a real answer. His instinct wasn't to roll his eyes and shrug it off as another one of my "silly moments."

"What does marriage material even mean?" he asks, but it seems rhetorical. "It's just wanting to spend your life with someone, right? It's not like there's a checklist." He must notice when I bite my lip because he continues. "I bet Ian had a checklist, didn't he?" I nod. "Actually, I bet he had a pro and con list. It was probably something like, 'con that she doesn't have a better title at work, but pro that she has family money.'" The voice he uses to mock Ian makes me laugh.

He continues, "Did he tell you that? That you weren't someone he'd marry?"

"Yes. Not that I was ever thinking about marrying him, but it still stung a little."

"He didn't even know you, Sparkles." Gavin brushes some hair behind my ear and urges my face up, to meet his gaze. "He had no fucking clue how amazing you are. I mean, did he ever tell you how adorable it is that you wiggle your toes when you have your first sip of wine? Did he ever notice how sexy you look when you're building a PowerPoint presentation? Or that perfectly serene face you make when you're listening to your favorite music?" He pulls me closer to him until his lips brush my ear. "Did he ever feel how soft and perfect you are after a second orgasm?"

I gasp and he catches it with his lips, kissing me deeply. "I know he missed all of that. Because no one would let you go if they knew you like I do."

This. *This* is what love feels like. I haven't won a prize or reached a goal. Fuck the ladder. I never needed to be perfect. Being understood is so much better. Love *is* a house. And ours is going to be magnificent.

"I love you, Scottie. A whole damn lot."

Tears threaten to spill again, but they're interrupted by a phone buzzing between us. Mine.

> TRISTAN CROSS:
>
> Are you sure I can't convince you to drive together?

I open the text so both Gavin and I can see. He's never even hinted at not trusting me, but considering that I'm definitely playing with fire here, I'm being as forthcoming as possible.

"What are you gonna say?" he asks.

"The truth of course."

> ME:
>
> I'm already in Sonoma. Spending the night with my family. I hope you're excited for tomorrow, though. I can confirm we'll be barrel tasting a few upcoming vintages

"Just in case he still needed motivation," I say.

TRISTAN CROSS:

> You and a wine thief sounds like quite the
> fantasy

Ugh. Does he have to make everything sexual?

"What's he talking about?" Gavin asks.

"Oh. A wine thief. It's a tool we use to pull wine out of the barrel. Like a pretty glass turkey baster...kind of. It's really fun to use, actually. I'll show you when we get back."

"Damnit," he swears under his breath. "Now I'm thinking the same thing as that asshole."

I laugh and type back to Tristan, wanting to end this conversation.

ME:

> See you at eleven!

"Let's head back," I say, just before I'm interrupted by my phone *again*.

ANDIE OH:

> Hey love bug! Daanesh wants to come with
> us tomorrow. He wanted me to check with
> you first though since I know you're planning
> a meal and everything

ME:

> Of course he can come. Does he usually
> attend stuff like this though?

"I swear I didn't say anything to him. Other than I was coming," Gavin says, his hands up in surrender.

ANDIE OH:

> Mario invited him. I don't know if he's a secret wine lover or what, but he seems to have really high hopes for this

ME:

> Honestly, I still can't believe Mario knows my name

"Why would you say that?" Gavin asks. "Our office isn't that big."

"I don't know. Mario just seems like the perfect executive. He's always getting written up in blogs on LinkedIn. Why would he have time for the little people like me?"

"Liv, you've been the highest producer on the global sales development team for a year now. You helped source the two largest deals we've ever closed as a company. And you took it upon yourself to plan this event, which is not only bringing three huge prospects, but several of our largest clients to help with retention. If Mario didn't know your name by now, he would actually be a shit executive."

My cheeks burn at so many consecutive complements. *Don't be ridiculous. That's nothing.* The words sit on my tongue, burning to be let out. I swallow them down along with their bitter taste.

And I find some new ones.

"You're right," I say. "I'm killing it. Plus, who could forget the name Olivia Diamond?"

"Exactly." He kisses my nose and my toes curl into the soft grass beneath us.

"Can I drive home?" I ask, battling my eyelashes. The sun is just starting to set, casting a blanket of gold over all the rolling hills. The perfect time for a joyride.

"Liv, you still don't have your license. I should never have let you drive in the first place."

"But I'll be so careful! And I made an appointment to get it next week. Please? Don't you want to be a rule breaker? Just a little bit?"

He grunts. "Fine. It's your world, Sparkles. I'm just living in it."

CHAPTER THIRTY-THREE

OLIVIA

"Are you sure your parents won't mind us being down here?" Gavin asks as we walk through the cellar.

"This is my home, Scottie. My brothers and I used to play hide and seek down here. It's like our basement. It just also happens to house a few million dollars worth of wine."

He gulps and takes my hand.

I lead us through the cellar and tasting room toward the dining area. Then I head for the double doors, the ones with the words *La Grotte* carved into them.

When I open them, he actually gasps. "Is this really a cave?"

I laugh. "It's man-made, but yeah it mimics a real one, at least the climate does."

"I love how cool it is in here," he says, looking around at the rows of barrels. "And it smells amazing."

"Oak. And I always found it a bit too chilly."

"Then I'll have to keep you warm." He wraps his arms around me from behind, spreads his legs to walk on each side of me.

We waddle toward the armoire that houses stemmed glasses and tools and he finally lets go of me. The door creaks when I open it, showcasing its age, a relic brought here from my great grandparents. I grab a glass and hand it to Gavin, and then I take out one of the thieves.

"What do you wanna taste?" I ask.

"You."

"Scottie!" I poke the wine thief at his chest. "Pick a barrel."

He licks his lips, raises a brow at me, but finally turns to face down the long hallway of barrels. "How do I know what's good?"

"Everything along this wall will be bottled in the next six months." I point to his left. "They'll all be good."

"This one." He places a hand down on one of the closest barrels. "It's gotta be your favorite for a reason."

"The Vega it is." I unlatch the barrel and slide the top over. "Hold out the glass." I insert the wine thief, making sure to cover the top of it with my thumb and pull out a decent amount of wine.

"It really is kind of hot. How do you make that look sexy?"

"Just taste the wine, Scottie."

He takes a slow sip, swishing it around in his mouth like my whole family taught him last time he visited. "It's sort of tart, I think? Compared to the one in the bottle, at least."

"Yeah, it mellows out the longer we barrel it." I take a sip. "Going to be perfect though."

We trade a few sips, and I let him test out using the thief for a second glass. Then I rinse everything in our little cleaning station so there's no evidence of our secret tasting session.

"Ready to—"

Gavin steals the words out of my mouth with a kiss, his arms coming around me in a tight hold. His lips brush mine softly, slowly, a little nip at the end before he pulls back.

"What was that for?" I ask through a grin.

"This has been one of my favorite days with you. I just wanted to make sure it ended with a kiss."

I *melt*. Will it always be like this with Gavin? I know our relationship is still new, but I can't imagine ever wanting him less, ever not going weak at the knees when he says things like that.

He backs me up against the same barrel we just tasted from and kisses me again, his hands wandering down to squeeze my ass. I think he's about to pick me up but stops short.

His hoodie is off a second later and he lays it down on top of the barrel. Then I'm immediately lifted up to sit on it.

"Can't have you getting splinters."

I laugh but he just kisses me again. He's so goddamn considerate.

"Did you mean what you said earlier?" I ask, pulling back an inch. "Do you really think you know me that well?" Because I haven't been able to get those words out of my head. *No one would let you go if they knew you like I do.*

"You doubt me, Sparkles?" He squeezes my ankle and runs his hand up my bare leg. Thank god we live in California, because I only ever want to wear dresses when I'm with Gavin. "I *know* you," he says, his voice dropping dangerously low. "I know that this house is your favorite place in the world, even if you tell yourself you wanted to escape it. I know that you're insanely proud of what your family does."

He kisses my neck and runs his hand further up my thigh, until he starts toying with the bit of lace under my dress, slips his fingers underneath it.

"I know that if I touch you here—" I gasp as his thumb presses against me— "You'll come in just a minute." My breath catches right as he pulls away, letting his hand rest back on my thigh. He licks the spot right under my ear and grins, his smile stretching against my skin. "But I know you'd rather I draw it out, make it last." This time he whispers directly into my ear. "You'd rather finish with me inside you."

My heart hammers against my chest as he drags his lips from my ear to my throat and back up again. His right hand squeezes my thigh as his other comes up to my shoulder and slides down the strap of my dress. He tugs until my breast is exposed and rolls my nipple between his fingers.

"So I'll touch you here instead," he continues, his words almost as teasing as his hands. "Because I know you love this spot too. But it won't get you there. This way I can keep you on edge a little longer."

"Scottie." It's all I can say, more of a breath than a word really, my brain short circuiting from this display of seduction. He chuckles in response, loving what he's doing to me.

But I don't give up control that easily.

I press a hand to the center of his chest. "You forgot something, Scottie. I know you too." I hike up my dress and throw each leg up until my ankles are resting on his shoulders. Satisfaction hits me like a drug when his eyes bulge. They grow even wider as I slide my hand between my legs. "And I know how jealous you get when I decide to take things into my own hands."

He lets out a rough, guttural sound. I think I finally understand what it means in books when the man growls. His teeth sink into his lower lip and he grabs my wrist, pulling it up to his lips. His tongue lashes out and he sucks two fingers into his mouth.

He smirks. "Told you I'd get a taste."

We both lose our patience after that. My dress goes first, then his pants, his shirt. I'm not even sure who removes what. The only piece of fabric I can feel is Scottie's hoodie that I'm still sitting on. He really thought ahead.

"Guess what I remembered to bring," he says, a smile playing on his lips. He bends down and pulls a condom out of his pocket.

"Look who's getting cocky."

"Not cocky. I just never want to disappoint you." His words are earnest, no longer teasing, even as he rolls on the condom. If it's possible, my whole body softens even more.

He pushes into me, slow and gentle, always waiting for me to set the pace. My head rolls back when his teeth sink into my shoulder, his tongue following with a languid stroke. Before I lose the ability to speak, I make sure to let him know, "You never do."

CHAPTER THIRTY-FOUR

GAVIN

I'M NOT SURE IF OLIVIA SLEEPS AT ALL.

"How long have you been awake?" I ask, rubbing sleep from my eyes. I look out the window and the sky is still a deep violet.

"Just an hour or two," she replies, typing away. "Just wanted to make a few last-minute changes to the presentation."

"Come here," I reach over to her side of the bed, trying to tug her away from the laptop.

"I can't," she says, staying put. "You have that look in your eye."

"What look?" I pout, feigning innocence.

"The one that says you want to do unspeakable things to me. It's the same look you had last night in the cave."

"Did you not have fun last night in la grotte?"

"Don't you dare start speaking French right now. I need to stay focused." She finally shuts the computer and leans down to kiss me. But it's just a quick brush of her lips. "I'm gonna jump in the shower. Do *not* join me."

I groan, pulling the covers back over my head. It's going to be a long day.

"THANK YOU ALL FOR COMING," LIV GREETS THE GROUP after everyone empties out of the shuttles.

"Has anyone visited Diamond Sky before?" A few hands raise, Andie's the highest. "That's great. I'm Olivia Diamond, and this is where I grew up. A lot of wineries claim to be family run, but we live right there." She points to their home on the west side of the chateau.

"I started working at Sizzl almost three years ago, and one of my favorite things about our company is our core values. One of those values is 'treat all our customers like family.' And in *my* family, we like to celebrate with wine."

She gets a few laughs with that one. I've never seen Liv more in her element than right now. We're all outside, hovering around the entrance, but I could swear there's a spotlight right on her.

"My brother Owen is one of our talented winemakers. He's coming around with glasses for everyone to start the day. I hope you enjoy one of my favorite wines, the Lyra rosé. If you end up here after dark, you can actually see the Lyra constellation from our telescope on the top floor."

Owen finishes handing out the glasses and comes to stand by me. My job today is to be his shadow, helping out where I can.

"Want one?" he asks. "I can open another bottle."

"I'm good. Maybe in a bit."

Liv continues to the group, "We're still waiting on a few guests before we start the tour so please introduce yourselves.

I'm sure Mario and Daanesh would love to meet you all as well."

A matte black Maserati pulls into the drive and grabs my attention. Owen's too.

"Damn," he says, practically drooling. I might be too if I didn't have a good guess as to who its owner might be. And when I see Liv grab another glass of rosé and head straight for it, I'm no longer guessing.

"Why do you look like that?" Owen's voice barely comes through with the ringing in my ears.

"Hmm?"

"You look like you're about to go on a murder spree. What's up?"

I grunt, nodding my head toward Liv and the man who just declined her extended hand and stole a hug instead. Bastard.

"Do you know him? What's the deal?"

I'm trying my best not to be annoyed with Liv's brother, but he's making it excessively difficult to read their lips. They start to walk toward us and I shove Owen behind a pillar so we can hide.

"What the hell are you doing?"

I explain the entire Tristan situation as quickly as possible. I know there's a few key pieces I've left out, but it seems to get the point across because now he's seething with me.

"What are we—"

"Shh," I whisper. "I want to hear what they're saying."

Owen follows my lead as I flex every muscle in my body, straining to hear them, like I can force some sort of superpower if I just try hard enough. Either it works, or they've moved closer to the other side of this giant pillar.

"I feel a bit tricked, Olivia."

"That was never my intention. I remembered how much

you said you loved our wine, and it's not often we open the private cellar for an event like this."

"When you said exclusive, I didn't think we'd be joined by so many of your colleagues."

If that asshole thinks he's getting her alone, he's delusional. The look Owen throws me lets me know he won't let it happen either. I haven't spent too much time with the brothers yet, but I'm glad to know at least this one's as protective as I am.

"I'm sorry if you're disappointed, but I hope you stay. I have a really exciting tour planned."

"I'm not going anywhere."

"Good, because I'd like to discuss the outstanding contract as well."

"Fuck. You're a little shark aren't you."

Owen takes a deep breath and gives away our hiding spot before I can stop him.

"Hey Ollie, last guest? Should we get going?"

"Sure," Olivia says. She turns back to Tristan. "Want to head inside?"

"After you."

"How the hell can you stand this guy being here?" Owen asks an hour later. While Liv started the tour, I was able to fill in the gaps of the full Tristan debacle.

"I can't." Tristan McFuckface hasn't left Liv's side once. He isn't doing anything outwardly inappropriate or disrespectful, he's just always fucking *there*.

She does a barrel tasting, he's first in line. She walks to the next place, he's reaching a hand to her back like he's guiding her or some shit. We've spent most of the time in the cave, so whenever I get especially angry, I just picture Liv from last night, propped up on a barrel with her legs wrapped around my neck. It's the best coping mechanism I've come up with so far.

"I need to go help Deacon and Phil set up for the lunch and presentation stuff. You should come with me."

"Then who will be watching Liv?"

"Nothing's going to happen with all these people here. I think you'll feel better if you can't see them anyway."

I grunt, not wanting to agree with him even though I know he's right. "Fine."

I follow Owen into the chef's kitchen to see if we're needed.

Deacon points us to a case of wine. "Just need to open those bottles. Food's all done. Can you check on Phil, too? He said he set up the projector but he's an idiot when it comes to that stuff. Guy's never left the vineyard."

I grab the case and bring it out to the table so we can pour them into the decanters already laid out.

"Was he serious about your brother?" I ask Owen. "Phil's never left the vineyard?"

Owen looks thoughtful for a moment. "Not really. Loves the land. We all do though. Ollie's the only one who hates it here."

"Hates it? Why would you say that? She loves this place."

"Could have fooled me."

Our conversation from months ago comes back to me. Olivia said she was the black sheep in her family. The only one who isn't an artist. She also told me Owen was the brother she was closest with growing up, but that he was angry at her for moving to the city.

"She does. I think she misses it a lot, actually. At least, she misses you and the rest of your family. I know she'd love to see you more. She just loves the city too."

Owen narrows his eyes like he's not sure if he should believe me, but I pin him with a pointed look. *It's true.*

"Thanks, man, for telling me that. You're umm, a lot better than the last one."

"Not much of a compliment," I retort. "The last one's a piece of shit."

"Amen," Owen says, handing me a full glass. We clink and down both glasses like we're chugging beer at a frat party.

Phil is nowhere to be found—"probably out in the vines sniffing soil," according to Owen—but a few minutes later, we have the projector set up.

Deacon comes out with huge platters of meats, cheeses and dried fruit just as Liv shows up with the rest of the tour group.

"Sit wherever you like," she says to the group. "My brother, Deacon, has prepared lunch for us and we're starting with some of my favorite charcuterie. All the cheeses are local to northern California. If you fall in love with any of them, let me know and I can tell you where to find it."

She really is impressive at playing host. Seeing her command the room like this has me falling for her even harder if that's possible. God, after our conversation last night during dinner, I felt like a proposal might slip out of me if I wasn't careful.

"We have three wines to choose from on the table. The red here is the Vega. This is the same one we just finished tasting from the barrels. It's the same grape from the same block of the vineyard, but we had much more rain the year this was produced. You'll notice a deeper flavor with earthier notes than the barrel wine."

"Where are you sitting?" Tristan asks Liv. I suppress the growl forming in my throat.

"I'm not. Take a seat." She coolly walks away from him and joins me and Owen where all the tech is set up.

"Are you okay?" I whisper. "He's on you like fucking glue."

"I'm good. I still need to get him alone to talk about the deal though."

"Alone? No way."

"Definitely not." Owen and I speak at the same time.

"I thought you trusted me?" She ignores Owen but looks at me, her face full of steel.

"I do. He's the one I don't trust."

"I can handle it, I promise."

Liv's presentation goes flawlessly.

I'm not sure why she wouldn't let me look at it before now. She put together an entire storyboard of how marketing a business mirrors creating a fine wine.

Each of her metaphors work seamlessly, comparing a/b testing different channels to mixing different grapes, and getting your hands dirty on your own "turf" instead of outsourcing to agency partners (or other winemakers). My favorite was the one where she compared choosing Sizzl as your platform to selecting the best terroir for farming.

I'm in awe of this version of her. She's never sparkled more than right now.

I look around the room to find every guest focused on her. Daanesh and Mario are both smiling, whispering back and forth and I already know they can see this for the success that it is. Part of me wishes Mitch were here to see too. The other part is glad he's still in Portland, unable to ruin such a perfect day.

"Thank you all so much for letting me share my wine obsession with you. I hope you've enjoyed your time with me and my family and that you've also seen how much our team at Sizzl cares about our partnerships with all of you. If you'd like to bring any wine home today, we're offering our friends and family discount on anything you'd like. Enjoy the rest of your lunch."

As soon as Liv concludes her speech I stand up, desperate to hug her. But she doesn't come to me.

Owen puts a hand on my shoulder, either to console me or stop me from doing something stupid. We both watch as she taps Tristan's shoulder, and then as he follows her into the cave.

CHAPTER THIRTY-FIVE

OLIVIA

"Alone at last," Tristan says, smirking.

I take another step away from him.

"How'd you like the tour?" I ask.

"Very much, actually. I've visited here before. But it's much more fun when I'm coerced." He folds his arms across his chest.

"Well, I'm glad you feel that way. I had to get creative."

"Don't tell me you did all this just for me? There are much easier ways to get me alone, Olivia."

"You've made that very clear," I murmur. "But you've turned down all my attempts to get you involved in business conversations."

"I told you, I'm letting Darnell handle it. He asked for more responsibility. Did you get the impression I was avoiding you?"

"I did, actually." My words come out a little softer than I'd like. I lean my hip against one of the barrels. "I've tried my best to keep our relationship professional, as hard as you make that for me. And I have been working well with Darnell. Unfortunately, all our recent communications have him saying he's waiting on leadership. And I'm pretty sure that's you."

He grins, like this is all just a game to him.

"Is this a kidnapping situation, Olivia? Are you about to lock me in the cellar until we agree to sign?"

"No," I breathe out, exasperated. "You'd enjoy that way too much and this deal would probably go on forever."

He laughs, nods in agreement. Does this man take anything seriously?

"Look," I continue. "This might all be one big joke to you, I honestly can't tell. But my job is on the line, and I need to know if this is happening or not. Darnell is frothing to get his hands on our platform, I can tell. It seems like the only blocker in this deal is you."

"You've got tenacity, Olivia. I might ask you to come work for me if you weren't so tempting." Oh, for the love of god. Another man treating me like Eve with an apple. "The truth is, I'm working on getting us out of our current contract. As soon as I do that, we'll sign with you. Patience is a virtue, even for someone as gorgeous as you."

"Are you for real?" The words come out abruptly, not exactly the professional tone I've been going for.

"That you're gorgeous? Of course."

"No, about the contract. You need to get out of your contract with MarketingStream?"

"Yes. They're being...difficult. We still have fourteen months left. The idiot who signed before I joined the team locked us into a five-year agreement."

"So," I start pacing. I can't help it. "You're saying that as soon as you can terminate your MarketingStream contract, you'll sign with us?"

"Yes, though I might add a clause to your service agreement that all future negotiations are held in this cave."

"Yeah, sure, umm, hold that thought!"

Rushing back into the main room, my eyes dart to every corner searching for golden hair and aqua eyes.

"Hey, you okay?" I jump when Gavin comes up behind me, wrapping his arms around my shoulders.

I turn into him. "Fine," I answer. "Just need you."

"What did he do?" Gavin's gaze turns stormy.

"Nothing. All good, I swear. I just need your expertise, that's all. Come on."

I pull Gavin with me back toward Tristan.

"Tristan, this is Gavin Scott. He's one of the original folks at Sizzl and I think he can help you with your problem."

"This is *Gavin?*" Tristan asks. It's then I remember I told him Gavin's name. Told him before we were actually even dating.

"Yes," I say with enough force to get my point across. *Don't you dare.* "And *Gavin* has helped many of our clients navigate early terminations at other vendors, specifically Marketing-Stream. So if you'd like to save yourself some time, and money, and make Darnell's team very happy, you two should talk."

Gavin looks at me. At first, I can't read his expression. But then I realize what barrel I'm leaning against and see him bite his lip. Is this conversation turning him on?

"All right," Tristan says, cutting off my current train of thought. "Let's hear it."

GAVIN GOES TO GET HIS COMPUTER AND WE SPEND THE next hour digging into Tristan's contract and finding the best solution for him to terminate early.

At first, watching Gavin and Tristan interact resembled a cock fight. They each took little jabs where they could, trying and failing to be subtle about it. But I refused to engage, and eventually we fell into a professional rhythm. Thank god.

We were busy working on this as the event wrapped up and the shuttles took everyone else back to the city. I got a text from Andie letting me know Mario and Daanesh thought the event was a huge success, then another asking if I'd ever consider joining her on the marketing team.

By the time Tristan leaves the vineyard, he has a finalized contract from me in his inbox, and a solid plan to have his current contract voided in thirty days. Somehow, by some sorcery of will, I pulled this off.

I feel amazing. I don't even care that I had to pull Gavin in at the last minute. I did this. Me. Olivia fucking Diamond.

"Sparkles, you're incredible," Gavin says, once we're finally alone. "Can we do unspeakable things to each other now?"

WE HEAD BACK TO THE CITY THE NEXT MORNING, AND TO my surprise, Owen asks if he can join us.

"Not on the ride, obviously. But our schedule is light this weekend and Dad said he could deal without me. I thought I could come down and spend a day with you."

"Yes!" I cheer. "That would be so fun. There are like a million places I've been dying to show you. We can get sundaes at Ghirardelli and go see the sea lions and Land's End and— can you stay the night? My couch is really comfy. One day isn't enough." I know I'm rambling. I can tell by the way Gavin squeezes my hand, but I don't care.

"Yeah, that sounds awesome. I'll go pack a bag and meet at your place?"

"Yes." I hug my big brother. "I'll text you the address and where to park."

Owen runs back inside, and I grin up at Gavin. "He's

visiting me!" I squeal. "I'm so excited. Will you play tourist with us?"

"Sure, beautiful. Ready to ride? Or are you gonna fight me to drive again?"

"No, you drive. I'm too happy right now to pay attention."

OWEN LEAVES LATE SUNDAY AFTERNOON AND IT'S THE first time I've been alone in three days.

Gavin spent Saturday with us, but today it was just me and my brother. I'm still in a food coma from our brunch, but Owen had never had dim sum before. I had to make sure we tried *everything*.

I fall into my bed, extremely bloated but my heart feeling fuller than it has in years. Owen said he wants to come visit more, even to bring Phil and Deacon sometime. He also asked me to come home more often. I think he might have convinced Gavin to join a bocce league in Sonoma for the summer.

I pick up my phone to respond to Gavin's last text, inviting me to sleep at his place.

ME:

> I can barely move. And I don't think you want to see what I look like after swallowing all the dumplings in California

GAVIN SCOTT:

> You could eat all the dumplings in the world and you'd still by the most beautiful girl I've ever seen

> Okay I know that was cheesy as hell, I'm sorry

> If you want to sleep alone tonight it's no problem

Hedge you later

I'm about to respond again when my phone rings, an unknown number glowing on my screen. I debate sending it to voicemail, but end up answering it, holding my breath for what awaits me.

"Hello?"

"Hey, Olivia. It's Daanesh, from work."

I stifle a laugh. *From work.* Like my CEO needed to clarify himself. I can see why Andie must like him. For a man in his position, he's incredibly humble, and he really seems to care about the people around him. What he said about his sisters wasn't lost on me.

"Hey, how are you?"

"I'm great, actually. I just wanted to congratulate you on such a successful event on Friday. Mario and I were both disappointed when we didn't get a chance to talk to you before leaving."

"Oh. Well, thank you. I thought it went well too."

"Better than well, Liv. Can I call you Liv? Gavin always calls you Liv."

"Yeah, of course. Liv is great."

"It was a huge success. Mario has been struggling to secure testimonials from a few big clients. After Friday, they all agreed, one even offered to speak at our next showcase. And Gavin told me it's possible you'll be closing your first deal? With someone as big as Surf and Stream. It's huge, Liv."

"He helped a lot," I reply and immediately regret it. He did at the end, but the event was *mine.* I can't let myself forget that. "But I put in a lot of effort so I'm really glad it paid off."

"Your effort hasn't gone unnoticed, and I actually called to talk to you about an opportunity."

"Okay," I say with a bit of trepidation. What kind of opportunity? I don't know how my family would feel if I asked to repeat this type of event regularly.

"First of all, Andie wanted me to make it very clear that this was not her idea, and it has nothing to do with your friendship. I thought it would be best coming from her, but she said you'd never believe it wasn't a favor, so I'm confirming right now, this is not a favor."

I laugh, having no trouble imagining Andie's voice when she told him that.

"Okay, not a favor. I understand."

"Good. Mario and I discussed this on the ride back to the city, and I went over it with Vaughn when I got home. We'd like to create a new position for you on the marketing team, as a Client Event Manager. We'll be setting aside a budget and don't expect your family to offer free services in the future. But we'd like you to plan similar events around the country, to help retain and attract more business. I can email you the full job description now, so you can see the details and what's expected of you."

He pauses, but I can't find any words. Is this real? Because it sounds a little too good to be— "Is this because of what happened with—"

"I'm still not sure about the details of what happened with Mitch. Honestly, I hope that one day soon you'll feel comfortable enough to tell me. I'm already looking into other behavior that we could terminate him for, especially considering he's been in *Portland* for the last month." He mumbles this last part and I wonder if Andie had a chance to share my suspicions yet.

"But this has nothing to do with him," Daanesh continues. "Mario and I both want you to know that your work is impressive, and we feel like your talents are being wasted right now. The fact that we've already determined a salary and event budget for you should tell you this is serious. Come talk to either of us tomorrow and we can discuss the details. I really hope you'll consider it."

"Okay," I say. "I'll consider it. Thanks Daan–"

"One more thing."

"Yeah?"

There's a long pause. For a second I wonder if the call dropped.

"Look, I don't know if this is inappropriate. I'm dating your best friend and vice versa, so I think some lines have been blurred already. I just wanted to say that Andie adores you. When I told her about the position and how Mario wanted you on the marketing team, she actually cried. And I know she's been feeling guilty about lying to you. But that's entirely my fault. I feel like shit about it, truly. I just hope it doesn't affect your relationship."

"Oh." It takes me a second to formulate my thoughts. "If anyone understands wanting to keep their personal life private, it's me. I just hope you can go public with it soon. Andie and I are both eager for a double date."

"Yeah, me too. Sorry for calling on a Sunday, but please consider the offer. We really want this for you."

"Thanks."

After we hang up, my first thought is to call Gavin and get his opinion on the position. Or maybe Andie, though she isn't exactly impartial. Instead, I throw on my noise-canceling head-phones and turn on my favorite playlist.

And I think about what would make me happy.

CHAPTER THIRTY-SIX

OLIVIA

Mitch doesn't return to the office until Friday.

He texted me last night with a thumbs up emoji when I emailed him the signed contract for Surf and Stream. When he called me at ten o'clock, I didn't answer.

Now, he comes barreling in like he's stepping into a welcome home party, expecting our whole team to cheer for his return.

"What's up," Gavin says to greet him, barely looking up from his computer. I can't help but laugh.

"Livy! I knew you could do it. You just needed the right motivation." He sits down at the empty desk next to mine. "Tell me what happened."

The right motivation? Give me a fucking break. I notice the way Gavin's jaw tightens across from me, trying his best not to defend me. I love him even more for staying quiet.

"We haven't had a one on one in a few weeks," I say cheerily to Mitch. "Wanna chat?"

"Sure, let's go to my office."

I follow him across the room, looking back once to throw Gavin a wink.

"I'm sorry I couldn't make it back for the event you put together," Mitch says, sitting down behind his desk. I follow his lead and sit across from him, leaving the office door cracked open. "Ellen was being such a bitch and—"

"I really don't feel comfortable talking about your marriage. Can we just discuss work right now?" I ask.

Mitch looks stunned. His nostrils flare with anger. He's not used to me speaking to him like this. I've always gone along with his rants no matter how uncomfortable they make me.

"Fine," he says curtly. "Why don't you tell me how you were able to close this deal. In record time at that."

"Record time? I'm so glad you can finally admit that, after the pressure you put on me."

"Hey, it worked. Like I said, you needed the right motivation."

"All I needed was the chance to prove myself. Hard work got me the rest of the way."

I cross my legs and lean back in the chair, curious to hear his next retort.

"You've always been a hard worker, Livy. Now if you can get your boyfriend to share a few more leads and show me this wasn't a one-trick pony, maybe we can talk about that promotion again."

Laughter pours out of me. I couldn't stop it if I tried. "You're serious? After all that, you still don't think I have what it takes to be in sales? There are other men on the team who have never closed a deal this big, not in years, but I'm still not ready?"

"Come on, don't get all crazy on me."

"You're really going to call me *crazy* right now?"

"Oh, you know what I mean," he placates.

"You're right. I do. Because you could have called me angry. Or mad, or frustrated, or a million other things. But those words would all imply that my feelings might be a justifiable reaction to something else. Those are the words you use with the guys. Because when they get mad, there's a reason, a *problem* making them feel that way. But when you talk to a woman, you use words like crazy or emotional. Their implication is real fucking clear—the only problem is me."

"Christ, Livy. That's not what I—"

"You know what? It doesn't matter. You're a monster, Mitch. And with or without the promotion, I'm done working for you. That's really all I needed to tell you."

"You can't quit. You're my best SDR."

I laugh again. "Thanks for finally saying that. Maybe you should have acknowledged my success before a different department beat you to it. I'm cleaning out my desk this afternoon. And I'm moving to marketing on Monday."

"You can't do that without my approval," he seethes.

"It's been approved by Mario. And Daanesh. And Vaughn. Do you want to go argue with them?"

"I always you knew you were a little..." he mumbles something I can't make out.

"In case you wanted to do an exit interview, it's been absolute shit working for you." I stand up and turn to leave, just as Andie knocks on the door.

"Hey, Mitch. Sorry to interrupt, but Vaughn and Daanesh asked me to grab you. They want to meet in conference room B."

Mitch's face pales. Andie grins at me.

"They want to meet right now?" he asks her, like he's just buying time.

"Yep," she says, cheerily. "Something about Vegas, some charges on the company card, I couldn't really understand all the details. But they seemed to think you could help sort it all out."

When I get back to my desk, I finish packing up my things. I had just been waiting to tell Mitch. Seeing the expression on his face was definitely worth it. Especially knowing what's happening to him right now in conference room B.

"I'm really happy for you, but I can't believe I'm not going to see your face across from me every day." Gavin pouts at me.

"We're dating now, Scottie. You will most likely still see me every single day." Then I lean over the desks to whisper, "Naked. In your bed."

"Yeah, okay. But maybe we can work together in a conference room sometime? Or at Fog & Foam? I'm gonna miss seeing your serious face. You're so sexy when you're making a PowerPoint."

"Scottie!"

"What?"

I sit back down and nod toward the computer. He smirks back, like he's expecting something salacious.

SLACK DIRECT MESSAGE
Olivia Diamond:
NSFW!
Gavin Scott:
Then let's go home
Immediately

"Okay, I'm ready to go," I say a few minutes later. "Actually, wait. Just got another email. Hold that thought!"

From: Tristan Cross < tristan.cross@surfandstream.com >
To: Olivia Diamond < olivia@sizzl.com >
Subject: Thank you

Olivia,

Did you get a new phone? My texts don't seem to be going through.

I wanted to thank you again for your help in my contract situation. Our board was thrilled with the money we were able to save and gave me a large bonus to show their appreciation. I'll be taking a trip to Paris next week and would love for you to join me. I know a hotel with excellent room service and sound proof walls.

Let me know
-Tristan

I guess some things never change.

CHAPTER THIRTY-SEVEN

GAVIN

6 Months Later

"Cheers!"

We all clink glasses, toasting to the official sale of Sizzl. Olivia planned a special getaway for the four of us at a resort in Healdsburg.

"To our first—*official*—double date!" she shouts. I guess I only thought we were celebrating the sale.

"This is so exciting!" Andie cheers. "Wanna jump in the pool?"

Daanesh reaches across the lounger to kiss her cheek. "You both go ahead. I need to talk to Gavin for a minute."

"Ominous," Liv whispers, squeezing my hand. She downs the rest of her flute and pops up. "I call the floating unicorn!"

We both watch our girls jump in the water, our faces covered in stupid grins. Daanesh catches it at the same time as I do. "Damn, we've gone soft."

Now that both of our secrets are out, we've gotten a lot

closer. This may be the first official double date, but he and Andie join game night every week.

"All right," I say. "What's this big thing you've been wanting to ask me?"

"I'm not gonna ask you when you have that attitude. This is serious."

Shit. He does look serious. "Okay," I say, sitting up straight. "I'm listening."

"As soon as the lockout period's over, I'm going to announce that I'm leaving Sizzl." This isn't a huge surprise. With the company now owned by Mojave, Daanesh is more of a figurehead than a true CEO. "I've been working on an idea lately. An AI platform that businesses can use to predict data outages. I already have some sample code to start pitching to investors."

"Wow, Daan. That's awesome. I'd say I'll miss you, but you know I'm gonna be looking for something else as soon as I can collect on my options anyway."

"That's the thing. I don't want you to miss me." I give him a quizzical look. Are we about to get all mushy about this? "I mean, I want you to work with me. I know you're done with sales. And I know you had your heart set on going to the investment side. But how would you like to be my partner? I need someone like you to help me *get* investors, and to help me hire the right kind of people to run the business side of things. After Sizzl, I just want to stick with the engineering part of the company."

I'm silent for a long moment, just watching Liv and Andie float together on their blow-up unicorn. A partner? It's a lot more responsibility, but that's what I've been wanting, right? And being the one pitching investors does sound fun. It sounds like a challenge. I haven't had one of those since I met Olivia.

"Well?" he asks.

"This is for real? You really want me to be running half of a company?"

"I really do. I think you'd be great at it. And I like knowing that you and I have the same vision for a culture. Some of the people Vaughn hired just ruined things for me at Sizzl. The sale couldn't have come at a better time. I know that won't happen with you. Also," he clears his throat. "You know I hate talking about money, but it will be public knowledge soon enough. I'll make around a hundred million from the sale, give or take, and I plan to invest most of it back into the new business. We'll be able to hire top talent right from the start."

"I was already sold, Daan. You didn't have to woo me with your newfound millionaire status."

"I figured. Just laying all my cards out."

"Do you have a name yet? For the company?"

"We've got two marketing gurus over there." He nods to the girls sharing the unicorn. "I wanted to ask you first, but I thought they might be able to help us with that part."

"Good call," I say, standing up and pulling off my shirt. "I'm in. But it's the weekend. Let's figure it out on Monday."

I jump in the pool and tip the raft, watching the girls squeal as they go under. Daanesh jumps in after me. "They might kill you for that."

"Nah, I'll be fine," I say just before Olivia pounces and takes me under.

"Ahem," Andie shouts. "This is a classy place. Let's try to act like we belong here."

"You're right," I say, pulling Liv against me. "Let's come back in three months when we're all rich."

"When you're all rich," Liv says. "My options are worth like ten grand."

"Good thing I plan to spend all my money on you," I whisper in her ear.

She knows I'm joking, mostly. Gabby and I have already started planning where the money will go. We've created accounts to pay for school and to pay off every loan or line of credit we've ever accumulated. The rest will mostly go into savings and investments.

But I might have a small fund set aside for Liv. For the ring I plan to get, for the house I'll buy us one day that has a huge yard for all our dogs, for the vacation to Mexico I've already planned where we'll celebrate the anniversary of our first kiss. Another trip that I still need to tell her about.

"Should we head inside and take showers? We have to be at the restaurant in two hours for dinner," Liv says to the group.

"How long does it take you to shower?" Andie asks.

Liv's eyes find mine, her cheeks turning pink. I save her from answering. "My fault. I take forever to get ready."

AN HOUR LATER, WE'RE DONE SHOWERING AND I TELL LIV about Daanesh's offer.

"You have to do it, right? I mean you don't *have* to do anything, and my opinion doesn't matter, but just in case you want it, I totally think you should do it."

"I love you."

"What kind of response is that? Are you going to do it?"

"Sparkles."

"Scottie."

"First of all, I always want your opinion. It matters to me more than anything." She bites her lip, trying to hide her smile. "And yeah, I'm gonna do it. But I think you should know, it means I'll probably be working crazy hours, at least at first. We might not see each other as much as we do now."

"Well," she says grinning. "That is actually perfect timing then."

"You're saying you want to spend less time with me?"

She grabs her phone. "I'm saying I think we should call Gabby and tell her the good news."

Still confused, I dial my sister and tell her everything about the job with Daanesh. I keep her on speaker, the phone far away from my face, so that she doesn't blow out an eardrum.

Liv bends toward the phone. "Gabby, I think now is a good time."

"A good time for what?" I ask.

"You're sure?"

"I'm sure," Liv says to her. What the hell is going on?

"So," Gabby starts. "Exciting news on my end too. "Kadesha asked me to move in with her. We're getting a place together closer to Stanford."

"You...wow...that's..."

"It's great! Right?" Liv offers, jabbing me in the chest.

"Yeah, it's great, Gabs. I'm really happy for you." And I am. Of course, I am. But damn, the thought of not seeing Gabby every day does something to me. For so long, it was just the two of us. Me and Gabby against the world. At least I know Kadesha will take care of her. There's no one I'd trust more to be there for my sister.

"Aww, don't think I forgot about you, big brother. I found you a new place too."

"You what?" I ask. Is she saying I need to downsize now that I'll be living alone?

"For you and Liv."

Liv grins at me, a twinkle in her eye. "I know you haven't technically asked me to live with you, but you also haven't wanted to spend a single night apart in the last six months, so —"

"Of course I want to live with you. I just..."

"Didn't know what to do about your sister?" Gabby chimes in. "Well, now your problem is solved. And Liv and I found the best apartment for you in North Beach, still walkable to downtown but so many better restaurants."

"This is real?" I ask Liv.

"Yep. Already signed a lease. You know how fast things go in the city. So please be happy." She bares her teeth, like there's actually a chance I wouldn't want this.

"I am incredibly happy."

"Yay!" Gabby cheers through the phone. "I will miss you so much, but you're coming over at least once a week for dinner, non-negotiable."

We easily agree, knowing there will be zero home-cooked meals in our place, though I'm looking forward to more wine and cheese nights with Liv. We chat a little longer, and make plans to see the new place when we get back to the city before hanging up.

I grin at Liv, imagining life waking up to her every single day. "How big is the closet? Will there be any room for my clothes?" I reach my arms around her and pull her toward me.

"Yeah...about that. I'll just be commandeering the whole second bedroom. You can have the closet. Well, I might need part of it for shoes—"

"We'll make it work." I silence her with a kiss, unhooking the towel still wrapped around her.

"Scottie," she whines. "I have to get ready."

"Good thing we still have time. We need to celebrate."

"I thought we already celebrated...twice."

"Not this."

"Not what?"

I lay her down on the bed, hovering over her. "Our future. And for no longer being co-workers."

"I thought you liked working together." She pouts.

"I do. I did. I never would have gotten to know you so well if I didn't sit across from you all that time." I kiss her nose. "But now I can text you whatever I want. I'll never have to see that annoying 'NSFW!' ever again."

EPILOGUE
GAVIN

My eyes squint, looking down the terminal at SFO. Bright red hair floats around Liv's head as she runs toward me, heels clicking loudly on the linoleum.

I take a few long strides to meet her, immediately catching her lips with mine.

"I made it." She breathes against me. After three different canceled flights from LAX, it feels like a miracle she's here. "I still can't believe there are *hurricanes* in southern California. What is the world coming to?"

I grab her bags and direct her to our gate to sit down. By a stroke of luck, this flight was delayed too. I can't even imagine how tired Liv is right now, after hosting a two-day customer event in Malibu and then another two days trying to get a flight out.

"Did you have fun with Lucy?" I ask.

"Yes! I can't even complain about the flight situation. Not only did I have a friend to stay with but she lives in an actual mansion. The weather was horrendous, but we spent the whole time in their basement. It felt like I was at a private concert."

"That sounds fun. I'm just glad you're here now."

She kisses me, a little slower this time. "Me, too. I missed you." Another kiss. "Like...a lot. You should come with me next time."

"Done."

An announcement overhead grabs our attention. *Flight 317 to Buenos Aires now departs from Gate G3.* Guess we have to move.

Grabbing all the bags again, we walk around the terminal to our new gate. One more hour until boarding.

"I can't believe it's finally happening," Liv squeals. We've been planning this trip ever since the day we moved in together, but it's taken me a year to work out all the details.

"Me too. It's weird to finally be going back after all this time. I just wish you could have met my mom." Because that's part of what this trip is for me, a chance to reconnect with my mother, my roots. I wish Gabby was coming but her schedule wouldn't allow it.

"I'm going to meet her," Liv whispers from the seat next to me. "Through everything we do. She'll be with us."

Fuck, I love this girl. Every time I think I've hit the peak, that this relationship is the best it's ever been, she surprises me and I love her even more.

How the hell am I supposed to wait a week to put this ring on her finger? The plan is to wait until we visit the vineyards in Mendoza, but I swear it's burning a hole in my pocket right now.

Liv's stomach rumbles between us. "Shit. I don't think I've eaten in...unclear. I'm gonna go grab some snacks. You want anything?"

I shake my head, tell her to go on and I'll stay back to watch the bags. It feels like I need a moment to collect myself.

It's not that I'm nervous. Liv and I are great together, and we've talked about the future enough for me to be optimistic about her answer. The commitment doesn't worry me either. I've never been more sure of anything in my life. I want to spend forever with her.

But my nerves still arise. This has to be *perfect*. I only get one shot at the proposal, one chance to make it the perfect moment for her, for us. Am I overdoing it? Are the fireworks too much? What if she hates wine from Argentina and the night is ruined? Shit, what if she *doesn't* say yes?

My fingers start dialing before my brain catches up.

"Let me guess. You're spiraling again?" Gabby's voice rings in my ear.

"Maybe." I gulp. I may have been faking some of the confidence lately, my sister having to talk me down on a regular basis. Sometimes it just feels too good to be true. It's hard to believe that everything's going so well when for so long, my life was the opposite. "You really think she'll say yes?"

"Why does this girl make you such an idiot?"

"Because I love her?"

"Fine, okay. Valid excuse. And yes! There is not a doubt in my mind she will say yes."

"But what if she hates the ring?"

"Jesus, Gav. We've been over this. Even Andie said she'll love that ring. It's unique and special and perfect for her. And even if she doesn't love it, she's not going to say no. You've got to stop worrying about dumb shit. You both love each other. That's it. Just focus on that."

I take a deep breath and listen to my sister. "Yeah, I can do that."

"Good. Please do not call me again until it's to announce your engagement." She hangs up.

A small laugh bubbles out of me at the conviction in

Gabby's voice. She's right. Liv and I love each other. That has never been in question.

I let out a deep breath and feel for the pearl in my pocket. For the thousandth time, I wonder if she'll be mad or confused that I didn't go with a standard diamond. This just felt more...her.

I should put it back in the box, but I also can't seem to let it out of my sight. I've had it on my body since the purchase was made five weeks ago, too worried about ruining the surprise if she finds it.

"Hey, beautiful," I announce when Liv gets back. I yank my hand out of my pocket and she gives me a funny look. Shit. "What'd you get?"

"Sushi." She holds up a bento box between us. "Wanna share?"

We nibble on nigiri and seaweed salad while she fills me in on all the details of her LA trip. As much as I miss her when she travels, nothing beats the way she loves her job right now. She's so much happier than she was in sales. Even her general anxiety has improved.

We're so lost in laughter we almost miss the boarding announcement, but make it just in time. I wouldn't want to miss my first experience flying first class.

Once we're settled in our private pod and up in the air, Liv grabs onto my hands. She tugs until we're facing each other, but she's just sort of staring at me. I wait for words and they don't come, nothing but a goofy smile on her face.

I'm about to ask if she's okay when she leans in and kisses me. It's not a quick peck, not even a loving press like she gave me earlier. It's the kind of kiss you only have in private, the kind that's full of promise and fire.

The amount of money we spent on these tickets was insane, but I have zero regrets right now with the privacy these seats offer. I'm about to pull her into my lap when she finally releases her hold on me.

"What was that for?" I ask, a little breathless. She licks her lips and I find myself leaning into her for more, but she pushes her hands gently against my chest.

"I just...I love you. And those words feel so insignificant sometimes. Like I *really* love you. I might have even cried to Lucy about how lucky I am to have you. I just need you to know that I think about it all the time. It's that one thought in my head that never goes away. Like a little fly buzzing around saying 'I love him!' 'I love him!' constantly." She scrunches her face. "And I'm just honored, really. That I get to go on this trip with you. That I even get to be with someone as kind and wonderful as you, and—"

"Marry me."

"What?"

Shit. Fuck. Did I seriously do it again? Is it impossible for me to hold anything in when it comes to Olivia? It's that damn "I kind of love you" all over again.

I'm frozen in place, not sure what to do next. Can I pretend she misheard me? Completely ignore it for another six days until we get to Mendoza?

"Scottie, what did you say?" Guess we're not pretending it away then.

Fuck it.

"Marry me. I mean, will you? Marry me?" Jesus, that was god awful. I pull the ring out of my pocket and she gasps, her hands flying up to cover her mouth. *Please be a good gasp.*

"Scottie..." She takes the ring and examines it slowly, her eyes wide as a doe's.

"I'm sorry. I had this whole wine thing planned and a speech and fireworks and—" I let out a breath. "I love you that much too. I think about it all the time. And I can't really imagine not spending the rest of my life with you. You're everything to me, Olivia."

Tears well in her eyes. Taking the ring, I hold her hand out to slide it on her finger. "Shit. Did you say yes?"

She laughs, tears streaming down her face. "Yes! Of course I will marry you."

She must be shouting a little because there are a few cheers and claps around us.

"Is the ring okay?" I ask. The pink pearl sits atop a rose gold band with lots of small diamonds of different cuts. "I showed Andie and Gabby but I wasn't sure—"

"It's perfect. I love everything about it." She beams. "And no one else will have the same one."

"It's one of a kind. Just like you, Sparkles."

She throws her arms around my neck and kisses me again. It's not as sensual this time, probably because she can't stop smiling. I'm getting more teeth than anything else, but I love it anyway. Her happiness is everything.

I'm exceptionally glad I waited until we're in the air to take my pills. I need to remember this moment forever.

We're interrupted when the flight attendant comes by. "Excuse me, did I hear we're celebrating? Care for some champagne?"

Liv looks at me, her arms still tight around my shoulders and grins back at the flight attendant. "Any chance you have a good pinot noir?"

ACKNOWLEDGMENTS

And just like that, I've written a third book! Honestly, no one is more surprised than myself.

This book was a labor of love, a story that mashed together a few pivotal moments in my life and made them into something entertaining and dare I say, empowering.

As much as I hate to do it, I have to thank my shittiest of all exes. Without you, {redacted}, I wouldn't have realized how amazing a healthy relationship can be and how fortunate I've been to find the man of my dreams. Now, crawl back into the hole you came from.

I'll also, very briefly, thank every misogynistic boss I've had to endure, all the mean girls I've worked with who love to put down other women, and that guy at {redacted (major television network)} who couldn't take the hint that I wanted to sell him marketing software without getting constant sexts and creepy snapchat requests.

Next, I want to thank all of the *amazing* women I have met through my years in tech. The people who motivated me to tell this story.

To Kelsey Mullaney, who may have started as my mentee but now inspires me every day. Can I be you when I grow up? You have dealt with all the bullshit that's come your way with so much poise, never letting it faze you and always being such a boss. ILYSM!

To Christina Oh, my inspiration for Andie. You might cook an amazing Korean feast but your raging positivity is why I love you. Some of my favorite work memories are the events we hosted together. You are truly an amazing travel buddy. Also, thank you for introducing me to Sushi Go.

To Michelle Novak, the best manager I could ever ask for. Thank you for always making work a safe space, no matter what insanity is going on at the time. I feel so fortunate to know you and work with you and don't tell anyone, but I'd follow you anywhere.

To my fellow author Amanda Blohm, who not only translated all the Spanish in this book but has been my trusted confidant, drafting partner and dear friend. I'm so lucky to know you.

Don't worry, I didn't forget my betas readers! As an indie author who doesn't have a publishing team of editors, these women mean *everything* to me.

You all killed it on this one. Seriously, there are at least three one liners in this book that I did not come up with my own. Sasha, Shay, Amanda and Kathrin, thank you thank you thank you for these contributions. Megan, your comments will forever live rent-free in my head, even if I'm a little annoyed that they are funnier than the book itself. Steph, Alyssa, Sammie, Taylor and Addy, your feedback is so appreciated. Thank you immensely for pushing me to make this book the best it could be.

I have to thank my wonderful husband, Erik. You have put up with many long days of me never leaving the writing cave and your support has not gone unnoticed. Wally and I would be lost with you. Thanks for being the best husband, dog-dad and partner I could have ever asked for. But to be clear, I never said perfect. We'll always continue working on ways you can improve.

Lastly, to you, my readers. Whether this is your first time reading my words, or you've stuck with me since Speechless, you are the best motivation. I hope to keep sharing my stories with you for years to come.

ABOUT THE AUTHOR

Lindsey Lanza is a romance author from Columbus, Ohio. She is a tech start-up enthusiast by day, a voracious reader by early mornings, nights and weekends, and now writes love stories when she gets a spare moment. You can most often find her laughing about nothing with her husband Erik, perusing a dessert menu, consulting clients on zoom calls or obsessing over her Sheepadoodle Wally. Not Safe For Work is Lindsey's third novel.

For more on Lindsey and to sign up for her mailing list: lindseylanza.com

 instagram.com/readwithli